INTO
THE
ABADDON

Wesley Newman

Wren With A Pen

Published by Wesley Newman
Augusta, Georgia
www.wesleynewman.com
Author imprint: Wren With A Pen

ISBN 978-1-7377638-0-2
ISBN 978-1-7377638-2-6 (eBook)
ISBN 978-1-7377638-1-9 (hardback)

Library of Congress Control Number: 2021925002

Cover Design by theBookDesigners
Author Photo by NewmanArtography

Cover Images © Shutterstock.com

Into the Abaddon

To my family.

CHAPTER ONE

January 8th, 2020

Wednesday

"I did it," Vincent whispers to himself. The computer light reflects off his glasses and greasy, black hair as he grabs either side of his head in amazement. "I did it!" Vincent says again with jittery excitement, but none of his sleeping colleagues hear him from behind his laptop.

Passed out at the table and surrounded by empty energy drinks and Chinese food delivery containers, Karl snores like a lawnmower while hugging his pizza box pillow. Lying on the floor, Grace lets out a "go-away-mom" groan and rolls over. Sarah is curled up on top of an adjacent table using her lab coat as a blanket and Vincent's black hoodie as a pillow.

"Guys, guys! Wake up!" One by one they all groggily snap out of it and crowd around him. They read an incredibly long series of mathematical formulas, graphs, and diagrams from over his shoulder.

Grace is the first to finish reading and shouts out, "Oh my God! We've done it!" Karl and Sarah similarly emote, and they all share a group hug before cracking open a bottle of champagne. "I'll call Mark! You back this up and make a soft copy!" Grace shouts before calling up Mark, the laboratory manager, forgetting that it's two o'clock in the morning.

All four of them read and reread the report, reviewing it with a fine-tooth comb and looking for any and all mistakes they could have missed. They run over the math together on the wall-mounted dry erase board while Vincent sits in the back of the room. He focuses on his notebook, trying not to get too excited about the rest of the team fawning over his latest finding. The door creaks open, and an obese man sporting a comb-over, tank top, and pajama bottoms shuffles into the research room.

"This better be good," he croaks.

"Mark! Get over here!" Grace's voice rises above the group's banter. Her boisterous attitude tends to appoint her as the *de facto* leader of this small think tank. "We've got it. Take a seat, and I'll run you through everything." As Mark shuffles up to the board, Vincent walks alongside him with butterflies floating up from his stomach.

"It was crazy, Mark! I-I was just sitting there, working on the data compression issue, and then it-it hit me out of nowhere! Boom! Like it was ju—"

"If you want to take a seat, Mark," Grace interrupts him, "then I'll go ahead and run you through what we've got so far." She pulls out a seat for him and turns back toward the board.

Vincent pauses for a second or two and whispers, "Oh, okay." He sits in the back of the room again and buries his nose in his notebook. He watches on as she presents his work to everyone. *She's definitely the better presenter... She doesn't trip over her words or sweat in front of a crowd.* Vincent focuses his attention on reading along with his notes.

Grace's caramel skin is freckled, and her hair is pulled back into a tight braid. She carries herself with confidence and poise. Her words are clear, and she communicates her thoughts carefully as she speaks. Even while discussing the translation of binary bits to usable information, she manages to keep the entire room's attention. From the back, Vincent wonders how she keeps herself so well put together. As she finishes the report, Mark sits silently as he processes everything that he has just heard.

"This is amazing. Genius. Who was it that figured out that last bit about the data compression?"

This is it! She's going to tell him I solved it! "Well, it's been a group effort, sir. We all have unique talents and worked very hard together;

all of our contributions led up to this conclusion." Vincent flinches as she says this. *Group effort?*

"Yes, well…" Mark stands and scans the board again. "This is the first step down a long road we're going to walk together." He turns to address the whole team. Vincent sits against the back wall, Grace at the whiteboard, and Karl and Sarah lean against a bookshelf. They all look back at him with a sense of gravitas. "If this stands up to scrutiny, your names will be famous. Universities around the world will teach their students about what you've accomplished here. Ladies and gentlemen, you just discovered the secret to teleportation."

THAT NIGHT, the four of them meet up at their go-to gastropub—The Ducky Luck—and sit at their favorite booth before sharing a "cheers" to their discovery. Many nights of laughter and revelry have been had here; however, they've seen far more nights of frustrated tears and desperate binges in their search for this moment.

As per tradition whenever they make a break in their research, Karl takes an empty beer bottle and spins it on the table. Whomever it points to when it stops spinning buys a round of shots. Vincent never liked this game; he doesn't like shots. He doesn't like drinking. In fact, he skipped the first few group outings after joining them in the lab three years ago, but he broke down after a few months of peer pressure.

Mark had received a government grant to hire this small team of researchers to build on the quantum teleportation theory: Karl, a theoretical physicist, Sarah, an astrophysicist, and Grace, a computer scientist. According to Mark, he noticed they were having trouble working together; the workload had them stressed out, they couldn't keep the math straight, and they would let their emotions run the lab. That's when he found Vincent, a mathematics wizard fresh out of M.I.T. who had become a bit of a local legend on campus for his ability to calculate complex equations faster than the computers he helped design for the school. Mark pulled the last remaining string he had at the Institute to hire Vincent. After the first week, he was already shouldering more of the workload than the other three combined, arguments about mathematics never even had a chance to arise, and he became an emotional sponge for the others whenever they needed an outlet.

"Vincent! It's your buy!" Karl says, as everyone lets out a round of laughter and sighs of relief. Vincent looks down to see the bottle pointing directly at him. *Of course, it is.* He sighs and walks through the scarcely populated pub to find the bartender busy watching a football game.

Vincent takes a seat and stares at her, but she fails to notice him. "Excuse me," he says quietly.

She shouts out at the television, "What are you thinking?! He slipped right past you, and you just WATCHED him!"

Vincent clears his throat and says a bit louder, "Excuse me!"

She turns around, but instead of addressing him, she greets a man that walks through the entrance. "Hey, Bobby! Rum and Coke?"

"You know it!" Bobby takes a seat three spots down from Vincent, then he and the bartender start talking about the football game.

What the hell! Vincent hangs his head in embarrassment.

"Hey, barkeep!" The only other person seated at the bar, an older man with a bushy, silver moustache, shouts out in a bold voice. She looks over with attentive gusto, and he points to Vincent. "My friend here needs something."

She looks at them both with a condescending attitude. "Okay. What?"

Vincent looks on with confusion and stammers for a moment, "Um, four shots of Fireball, please."

"Fine," she huffs, reluctantly pulling herself away from Bobby. The silver-mustached man raises his glass and nods to Vincent.

Mimicking his nod, Vincent grabs the drinks and returns to his table, but he sees Sarah off in the corner on her phone. When she returns, her eyes are slightly puffy, but nobody asks her what's wrong, so he doesn't either. With much chagrin, he follows his friends' examples in celebration.

Grace picks up her shot glass and announces, "I propose a toast! Three years of blood, sweat, and tears, and we finally did it. Each of us played an absolutely vital role in this, and none of us could have done it without each other." She pauses and looks around the table, then smiles. "Thank you all. Now, down the hatch!"

A few hours of darts, nachos, and begrudged merriment pass late into the night. Vincent never knows how to make himself feel included during these late-night drinking sessions, so he tends to turn invisible while the others get drunk. Intermittently, he looks back to the man watching the game. Constantly there, sipping away at his whiskey, occasionally he would look over and smile at Vincent before looking back at the screen.

"Hey, you all up for some beer pong?" Karl asks the group for the tenth time.

"Fine!" Grace finally acquiesces. "If it'll shut you up about it already."

Bobby appears out of nowhere and shouts, "Hell yeah!" He and Karl then share a resonating high-five. "Me and the red-head versus you two!" He gestures to Sarah and wraps his arm around her shoulder. "Watchu say, girl?" Sarah returns an uncomfortable glance.

"Let's kick their asses, Grace!" Karl and Grace clank glasses.

I guess that's my cue to leave. Vincent wanders back to the table, sitting for a moment before realizing how stupid he feels. *I should just go home.* With a pit in his stomach, he stands up but feels a hand touch his shoulder.

"You're not leaving yet, are you?" Vincent looks back to see the man from the bar smiling at him while palming two glasses of whiskey in his other hand.

"Oh, well, I was just…" Vincent stammers.

"Just because your friends over there abandoned you doesn't mean you have to leave. Here, I'll sit with you." He takes a seat in the opposite booth, offers him the second glass, and asks, "What's your name, friend?"

After a short hesitation, he sits back down and says, "Vincent."

"It's nice to meet you, Vincent. My name is Leonard, but you can call me Leo." He raises his glass, to which Vincent raises his own, but he sniffs what's inside and winces. "It's okay, you don't have to drink it." Leo chuckles before pouring the drink into his own glass. "It's a bit strong for some, I understand. Drinking isn't really your thing, is it, Vincent?"

He looks around before answering to see Bobby slide closer to Sarah, accidentally spilling some of his Bud Light on her shoes. "No. I don't really see the appeal."

Leo nods solemnly and follows Vincent's gaze. "Fair. Who's the girl?"

Vincent's head spins back quickly as his face flushes. "Girl? What girl?"

"The redhead who that Bobby guy has been throwing himself at. You fancy her?"

"Oh no, no. That's just Sarah. We're lab partners. That guy's just a jerk." He looks down at the table and fidgets with the empty glass in front of him.

"That's for damn sure. So lab partners, huh? You guys in med school or something?"

"No, we work in a lab," Vincent pauses and squints. "Why are you being nice to me?"

"Well, I saw the way you let that bartender walk all over you. I figured you might appreciate someone showing you that jerks aren't the only people who come to bars."

"Thanks."

"I used to be like you, Vincent. I used to mope around with no sense of self, doing everything I could to meet others' expectations of me."

"Really?"

"Yeah! I was about your age, too. My old friends were kind of bull-dozers. They would take advantage of how good I was at my job and give nothing in return. It kind of sucks, doesn't it?"

"Yeah. It does."

"Let me guess, you do most of the work for them down at your lab, go to all of their little outings, but they never turn around and pay back the favor?"

"Well, yeah," Vincent agrees, but instantly feels bad for bad-mouthing his friends. "But I never really give them a chance to return it. I don't really ask them for anything in return."

"You shouldn't have to! When you do someone a solid, they should do you a solid, right?" He raises his eyebrows and gives Vincent an intense, questioning stare. "I don't want to tell you about your own business, Vincent. I just know how it feels to be stepped on like you. If you disagree with me, by all means, tell me to shove off."

Feeling like he's back in the lab watching Grace present his work to Mark, Vincent dares not disagree with Leo, but those are his friends. *I'm not the kind of person to talk shit about my friends behind their backs… am I?* "I mean, it's just the way things work for us. That's how we've always been. It's normal. I like my friends."

"Is normal always a good thing? Look where trying to be normal got you, cast out by your own friends." Leo leans on his forearm, giving him his full attention. "Tell me something, Vincent, what does normal look like for you?"

Vincent thinks back over the past several years and how they've shaped his everyday life. *I wake up in a crappy apartment, go to a lab where I'm the whipping boy who does everybody's work for them, and then I pay for everybody's drinks at a crappy pub that I don't even like.* "You know where normal has gotten me?" Vincent looks deep into his glass, then his eyes meet Leo's intense glare. "I do everybody's work and get no credit for it. I buy everybody's drinks, and they kick me to the curb when a more interesting guy comes along. I make the biggest scientific discovery of our generation, and suddenly it's a *group effort!*"

He notices his voice slowly rising, so he brings it down to a whisper, pointing his finger at Leo as he speaks. "Who corrects their math when they just throw numbers out there and hope something sticks? Me. Who listens to everyone's petty, little squabbles about each other's bullshit drama? Me. Who was it that stayed up late every night for the past three goddamn years fixing their mistakes and earning their paychecks? Me!"

Vincent, nearly out of breath and panting, looks embarrassed and withdraws into his chair. "I'm sorry, I-I don't know where that came from." Leo has a proud smile on his face but lets him stew in the moment. Eventually, Vincent looks up at him. "I'm just not confident."

"Can I give you a hint, Vinny?" Leo lowers his voice and leans all the way across the table, causing Vincent to lean in curiously. "It's all a mind game. If you want to be confident like Bobby over there, it's all in your head."

Vincent looks down, unconvinced. He sits back and stares into his glass for a few minutes, then looks up at Leo. "What does that mean?" Vincent asks.

"Well, look at Bobby," Leo says. Vincent looks over to see Bobby sloppily drinking beer and flirting with Sarah. "He's a complete stranger to Sarah, but he just came bumbling into your circle of friends, took your spot next to her at the pong table, and pushed you out like she doesn't even know who you are. Do you think he lets people at work walk all over him?" Vincent sighs, trying to recover from his outburst. "How do you think he does that?" He pauses, but Vincent has no answer. "He demands their attention. And look where it got him, a hell of a lot further than I'd reckon you ever got with her. Do you demand attention, Vincent?"

Vincent blushes again; he shakes his head.

"Do you want to be confident, like Bobby over there?"

Channeling his overwhelming discomfort into the empty glass in his hands, he continues fidgeting with it, twisting it in his fingers, biting the inside of his cheek, and blinking hard over and over so he doesn't accidentally let out an uncomfortable tear. He nods weakly.

"Then go buy me a glass of the finest whiskey they have." Leo pulls out his wallet and throws a fifty-dollar bill on the table.

Vincent inhales choppily and swallows hard before wiping his eyes with his sleeve. He looks at the cash confused. "Wh-What do you mean?"

"You want to be confident, right? Well, nothing says confidence like standing up to that bitch of a bartender and ordering the finest drink they have. Take the cash and go get my drink."

"That's ridiculous, I'm not going to—"

"Yes, you are, Vincent." Leo glares into Vincent's eyes, his silver moustache projecting decades of wisdom and experience.

Vincent stares back, but he doesn't have the wherewithal to hold it. Slowly, he lifts his hand to grab the cash, then stands up. Walking past his friends playing pong with Bobby, he shakily steps toward the bar. Leo takes note of Sarah looking quickly over her shoulder to watch Vincent as he walks away. The bar seems so far away; he can see the bartender flipping through the channels until landing on a replay of the earlier game. Walking for what feels like hours, he makes it to the counter.

"Excuse me," Vincent immediately regrets saying. Looking in the mirror behind the bar, he can see her eyes roll. He chokes on his own nervousness and practically screams across the entire pub, "Hey!" He feels everyone's eyes on him when she looks back.

"What do you want, creep?" she asks.

Shit, what did I want? He looks at her with wide eyes, then panics. "Can I see a menu?"

"There's one right in front of you, Einstein."

"Oh, right." He shrinks into himself and looks through the menu, finding the most expensive whiskey he can find. *Macallan 18. Forty-five dollars for a glass? Holy shit, I bet it doesn't even taste good.* He stares at the menu for a few moments, formulating what he's going to say before he says it. *Just go.* "Can I, um, c-can I get a glass of Macallan 18?"

"Really? You sure about that?"

"Um, yeah. Yes."

"Whatever, dude. It's your money."

She pours the drink, and Vincent smiles triumphantly as he walks back to the booth. His smile fades to find the booth empty, except for a napkin with three words written on it. "Enjoy it, kid." He sits down, folds up the napkin, pockets it, and follows the instructions. He celebrates.

Chapter Two

January 13th, 2020

Monday

The following week, the team finds themselves a few towns away from their own laboratory, wearing suits and ties in lieu of white coats. Hiding out in a college locker room while they get into their Sunday best to look television-ready, the team shuffles around nervously. Grace adjusts the collar on her button-up. "Do you think we're ready for this, Mark? We haven't exactly worked all the kinks out; we're not even ready to publish our findings."

Mark brushes what little hair he has in the mirror and answers, "That's what I told them, but the government wants to drum up some public support before we start testing. Don't worry, this is just a preliminary announcement, you know, for transparency's sake." This answer doesn't seem to satisfy Grace, but her nervousness and excitement dull her skepticism. Sarah adjusts Vincent's tie while Karl lint-rolls Grace's trousers.

Sarah grabs Vincent by the shoulders and takes a deep breath. "There's nothing to it. We just go up there, Mark says a few words, then we leave. We got this, right?"

Her smile radiates through him as he momentarily forgets about the others in the room. But his eyes widen as what she said settles in. "Totally. We just go up and stand in front of a hundred strangers"—his voice cracks—"while they look at us and ask us a bunch of questions. Super easy."

Sarah chuckles. "Oh no, no, no. Mark's the one who answers questions. We're just up there to look pretty. Easy day."

Vincent smiles and says shyly, "Well, that's easy for you, not so much for the rest of us." He feels the sweat drip down his forehead as he blushes.

"Hey now!" Karl yells from across the locker room. "If anyone here is the pretty one, it's gotta be yours truly. Sorry, ladies." He flashes a cocky smile before Grace "accidentally" chokes his tie up a bit too much.

A woman with a headset and a clipboard peeks inside the dressing room. "Two minutes to air—are you guys ready?"

"A bit nervous, but we're ready," Mark replies, and she makes a brisk exit. He addresses the group, "Alright, guys, remember that we're just out there to put a face to this project. You guys are the smartest people in that room. There are no scientists trying to criticize you, and there's nobody out there interested in the actual research. They all just want some fluff pieces about the magic behind science. I'll answer whatever questions they've got for us. Sound good?"

Everyone sighs before quietly agreeing. The headset and clipboard lady returns. "Ten seconds to air. Let's go."

Mark leads the team of researchers through the conference room door to find a large room full of cameras and reporters. A barrage of flash photography immediately blinds them as they file in and walk onto a hastily thrown together stage. Vincent pores over the sea of onlookers. In a room like this, a hundred people feels like a thousand. His movements become stiff and deliberate before lining up against a black curtain and an American flag. Mark stands downstage and steps up to the microphone. The room falls silent.

"Years ago, as a species, we discovered the secret of teleportation on the nanoscale. Quantum bits of information. Individual atoms. We managed to bend reality just a little by moving information from one place to another without crossing the distance between them. Well, today I am proud to announce that my team—"

Vincent's attention shifts to him. *Your team?*

"—at the Marysworth Institute of Nanoscience has taken that secret and brought it to the macroscale. What does this mean, exactly? Well, we aren't just teleporting information anymore. We are teleporting matter itself. Imagine a world without traffic. No cars backed up on the freeway during your commute to work. No more sitting in cramped seats while watching a crappy movie on a long flight. No more waiting for the delivery person to bring you that package scheduled to arrive tomorrow."

What is he doing? That's not how this technology works at all; he's overselling it!

"Today marks the dawn of a new era. With generous funding from the Department of Energy, we are thrilled to be moving forward into the experimental phase of our project. Thank you for your attention; we will now have time to answer a few questions before departing." The room erupts into a game of 'pick-me, pick-me.'

"Yes, you in the front."

A woman in a leather duster raises her pen in the air and says, "Miranda Barkstoff, *Huffington Post*. Why have you focused so heavily on this aspect of research?"

"That's a great question. Science has long considered teleporting humans to be nothing short of an impossible task, and we at the Marysworth Institute of Nanoscience are constantly on the lookout to prove the impossible possible. Next question. Yes, you in the fedora."

A shorter man carrying a notebook pushes through the crowd. "John Haverford, *New York Times*. How soon can we expect commercial products using this technology to hit the market?"

"You know it's tough to gauge things like this sometimes. We still have a few steps to take before you see teleportation pads at Best Buy." The room shares a half-hearted chuckle. "But we are hoping to be out of the testing phase within the next six months. Next question, you in the back?"

Six months? What is he talking about? We have years before we can even think about testing on humans. Vincent feels a tap on his elbow and looks to see Grace with a confused scowl on her face, along with Karl and Sarah sharing her expression behind her. Grace mouths the words, *"What the fuck?"*

A woman with a sadistic grin on her face speaks slightly slower than the rest when she says, "Shelly Robertson, *Wall Street Journal.* Do you care to comment on the ethical implications that arise from killing people for the sake of your research?"

A hush falls over the room. Mark's eyes open widely as he stammers. The room instantly heats up to a thousand degrees as Vincent sweats bullets. *He has no idea what to say to that. Someone has to go up there.* Vincent looks to Grace, whose jaw just goes slack. No action is taken. Mark stands at the microphone unsuccessfully trying to form a coherent sentence.

"Um. Well, I-I don't…" The team all look at each other for a few more moments while Mark flounders. "You see, that's a good question because… um…"

Do you demand attention, Vincent? Vincent closes his eyes and takes a deep breath before his legs act of their own volition. He steps up to the microphone where he awkwardly tries to stand right where Mark is already standing. Mark whispers, "What the hell do you think you're doing?" They shuffle for a moment before Mark finally steps aside.

Vincent stands there frozen for what feels like an hour, just watching the crowd. Eventually he coughs and manages to say, "What, uh, what Miss Robertson is referring to is, uh, a technique known as d-destructive scanning. Is-Is that right, miss?"

She nods subtly with a pompous smirk still on her face.

"Well, it's true that my—well, *our* hypothesis does kill…" He clears his throat and notices sweat dripping down his back. "Our hypothesis does utilize this technique. When we scan an object's atomic structure, it destroys the object." He focuses on his breathing as he speaks. *She's questioning your research.* The rest of the room fades to black. His attention lies solely on the woman in the back of the room. *She's saying you're a bad scientist.* "But it's not like we're going to just test this out on people based on a hunch. We have research! And we'll do more! Other scientists are going to check our work." He feels a fiery rage fueling in his gut. "We're going to test it on inanimate objects first. We're not going to just flagrantly do whatever we want without considering every possible consequence of our actions! That's not how science works!"

Mark slides in front of Vincent to cut him off, "Okay! Thank you very much, that answer comes from my esteemed colleague, Dr. Vincent Creighton, and will conclude today's press conference." The room erupts into a cacophony of shouts and flash photography. "There will be no more questions! Thank you for your attendance!"

They quickly depart the stage and make their way outside to the parking lot where a van awaits them. They pile in and shut the door. At the first break in shouts and screams, Grace exclaims, "What the hell was that, Mark?! You promised those people far more than this project will ever deliver! Teleporting *people*? We haven't even been peer-reviewed yet, much less ready to put airlines out of business!"

Mark avoids eye contact and responds calmly, "Look, Grace, nobody believed in this project. The only reason we were able to get our hands on it was because nobody else would stake their reputation on an impossible theory. But look at us now! We did it!" Vincent, still shaking with adrenaline, scoffs. *He says "we" like he had anything to do with it.* "We needed to take a victory lap for anyone to take this seriously. We're starting up an ad campaign for this technology, and it was going great until that bitch of a reporter asked that stupid question."

"What the fuck do you mean an 'ad campaign'? This isn't a product; it's a hypothesis. There *is* no technology yet. And by the way, that reporter was right: it would literally kill a human person and rebuild them from scratch. That's some serious shit to consider!"

"You're right… and that's why the four of you will be joining the R&D team at DARPA." The van falls silent as everyone glances at each other with amazement.

Sarah speaks first, "Research and Development for DARPA? That's my dream job!"

"Well, you'll be working alongside them from a remote lab, but yeah. They can't do it without you. Six months will pass in the blink of an eye."

Karl says what everyone else is thinking, "I don't know if we can do it, even *with* their help."

Grace tacks on, "Yeah, he's right. Even with DARPA's help and resources, six months is the most ambitious deadline in history. It took NASA eight years to get to the moon, you think we're going to be teleporting by August?"

"The hard part's the theory, right?" Vincent notices Sarah eyeing Mark insightfully, who still appears sweaty and nervous, with just a twinge of guilt. He looks more nervous now than he did during the press conference. "Now all you gotta do is make the damn thing." The rest of the hour-long van ride back to the lab goes by with giddy anticipation for this new chapter of their lives. Vincent shares a beat of cautious excitement with his colleagues, but the worry of Mark overselling his breakthrough lingers.

After arriving back at their own lab, the team bids each other good night and heads home. When Vincent unlocks his car, however, he hears Sarah's voice call out, "Vince! Hold up a second!"

Delighted, Vincent obliges. He has always felt comfortable around Sarah, never feeling the drive to compete with her at anything. She looks at him through emerald eyes and carries her ginger complexion bashfully. A bit shorter than average, Sarah stands about shoulder height to Vincent, but he barely notices. She flashes him a smile. "Hey, I just… I wanted to tell you that you were amazing during the conference. When that reporter asked an ethics question, Mark totally froze up. But you stepped up. I'm really proud of you."

Vincent's heart pounds, but he doesn't know whether it's from the excitement of her compliment or him just reliving the moment. Standing a bit taller, he puffs his chest out. "Thanks, I don't know how much credit I can take for it though. My legs just took over, and my mouth just started talking. I'm about as surprised as you are." They both chuckle at his self-deprecation. As they stand there, he remembers watching Bobby fawn over her. *Do it. Say something.* "You did a good job at looking pretty."

She grins. "Yeah well, someone had to pretend we were all professionals, right?"

"It definitely wasn't going to be Karl, was it?"

"Definitely not! Although, the twenty minutes he spent teasing his hair did pay off." They both laugh and look down at their feet. A moment passes before Sarah says, "So I know you already answered this, but what *do* you think of teleporting people? Obviously, it's going to take forever before we need to think about it, but just out of curiosity, do you think it's a good idea?"

He wrinkles his brow as he thinks about it, then says, "Well, maybe. There's so much that can go wrong, but the same can be said about flying an airplane."

"Yeah, but let's say we did it perfectly. Let's say we use destructive scanning to 'destroy' someone's body and rebuild them somewhere else. Wouldn't we be killing them and then animating someone else?"

Vincent sighs. "I guess we would be, but if we manage to rebuild them as good as new... would that be a bad thing?"

"I guess not. It just seems... weird to me."

"It does seem weird, but..." He thinks back to how stupid he felt sitting by himself at the bar. "Weird isn't always bad, is it?"

Her eyes meet his, and she grins. "I guess not." A comfortable silence passes. "Well, I better get going. You drive safe, okay?" She starts to walk away, but Vincent stops her.

"Wait!"

She turns back around, brushes a lock of hair behind her ear, and smiles expectantly. "Yeah?"

"Um..." *What are you doing?* "The other night... at the Ducky Luck... uh, who were you talking to?"

She instantly crosses her arms. "What's that now?"

"Oh, sorry, um, you went off to talk on the phone, and when you came back, your eyes were red and puffed up. What happened?"

Her body tightens up, and she holds her elbows in each hand. "Oh… that. Um, that was… you know, I'd rather not talk about that, if that's okay?"

"Oh," he blushes, and his face feels hot. "I'm sorry, sure. My bad."

"No, no, no, it's not your bad. It's just, I'm not ready to talk about it."

"Okay… I'm sorry…"

"It's really okay," she smiles at him, which brightens his whole day. "I appreciate your asking."

They bid each other "good night" before parting ways. Vincent puts the key in the ignition and just sits there for a few seconds, bathing in the moment. He looks over his steering wheel to see Karl's truck still parked, from the driver's seat he's flashing double thumbs-up along with a wide grin. Vincent blushes and buries his face into his hands with embarrassment, then fires up his Honda Civic and speeds out of the lab's parking lot.

Flickering street lights barely illuminate the crowded parking lot of Vincent's apartment complex. Watching his breath condense in the cold air keeps his mind occupied as he walks to his building. After trudging up several flights of stairs, he flips the lights on and hangs his keys up on the entryway shelf before he hears a calm voice pipe up from inside his living room.

"Hey there, Vinny."

His eyes dart over to a mysterious figure fiddling with the Rubik's cube he keeps on his bookshelf, but no words manage to escape his lips. Vincent's stomach drops as his brain blazes through the options that are available to him while subtly grabbing at the umbrella posted up against the door. *Turn around and leave? Does he have a gun? Should I say hello?* The umbrella fully in his grasp, he now doesn't know what he should do with it.

"Oh, you won't need that," the man says without looking up from the puzzle. He's wearing black leather gloves, a black turtleneck, and a black blazer. He gives up on the puzzle and sets it on the coffee table. "Though I must say, I admire the instinct. Do you mind if I make myself at home?"

"Uh, s-sure," the word slips out. "Who, uh, what do you want?"

The man chuckles before looking at his seating choices. Recliner or sofa. He chooses the sofa and puts his feet up on the coffee table. "I'm not here to rob you or hurt you. So don't you worry about that." As the man gets comfortable, Vincent sees under his blazer the grip of a small handgun strapped under the man's arm. "I'm here on official business. Are you gonna sit?" He asks, gesturing to the recliner.

Vincent's legs refuse to move as his breathing becomes labored. Mark has everybody take online trainings for active-shooter situations, but none of that comes to mind as he stands there frozen.

"Look, Vinny, you're making me real nervous here. Why don't you just take a breath, sit down, and we'll have a little chitchat. Then I'll be on my merry little way. What do you say?" Vincent blushes with a burst of social anxiety. The tone of his voice is pleasant, but Vincent can't take his eyes off the gun. *Just breathe and do what he says.*

He lifts his concrete legs and steps toward the recliner, shakily sitting down.

"There we go, that's not so bad, is it?" The man takes his feet off the table and leans on one knee, gun displayed in full view. "Now that we're both comfortable, my name is Trent. It's nice to meet you, Vincent." A moment of quiet. "And then you say—" He gestures for Vincent to speak, but Vincent fails to produce a response.

"I know you're nervous right now, but let me tell you this: I think you're gonna be glad that I dropped by today. You see, I watched that press conference. You stood up to that reporter like nobody's business! You're a hero, Vinny!"

I don't feel like a hero right now.

"And I heard you just got a new job. In a cool new laboratory, right?

That's a pretty sweet deal. What's not a sweet deal, though, is the way your peers have been treating you."

Vincent's eyebrows perk up slightly.

"Some government friends of mine saw your report. Well, I should say 'your *team's* proposal', but I think we both know it was mostly you who wrote it, right?"

Vincent glares at him, seemingly interested.

"I thought so. The others contributed, sure, but without you, there is no project, is there? They're only getting this job because of you. How does that make you feel, Vincent?"

His voice is frozen, but he doesn't break eye contact with Trent.

"Yeah, I'd feel pretty upset, too. Especially considering they don't even acknowledge the fact that you're the better scientist and deserve more of the credit. I saw the way they treated you; they made it sound like all four of you contributed equally across the board." He leans forward, giving Vincent another view of his sidearm. "That's just not how the world works, I get it. My friends and I see the world for how it really works. Like you do."

Vincent's eyes fall to the Rubik's cube on the coffee table. Closing his eyes, he takes three deep breaths and wishes for everything to go back to normal. He opens his eyes to see Trent still sitting there, his gun still visible from inside his jacket.

"I used to work with some people who were like your friends, Vinny. They put on a trustworthy façade, but then the first chance they get, what do they do? They stab you in the back. They leave you out to dry." The moment lingers for a while. "I'll tell you what though, I learned a lot from those people. I think you can, too."

Listening as best he can through bated breath, Vincent makes eye contact again with Trent.

"You've got a good head on your shoulders. Trust your own eyes—your own instincts. And if you're ever in the market for some new friends, give us a call." He reaches into his blazer's inner pocket, but Vincent stands up, nearly tripping over the recliner as he does so.

"Relax, Vinny! You're so jumpy. I'm just reaching for my card." He cautiously pulls out a small business card and tosses it on the coffee table. It's a thin piece of cardstock printed simply with a phone number. "Give us a call if you feel like you need a friend." Trent stands, straightens his blazer, and walks toward the door. Vincent eyes the card on the table for a moment.

"Wait." Vincent barely even registers that he was the one who just spoke.

Trent freezes before turning the doorknob, then he looks over his shoulder.

"Who are you?"

Trent smirks. "We're big fans of your work." His leather glove turns the doorknob, and he leaves, closing the door behind him.

Vincent stands frozen for a minute before letting out a deep sigh. He steels himself and sprints to the door, locking the deadbolt and watching through the eyehole to see the headlights of a black sedan illuminate. Closing up all the window blinds and turning off the lights, he considers his next move. *Do I call the police? Do I call Mark?* He pulls out his phone and starts dialing nine-one-one, but hovers over the "call" button. *What would I tell them? What if he hacked my phone? What if they are the police? Do they know Mark? Was I the only one he's come to?*

Calculating the risk, he cautiously begins typing a text message. *Gotta choose my words carefully.*

"Hey, Sarah, did you make it home safely?"

Is that weird? I don't want to tip anyone off, in case I am being watched. He stares at the cursor blinking at the end of the sentence for about five minutes before erasing it, typing it again, and eventually sending it. Pacing in his living room, he does a check around the rest of his apartment, just in case. He finds nothing, so he sits in his recliner, clutching his umbrella. He intermittently peers out of his blinds before hearing a bell sound from his phone.

"I did! Thanks for checking :)"

He lets out a sigh of relief. *She probably wouldn't send a smiley face under duress.* He sits in his recliner armed with his umbrella, texting the other two members until he is convinced that nobody else was met with a strange visitor. Daring not to turn the TV on or get distracted by reading a book, he takes a deep breath and dwells in his anxieties until finally falling asleep, all the while thinking one thing over and over.

Why me?

CHAPTER THREE

January 16th, 2020

Thursday

Mark calls for a team meeting at the Marysworth lab. Vincent decides not to tell anyone about his late-night visitor, figuring it might be too dangerous to show his hand in case he is being watched. They meet at the lab in the morning, but about twenty minutes later, a large, broad-shouldered man wearing a military uniform enters through the front door. Taking his flight cap and black aviator sunglasses off as he comes inside, his face stays contorted with the scowl of enduring a bright, sunny day.

"Good morning, Colonel Bartram." Mark anxiously walks over to shake his hand. "Welcome to the Marysworth lab. This is my team." Grace is the first to be introduced, followed by the rest of the team. "Colonel Bartram is here to brief us on your new job."

"Good morning, ladies and gentlemen," he says with a curt and husky voice "The United States Air Force is proud to have you four bright minds join us on this project." Everyone smiles and nods politely, forgiving his tardiness despite him not apologizing. The colonel opens the briefcase he's carrying in his left hand and passes out a few manila folders with stacks of paper inside. "How do you folks feel about the desert?" Everyone exchanges unsure looks. "You will be relocated to Wyoming. We have a small base out in the Red Desert we use for tech development. It's isolated. It's quiet. You can focus on your work out there with the rest of the R&D team for the duration of this project." Everyone looks over the stack of papers as he gives them an overview; background check consent forms, personal and family history information, non-disclosure agreements, and an incredibly long employment contract.

"I know this all looks intimidating, but it's just a bunch of red tape. I guarantee you, the faster we cut through it, the faster this teleportation machine comes to life."

They spend the next several hours filling out these forms, but Vincent feels uneasy about the whole situation. It seems so quick. The whole group intermittently looks up to Mark for affirmation. He always nods and smiles, but Sarah doesn't seem terribly convinced. Never wanting to be the squeaky wheel, Vincent pushes through. Signing this, providing that, and trying to read everything as thoroughly as possible, but there is just too much for a normal person to fully comprehend in one sitting.

When they finally finish reviewing everything, Colonel Bartram collects it all. "Thank you for your cooperation. There will be a car waiting for you at your homes in exactly ten days."

"Woah, wait a second, ten days?" Grace says cautiously. "We only get ten days' notice to pack up our shit and make the necessary arrangements? Seems a bit quick, doesn't it?"

"What were you hoping for, a whole month?"

Grace gawks at him with her trademark attitude. "Yes. At least. Or even two to three months would have been better."

"That's not how we work in the military, princess, we have deadlines. You can't just dink around for months at a time wistfully reminiscing about your past, you see? We have work to do."

"And we have lives to live. I have to give my apartment adequate notice, I have to pack, I have to work things out with my family. My world doesn't revolve around you, you know that, right?"

"You don't need to worry about your housing, or change of address, or any of that. We have an administrative team that handles everything. You won't need to pack much anyway; you'll be staying in a fully furnished barracks room, and your meals will be provided."

"Did you just say *barracks*? I'm not staying in barracks like a soldier in the field."

"You'll find your stay quite comfortable. I assure you."

"You're not doing a great job of making me feel assured. Mark, did you know about this? The deadline, the barracks?"

Mark looks up at the colonel with fear in his eyes and hesitates. "Um… yeah." He fails to make eye contact with anyone. "I thought I sent you an email about the timeline? I must have forgotten."

"What the fuck, Mark? You forgot to tell us we're leaving for a desert in Wyoming next week? That's not something you just forget!"

The colonel cuts her off, "Listen, you can bicker about it if you want, but either way, there's going to be a car picking you up ten days from right now. You can spend your time here arguing or at home packing. It's up to you."

Grace looks at the rest of the team with fire in her eyes. "Can I talk to you guys outside, please?" Then she storms outside into the parking lot. The others quietly dismiss themselves and follow.

Pacing back and forth, taking laps around their parked cars, Grace shouts in a hoarse whisper, "I don't trust that guy! He comes in, makes us sign a bunch of bullshit, then tells us we're leaving in ten days? Who the hell does he think he is?!"

Sarah's face bore a terribly concerned look. "Yeah, I can't just up and leave that soon. I have… things to take care of. Also, the way Mark was acting kinda gave me the creeps. I thought you all were cool with it so I just went with the flow. I'm glad I'm not the only one."

"Aw, c'mon guys," Karl speaks up. "That's just how the military works. My dad was in the Army, and he's the same way—direct. That's how things get done, his way or the highway. When you say you're going to do something, you don't stand around for a month talking about it. You just do it."

"Being direct is one thing. Telling someone they're moving with less than a two-week notice is another thing altogether. It's poor planning…

and inconsiderate!" Grace takes another lap around their parked cars. They stand there for a moment, thinking about what to say. Vincent's eyes wander, landing on the doughnut shop across the street. A black van with tinted windows is parked in front of it. He squints. A man wearing dark sunglasses sits in the driver's seat, holding a phone to his ear. He doesn't seem to be talking at all, but his head is on a swivel, watching everything in sight—especially the Marysworth parking lot.

Vincent barely notices as Grace goes off on something else the colonel said earlier about it being 'his project.' *He isn't talking. He's listening. I wonder...* As subtly as he can manage, Vincent slides his phone out of his pocket and palms it. He sneakily looks down to find a green light illuminated on the phone. His microphone is active.

Oh shit. Panicking, he turns the phone off.

"Who are you texting, Vince?"

His eyes dart up to find all three of his friends giving him quizzical looks.

"Oh, uh, nobody. Just checking the time." Back at the doughnut shop, he finds the man still with a phone to his ear. His mouth moves a few times. Then he hangs up as somebody exits the shop to get in his car. A box of doughnuts in hand, they drive off.

"You haven't said much about this whole thing, Vince. What do you think about the colonel?" Sarah asks.

He shakes his head. "W-Well, uh, I mean, Grace is right." She mouths the words *"thank you"* in vindication. He looks down at his feet and adds, "The whole thing is, um, weird and off-putting, but... it sounds like they're going to do it with or without us." He pauses for a moment, considering what Leo would say in this situation. He looks up into Sarah's eyes. "But um, but it's our research. If they build this thing without us, they're going to erase our names and credit some other scientist who has no idea what they're talking about."

Sarah nods in agreement. "That's true. They're going to move forward either way, and if they test it on someone using some other schmuck's data, someone's going to get hurt."

Getting frustrated, Grace says, "But that's not our responsibility, is it? If someone volunteers for a half-assed experiment, that's not on us."

Karl says, "Isn't it, though? I mean, we discovered this thing." *I discovered it. You were passed out in a pizza box.* "We should see it through to the end, shouldn't we?"

Sarah seems to be deep in thought as she looks at her feet. "Yeah… if whoever takes over the project decides to—I don't know—pay college students a hundred bucks to volunteer for an incomplete experiment, that's kind of on us, at least to some extent," she admits.

Grace sighs deeply. "You're right." Defeated, she breaks away and paces. "We have to take ownership over whatever happens with our research." Everyone shuffles for a moment in silence until Grace breaks the ice. "Let's get back in there."

Though he hides his expression, the colonel is thrilled to hear that they will join the project. They all depart for their homes to manage their affairs. However, Vincent stops by for a jelly doughnut as he leaves. He looks for anything out of place, any person who seems a bit more attentive than others, or anything that might pop out to him, but… nothing. *I'm just paranoid. Phones turn on for no reason all the time.* Receiving his order, he leaves feeling uncertain.

CHAPTER FOUR

January 26th, 2020

Sunday

Vincent is jolted awake by the sound of banging at his door. Startled, he grabs the kitchen knife he started sleeping with and takes a few breaths. He slowly walks through his house and checks every room before looking through the door's eyehole. A man wearing a military uniform is visible through the fisheye lens. *Is it time already?* He looks at the clock. Four-thirty in the morning. He replaces the kitchen knife and opens the door.

The man greets him, "Good morning, Mr. Creighton. I'm Technical Sergeant Martinez, are you ready?"

Vincent rubs his eyes. "Yeah, let me just..." He looks back at the clock. "Do you want some coffee? It'll only take a minute."

"Unfortunately"—Sergeant Martinez looks at his watch and clicks his tongue—"we're on a bit of a tight schedule. We have a long drive ahead of us."

"Of course, we do." He gathers his bags, and they head down to a grey van with government plates. Loading up his bags into the back, he notices another military person waiting in the driver seat, along with Grace and Karl asleep in the back.

"That's Senior Airman Little. He'll be our driver today."

Karl stirs at the sound of the sliding van door, his blonde bed-head spiked up all over the place. "Hey, buddy. Welcome to the, uh"—he yawns—"the party." He then passes out into the sweater that he's fashioned into a pillow.

Vincent takes a spot in the back and tries to follow suit with the pitch-black sky lingering overhead, but as they leave his apartment complex, something catches his eye. They're being followed. A black sedan with its lights turned off follows at a distance while still maintaining visual contact with the van. Vincent looks to their military detail, but they're both too busy talking about something called their "Senior NCO" to notice anything. *Do I say something?*

As they pull into another apartment complex, Vincent loses track of the sedan and panics silently. They park, and Sergeant Martinez gets out. Sitting there with only the sound of the running engine to focus on, Vincent looks through the tinted windows to get a glance of anything that might be moving out there. *Nothing.*

The back door opens to let Sarah put her bags in with everyone else's. Vincent quickly turns back around and pretends to be stirred awake at the disturbance.

"Oh hey, I'm sorry to wake you," her tired voice croaks before walking around to get in the van. The only empty seat left is next to Vincent, so she settles in and yawns. "I didn't know there still was a four-thirty in the morning; I thought they got rid of it after grad school." She stretches and settles her head against Vincent's shoulder, causing his stomach to erupt into butterflies. Her curly red hair falls across his chest. Vincent, having never experienced anything like this before, tenses up as his eyes widen.

Departing for the San Francisco airport, Vincent tries watching for signs of movement. This proves difficult as he attempts to keep his shoulder as still as possible, severely limiting his range of vision. Fortunately—or maybe unfortunately—they aren't followed. An uneventful two-and-a-half-hour flight later, they find themselves back in a Grand Caravan with government plates driving down a dirt road. The road extends endlessly into a sea of sagebrush-covered fields surrounded by massive rock formations and dunes of white sand blowing in the wind. In the greener stretches of land, herds of deer cross the road ahead of them, a distant pack of coyotes settles into a crack in a rock formation, and prairie dogs, ferrets, and all sorts of other small animals scurry in between the brush.

A few grueling hours of driving through the harsh North American desert pass, then they finally see civilization up ahead. The closer they get to it, however, the less civilized it appears to be. It's a small gated area sitting at the base of a rocky mountain. The gate stretches a little over a quarter-mile in length on each side and surrounds what looks to be a few concrete buildings and a smattering of old, decrepit shacks that look as if they haven't been maintained since the shooting at the OK Corral.

Grace is the first to address everyone's thoughts, "This is where we'll be living for the next six months?"

Sergeant Martinez grins. "It sure is. I know it looks a bit, well, cozy. But I promise it's a lot more comfortable than it appears."

Sarah asks, "What are those old shacks?"

"The ruins of an old general store and a small armory. This used to be a military fort during the Oregon Trail days. We believe they used this fort to protect the emigrants against bands of Shoshone Indians during the Westward Expansion."

"Oh my gosh, that's awful."

"Awful?" Karl interjects. "Don't you mean awesome? Could you imagine walking for months on end only to have your wagon burned to the ground and you get speared in the chest in front of your family? Those men were providing an invaluable service to their country."

"I suppose..."

Sergeant Martinez cuts back in, "Yes, well, across the street from them, you'll see your new homes. Two barracks buildings and the work space."

Grace says, "Wait, only one of those is for working? How small is this lab? That looks even smaller than our office back home."

"You'll see once we get inside," he says as they approach a security checkpoint at the gate, which simply looks like a cramped booth. Two Airmen sit inside the booth, and one of them comes out to greet the van. As he walks, his right hand cradles the grip of an M16 strapped around his shoulder, and his sidearm pistol bounces on his thigh. Both Sergeant Martinez and Senior Airman Little produce identification cards. The gate guard scans both IDs, then peers inside the van. He shines a small flashlight on each of them in the back.

"Afternoon, sir, just the six of you?" he asks skeptically.

"Yeah, the old man should have called yesterday," Sergeant Martinez answers. "There was a scheduling conflict, so he's going to be late."

The gate guard turns back to address the other guard and asks, "Did you hear about this?"

He rolls his eyes. "Yes, did you check your email?"

As they bicker, Vincent looks inside the booth to see a wall of closed-circuit TV screens watching camera feeds of every corner of the base and the perimeter around each of the buildings on the campus.

He hesitates, then says, "How can I check every single email? There's too many!" before handing back the credentials. "Anyway, you gentlemen have a lovely day."

They pull into a small parking lot containing three other Grand Caravans and a small fleet of pick-up trucks. The January air feels relatively cool and refreshing as they exit the van. They unload their bags and are shown to their rooms. The barracks buildings have a faint yet persistent aroma of sand and cleaning products. Vincent is surprised to see how many people there are roaming the halls. There are several floors of rooms, each of them with a common area where people might gather to socialize or watch one of the six VHS tapes that are provided.

"We have more scientists and engineers than we have rooms, so you will need to be doubled up, unfortunately." Vincent and Karl are led to a room while Sarah and Grace get one across the hall from them. A dry erase board outside their rooms has their names written on it. Inside, they find two twin beds, two wall lockers, and a window that overlooks a small gazebo, volleyball court, perimeter fence, and miles of open desert. "You have the rest of the afternoon to unpack and settle in, but I will meet you at the gazebo at zero-seven-hundred tomorrow. We'll get you through indoc, then you'll get to work. Welcome to DARPA."

Chapter Five

January 27th, 2020

Monday

The brisk, early morning air gives Vincent a chill down his spine as he stands alone at the gazebo. The cold doesn't bother him as much as it used to; Massachusetts weathered him to it well enough, but he wasn't prepared for how dry it would be. His skin feels crackly, and he feels like he's constantly on the brink of a nosebleed. He had woken up earlier than the others so he could take a hot shower before the rest of the floor had a chance to ravage all of the warm water. *This will be my me-time from now on, I suppose.*

"You're here early," Sergeant Martinez says as he exits the second barracks building. Vincent looks down at his watch. Six thirty-two A.M.

"I guess so, yeah. Just, you know, wanted a hot shower. You too?"

Sergeant Martinez leans against the gazebo's handrail and dons a pair of military-issue gloves. "No, me and the other security guys have to wake up before you smart types. We can't protect you from coyotes and mountain lions if we're asleep, can we?"

"Mountain lions? Is that a fun job?"

"Too fun. Sergeant Cesar and his dog are excellent hunters," he grins brightly. "But the military guys and I have a few different jobs: we watch the gate, do patrols in the trucks, and most importantly—groundskeeping." He gestures out to the sandy parking lot and unkempt tufts of sagebrush here and there and laughs. "It's hard work. Plus, with the supply deliveries coming in every week, we have to help them unload and move crates."

"So… you guys are kind of the work horses around here then?"

"That's one way to put it, I suppose." They sit in silence until the top of the hour when Grace and Sarah join them, followed by Karl, who is characteristically fifteen minutes late. They all shuffle over to the single-story workspace building, the door to which is accompanied by a large, armed guard who lifts his chin and steps up to them as they approach.

"Hey, Murphy, these are the new guys." Martinez taps him on the shoulder. Murphy nods and backs down. Martinez pulls out his identification card and presents it to the scanner mounted on the door. It beeps, and they hear a click as the door unlocks. Martinez then holds the door open for everyone as they enter the foyer of a typical municipal building. Chalky, white drywall surrounds them in a corridor that leads to a security checkpoint with a large locker containing multiple cubbies, a conveyor belt X-ray machine, and a metal detector staffed by a single sergeant and his canine partner. A bloodhound sits attentively, its droopy ears and sad eyes lazily looking them over while sniffing and licking at the air.

"Oh my gosh! Such a beautiful puppy!" Sarah coos as they enter.

"That is our resident good girl, Dolly. You'll see her doing her rounds, playing her part in keeping us all safe. You all left your phones in your rooms, yes?"

Grace pulls her attention away from Dolly. "Were we supposed to?"

"Absolutely, this is a secure facility. No phones, nothing with Wi-Fi, Bluetooth, nothing. It's okay if you brought them with you, you can just lock them up in the cubbies, take the key with you, then just grab it on your way out." Vincent's heart beats faster at the thought of leaving his phone here. *What if they go snooping and somehow find out about Trent?*

"You really should have mentioned that yesterday or even, I don't know, ten minutes ago in front of the gazebo."

"It's really no big deal, you guys," Karl says, happily locking his phone up and pocketing the key. "C'mon, let's get to work." He empties his pockets for the X-ray machine and walks through the metal detector. Grace and Sarah sigh and follow suit, but Vincent sweats a little before acquiescing.

Sergeant Martinez leads them past the checkpoint to a split hallway. On their left is an inlet with four elevator doors, and to their right is a door printed with big, bold letters spelling out the word "Admin" on it. Sergeant Martinez opens the admin door and leads them down a series of hallways, each with portraits of people in suits and ties, display cases with Meritorious Unit Commendation awards, and several offices and placards with corporate sounding names and titles:

Bryan Forsyth, Accounts Manager

Dr. Delilah Abbott, On-site Psychologist

Richard Tasker, Supply and Acquisitions

As they walk, Sergeant Martinez gives them a spiel about the history of the base. "After the Westward Expansion, this base, Fort Chivington, was forgotten until it was reestablished in 1939 upon the discovery of nuclear fission. The researchers here were tasked with creating what the world feared the most: the first atomic bomb. Unfortunately, they failed in this endeavor. The incident was buried and revived in 1942, renamed The Manhattan Project. Ever since then, this place was turned into a black site and has been used for the initial development of the most cutting-edge technology."

"They failed? What happened?" Grace asks.

"Well, frankly, they didn't have an Oppenheimer. They didn't have a leader. They were a band of misfit scientists excited to blow stuff up for their country."

"Do we have an Oppenheimer now?" Vincent asks.

"We do," he says with a knowing grin. "Dr. Russell Smith. He is the DARPA civilian project manager. He's responsible for finding and directing the best and brightest minds that the country has to offer. We then bring those minds here to help develop the greatest technologies that mankind will ever create." He stops in front of an office door labeled "Master Sergeant Tzofiya Kritzman-Director of Security."

"Wait, *the* Dr. Russell 'Runs With Fire' Smith?! We used some of his findings on energy conversion in our research," Grace exclaims. "That man is a visionary!"

"Well, he must have thought the same about you all, because he was the one who sent Colonel Bartram out to recruit you." As Sergeant Martinez says this, Vincent smirks at the rest of his team. *You're welcome.*

"I'm going to pass you guys off to Master Sergeant Kritzman—she is our head of security; she'll get you set up with your ID cards and get the ball rolling on all the administration crap that needs to get done. I'll see you guys in a few hours."

The first part of the day is spent in-processing; getting pictures taken for their ID, network accesses, general administerial work. While his friends are on autopilot, filing paperwork and signing documents, Vincent's eyes are peeled. As he sits with Master Sergeant Kritzman, he notices several binders on her shelf. Twelve of them are labeled B1 through B12. She pulls out B1 and files their personal information in it before assigning them ID cards. They finish at about noon, at which point Sergeant Martinez escorts them out of the admin spaces and into the elevator inlet.

"Is the lab in the basement?" Grace asks, as Sergeant Martinez calls for the elevator.

"It is, along with the cafeteria, the library, the atrium, more barracks, and the gym," he says coyly as Grace shares a confused look with the group.

"Atrium? Um, how big is this basement?" she asks as the elevator door opens, and he ushers them inside.

"You'll see. Have you ever been to the top of the Empire State building?" He presses the only down arrow, and the doors shut. They begin descending, and everyone's ears pop a few times. "The lab is three times deeper in the Earth than the Empire State building is tall. Sitting nearly four thousand feet below the surface, it provides us with the protection we need from the elements, which is absolutely critical for the precise work that you guys do every day."

"How..." Karl stammers, "How have I never heard of this before?"

"We're good at keeping secrets." He grins suspiciously. "Speaking of secrets, you all remember the non-disclosure agreements you signed?" They all nod. "This building is a black site. It does not exist. Even when speaking about the workspace above ground, on the phone, to any other human being, you will not refer to any underground structure or discuss any of the work that is done here. Any discussion of work, on-site amenities, or even inter-workplace drama must be conducted within the confines of the lab. Is that understood?"

The group all look at each other. Grace seems visibly disturbed, and Sarah looks uncomfortable, but Karl has a childlike twinkle in his eyes. He excitedly nods his head and proclaims, "Sir, yes, sir!"

Martinez chuckles, "You don't have to call me 'sir'; only my subordinates do that."

As the elevator comes to a halt, the door slides open to reveal a massive oasis garden twice the size of a football field containing granite-laden dirt pathways cutting through the trunks of hundred and fifty feet tall Giant Sequoia trees that soar into a blue sky. Rays of golden sunlight streak down on them through the Sequoia canopy. The garden is surrounded by blue marble walls that stretch up, disappearing into the simulated sky. The faint roar of a waterfall hums off in the distance as it splashes into a pool of crystal-clear water, but the scent of blooming gardenias draws attention to the myriad of colorful plant life that are scattered across the gardens.

The group exits the elevator inlet and watches on, jaws agape, as they see dozens of scientists walking through the garden and discussing the various experiments that they're working on; a pair of individuals that Vincent remembers seeing in the barracks from the day before walks past them and steps into the elevator from which they just departed.

Across the way, however, Vincent catches eyes with a few older scientists with less than optimistic faces who avert their gaze and walk in the opposite direction.

"Wh... how... where are we?" Sarah asks with wonderment in her voice.

"Welcome to the Abaddon," a female voice says from behind them. A middle-aged woman wearing a white lab coat approaches them, her eyes glistening with sincerity and her hair pulled back into a tight bun.

"Dr. Blackwell!" Sergeant Martinez welcomes her. "These are our newest neighbors. Guys, this is Dr. Mavis Blackwell, supervisor for the teleportation project. She is a... biomedical engineer?"

"You got it that time! Congratulations! However, I do have a slight correction, it's more like *I* will be joining *them*," she remarks, her voice warm like a pitcher of sun tea on a summer afternoon. "Your names have created quite the buzz in the scientific community! It's an honor to have you join us. Please, call me Mavis, the scientists all use each other's first names down here."

"It's a pleasure to meet you, Dr. Blackwell, er, Mavis. But... where exactly *is* here?" Grace asks, still sounding awestruck.

Sergeant Martinez answers, "This will be your home for at least the next six months. If you decide to stick around after your contract is up, you can choose to move underground, joining your brothers and sisters inside the Abaddon. The rooms, of course, are a lot better. Private bed and bath, better entertainment setups, just a real treat all around."

Sarah steps lightly through the dirt pathways, bending over to smell the gardenias. Grace and Karl approach one of the Giant Sequoias, feeling the trunk and admiring their overwhelming size. Vincent stays back next to Sergeant Martinez and asks, "How did they create the illusion of the sky?"

"Well, I'm sure Dr. Blackwell is more capable than I am at answering any questions you may have, so I'm going to leave you with her for the rest of the afternoon. Enjoy your work here at the Abaddon, guys." Everyone says goodbye as he departs for the elevators.

"Before I answer your question, Dr. Creighton, can you all tell me your first names? I think I remember most of you from your files." She points to each of them as she says their names. "I believe it's Karl, our local quantum theory expert. Sarah, our stargazer. Grace, the computer whisperer. And Dr. Creighton, I am so sorry, dear! I'm afraid I don't remember your first name."

Are you kidding me? It's Vincent. Like, Van Gogh! Visionary of his generation!

Vincent doesn't realize how long he stands in silence before Sarah saves the day. "His name is Vincent. He's our math wizard. He was actually the one who found the missing puzzle piece in our research." Vincent's face flushes as she says this. Grace, however, rolls her eyes.

"Well, Vincent, it is an honor to have you join us in the Abaddon." They continue walking through the garden. "Back to your question—one of our projects was to create an artificial microcosm of the sun and atmosphere to use on the International Space Station, and hopefully, on our future Mars colony. It's hard to tell, but there's a sophisticated environmental control system built into the walls that surround the garden. The 'sun' is programmed to replicate the way the real sun moves, mimicking the time of day, the seasons, and the weather. You can even get a sunburn if you're out here for too long." Vincent listens carefully as the others walk ahead, oohing and ahhing at the beautiful flowerbeds and commenting on how realistic the warmth of the sun feels.

When they reach the center of the garden, Mavis gathers everyone for an orientation. "If you look ahead of us through the trees, do you see that large set of glass double doors near the pool? Right above it, there's a letter 'N' printed over it. You guys see it?" Everyone nods. "That 'N' is for the north wing. We have north, east, south, and west wings. You'll get your chance to explore each wing later, but for now I'm going to take you to the south wing. That's where the food's at! The cafeteria makes up the entire south wing, and I'm sure you guys are starving after a long day of admin work," she says, smiling with prominent dimples. Vincent notices that her happy demeanor seems to have a calming presence on the others, but it puts him on edge.

The glass double doors automatically slide open as they approach, revealing a fine dining hall apparently suited for several hundred diners. They are met with the aroma of freshly baked bread and roasted chicken as they look out over a sea of round tables populated by scientists in lab coats. People retrieve plates of food from several stations catered with a wide variety of meals. In the back of the room, two private dining areas frame the path that leads into the bustling kitchen.

"You guys just get comfortable here and enjoy your lunch. I need to go take care of something in the lab, but I'll meet you back in the atrium in an hour." She politely excuses herself and shuffles off. The four of them grab a few plates of food and sit at one of the few empty tables.

"Can you guys believe it?" Karl says giddily. "How did we score this huge? This is the most beautiful place I have ever seen!"

"It is very pretty, I suppose," Sarah mutters.

"You've got to be kidding me," Grace addresses Karl condescendingly. "This is weird. How the hell could they have kept this a secret for this long? I mean, them being 'good at keeping secrets' is one thing. This is something else entirely."

"Guys, c'mon! We're in the middle of the desert," Karl says with a mouthful of mashed potatoes. "How often do you drive out to the middle of the desert to look for secret government buildings? This place is perfect!"

"It's not the fact that we're in the desert, Karl! It's the fact that we're in a city four thousand feet underground in the middle of the desert!" Grace realizes she's raising her voice so she brings it down to a whisper. "Does this not feel the slightest bit suspicious to you?" Karl just shrugs his shoulders as he wolfs down his food.

Sarah nods in agreement. "Yeah, it is kind of weird. How many people do you think live down here?"

"Five hundred and seventy-six," Vincent says abruptly. "Approximately."

They look at him, confused, and Grace asks, "How do you figure that?"

"Did you guys not see the binders in the security office? There were twelve binders. Our information was filed into B1. Barrack one, or Building one, I'm not sure. But our building has sixteen rooms per floor and three floors. That's forty-eight rooms per building. If there are twelve buildings, that's five hundred and seventy-six rooms. They double up the newbies in B1, but I assume there are a few vacancies down here that about evens it out. Although, if they doubled up in every building, it would be one thousand one hundred and fifty-two people, but I'm not sure if they'd be able to sustain that many people here." He looks around at everyone with a blank expression. "Also, those Giant Sequoia trees ranged from one hundred and fifty-eight point two to two hundred and four point eight feet tall, and twenty-seven point five feet to thirty-two point eight feet in circumference—meaning they must have been planted circa 1945. So… they built this place during World War II, but there was no technology capable of all this at that time."

"Right… well… that just feeds my point," Grace says, brushing off Vincent's monologue. "They somehow manage to keep almost six hundred people and several giant trees down here, but no one knows it exists?"

"Oh my God!" Karl rolls his eyes at them. "You guys are overreacting. You have no frame of reference. Tell me about all the other secret science labs you're basing this judgment on, please. Go ahead." Nobody says anything. "Exactly. We've been here for a total of like, what? Twenty-four hours?"

"Twenty-five hours, seventeen minutes, and forty-seven seconds."

"Thank you, Vincent." Karl chuckles. "We've only been here for a day, and all we've really learned is that we're not always the smartest people in the room." Vincent snorts. Karl gestures to the crowds of other scientists around the cafeteria. "Everyone's been here longer than us. Let's get a lay of the land before jumping to a conclusion."

Grace and Sarah share a look of concession, then Grace says, "He's got a point."

They silently enjoy their lunch for a while before Sarah says, "I wish Mark would have come with us. He's kind of a jerk, but it was nice to have someone to make the big decisions."

"Yeah, did he ever tell you guys why he stayed back?" Grace asks, but everyone shakes their heads and keeps eating.

AFTER LUNCH, Mavis brings the group to the west wing. Similar glass double doors automatically slide open, revealing a grand foyer of the blue marble walls in the atrium. Two sets of staircases frame a large oak door engraved with the phrase "*E Pur Si Muove*" over a stained-glass window. The stairs lead up to a platform that splits at the top.

"We're heading upstairs and to the right," Mavis says. "But when you get some free time, you should check out the library," she gestures to the oak door on the first floor but leads them up to the second. They take an elevator to the third floor, and Mavis explains, "We have six laboratories here in the Abaddon. Three on each side. They're stacked on top of each other, and unfortunately, our lab is at the top."

"Why is that unfortunate?"

"Well, I guess it isn't anymore, but we used to have a stairwell that was a pain to climb several times a day. We're constantly working on something or another, always developing the most bleeding-edge technology. Right now, in addition to teleportation, we have labs dedicated to developing invisibility tech, anti and artificial gravity, telepathic communication, light-speed travel, and the lab I actually transferred from, the CRISPR lab, where we worked every aspect of DNA research we could imagine."

"Wow," Grace cuts in. "You guys are incredibly busy. Does each scientist have a similar story to us?"

"To an extent, yes. Everyone here distinguished themselves in a specific way that we thought might be of value to one of our projects. You guys, however, made a breakthrough on a tech that we were already working on."

"We beat you to the punch?" Grace asks.

"Essentially, yes." *I beat them to the punch, thank you very much.* "And we're happy you did, because with your help, we should be able to send out some useful tech to our troops overseas by August."

"Hell yeah!" Karl exclaims fervently.

"Actually, about that. Don't you think that timeline is a bit… ambitious?" Grace asks.

"You would be surprised at how much you can get done when you get a team as smart as ours together, eating, sleeping, and breathing this stuff. Not to mention our wealth of resources." Grace, Sarah, and Vincent share a skeptical look, but Karl just has an excited grin on his face.

Entering the third-floor lab, Vincent finally feels some semblance of being at home. He feels like a kid in a candy store as he peruses aisles of workstations, dragging his hand along pristine, beautiful tables. The room is filled with top of the line computing equipment, every article of safety gear imaginable, and ream upon ream of every shape and size of graph paper he's ever dreamt of.

"So this is our research center—three thousand square feet of pure, nerd heaven." As the group explores the room, Vincent takes in the scent of chemical sanitation, the brisk, still air around them, and the clean whiteboards with multi-colored markers mounted on every wall. "Sarah, if you look at this display on the wall, you can access our observatory. That station lets you remote into all of its various telescopes, and you can direct them however you need. There's also an astronomical calculations suite programmed in."

"Observatory?" Sarah asks in astonishment.

"Indeed, it's located several miles off-site in the desert. Every astronomer and astrophysicist here has access to it. Oh! And Karl, see that cabinet over there? That's the optics storage. Every type of beam splitter your heart can desire is in there."

After a few moments of blowing minds, Mavis says, "The walls are soundproof, but if you head through the back door, you'll find our workshop." They exit through the back to find what looks like an aircraft hangar full of machines and high-tech equipment, some of which they have personally used, some they've only heard of, and others they've never even imagined before.

Grace tugs on Karl's shirt and points to the far corner. Karl turns and shouts out, "No way!" They both rush over like children chasing puppies through a field. "Is that the IBM Q System One?!" They stand around what looks like a metal punching bag made of gold plates and silver wires being supported by a four-legged steel frame. "This is one of the most advanced quantum computers in the world!"

"Not exactly, that's our version of it. We've bumped it up to one hundred qubits with a zero point two percent error rate." Grace and Karl look at her in disbelief.

"Impossible," Vincent says definitively.

Mavis looks at him and grins. "You're right, Vincent. It was impossible. But not anymore."

MAVIS GIVES THEM A TOUR OF THE EAST WING. The blue marble hallways and curved architecture give them the sense of walking into a fancy hotel. The entrance splits off in two directions—the barracks and recreation. They explore the barracks first. In one of the common rooms, they find a gathering of off-duty researchers huddled around a TV screen watching the first episode of *Firefly*. As they pass by, Vincent quotes the dialogue line for line, finding it difficult to walk away before noticing people greet him. He neglects to reply and quickly follows behind the tour group. In the distance behind him, he can hear someone call out to him, "Everyone knows these lines word-for-word, buddy!"

"As you can see"—Mavis continues her tour despite the

interruption—"the east wing is the central hub for all things non-work related. We have the rest of the barracks buildings here, and on the recreation side, we have a gym, a small theatre where they show movies and put on plays, and we have a few different general rec rooms where people get together to play board games and the like." When they return to the atrium, she continues, "Well, that concludes the tour. I don't really have anything else for you until tomorrow."

"Wait, what about the north wing?" Grace asks.

"Oh, well that's just the Executive Suites and testing facility. Dr. Smith and Colonel Bartram live there. They and the other military are the only ones with access. But whenever it comes time to do tests, security will escort us to the facility."

"Why doesn't everybody have access to the north wing?"

"It's just a security thing. The testing facility is a sensitive place requiring compartmented access for regular visits."

Karl sees Grace's skeptical look, but he rolls his eyes at her. "Totally reasonable. You can't have too many cooks in the kitchen, right?"

"Exactly," Mavis says and looks at her watch. "Well, I'm going to call it for the day. You guys are free to roam about as you wish. The bars in the cafeteria open up at seventeen hundred hours, and dinner is served from eighteen hundred to twenty hundred."

"I'm sorry, twenty-what?" Sarah asks.

"Oh, I'm so sorry! 'Twenty hundred' hours. It's military speak for eight P.M. That's how all the guards tell time around here, you'll get used to it. Anyway, you guys enjoy your evening! Feel free to find me if you need anything. My barracks are in building three." She turns and goes back to the east wing, leaving the group to get comfortable in the atrium. Taking a seat in one of the patio sets spread out across the garden, they discuss their anxieties and excitement over their new home. Vincent leaves almost immediately, but when Sarah tries to say "goodbye", he's already halfway to the elevators.

The long elevator ride gives him plenty of time to worry. *Please, please,*

please. He steps out of the elevator and tries not to rush as he goes through the metal detector. Dolly gives him a droopy side-eye as he puts his key in the locker, hesitates, and opens it to find his phone screen-side down. He flips it over to find it turned off, the battery completely dead. *What the hell?*

"You alright there, buddy?" Vincent jumps at the security guard's gruff voice.

"Oh yeah, I was just, uh, expecting a call from… my mom. She wanted me to call yesterday, but I forgot… you know how it goes."

"Uh-huh," he says unconvinced.

"Well, I… better get going." He turns and exits the building abruptly. Walking away from the administration building, he sees a van pull through the gate and into the parking lot. A few military guards get out, along with the burly frame of Colonel Bartram. Sun reflecting off the medals he wears on his Air Force blues, he slips on a pair of black sunglasses and his flight cap.

"Ah! It's good to be home, isn't it, boys?" His bold voice echoes off the mountains behind the base.

"It sure is, sir," one of the military yes-men who was in the car says.

Vincent lowers his head and walks toward his barracks as quickly as possible; he hears them quietly discussing the loss of something before his name is called.

"Dr. Creighton!" Colonel Bartram shouts as the other guards trail behind him.

Vincent stops in his tracks and turns ninety degrees to look at him. "Uh, h-hi, Colonel, w-welcome back."

The gaggle of military walk over to meet Vincent, and the colonel offers him a handshake. Vincent extends a sweaty palm and gives a weak shake as the colonel strikes up conversation. "How are you liking it here at Fort Chivington?"

"Good. It's nice." He has a million questions he wants to ask, but he knows to stay quiet about the Abaddon while above ground.

"I couldn't agree more. The scenery is gorgeous, the work is rewarding, it's a great place to work, don't you think?"

"Um, yes…" *Am I supposed to say 'sir'?*

"Let me tell you something: the longer you're here, the more you like it. I know it sounds crazy, but it's true." He gives Vincent a convincing grin. "Well, we got some work to do, but I wanted to apologize for Mark not being able to come with you guys. I know you must be pretty busted up about it, but we only want scientists with a passion for their art and expertise in the field." It's difficult for Vincent to get a read on the colonel through his sunglasses.

"Oh. It's okay, I-I didn't know he even wanted to come."

"Right, he was more of a pencil pusher, anyway. He was never a nose-to-the-grindstone type of scientist like you, was he?"

"Um…" *He was actually an accomplished biologist back in his day.* "I guess not?"

"Exactly," he says definitively. "Well, we have some things to take care of. You have a great day, Dr. Creighton."

Vincent watches Murphy pop a smart salute as the gaggle walks into the admin building before turning back to his barracks to charge his phone. Inspecting it carefully, he finds no evidence of tampering or any reason it should have died. *Did I not turn on battery saver mode or something?*

Chapter Six

January 28th, 2020

Tuesday

Vincent's morning shower is warm, the cafeteria's breakfast is hearty, and he's the first person to arrive at the lab. Having full reign of the research center, he takes some time to memorize where everything is located, wipe down every surface he can find, and organize the cabinets. Logging onto his computer, he prints out a copy of his published report and pins it to the corkboard at the head of the room. *My blueprint.*

"I had a feeling you would be here early." Mavis's voice startles him. He looks over to see her with her tight bun and morning-person cheer carrying two paper cups of coffee.

"Oh… hi. Uh, yeah, I like to be the first one in the lab. Clean everything up… make sure there's nothing for the others to argue about."

"Well, Vincent, you certainly clean up nicely. The room looks great!" She hands him one of the cups and sits across from him. "I thought you might need a pick-me-up for your first day. It's going to get pretty busy in here with the amount of people we have at our disposal."

"Oh, thanks." He takes the cup. "I'm not really the biggest fan of crowds."

"I figured not," she says, sipping her coffee and looking at the corkboard. "I like your style, you put up the report for quick reference. Not that you need it, though, I'm sure. You could probably recite this report by heart."

Of course. Can you not?

"So you're the math-magician of the group, huh? Must be tough keeping all those numbers straight in your head."

"No, it's not really a task for me. It feels just like breathing. It's just something that I do."

She chuckles. "Wow. Well, I am quite jealous. I had to retake calculus. Twice."

"That's okay. Most people aren't good at it."

"That is true, it's good I passed at least," she says, but Vincent doesn't respond. She watches him read over the report. "Vincent, tell me something: what excites you most about being here?"

He keeps his eyes on the report, unsure of how to answer. "What do you mean?"

"I mean, this is a pretty cool place. A lot of cool stuff, smart people, close friends. What about all that is interesting to you?"

As she asks the question, he looks at her from over his glasses. "The results. I want to see my, uh… our research come to life."

His trip up tells her everything she needs to know, but she just smiles at him. "So do I, Vincent."

A swarm of researchers and engineers start to file in as they finish talking, and Sarah is among the first to enter, her eyes flitting back and forth between him and Mavis, who grins and turns away from them. She furrows her brow for a second before saying, "Oh, there you are, Vincent. We looked all over for you, but Karl said you were gone before he woke up."

"Yeah, I wanted to get a head start on cleaning." Vincent notices Sarah's shoulders deflate as he says this.

"Oh, okay. Well, good job, the lab looks very nice." She paints a smile on her face and takes a seat next to him.

"Thanks." He wishes he could say more to her, but the chatter is loud and abrasive, so his shoulders tense up, and he tries cracking his neck. Focusing on the computer, he reads the report over and over to distract himself.

Mavis waits for the cacophony to settle before standing at the head of the room. "Good morning, everyone!" The group immediately hushes when she speaks. "Today is the day! Our new friends have finally joined the team, so please welcome Vincent, Grace, Karl, and Sarah!" She leads a round of applause, causing the four of them to blush. Grace waves sheepishly for them.

"We've been working on the teleportation project for four years now, but we hit a rut about two years ago. Day in and day out, we test hypothesis after hypothesis, never moving past the hump. Then a few weeks ago, we saw a report published out of the Marysworth Institute for Nanoscience that revolutionized the project on a fundamental level. Then yesterday, the writers of that report show up on our doorstep." The more than two dozen people in the room scan them carefully, and Vincent's not sure if they're just sizing him up or if he senses a trace of pity in their gazes. Either way, he uncomfortably sinks into his chair.

"Please make them feel at home, and help them integrate with the team as we transition into our new phase of development."

That morning is spent getting caught up on the Abaddon team's progress and familiarizing Grace's team with how things operate. Vincent sticks close to Sarah. She always finds the perfect way to help him break into a conversation, the perfect way to make him feel socially useful to others. When they break for lunch, Grace, Sarah, and Vincent all find a table together like the day before, but Karl seems to have found himself blending into one of the rowdy cliques, and he lunches with them instead.

"Well, he found friends pretty fast, didn't he?" Grace asks bluntly.

"Good for him. He always seemed like he was stuck in his cocoon phase with us. It's nice to see him spread his wings," Sarah says in a hopeful tone.

"So what do you guys think of the lab?" Grace asks excitedly.

"Oh my god, it's so cool! They have all the bells and whistles! That six-month timeline is looking a lot more realistic. What do you think, Vince?"

"It's really cool. I like how Mavis lets us work stuff out on our own."

"Yeah, I saw you two hitting it off this morning, that must have been nice," Sarah says, looking into her Caesar salad.

"Um, yeah I guess so," he says without making eye contact. "She brought an extra coffee, so it was nice." Sarah doesn't say anything.

Grace watches this interaction and chuckles to herself. "Do you guys want to check out that recreation center after work? We could catch a movie, then get some dinner. I'll try to get Karl in, but I don't see that happening."

"Yeah, that'd be fun…" Sarah glances at Grace, who discreetly gestures to Vincent and mouths the words, *"You guys good?"* Sarah responds with a shoulder shrug.

After lunch, Mavis gathers up the entire research team to discuss their next steps. Grace is the first to offer an idea.

"So the way our theory works is: we take an object, and using destructive scanning, send that object's quantum superposition data to the intended location, then essentially… we 3-D print the sucker."

"Right, we all read your report," a muscular man with a chiseled jaw and perfect eyebrows speaks up with a cocky attitude. "But even with a quantum computer, we physically can't process that much data."

"Did you read all of the report? Because we found a way to compress the data, effectively cutting down the processing time to a fraction of a fraction of a percent of what it would be otherwise," Grace says smugly. Vincent squints. *I found a way. I found the way. It was me.* She continues, "Granted, it would still take a long time."

"Years. Not a long time. Years," the jock says, and Vincent stares daggers at him. *Years? Nuh uh. Did you even look at my equation?*

Mavis cuts in, "Look, Chad, let's try to be constructive with our feedback. We're not here to shut down the process, we want to encourage it."

"Mave, I agree, you know I agree. I'm just throwing it out there that I don't think this is the right approach. Unless we cut that processing time down to absolutely fucking zero, it just won't work."

Stop talking shit about my theory.

Chad continues, "You can't print off a person like a damn picture. This theory you guys wrote is neat and all, but in practice, it's totally useless."

"That's not true," Vincent speaks up for the first time. All eyes fall on him. Sweat drips down his neck. *Yeah, look at me. I demand your attention.*

"Oh, really?"

"Yes, really." Vincent stares daggers at Chad.

"Prove me wrong, Babbitt," he says. A few of Karl's new friends laugh.

"Okay," Vincent says assertively and stands up. "First off, your math is wrong. It's not years. It's hours." His hands are shaking, but he walks to the whiteboard, grabs a marker, and writes an equation that takes over the entire board, then a second board, and even a third. By the time he finishes writing the equation, the crowd of scientists has grown as the engineers who were out in the workshop join to listen. They all murmur amongst each other, discussing what they're being shown. Vincent turns, barely registering the rest of the room, to face Chad. "After surveying the resources we already have in the workshop, I've determined that in the next two months, we can build a machine capable of teleporting an inanimate object inside of two hours."

"Whatever. Even if that's true, the project's goal is people. Human people. Is your plan to print a person out, atom by atom, over the course of two hours? They'll be a corpse by the time you finish."

"I've thought about that, too. I designed my equation"—he looks over to Grace, Sarah, and Karl and corrects himself—"well… we… we published that report with inanimate objects in mind. But with biological entities, we don't need to create them all at once." Mavis lifts her chin curiously. "We can prioritize certain functions over others. Build the brain and nervous system, then the circulatory system, then the respiratory, and so on. That way, we wouldn't need to instantaneously create the entire body."

Mavis steps in, "The brain can survive for six minutes without oxygen.

Obviously, we'd like to get that down by a factor of… well, a lot, but I can see it working."

Grace adds on, "The data compression equation allows for exponential increase in processing power. When you deal with exponents like that, a little can turn into a lot very quickly. If we make our computers a little better, it might cut that two hours down by the requisite factor of a lot."

Chad stands up and cries out, "How are you guys even humoring this? You really think you can just improve the quantum computer? Just real quick? That's ridiculous!" He laughs and looks back at his crew, then they all join in. Karl snickers for a moment before coughing and righting himself.

Mavis says, "Chad, you know that we can already improve a quantum computer because we've done it before. This is just on a much bigger scale." She smiles at Vincent and continues, "Karl, why don't you take Chad and the rest of the quantum theory experts? Work together with Grace and the other computer engineers to cut down our processing time. Sarah, you take the astrophysicists and geologists and start charting out a map of every known cosmic event that will occur in the next six months. We need to know about anything and everything that will affect Earth's gravity on even the smallest scale."

Sarah says, "Yes ma'am, but what about Vincent?"

"He is going to help me devise a way to stabilize the subject's vitals for as long as possible." As Mavis says this, Sarah glowers at her. "What do you say, Vincent?"

Vincent seems disoriented by this. "Um, sure." Sarah looks at him, slightly disappointed, but knows how triumphant he must be feeling. So she chooses to just smile and get to work.

CHAPTER SEVEN

February 25th, 1954

Thursday

Charred cigarette ash flicks to the ground as a man wearing olive drab fatigues with "U.S. Army" emblazoned over the heart walks through the street. Smoking his cigarette in his left hand and carrying a duffel bag in his right, he feels comfortable in this uniform despite the fact that it feels slightly too small for him. It's been years since he's donned his military uniform. His post-military career didn't require one, at least not one that's so identifiable to the public; he was taught how to blend in with the crowd, how to look just like everyone else, how not to be unique. Today, he is ignoring those protocols. Today, he wants to be seen. Today is the day he becomes unique.

Walking across the hospital courtyard, he takes a look up at the American flag hoisted in the center of the lawn. He sets down his duffel bag, looks up at the flag, and pops a smart salute as patriotically as he can before continuing inside the ten-story boxy hospital building. With the natural swagger that he's practiced over the course of several years, he walks up to the reception desk, pulls out a cigarette, and says to the person working the desk, "Do you have a light?"

"Sure thing." She pulls out a matchbook, lights the cigarette, and asks, "Is there anything else I can do for you?"

"Actually, there is, which floor is the ICU? I have a friend who recently transferred here from Germany. He came back from Korea, and I was hoping to surprise an old war buddy."

"That's so nice! I'm sure he'll enjoy the surprise. Third floor, follow the signs." He follows her directions to the elevator, admiring the wood paneled walls and linoleum flooring. *They should really get some more color in these halls.* He takes the elevator to the third floor, making small talk with a nurse he meets along the way, and follows the signs to the nurses' station outside the door marked ICU. *It's secure. Not a strong door, though.* He sees there is only a single nurse manning the station, so he places his duffel bag on the floor and leans over the counter.

She asks, "Can I help you with something?"

"Yes," he says and looks around to find a doctor conducting rounds with his residents. "I have an old war buddy in there I'd like to visit. Could you let me in?"

"What room is he in?" She looks down at a clipboard.

"Actually, I was sort of hoping you could tell me that." He chuckles and puts on a smile.

"What's his name?"

"If I had a name to give you, I would have led with that." He looks at her with an impatient grin, then over at the doctor to see him and his residents walk down an adjacent hall.

"I'm sorry, sir, if you don't have a name, I can't—"

"You know what? This is taking too long," he says. He then pulls the duffel bag up onto the counter, unzips it, and pulls out a suppressed M1911 Colt Government pistol and paints the wood paneled walls with the back of the nurse's skull. She falls out of her chair and hits the floor. He reaches into the duffel bag past the M16 rifle and extra magazines to find an MK2 "pineapple" grenade.

Behind him, he hears a woman gasp and the sound of a clipboard slamming against the ground. Before she can get any words out, the man turns a hundred and eighty degrees, points the gun at her, and fires. She drops in a crumpled pile of paperwork and blood. *I gotta hurry, someone else is going to walk by.* He places the duffel bag on the ground and holsters his sidearm, then he palms the grenade in his right hand before walking up to the locked ICU door. He braces himself, then lunges forward with a kick that breaks cleanly through the deadbolt as the door swings wide open.

"What is the meaning of this?!" A man in his early fifties wearing a white lab coat comes rushing out of his office as a bay full of doctors and nurses gasp in shock. The man pulls the pin on the grenade.

Four.

Slides it through the open doorway, and the spring is released.

Three.

Ducks to take cover behind the nurses' station.

Two.

Draws the M16 and shoulders the sling.

One.

A concussive pop blasts in the ICU, causing screams to instantly be stifled then turned to groans of agony.

The man slides the duffel bag into the room, then storms inside, gunning down any survivors within sight. Each time he pulls his trigger, a three-round burst lights up the room. Broken glass and shredded hospital beds litter the path as he steps over bodies. He rounds a corner and sees two nurses and two doctors stumbling around in a disoriented state. He drops one of the doctors first, then targets the nurses. He fires at their kneecaps, being careful to avoid arteries. They both drop to the floor crying out in pain.

The surviving doctor, deciding to be a hero, lunges at the sound of the gunshots. Unfortunately for him, the gunman isn't as disoriented. The gunman nimbly dodges out of his path and bashes the butt of his rifle into the back of the doctor's head. The doctor crumbles to the floor, landing in the bloody pile that used to be his boss.

That's a brave one. Army medic maybe? The gunman puts his rifle on safety, then lets it hang on the sling behind him before drawing his pistol again. He searches each of the patient rooms, firing on anyone that may have survived the initial blast. His first victim is a young man attached to an iron lung, followed by a few other bedridden individuals. After checking that the nurses aren't bleeding out, the gunman cuffs both of their hands behind their backs and walks to the doctor. He drags him by the collar to where the nurses are lying and stands a few feet away from them, asking, "Can you hear me, doctor?" The doctor clutches at the back of his head and tries opening his eyes. "What's your name, doctor?"

"Wh-What's happening?" the doctor asks as his vision comes into focus.

"*What* is your *name*, doctor?"

The doctor opens his eyes to notice the nurses' conditions. "Holy shit, we-we need to get a crash cart! Nurse!" He barely registers his own voice as the ringing in his head begins to fade away, but he turns his head to see the rest of the gore inside the ICU. His eyes widen, then he looks up to see the gunman—a man in his early thirties sporting piercing blue eyes, a James Dean pompadour, a fresh shave, and U.S. Army fatigues that don't seem to fit him as well as they used to—looking down at him with a silenced pistol.

"I'll ask you one more time: what's your name?"

"Ha-Harrison. Doctor Harrison."

"Good. Now, Doctor Harrison, you need to fix up these nurses here. They're fine for now, but they are losing a lot of blood." The gunman walks out of sight and returns with a crash cart. "Now. Get to work."

The gunman walks over to the blown-out windows that overlook the courtyard and hospital parking lot. Police cars and news crews have begun arriving on scene. *It's showtime.* He smiles and drags a few of the bodies to the entrance doorway, shuts the door and begins stacking bodies in front of it, creating a makeshift barrier. He also slides hospital beds in front of the barricade for reinforcement before tying a wire to the safety pin of another grenade and attaching it to the doorknob. From his duffel bag, he reloads his weapons and dons a belt carrying extra magazines. Once triage is complete on the nurses, Doctor Harrison begins whispering instructions to them, but the gunman fires a bullet dangerously close to the doctor's ear.

"No, no, no. None of that, now. None of your Army tactical planning over there. I don't want you thinking you'll be breaking out of here without my consent."

"How did you know I was in the Army?"

"You can't hide it, Doctor," the gunman says without further explanation. He looks out the window one last time to see camera crews getting set up and the police establishing a perimeter.

"Alrighty, it's go-time people! Move into that patient room." He steps away from the window, out of sight, and sits in one of the empty patient rooms.

"Go-time for what?" one of the nurses asks through strained grunts.

"The big show! We're gonna give them something to talk about." The three of them look at each other with concern before he notices and tries reassuring them. "But don't worry. You two don't have to do anything. Just… hide in that room, and you'll be fine. You, however, do have a task." He reaches into his duffel bag and hands a folded letter to Doctor Harrison. "When I give the command, you will take that letter to the window, unfold it, and read it aloud for everyone down below to hear you. Understood?"

The doctor grabs the letter, scans it, and acknowledges by saying, "Hooah." They share an uncertain look, the gunman chuckles, then Doctor Harrison says, "What's your name, son?"

"Why do you care about my name, Doctor Harrison?"

"Probably the same reason you care about mine, I suppose. We're going to be spending some time here together; I'd like to get to know who you are."

The gunman looks at them and thinks for a moment. "I was called Sergeant Sideris when I was in the Army."

"Sergeant Sideris. Where did you serve, Sergeant Sideris?" Doctor Harrison asks, but Sideris abruptly stands up, readies his rifle, and takes up a defensive position pointing his rifle at the door. They all hear a voice speaking through a loudspeaker coming from the window.

"You're up, Doctor Harrison."

Doctor Harrison looks at the letter, then at the nurses. He can see terrible panic in their eyes. "What if I don't do that, Mr. Sideris?"

"How did playing the hero work for you last time?" Sideris asks without moving his eyes from the door.

"Well, at the time, I thought you were going to just shoot me along with the others. So what other choice did I have?"

"Not much of one, really. What makes right now seem different than before?"

"Well, before, you didn't need me to do something for you. But now, you need me to read this letter, so I have leverage over you." Doctor Harrison holds up the letter.

"I mean, you could play it that way. If you don't show the police that I have hostages, however, then they have no proof of life. And if they have no proof of life, they have significantly more reason to use hostile force when trying to break into this room. Either way, I get what I want."

"And what is it that you want?"

"Go read the letter, and you'll find out."

Rushed footsteps pitter-patter outside the ICU entrance, and whispered commands are audible through the wall.

"It's your call, Doctor Harrison."

The doctor carefully weighs his options, then stands, walks to the window, unfolds the letter, and reads the typed words:

"To whom it may concern"—Doctor Harrison clears his throat and projects a little louder—"this is not an act of aggression. This is a challenge. For years, the strong have manipulated the weak. The powerful have exploited the powerless. The vocal have squashed the voiceless. I spent years in the Army being silenced by those who stood atop the people who did their dirty work for them. I spent years as an assassin killing those that others wanted dead. Why? Because I'm good at it. I'm good at killing, therefore, people make me kill. I'm sick of playing the game for others. It's my turn to choose who lives and dies. I have three hostages. This means you have three chances to save them. Every five minutes, I…" The doctor halts, looks back at Sergeant Sideris, who has the most intense, passionate face he has ever seen. "Every five minutes, I will kill a hostage." An audible gasp is heard from the parking lot, and the nurses burst out in tears. "If you manage to outmaneuver me, I will surrender immediately, and no harm will come to the hostages. However, if you don't outmaneuver me within fifteen minutes, then I will escape, and you will get a second opportunity to stop me. The clock starts now."

As Doctor Harrison finishes the final sentence, Sergeant Sideris looks at his watch and shouts out, "It might behoove you to rejoin your coworkers in hiding." The doctor runs across the room, through the blood, and past the barricade of bodies to the room with the nurses. As he takes cover, he hears commands being called from behind the entrance, and then suddenly, the door shakes with loud pounding. *A battering ram. Interesting, I would have gone with C2 plastic explosives.* After the second bash with the ram, the door bursts open and the bodies crash into the hospital beds. Sergeant Sideris takes cover inside his room as the grenade's pin is pulled by the wire.

Four.

Half the police squad rushes into the room, shouting and screaming orders.

Three.

They stop to ogle at the gory mess of bodies tangled up in the hospital beds.

Two.

Doctor Harrison shouts, "Grenade! Grenade!"

One.

A handful of officers grab the frontline and pull them back, but it's too late.

Another concussive pop blasts the ICU, splattering the walls with blood and ash. Sergeant Sideris stands to watch the entrance. Survivors are taking cover in front of the nurses' station. He turns to find

Doctor Harrison rushing in his direction. Sideris pulls his trigger. Doctor Harrison collapses before he makes it halfway to Sideris. The nurses watch on in silent horror. Sergeant Sideris's attention switches back to the entrance. A young police officer hears the gunshot and seizes his opportunity, rushing in and firing his revolver in the general direction of the sound before Sideris's M16 hits him center mass. The officer falls. Sergeant Sideris notices him twitch. Another three-round burst. The body stops moving.

Sergeant Sideris reloads. It's quiet. He looks at his watch. Three minutes and fifty-four seconds. It's quiet until the five-minute mark. *Well, looks like Doctor Harrison sacrificed his turn for another chance to be the hero.* He turns and fires on one of the nurses. She goes limp, and the nurse next to her screams, hyperventilating as she begins to lose her senses. *Crazy bitch. You know what? Fuck this. They don't stand a chance, and this isn't as much fun as I thought it would be.* He fires again to end her insufferable screaming. He then unloads the rifle, takes his ammo belt off, unloads his pistol, places everything he has on the floor, then walks to the entrance with his hands on the back of his head. There's nobody around to stop him. *I must have killed them all. Well, the second wave is coming, so I guess right here is good.* He lies on the floor, stomach down, waiting for the second squadron to arrive.

They burst through the stairwell door and cautiously approach him. They cuff him and lead him down to the empty lobby. As they exit the hospital, they walk across the courtyard where they are met with a flock of reporters all taking desperate notes. Everyone pushing and shouting over each other makes it difficult for the police to keep a perimeter, then one of the reporters gets a foothold and shoves a microphone in the gunman's face. "Do you have anything to say to the public?" The police shout at the paparazzi to move on, but it is of no use.

As the arresting officers shove Sideris into a police car, he manages to get off one quote: "My name is Leonard Sideris—and I demand your attention!"

CHAPTER EIGHT

January 31st, 2020

Friday

The first week in the Abaddon is a productive one. Sarah embraces her place as a leader in her section, directing workflow, delegating responsibilities to others, and finding time to be friends with each of them outside of work. Grace and Karl lead their team of computer geeks and quantum theory jocks in redesigning their super-computer; Karl, however, spends more time playing volleyball with his buddies than in the laboratory. Vincent finds his place at Mavis's side working on the medical aspect of the project. He finds that she shares a work ethic with him, which feels like a first. It was easy for him to waste an afternoon with the others when they all went out for lunch, or took breaks every half-hour, or talked about bullshit until late at night. But Mavis takes her work seriously, and it shows.

Friday afternoon, after staying late in the lab with Mavis, they leave for the atrium to find it infested with people setting up decorations and speakers, along with the cafeteria staff setting up food and drink stands.

"What is all this?"

"Oh, right, this is your first weekend! Every Friday, the staff likes to hold a party in the atrium. People go absolutely wild, but they always respect the premises. It's not a mandatory thing by any means, just a way for the more rambunctious staff members to blow off steam."

They have to dodge party preppers and cafeteria staff to navigate the area. Vincent says, "That sounds… not fun."

"I completely agree. I usually just hang out in my room, but every now and then I'll come and partake. It's really a great way to get to know people."

Vincent takes the elevator upstairs. As he goes through the security checkpoint, he notices Dolly and her handler are off shift. Senior Airman Little is standing watch tonight. They exchange quiet nods, and Vincent keeps walking. As he steps out, he sees Dolly running around the parking lot, getting some exercise. Seeing her floppy ears bounce around makes him smile. He retreats into his barracks to read and watch the sunset before his bedtime. He feels nervous for tomorrow, the first weekend after arriving at the base. *What am I supposed to do? Will the library be open?* A knock at the door startles him.

"Vincent?" Sarah's voice cuts through the door. "Are you in here?"

They've barely spoken all week, so he doesn't answer at first. *What if she's mad at me for spending so much time with Mavis?* "I'm in here."

"Can I come in?"

He marks his page in the book and puts his shoes on. "No, I'll come out." He opens the door to find her wearing her street clothes and an excited grin.

"Hey! Grace and I are going down to grab dinner and a drink. Do you want to come?"

"Um…" Despite wanting to be with her, he looks for any excuse to get out of being anywhere near that party but comes up short. "Sure," he finally says.

Heading down to the cafeteria, it seems like the party has already overtaken the atrium; nearly every single scientist in the building is either drinking, eating, or making out. This presents a social obstacle course for Vincent as he steps through the crowd. Keeping close to his friends as they walk, Sarah extends her hand for Vincent to grab onto.

She looks back at him and has to shout over the music. "Keep close to me! You'll be okay!"

He panics but manages to grab ahold of her hand, and when he does, something wonderful radiates through him. She drags him through the sea of drunkards, past a food and beverage stand next to the elevators, then into the cafeteria. As soon as the double doors close behind them, all of the music and noise seem to disappear completely. This leaves the three of them standing in a less-than-crowded cafeteria with light jazz playing over the speakers. The two private dining rooms have "Quiet Room" signs posted over each of them. Sarah squeezes Vincent's hand gently.

"Holy crap! That was fucking wild!" Grace exclaims to Sarah.

"I know! I heard it gets kinda crazy down here, but that was insane! And it hasn't even started yet!" She notices Vincent's lack of comment and says, "Hey, let's get our food and eat in one of the quiet rooms."

"Totally, I need to warm up to that level of activity."

The food is served à la carte as it usually is, but at the end of the serving line is a full-service bar. Vincent was usually still working or had turned in for the night by the time the bar opened up, so this is his first time seeing it. He doesn't feel like having a drink right now though, so he just grabs a soda and follows his friends to the table.

"So! How was everyone's week? What have you guys been up to?" Sarah asks enthusiastically.

"Oh. My. God. Karl is getting on my last nerve, I swear!"

"Yeah? I haven't seen him around the lab much lately."

"Cause he's never there! He and that Chad guy are always at the gym or outside playing volleyball! I'm good with computers, and my quantum theory knowledge is about as good as the next guy's, but I need him and his team to crack down and do their work."

"What a jerk! I never thought he would just ghost you like that," Sarah says with a sympathetic expression.

I did. He's always been a jerk.

"Right?! Whatever, though. We'll figure something out. What about you, though, Sarah? You seem to be pretty popular with your team."

"I know! They love me! They're all so smart and cool, too! We found evidence of a pattern of seismic activity that seems to be recurring near the observatory. It's been messing with their astrometric readings for years, and they never even knew!"

"Good job, Sarah! Could you imagine if we went into testing, and our subject ended up, like, inside the earth or something?"

"That would be terrible! How about you, Vincent? How is working with Mavis?" Sarah tries to include him in the conversation.

"Oh, it's, it's good. She's smart. She works hard, and it's nice to have a partner who likes working, instead of just talking and stuff." Sarah and Grace look at each other trying not to be offended.

"I think she means at *work*—how is the *work* coming along?"

He looks up and sees Sarah's face. *Did I say something wrong?* "Oh, well, we established our priority scheme for the post-teleportation anatomical structure reintegration process. We need to write algorithms that tell the computer how to lay the framework for the human body and then layer each anatomical system in a way that keeps the subject alive for the duration of the teleportation." They both look on with glazed eyes.

"That's incredible. You think you guys are going to figure it out soon?" Sarah tries to show her interest as overtly as possible.

"Mavis understands the human body better than anyone," he replies, and Sarah winces when he says this. "And I've already written algorithms for five out of the eleven main systems. I think we'll have it nailed down within the month." Sarah can't help but push her tongue against her cheek and look down at her plate.

"Well, good for you, Vincent. I'm happy things are going well for you," Grace says, then she looks over at Sarah and twirls some spaghetti around her fork. "So… Sarah, how have things been going with you and that Brian guy?"

Sarah's head pops up, and she fails to hide a bashful grin. "Oh, you know, pretty good. He invited me to join his Dungeons and Dragons party this Saturday."

Grace shoots her a face that says, *"Really? D&D?"* but she looks at

Vincent and plays along. "Oh yeah? You think you'll take him up on that offer?"

"Maybe, if I don't have anything else going on this weekend." They both shoot a meaningful glance at Vincent, who fails to notice any of these hints and instead focuses on his food. *What did I do wrong? She asked how it was working with Mavis and I told her.*

"What are you doing this weekend, Vincent?" Grace asks bluntly.

"Oh, I'm not sure. I was going to work in the lab, but Mavis doesn't work on weekends, so there's not really a point to it." Sarah rolls her eyes and drops her fork, then Grace pinches the bridge of her nose. "Probably read. Why? What are you doing?"

"Just hanging with some friends," Sarah says, sounding defeated. She picks up her plate and leaves.

"I hope that book is worth it," Grace says before following Sarah.

"Worth what?" Vincent sits there, confused as to why his friends are leaving. *Now there's something wrong with reading?*

When he finishes his dinner, he takes a seat at the bar. The bartender asks what he wants, and he says the only thing he thinks to ask for. "Macallan 18."

"On the rocks? Or neat?" the bartender responds.

Rocks? "Um, surprise me?"

The bartender pours his drink and lays down a coaster, but Vincent replaces it with a napkin he removes from his wallet. The bartender, confused, sees the writing on the napkin.

"…'Enjoy it, kid'? Who wrote that?"

"A friend."

Vincent takes a sip of his drink, but nearly spits it up as the alcohol burns his throat. It's not as sweet as he remembers it. He chokes down the drink and turns in for the night.

Chapter Nine

February 2nd, 2020

Sunday

The weekend proves to be an uncomfortable time for Vincent. Grace and Sarah are off with their new friends and Karl with his frat. He spent most of his day reading in his barracks, alone. He is enveloped in his favorite Sanderson novel for most of the day until he finds himself reading the same sentence over and over again. He is stuck inside his own head.

Every week for the next six months. This is what every weekend is going to be for six months. *They're annoying, but… they're my friends. It hasn't even been a full week, and they're getting sick of me.* He just tries to get through the next paragraph of his book, pushing out each subsequent thought until he can't manage it. Shutting the book, he slams it on his nightstand, causing his phone to bounce off the table. He picks it up. The image of Trent standing in his living room flashes into his mind. *"If you're ever in the market for some new friends, give us a call."*

"No."

Pacing around his room, he does another lap, and gazes out over the desert landscape. Down below, he can see Chad and Karl with their clique rallying the volleyball. He sits back down and tries to finish his book. Though he reads through the words, he fails to grasp more than a few paragraphs. *You know what? I should get more books.*

On the way down to the Abaddon, he notices Senior Airman Little standing watch outside the admin building. He seems antsy, nervous about something. Vincent ignores this and continues. Reaching the bottom, his nerves are on end just entering the atrium. There's so many people strolling around, talking, and walking through the gardens. He speed walks to the west wing and enters the door marked *"E Pur Si Muove"* to find the library.

The oaken walls contain more books than he has ever seen in his life. In the center of the library, circular walls extend over a hundred feet in the air. He spends a few hours perusing the aisles looking for new books and finds some interesting historical fiction stories that catch his attention. After checking them out, he sits in the reading area, which is furnished with old Victorian furniture and a fireplace, then he settles in.

Reading the first page becomes a chore as another library patron seems to be laughing his head off at a Calvin and Hobbes comic that he's checked out. Vincent tries to focus but fails miserably. Frustrated, he gets up and leaves. On his way out, he passes by a face that he hasn't seen much since arriving.

Master Sergeant Kritzman breezes past him, making a beeline for the library. She carves an intimidating figure with her olive skin and long, dark brown hair curled up into a bun. Her face always seems to be morphed into a permanent scowl. There's a rumor circulating in the Abaddon that before she moved to the United States to join the Air Force, she was drafted into the Israeli Defense Forces. Others say that that's ridiculous because of her Russian accent, claiming that she was Spetsnaz. She refuses to comment on this rumor to anyone.

"Murphy!" Her booming voice catches enough attention inside the library, but piled on is her heavy accent.

"Ma'am?" Sergeant Murphy pokes his head out from one of the aisles.

"You! Where you been? Little waiting at post for two hour!"

"Oh shit, is it my watch?"

"Is it your watch?! Resupply arrive in fifteen minute! Go!" Sergeant Murphy drops all his books on the nearest book return cart and sprints out of the library. As far as Vincent can tell, Master Sergeant Kritzman prefers to be nice and kindhearted, like she was when they met, but she has to let out her inner demon to scare her underlings more often than not. She shouts after him as he runs, "Third time this month, Murphy! I shoot you myself if this happen again!" She grumbles to herself about Sergeant Murphy as she leaves.

Vincent catches the next elevator after Murphy and heads topside. When he leaves the admin building, he sees Sergeant Martinez park a pickup truck before three semi-trucks park behind him. Sergeant Martinez, wearing full tactical gear with his rifle and sidearm, flags him down. "Murphy! Where the fuck were you?!" Martinez's voice booms out. Vincent has never seen him so intimidating before.

"Sorry, sir! I, I just forgot it was—" Murphy bumps into Vincent as he rushes to relieve Little on watch.

"If I hear you forgot one more fucking time, I'll dump your body in the fucking desert myself, Murphy!" Finally noticing Vincent, his countenance lightens up, and he waves. "Hey, Vince! How you been?"

Vincent's eyes widen, and he uncomfortably waves back. "G-Good… you?"

"It's resupply day! Always a great day!"

"I suppose."

"Vincent! Yo, come join us!" Karl's voice carries across the dry air. Vincent looks over to see him in the volleyball court. Karl's buddies are whispering to him, but he pushes them off and jogs over. "Hey, man! I barely ever see you, how you been?"

Vincent doesn't know how to respond. *Yeah, because you're never at work.* "Good. You?"

"You know, things are pretty great. This place is freaking cool, right?"

"I guess. How is the project coming?"

He looks over his shoulder at his clique and says, "Uh, not too bad. It's a bunch of rowdy boys over there, you know?"

"Yeah, they're… they're cool." Vincent looks at his feet, not sure what is happening.

"Well… did"—Karl's voice cracks—"did you hear about Chad?"

"No, what'd he do?"

"I guess his daughter got hurt. It's… it doesn't look good. He shipped out this morning to go see her." As Karl says this, Vincent struggles to fight off the urge to be excited for Chad's leaving.

"Is he coming back?"

"I'm not sure… from the way he sounded, this all came about so suddenly. Plus, I don't know, I thought the guys would be more bummed about it, instead they just pretend it never happened. It's weird."

"That's sad, what are you going to do?"

"I guess there's not much I can do about it, is there?"

"Not really." Vincent looks back toward the semi-trucks as Sergeant Martinez helps the team of jumpsuit-wearing truckers unload crates from the back of the trucks. Dolly and her handler inspect the crates as she sniffs them diligently.

"Well, it was nice talking to you, Vincent. Maybe we can chill in the barracks later, watch some Monty Python or something?"

Vincent snaps back to the conversation. "Sure, yeah, that sounds good."

When he reaches his barracks room, he watches the resupply trucks unload from his window. He notices Sergeant Martinez directs them around to the back of the admin building. *There must be a service elevator back there that leads to the south wing?* But then he sees Sergeant Martinez direct one of the crates to inside the old armory building. *Oh? Where might that go?*

Finding this mildly interesting, he digs his nose into his stack of new books, excited at the prospect of Chad not being around anymore.

Chapter Ten

March 31st, 2020

Tuesday

The following weeks pass by in the blink of an eye. Without Chad in the picture, Karl becomes more focused on the project—at least for a few days until he falls back into the habit of disappearing after lunch with his buddies as their new ringleader. Grace attempts to wrangle in the rowdy group of quantum theorists, but she winds up crying herself to sleep most nights out of exasperation. While the team does manage to cut down the computer's processing time from two hours down to thirty minutes, Grace was hoping to be much further along than they have gotten.

Sarah's team is successful in creating a chart of every celestial body that will come anywhere near enough to noticeably affect the Earth's gravity. Her Dungeons and Dragons party meets up every Saturday, but she and Brian tend to spend the rest of the week together, too. The two of them study techniques that might help their projects, visit the library to read fiction novels and fantasies that take them far away from where they are, and they watch movies with friends from other projects. Grace often finds herself being the third wheel around them.

Eventually, Vincent stops talking to Grace and Sarah altogether. Instead, he makes breakthrough after breakthrough by spending nearly all of his time in the lab. Days at a time pass by with Mavis as they power through the workload. Within the first two weeks, they manage to write an algorithm set that allows for all eleven anatomical systems to be rebuilt with no damage to the subject. The two of them even begin working on other aspects of the project; providing Grace with a technique that improves computer efficiency by ten percent, creating an organizational system that increases the engineers' efficiency by thirty-five percent, and Mavis even creates a coffee machine that roasts, grinds, and brews coffee beans to perfection based on each of the individual team members' preferences.

Every night, Vincent returns to his bed alone. Sometimes, Karl is there already asleep, but most of the time, he is off in someone else's bed. On those nights, when Vincent is completely by himself in the room, he looks at his nightstand. His phone lies there, staring back at him. He just stares at it until he falls asleep. When Karl slipped away from the group, it made sense. Karl was kind of a jerk, anyway. When Grace stopped talking to him in the lab, he was fine with it. He always resented the control freak in her. But when Sarah drifted away from him, he didn't realize it at the time, but he had lost his best friend in the world. He felt uncomfortable in his own skin. In his room. On his way to work. At breakfast, lunch, and dinner. Now he lives that discomfort all the time except for when he's in the lab.

At the end of the second month of being at the Abaddon, Vincent and Mavis sit in the lab. Vincent diligently writes an algorithm on the board. Mavis watches on with a cup of coffee in her hand.

"How do you do this every night, Vincent?"

"Four hours is enough sleep for me. I usually go to bed after midnight."

"No, I mean… how do you spend so much time in here? With me? Don't you ever spend time with your friends?"

He stops. "Not really. They're all into things that I'm not into."

"Have you tried?"

"What?"

"You said you're not into the things they're into—have you tried those things?"

"You mean drinking all night and talking about drama? Yes."

She chuckles. "No, I mean Dungeons and Dragons, volleyball, and… well, whatever Grace is into."

"Don't get me started on Grace," he says as he continues writing on the board. "When we first told Mark about the discovery, she made it look like they all did just as much work as I did."

She looks at him skeptically. "Do you disagree with that?"

"Yes! I did way more work than her, more than all three of them combined."

She takes a sip of her coffee. "I believe that to be literally true. Some people are only out for themselves. You especially gotta watch out for that Karl."

"Yeah, he gets distracted super easily." He finishes up the problem and turns to her. "Well, looks like we just helped Grace's team cut that processing time down to ten minutes."

She laughs in amazement. "You really are something, Vincent. You know that?"

"What do you mean?"

"You're a jack of all trades, well, you're the master of all trades! You're very good at what you do. You're a real asset to this team."

He smiles and says, "Thank you."

"You know, I heard Dr. Smith talking about you the other day."

"Oh yeah? What'd he say?"

"He's impressed. He says he wants to see a practical demonstration on Monday."

"A test? He wants to see a test? Don't we still have a month before we start testing?"

"Don't worry, he won't judge us on the results—he's just curious. He's been paying special attention to the project and wants to see it in action. We're just going to test on an inanimate object, which is something we've had in the bag for weeks."

"Oh, well, great. That sounds good."

She sips her coffee again. "He wants to meet with you."

He looks at her seriously and asks, "Me?" His stomach drops.

"Yeah! Like I said, you've made a real impression on him. He wants to meet with you after the test."

His smile stretches from ear to ear. "That's… wow. Dr. Smith wants to meet *me*."

"You should be proud of yourself, Vincent. You've put your heart into your work, and people are noticing. I do need to warn you though. He and Colonel Bartram have had some… disputes in the past."

"Disputes?"

"Yes. Smith has a tendency to, well, manipulate people. He's a heartless opportunist who picks a favorite scientist, treats them well, praises them, and then he tries to promote them."

"Promote them? Like making them a supervisor? Is that not how you got to be a supervisor?"

"Not exactly. He tries to transfer them out of the Abaddon. Ripping them away from us and the cause that we are promoting here. Pushing them right into the hands of corporate science."

"Cause? What cause are we promoting here?"

"We protect people, Vincent. We use science to make a safer world so people don't need to die or suffer. The corporate slime that Smith represents is all about greed, keeping things to themselves. He doesn't believe in sharing knowledge to make a better world."

"How is it that we're making a better world?"

"We create technologies that fight evil. Our projects are sent to troops down range, fighting wars, ending wars so they don't reach the shores of our homeland. Winning battles before they even begin. Dr. Smith doesn't believe we should be sharing our military tech with the world."

Vincent pauses to consider this. "How do you know all this?"

"I used to be his protégé, but then he got me a job at a huge pharmaceutical company. I couldn't take him up on it because I wanted to stay here. Ever since, he's been biased against me."

"Why did you want to stay here?" He grabs a cup of black coffee from the machine.

"Because I was doing amazing things here. I had already worked on multiple projects using CRISPR to improve life expectancy; we made huge strides in battlefield medicine, genetic engineering, weapons' optics, and so much more. I was the driving force behind some truly great technologies. Life was exactly the way I wanted it to be. But Dr. Smith wanted to rip that away from me, just so I could be a corporate cog in the machine that profits off the sick."

Dr. Smith wants to profit off the sick? "What did you tell him?"

"Colonel Bartram stepped in on my behalf. He and I have worked together for a long time so he was willing to stand up to Smith for me." As she speaks, Vincent studies her body language. She keeps her arms open as she speaks, moving toward him inch by inch. "If he tries to pull the same crap with you, let me know. I'd like to keep you around." That last sentence excites him in a way he hasn't felt since Sarah held his hand in the atrium.

"Well, thank you…" he blushes. "I'd like to keep working with you too. It would be cool to create great things here." She smiles at him gently, and after quietly cleaning up together, they both turn in for the night.

Throughout the week, they make their preparations for the test, getting all their ducks in a row before the weekend. Vincent avoids confrontation with his friends to focus on preparation. At this point, he's afraid to find out if they are mad at him. Karl still shows up late every morning and tends not to return after lunch. Vincent often overhears Grace venting about this to Sarah in the cafeteria, but he usually walks right past their table without making eye contact.

CHAPTER ELEVEN

April 3rd, 2020

Friday

After work on Friday, while everyone is packing up to leave for the day, Vincent and Mavis finish up some work. Collaborating on a single computer, they sit next to each other, shoulder-to-shoulder on one side of the table. From across the room, Sarah eyes them as she hangs her lab coat on her way out the door. Vincent sees her watching them, but her attention is pulled away as a muscular guy with a clean haircut and short beard walks up to her.

"You ready, Sarah?"

She looks away from Vincent and grins. "Hey, Brian. Yeah, I'm ready."

Vincent focuses his attention on the computer as they leave. Mavis, having seen the whole ordeal, just grins victoriously.

Once Sarah leaves, Mavis says, "I think I'm going to turn in early today, get an early start on the weekend."

"But the test is on Monday. Don't you want to look over everybody's work?"

"Nope. I trust my team. We've been doing great work," she says, but Vincent doesn't respond and just keeps working. She hangs up her coat and pours two cups of coffee. She hands him one. "You should get out of here too, enjoy the sunlight."

"Yeah, sure," he replies without budging.

Mavis watches him toil away and grins. "If you'd prefer to work though, who am I to judge?"

As soon as the lab is clear, he grabs a clipboard and starts reviewing everybody's work, checking boxes on a list he printed out the night before. As expected, Grace and Karl's side of the project are missing several points, but Vincent squares them away. After conducting his survey, he hangs up the clipboard and admires the lab with its various industrial islands, advanced equipment, walls of computers, and organized shelves. He looks through the window of the back door that leads to the workshop and sighs. Usually, he feels more at home here after everybody leaves. Not today, though.

Realizing he's been in the lab by himself for nearly an hour and a half, he hangs up his lab coat and heads down to the atrium. There are already people hanging up banners, setting up a stage, and making preparations for the Friday night bash. Looks like they're doing a full-on concert. *Gross.* Dodging groups of party planners along the way, he passes by the south wing. When a hot dog stand is carted out of the cafeteria, Vincent catches a glimpse of Sarah and Brian at the bar. They seem to be talking to each other with none of their other friends around. Vincent notices Sarah laughing and playing with her hair as Brian talks. *What are they up to?*

Taking the elevator topside, Vincent wonders about them until he gets outside. The fresh, afternoon breeze jostles his hair. *I'm sure it's fine. They're just starting the weekend early… like Mavis.* He goes to his room and falls back into his reading habit. Having finished the last stack of library books he was working on, he decided to pick up *The Lovecraft Compendium* from the library. From the halls of his barracks, he can hear people talking and getting ready for the party. Based on Karl's destroyed half of the room, Vincent figures Karl had already been pregaming before lunch was over.

It takes thirty-seven pages for his foot to start tapping. Another twenty-four for the pangs in his stomach to flare up. Then twelve more pages before the words start losing meaning. Each word he reads turns into an illustration of happy couples dancing through a garden. He sighs. Brian's dirty fingernails grab at the small of Sarah's back as they waltz into the night. Karl and his band of goons mosh and crush beer cans against their foreheads. Grace, finally having people to dance the bachata with, dances her heart out. His face flushes as he pushes through Lovecraft's short stories.

He. Vincent says the title of the book in his head to ground himself. *"I saw him on a sleepless night…"* It takes everything in him to drive his eyes from one word to the next. *"My coming to New York had been a mistake."* Sarah laughs and leans against the trunk of a redwood as Brian picks her a gardenia, her favorite. *"…there came only a shuddering blankness and ineffable loneliness."* Its scent is hypnotizing, the music fades away, the smell of the dancers' sweat disappears. *"Shuddering blankness and ineffable loneliness."* They lock eyes. *"Shuddering blankness."* He grabs her waist. *"Ineffable loneliness."* She pulls him close.

Crack. The book slams shut. Vincent gathers his breath, looks at the phone on his nightstand, then rushes out the door. As the elevator descends, the bumping of an upbeat rhythm vibrates through the walls. The further he drops, the louder it gets. The doors open to let in a burst of electronic dance music; he feels the beat rattling in his heart. A sea of sweaty, science-minded bodies has taken over the entire atrium, bouncing in sync as the DJ on stage gradually speeds up the tempo. The sky overhead has been programmed to replicate a brisk, cool sunset evening. Breathing deeply, he tastes the concoction of body odors that he has been avoiding for two months. Gathering up his nerves, he steps into the crowd.

Shoulder-first, he slides between grinding couples, skirts around a dance circle, and pushes through to the dirt path of the garden. *Why did I come down here?* A thousand voices shout over each other, intensifying the bass's destabilizing tremors. Vincent looks up; the Sequoia canopy filters out the red sky as the illusory sun sets. His heartbeat matches the escalating rhythm as he fights off the push and shove of those around him. The dirt path leads to a tunneled-out trunk. Inside the tunnel, he sees a couple behaving as couples do in relative privacy. His stomach drops. Pushing forward, he recognizes them as Megan and Beth, both assigned to the invisibility project. *What was I expecting? I'm just… paranoid.* He fails to hear his own thoughts just as a voice cuts through the cacophony around him.

"Vince!" Karl's voice is bold, and his hand grabs Vincent's shoulder.

"Karl, hey."

"What are you doing here, man? You've never come down here before!"

He looks around for a moment. "Yeah, I… I don't even know."

"Well, shit, since you're here, c'mon! Follow me!" He pushes Vincent through the crowds to the epicenter of it all: the pit. *No, no, no, no, no!* Karl pushes him into a small circle that forms up in front of the stage, where he notices Grace, Sarah, Brian, and their D&D friends standing on either side of him. *What have I done?*

"Vincent! You came out!" Sarah shouts out and sloppily hugs him, which would excite him deeply if he didn't smell the alcohol on her. "Oh my God! I thought you were never gonna loosen up! Whoo!"

"Um, yeah…" he stammers as Grace tries to goad him into a dance. "Oh, no thanks. I don't—"

"Come ON!" Grace shouts at him. "It's just one dance!"

Behind him, someone steps on his heels. He looks back to see three drunkards moving in. The crowd is getting tighter.

One of Brian's D&D friends manages to dig her elbow into Vincent's hip and shouts, "You HAVE to play the new Ravnica module!"

"Rav—What are you saying?" A cold can of beer appears in his hands as Karl shouts something at Vincent.

"I can't hear you!" Vincent shouts. He thinks Karl mouths the words *"drink it"* to him, but he can't be sure.

Grace crashes into him and shouts, "Vin! Vinnay! You know the steps! Let's daaaaance!"

His heart beats in his head as he tries to process every individual noise that he hears. The music gradually overtakes every sensory input. The room begins to feel like it's a thousand degrees. The collar of his shirt irritates his skin as the sweat drips down his back, making the fabric stick to him. His breathing becomes labored, and his body takes over as he involuntarily begins shoving people out of his way. Vincent doesn't expect them to shove back, however, and a mosh gradually begins to form. In a panic, Vincent locks his eyes on the nearest exit. *The east wing.*

Losing control of his breathing, he pushes and shoves his way to the exit; partiers respond in a variety of ways. The tempo rises up and up until it reaches a crescendo, and suddenly a silence befalls the entire atrium. In this momentary beat of calm, Vincent reaches up to climb atop those around him, but a steady arm takes a powerful hold of his wrist.

The bass drops, and the dancers go wild. Vincent is forcibly dragged through the crowd and into the east wing corridor. The music becomes muffled as the door shuts, and Vincent is thrust against the blue marble wall, being held in place by his chest.

"Hey, man, you gotta chill out for me, okay?" a male voice says calmly, but Vincent barely registers his words and keeps flailing. His weak arms attempt to bash and thrash his captor. "You're gonna be alright, just calm down for me. Deep breaths." The man holds him in place with one hand and gently rests the other around the back of Vincent's neck.

It takes a while, but Vincent's head begins to cool down. Taking deep breaths with the man, he eventually recognizes him as Sergeant Martinez. The desert camouflage he wears stands out to him in front of the marble wall. His weapons firmly stowed, he lets go of Vincent, who promptly takes a seat and rests his eyes. Sergeant Martinez hikes up his gear and sits next to him.

"Don't worry, you're not the first."

His vision blurry, Vincent rubs his temples. "Really?"

"Yeah, every now and then, we'll see some of the more… what's the term… *sensitive* people with shitty friends get dragged to the party. They get overwhelmed and end up freaking out."

Shitty friends… "If this is common, why do you let them go crazy like that?"

"It keeps them focused. Those who don't enjoy it just find something else to do on Friday nights."

Vincent, feeling exhausted, rests his head against the wall and exhales.

"Whenever you're ready, we'll get you back upstairs."

After a short rest, Vincent has a tough time standing but manages to keep up with Sergeant Martinez as they make a hole through the crowd. He makes it through the checkpoint, where an airman named Ashley is standing watch, and goes outside. The quiet, cool, desert air is a welcome relief from the chaos downstairs.

"You feeling alright, Vince?"

"A bit… bruised. But I'll be fine. That hasn't happened to me in a long time."

"That's okay, man. That's why we stand watch down there."

"That's good, how many of you does it take to guard everyone? I imagine that's pretty taxing on you guys."

"Yeah, we keep the more experienced people down there, me, Little, Cullen, Peterson, Gibson… a few others." As they get out of earshot of Ashley, Martinez whispers, "Our B team takes over on weekends. Murphy… I don't understand how that boy made Staff Sergeant."

"Yeah, he seems forgetful."

"You don't even know the half of it. He's a total mess." They stop in front of the barracks building. "Well, I hope my talking your ear off helped a bit. Have a safe night, Vincent."

He takes a slow walk back to his room, wishing that he felt like he fit in a bit more than he does. That is not the case though.

The popcorn ceiling stares at him as he lies atop his covers. *Why can't I just be like them? Why do I have to shut down or freak out when there's more than ten people in a room?* He listens to the coyotes howling with the moon rise, signaling their nightly hunt. *Why do I have to be saved by someone… stronger than me?* Dwelling in his lament, many hours pass until he hears the laughter and merriment of less socially inept people gathering outside and filtering back into their rooms, and then the silence falls around him again. Sleep never finds him, leaving him in a cesspool of self-pity for another night.

82

CHAPTER TWELVE

Saturday

The following day, Vincent walks through the halls of an unwelcoming home. His dinner is lonelier than normal. His book is uninteresting. The lab is empty. He sits in his bed again, staring at the ceiling. His eyes fall on his phone again. Normally, he would reach to find some reason not to dive into it… but not today. Today, he picks it up. Pulling out the business card from his wallet, he hesitates before calling the printed number.

A bead of sweat drips down his neck as he hits the "call" button. He stands up, pacing around the room. The line rings only once before someone picks up.

"Hey there, Vinny," the familiar voice of Trent answers.

Vincent's breath turns to static in the receiver as he remains unsure if he should speak.

"How's the Abaddon treating you?"

His eyes widen. *He knows about the Abaddon?* "Not great."

"Your friends turn their backs on you?"

He nods, but realizes he needs to speak. "Uh-huh."

"I thought they might. You looking for some new friends?"

He nods. "Uh-huh."

"Well, lucky for you, I got a whole mess load of friends just itchin' to meet you. What do you say?"

Not knowing what this means, he utters, "Uh-huh."

"Well, good, that'll happen in due time. For now, let's just talk. How's the project coming?"

He looks at his feet. "Um, good."

"That's good. Has Mavis been up to her usual tricks?"

"You know Mavis?"

"Quite well, her and her misplaced loyalty."

"What do you mean?"

"Has she not talked to you about Dr. Smith yet? If she hasn't, she will. He's gonna want to meet you, but she's gonna make sure to get her claws in first."

"…She did that already."

"Ah. Did she give you her spiel about him being a slimy corporate sellout?"

Vincent furrows his brow. "Something like that, yeah."

"Well, that's all bullshit… I suggest you talk to him yourself, then come to your own conclusions."

The line is quiet for a while.

"Are you old friends with Colonel Bartram?"

Trent chuckles. "I have to go now, Vinny."

"Wait!" He waits. "Why were you spying on me?"

"What?"

"I saw your car following us to the airport. Before that, you were at the doughnut shop. You were listening to me on my phone. Why were you spying on me?"

Trent doesn't respond for a minute. "That wasn't us, Vinny. Call us again soon. And uh, stay safe."

The line goes dead before Vincent can say, "Wait! Damn it!" *What does that mean?* He sits and thinks for a moment. *If Trent wasn't spying on me, then who was?* Putting his phone away, he rushes down to the gazebo and sees Dolly and her handler, Sergeant Cesar, doing some routine training. Vincent walks over to them to ask, "Hey, Sergeant Cesar, do you know where I can find Sergeant Martinez?"

Cesar stands up from petting Dolly and says, "I think he's patrolling the observatory right now. Why do you ask?"

"Well, maybe you can answer my question. Have you ever been sent out on a recruit pick-up detail?"

"Not really, no. I'm the only one who knows how to work with Dolly, so I get to hang out by the checkpoint most days."

"Okay… how long have you been here?"

He squints at this question. "A couple of years now, about. What are you getting at?"

"Are these pickup trucks and vans the only vehicles that come on base?"

"The only ones I know of, outside of the resupply trucks, of course."

"Of course, well… okay. Thank you." Vincent rushes off to the admin building.

Cesar shouts out, "Why? What are you talking about!?" When Vincent doesn't respond, he squints suspiciously, then continues training with Dolly.

Vincent takes the elevator into the Abaddon and goes to the east wing. *Mavis has been here a long time, and if she was in the military like Trent said, she might know why a black sedan was following us.* He knows she's in building three, but doesn't know which room. Searching through the bottom two floors, he passes by a few common rooms where people are having movie marathons. Luckily, each room has a digital placard that displays the occupant's name. 325: Goodman, Jeffery. 326: Silver, Lonny. 327: Reid, Brian. As he passes by room 327, he hears a familiar voice.

Sarah? What is she doing here? Maybe she remembers something about the trip.

Upon knocking on the door, he hears some shuffling around inside before the door opens. A shirtless Brian wearing only boxer-shorts cracks the door open; Vincent can tell he visits the gym every day.

"What! What do you want?" Brian asks curtly.

Vincent, confused by what he is seeing, stammers, "Uh, is… is Sarah he—"

"Vince?" Sarah's voice cuts through. Vincent looks past the door to see her covering herself in only a blanket on the bed.

"Uh… um… I don't…" He steps backward until he bumps into the opposite wall.

"What are you doing here, Vincent?" she asks sternly.

Brian's eyebrows are raised uncomfortably. "Do you… you guys need to talk?"

Vincent stammers a bit more before he takes off down the hall, sprinting as fast as he can for the atrium. *What… why was she…* He accidentally stumbles through a group of scientists in the garden. His mind flashes back to her grabbing his hand in the party filled atrium. He remembers the way her vibrant scent brightened his day in the Marysworth parking lot. He leans against one of the redwoods to catch his breath while images and thoughts rush through his head. His eyes shut, and he remembers the way she was psyching him up just before the press conference. His mind races, but so do his feet as he runs, not knowing where he's going.

SARAH BUTTONS HER PANTS AND SLIDES HER SHIRT ON. "I've got to find Vincent; he's going to have no idea how to handle this."

While she gets dressed, she can hear Brian at the door complaining, "Why are you going after that weirdo? The dude was seriously creeping on you."

"He's my friend, Brian! And he's not weird, he's just… different."

He laughs disrespectfully. "Yeah! Different. That's a generous way of putting it."

"Fuck off, Brian. I don't talk about your friends like that, you don't talk about mine."

"He's not your friend! He hasn't talked to you in months!"

As she puts her shoes on and leaves, she shouts, "We don't need to hang out all the time to be friends!" Then she slams the door behind her and takes off down the hall.

She makes it to the atrium and finds nothing but crowds of people enjoying their weekend. *Where'd you go, Vince?* She heads to the cafeteria for a quick look around, but nothing. *Saw that coming. Maybe he went to get some fresh air.* She takes the elevator upstairs, and on the way out, she sees Senior Airman Little standing watch.

"Hey, Little, did you see Vincent come this way?"

"Vincent? I'm sorry, I'm terrible with names."

"Urgh!" She storms out and rushes to their barracks building. She knocks on the door and shouts, "Vincent! Are you in there?"

Karl opens the door, and his eyes are puffed and slightly red. "Hey, Sarah, Vince isn't here. What's up?"

"Oh, I was just… why aren't you out with your friends?"

"Well… I was just on the phone with, um, someone."

"Someone? Is everything okay?" she asks sincerely, but with a clear urgency in her tone.

"Uh, yeah. It's just family stuff; don't worry about it. I can tell you're in a hurry, so go ahead. Your shirt's inside out."

"Shit! Thanks, I'm going to leave, but we'll talk later!" She tears back through the barracks and makes her way to the atrium. *Where are you, Vincent?* Then it hits her. She feels like an idiot as she heads for the west wing. Stepping out of the elevator as she reaches the third floor, she holds her ear up to the lab's entrance and listens to the sound of marker click clacking against a whiteboard. She stands there for a moment to gather herself, takes a deep breath, then opens the door.

"Hey, Vince."

He ignores her and keeps writing his algorithm on the board. She closes the door behind her and says nothing. She waits to see how he reacts. He doesn't. She moves to sit atop one of the tables. The echo of his writing is the only thing either of them can hear, but Sarah can taste the bitterness in the air. He erases the entire equation and starts over.

"I'm sorry about the way I was acting last night, Vincent."

He hesitates. "I know."

She looks at her feet dangling off the table, then watches him write his comfort math.

"I've seen how you've been helping Grace's team. That's really nice of you."

"Thanks… Why did you sleep with Brian?"

She bites her lip and looks away, then thinks about what the right thing to say is for quite some time before finally asking, "Do you remember that night in the Marysworth parking lot, when you asked me about that phone call?"

"I remember every night."

She chuckles. "I'm sure you do… well, I should have told you then, but I wasn't ready."

"Told me what?"

"The reason I joined the teleportation project. That night in the Ducky Luck, I was on the phone with my mom. She had just gotten some tests back from the doctor."

"Tests?"

"She has brain cancer. It's growing slowly, but there's nothing we can do."

"Oh." She sees him thinking hard about what he's supposed to say until he stammers, "I'm-I'm sorry…"

"Thank you, but you really don't have to say anything. It's really not necessary. I joined the project because… well, I'm a scientist! I should be able to help her, right? But a lot of good my astrophysics degrees will do in that operating room, huh?" She fakes a laugh. "So I decided to take a long shot. I heard about this teleportation project, and I figured, why not? Maybe I won't be the one to cure cancer, but I could at least help figure out how to pull it straight out of the body."

"I… I hadn't even considered cancer treatment as a potential use for teleportation. That would be huge." She can see his mind reeling with possibilities but cuts off his train of thought.

"Yeah, it would. For the world and for my family. So when Bartram told us we'd have to leave for six months, I wasn't sure if I could leave her for that long. She's a ticking time bomb and"—she takes a choppy breath—"she might not even have six hours left. But what you said was right. It's our research. We need to be responsible for it." Vincent looks at his feet. "I need to make sure this gets done the *right* way, even if I never..." She swallows hard. "Even if I need to leave my family for a little while."

While she fights back tears, she can sense him standing awkwardly at the whiteboard. He quietly says, "I'm sorry that I didn't know about that, Sarah..."

"It's not your fault..." She breaks the tension with a cough. "Anyway, kind of went off on a tangent there... when I came here and couldn't talk to my mom as much, I... I got lonely. And Brian was there and... it just kind of happened. He was there for me, and we just get along pretty well."

"So do we..."

"Do you think so?"

"Do you not?"

"I do. But... I don't know. It's different, I think, with us."

"Different how?"

"It's sometimes hard to..." She takes a deep breath. "It's hard to read you, sometimes. I sometimes get the feeling that you aren't interested in... romantic relationships. Which, you're allowed to not want romance, but... did you want... that?" She looks at him with sincerity.

"...I never thought about it."

"I did," she says in her small voice.

"Then why didn't you—"

"I tried. I was trying to go at your pace. You're not like Brian." He grits his teeth, squeezing the marker in his hand. "But that's a good thing, Vincent."

He looks back at her. "How?"

"Cause he's just a guy, you know? There's a million of him out there.

But there's only one Vincent Creighton. You're a special person and you deserve another special person."

"You're special."

Her heart flutters. She sits up a little straighter. "I didn't feel special."

"Really? But everybody likes you. Your team sees you as a godsend, you have friends."

"Yeah, but *you* didn't make me *feel* special. You seemed wrapped up in your research—in Mavis. I felt like I had lost my best friend. I mean, Vincent, you haven't looked me in the eyes for weeks. I never see you except for when you're with Mavis."

"We were just doing work on the project…"

"And I'm proud of you for what you've accomplished. Unfortunately, the cost of those accomplishments… was us." She wipes a tear from her eye with the sleeve of her red hoodie. "I felt like you had thrown me away."

"I… I didn't know that. I thought you wanted me to leave you alone."

"And I… Well, I did. But… I didn't *really* want that." She laughs through a few tears, realizing how he must be hearing this. "That's probably even more confusing, but listen…"

"I like you."

She looks at him and smiles. "What's that?"

"I like you. I've never said that before and… didn't know how to say it."

"Like, to anyone?"

His face turns pink. "Well, no. But I meant to you. I expected you to choose me as a romantic partner because of how nicely you treat me. You stand up for me when others don't. I like you because of that." Sarah's eyes dance back and forth between each of his bespectacled irises. "But that doesn't mean you reciprocate those intentions, and that's okay."

She bites her lip. "You're right, Vincent. Just because you like me, doesn't mean I like you back." She gives him a knowing look.

He walks away from the board to get closer to the table she's sitting on, then looks at his feet. "But you're here. Which means you left Brian's room to come talk to me. That means… something. I'm not quite sure yet."

She grins and interlaces her fingers with his. "That means I like you, too, Vincent."

He looks up into her emerald eyes and whispers, "Really?"

"Of course, I do," she smiles tenderly. *Kiss me, you idiot!*

He doesn't know how to respond to this, but a stupid smile is plastered on his face. He notices her pulling him closer to her and happily lets her. He finds himself leaning in and when a waft of her perfume passes by him, he is momentarily transported to a beautiful garden filled with lilacs and lavender. But that garden is swiftly replaced by his high school locker room as the telltale scent of Axe body spray overtakes the perfume. His hand snaps away from hers, and he leans back.

"I have to go." He walks away but stops at the entrance and looks over his shoulder. "Thank you, Sarah." Then he rushes off.

Alone in the lab, she grins and says to herself, "That's okay…"

Chapter Thirteen

April 5th, 2020

Sunday

"Vince!" Karl's voice shakes him from a deep sleep. "You want to grab some breakfast?" He looks over to see Karl fully dressed, showered, and shaved.

"You're up early," Vincent says groggily.

"Yeah, I didn't sleep very well last night." Karl combs his hair in a mirror that hangs inside his wall locker.

"Why is that?" Vincent rubs his eyes and checks the time.

"Been thinking a lot."

"What about?"

"Talk about it over breakfast?" He finishes combing his hair and throws Vincent his jacket.

Thoroughly disturbed with how solemn Karl's voice is, Vincent agrees. He gets ready, and they head outside. The sun rises over the desert landscape, painting the sky with a gorgeous shade of red. Nobody else, save for security and the kitchen staff, is awake this early on a Sunday morning. There is no line in the cafeteria, so they get their bacon, egg, and pancake breakfast made to order. They have their pick of which table to take, and Karl casually eats his food while Vincent sits with bated breath, pretending that he isn't expecting him to say what kept him up so late.

"Karl, what's going on?"

"I got a call from my sister yesterday."

"Is she okay?"

"Yeah, she's fine, but I guess our dad was in a car accident." He doesn't look up from his plate. "He died on impact."

"Oh, I'm sorry to hear that." Vincent's head falls, and he twiddles his fork in his fingers. *Jesus fuck! I have to say more than just "oh, I'm sorry", but what the fuck am I supposed to say to that?*

"I need to go to Ohio for the funeral but… I don't know, it's weird."

"What's weird?"

"Well, before he retired from the Army, my dad went on deployment, and his patrol was struck by an I.E.D. Though he managed to get out mostly unscathed, he had pretty severe P.T.S.D. from it. He didn't drive anywhere unless it was absolutely necessary and *never* by himself. According to the report, he was driving by himself in the middle of the night. It… I don't know… it just doesn't feel right."

"That is weird, but I mean stuff happens, right? Maybe it was an emergency, and he just needed to do it."

"Right, that's what I was thinking, but… that's not the weirdest part. She said she got word of the accident from the military. A couple of Army personnel showed up to her door and gave her the news."

"Okay… so?"

"I asked who they were, and she couldn't remember their names, but she described two people who sounded just like Sergeant Martinez and Airman Little."

"Oh… that is weird."

"I agree. I mean, it could be a coincidence, but it got me thinking about Chad. I did an online background check on him, and in every file that I could find, there was no record of him being married or having a child. That's not to say Chad didn't go around his hometown making babies with every girl that would let him, then skip town for a secret lab mission. But there's definitely nothing in the public record about it."

"So… what are you saying?"

Karl puts his fork down and looks around the cafeteria. People have started filing in to get breakfast, but nobody is within earshot.

"I don't know. But I do know that Chad was a cold-hearted dude. He didn't suddenly grow a heart and rush off to the side of some sick daughter he probably didn't even know he had."

"He wasn't… the greatest of people."

Karl laughs. "No, he was not. But he made the days interesting."

"Have you heard from him since he left?"

"I don't think anyone's even tried reaching out to him. It's like people are actively forgetting he exists."

Vincent stifles a grin. *Good. He's a jerk.* They share a quiet thought before Vincent asks, "Are you going to Ohio?"

Karl looks at him with a concerned look. "I don't know, should I?"

Uh… "I… I don't…"

"You don't have to answer that. It's not fair to you." He moves scrambled eggs around on his plate. "I think I'm going to stay." He looks to Vincent for a reply that he doesn't have. "Does that make me a bad person?"

"I can't… that's not for me to say."

"I guess it's not."

Vincent struggles to find the words that Karl is looking for him to say.

"Look, man, you don't have to stay here. I just appreciate having someone… I guess… rational to hear me out."

"Are you sure? I feel like I haven't really helped."

"I don't know that there's anything you can do to help. Like I said, just having an ear to talk to is nice."

"Okay…" He hesitantly stands up, pushes his chair in, and turns around. Before leaving, he turns back to ask, "Karl… do you remember the drive to the airport last month?"

"Kind of, I was conked out from Berkeley to San Francisco."

"Well, when we left my apartment complex, there was a black sedan following us."

He gives a suspicious look. "Are you sure they were following us and not just driving behind us?"

94

"They had their lights turned off and kept driving just barely out of sight. I'm fairly certain they were following us."

"Hm, I don't remember seeing anything like that. Do you think they could have been, like, scouts? Maybe they were part of the detail that ensures safe arrival of VIPs."

"Maybe… I didn't see them following us during the second leg of the trip, but I'm not sure."

"I'm not either, man. Wish I could have been more help."

"It's okay. Me, too." Vincent turns around and leaves for the atrium.

Walking through the gardens, Vincent eyes the east wing. *Is she with Brian again? What am I to her now?* He doesn't know where he wants to be. Having grown sick of his room, he loathes the idea of spending another day in there. The prospect of spending it with Karl is not attractive, considering the way Karl enjoys spending time. Grace would never want to do anything with just him; she always needs a social buffer to absorb his lack of conversational skills. Instinctively, his feet lead him to the west wing, wanting to triple-check all of their preparations for tomorrow's test, but he knows he would be wasting his time.

I have a whole day to waste… there has to be something I can do that I… enjoy. He decides to spend the morning in the east wing theatre. A small population of the scientists have made a drama club—or as they call it, an "acting guild"—that performs renditions of plays, movies, and musicals. A few of the performers are good at singing—a few are not—but they hold open rehearsals on Saturday mornings, where people can come to watch them prepare for whatever play they end up performing that night. Tonight, they will be performing a rendition of *Back to the Future*.

Vincent could never get into the idea of live theatre; the acting is always less clean, the directing less refined, and the performances are always too rehearsed. However, *Back to the Future* was always one of his favorite movies, and he would watch it as a kid until he could recite every line of it perfectly, which took only one watch. While the physics and rules of time travel were utterly ridiculous, he enjoyed the portrayal of the underestimated, wacky, and weird scientist being the genius mastermind who solves everyone's problems.

Following the maze of staircases and elevators through the recreation complex, he finds a side room outfitted with bleachers and a stage small enough that it could fit inside his apartment's living room. When he takes a seat at the back of the bleachers, he watches the actors read lines. He recognizes one of them from walking to and from the lab, but most of them are just faces he has never encountered; in this moment, he realizes that any of them could be teammates on his project, and he would have no idea. This upsets him. While he is proud of himself for the distance he has sprinted in the name of his research, he realizes what Sarah said was right: pouring all his time into work gets a lot done, but it comes with a price.

There are at least five hundred and seventy-six people who work here whom he has never even tried to befriend. He knows next to nothing about most of his coworkers. Even with his own friends, he only has surface level knowledge about who they are and where they come from. *How could I not know her mother had cancer?*

"Great Scott!" The actor portraying Doc Brown yells his line during the third act finale, then the props department drops a fake tree branch, which passes right by a fake wire and hits the ground unobstructed.

"Cut! What happened?! It missed the wire completely! It's supposed to cut the wire in half!"

"Sorry!" A voice backstage calls out. "The wire was a little off; we'll fix it!"

Memories of the Ducky Luck flash. Tons of memories. *We spent a lot of time in that bar. I don't even like bars, but I still went with them. Why is it so much harder for me to connect with them than it is for them to connect with each other? They never do the things that I want to do… but I also don't really want to hang out with people when I'm doing things that I like to do…*

"Don't worry!" Doc Brown says again once the stage is reset. "As long as you hit that wire with the connecting hook at precisely eighty-eight miles per hour at the instant the lightning strikes the tower… Everything will be fine." The actor reaches into his trench coat pocket and pulls out a prop letter. "What's the meaning of this?!" Vincent is actually quite impressed with the actor's commitment to the role.

"You'll find out in thirty years!" The actor playing Marty is considerably less committed to his role it seems; he mostly mumbles his lines as he speaks.

"*Vince! Hold up a second!*" Sarah sparks in his mind's eye as he turns to see her in the Marysworth parking lot calling out his name. *Maybe she has always cared about me… but she might need something that I can't provide. Maybe it takes something special to be friends with people, something that people like Brian have… but I just don't.* He can clearly picture her in the corner of the Ducky Luck on the phone, tears welling up at the updates of her mother's condition. *But… maybe I can do something that they can't do.*

"It's about the future, isn't it?! It's information about the future! I warned you about this, kid! The consequences could be disastrous!"

"Doc, that's a risk you're gonna have to take! Your life depends on it!"

Sarah came here to help her mom, but she doesn't have what it takes to get this teleportation tech up and running. I do. There's no way I can do this while catering to her emotional needs, though… would Sarah rather be in a relationship with me or save her mom's life? Would I be able to live with myself if I let her die without doing my part?

"No! I refuse to accept the responsibility!"

"In that case, I'll just tell you straight out!" The actor stiffly squares up to Doc Brown, but when the fake tree branch drops, it successfully cuts the prop wire in half.

"Great Scott!" The Doc Brown actor has a real knack for matching Christopher Lloyd's facial elasticity. Vincent watches Doc Brown and Marty try to fix the downed wire and realizes something that he had never thought about before. *Doc Brown says he refuses to accept the responsibility, but in the end, we find out that he kept the letter. When it came to a life-or-death situation, he accepted the responsibility of messing with the time-space continuum. If Sarah's mom is going to survive… then someone needs to take up the responsibility of getting this tech built.*

Vincent comes back to watch the full show that evening. It's usually difficult for him to connect to most of the actors' performances, but Doc Brown really connected with him during this particular show.

Chapter Fourteen

September 17th, 1954

Friday

A field of denim pants and white T-shirts litters the penitentiary yard. Leonard Sideris sits on a bench in the center of the yard as gang members walk circles around the inner fence. Most people leave him to his business, which usually consists of staring at the sky for the entire duration of their recess, since the last inmate who prodded him to "be his friend" ended up being wheeled out of there on a coroner's gurney. Today, however, is his last day on the yard… and word of this has spread.

A recently admitted inmate has decided to make a statement to his new colleagues. Sitting on his bench, Leo watches a bird fly overhead as a scrappy-looking bald man crosses the yard and stops in front of him. Eyes all around turn to watch. Most of them scoff and laugh.

"Bird-watching, huh?" The man's shadow appears on Leo's face, hovering over him.

Leo looks at him and sighs.

"Sounds like a pleasant afternoon, especially since you've got the best seat in the house."

Leo makes eye contact and says nothing.

"I think I'll join you." The man looks around at the other inmates chuckling in their direction. He laughs. "Yeah, slide on over. We'll watch these birds together."

Unmoving, Leo stares at him.

"Slide over."

Leo stares.

"That's fine; I'll just sit next to you." Taking his seat by Leo's side, he leans back, puts one foot on his knee and rests his arms along the backside of the bench, his right arm behind Leo himself. "Ah! Very pleasant. Oh! You see that one?" He points at a falcon passing by.

Leo turns his head to watch him.

"This is nice, isn't it? In fact, it's so nice that I think I'm going to pick it back up tomorrow. Right here in this seat. What do you think? You in?"

Eyes squinting, Leo stares at him. Other inmates' eyebrows raise, clearly entertained at this display.

The man leans in as if struggling to hear Leo's response. "What was that? I didn't hear you."

Leo keeps watching.

"One more time, do you want to join me tomorrow?" Not receiving the rise that he was hoping for, he continues, "Oh that's right! You have a date tonight, don't you? Well, with that being the case, you must be nervous. Why don't you get up and go walk off your nerves? I'll keep your seat warm for you."

No response.

"Go on." He waves his hand to shoo Leo away.

Blinking once, Leo slowly gets to his feet.

"Enjoy your date."

Leo turns and walks behind the bench; the man keeps one eye on him. Up close, Leo can tell the man's jaw is trembling. Directly behind the man, Leo places both hands on his shoulders and bends over to whisper in his ear, "Stand up and earn this bench from me. Then they'll respect you."

The man chuckles. "You want me to earn the bench?"

"No. They do."

The man looks out across everyone's gazes, then he nods, stands up, and walks around to the backside of the bench. Squaring up to Leo, he almost expects a tumbleweed to blow in the wind between them.

The man puts his fists up and begins bouncing from side to side as if they're in a cartoon boxing match, stepping toward him with each bounce. Leo gets into a similar stance, minus the ridiculous bouncing. The man throws a few jabs with his left before hooking with his right, but Leo nimbly dodges each of them. Getting his bearings again, the man throws another jab, but Leo grabs his wrist, pulls him close, sweeps his legs, and as the man falls, Leo grabs his jaw to plunge him onto the back of the bench. The man's neck snaps, and his body crumples to the concrete floor below.

MIDNIGHT. Leo is properly restrained and led to a small, cement room with nothing but a simple wooden chair, wired up with straps and a variety of electrical instruments. The guards, cold and callous, sit him in the chair, then fasten the leather straps to his wrists, ankles, and chest. Damp sponges are placed under his bindings, then applied to his temple and calf before being wired up with the electrodes. Then he is asked a simple question.

"Would you like a blindfold?"

Leo gives him a deadpan stare. "No. I want to know you're watching."

"Oh, well, nobody wants to see you squirm." The guard slides a black bag over his head and chuckles.

Leo sighs. *Of course, they don't.* Splinters dig into his forearms against the unfinished chair. He can't get comfortable in the terrible seat. The bindings were pulled a little too tightly, so he can't scratch the itch on his wrists. The sound of shuffling of feet leaves the room. All he can see is black fabric, but he hears two voices bickering just outside.

"Let's start at fifteen hundred volts. If that doesn't work, we'll kick it up to two thousand."

"Do you want to just start at two thousand?"

"Why? Spare him a less painful death?"

"Well… yes."

A third, bold voice enters the conversation. Boisterous and familiar, Leo can't help but smile as the voice speaks.

"Good evening, gentlemen," the bold voice greets them as the door shuts, and the voices become too muffled to understand.

The door opens again and the guard who covered his face asks, "Leonard Sideris, do you have any final words?"

"Well, now that you mention it, I do." Smiling wickedly, he shouts loudly enough for everyone to hear, "Bartram! It's good to see you again. Now that I have your attention, I'd like you to take a close look at what you've turned me into. My story is one of tragedy that will echo through the annals of history. The unlikely hero, risen from the debris of a shattered life, ravaged by the insufferable greed of the powerful seeking power! People will hear my story and revolt!" His echoing words dissipate into silence as they are absorbed by the concrete walls.

"Administering the first shock in three... two... one." Leo gulps and hears a mechanical lever being pulled. He tenses his muscles up and shuts his eyes tightly. Then he waits.

Fifteen seconds later, the same voice says, "Administering the second shock... now." Then he hears the lever being pulled again, another fifteen seconds pass.

"Time of death, twelve fifteen A.M."

Leo turns his head left and right in confusion, then corrects them. "What? No, it isn't! I'm not dead yet!" From underneath the black bag over his head, the electrodes are ripped off, and his straps are loosened before being dragged from the chair onto a gurney, and his hands are cuffed. "What's happening?! Where are you taking me?!" The crumpling of plastic surrounds him.

The boisterous voice says, "Knock him out; I don't want any guerilla journalist to get a picture of him struggling."

Leo tries to lift his hands up, fighting against the leather straps as hard as he can. "Wait! No! What are you—" The sweet scent of some kind of alcohol cuts off his train of thought, and he ends up babbling nonsensically trying to get back on track before falling asleep.

Swaying from side to side and an abrupt jostling suddenly wake him up. His eyes open to blackness, which he stares at for quite some time before regaining the strength to turn his head. Skull throbbing, he tries to cradle it from the rocky movement but finds that his wrists are still cuffed and chained to his waist. Pulling harder against the restraints proves impossible as his muscles are still quite sore, and in the movement, he can hear the crinkling of plastic all around him. The realization suddenly makes the air he's breathing incredibly stuffy, and his struggle gradually turns into a tantrum until a hand steadies him in place.

Calm though his body becomes, his mind races with anxiety. He is startled by the sound of a plastic bag unzipping, then the bag over his head is quickly pulled off. Once his eyes adjust to the dim light, the face of a young Major Henry Bartram stares down at him, sporting a wide grin. Broad shoulders nearly bursting out of a white, collared uniform shirt make his necktie look razor-thin and his greased back, bleach blonde crew cut glistens in the street lights shining through the windows of a Chevy van.

"Oh… fudge." Leo's heart sinks.

"Sergeant Sideris, it's been a while, hasn't it?"

"What are you doing? Why am I not dead?!"

"Is that any way to greet an old friend? Hell, you should be thanking me!"

"You should have let me die!" He struggles against his restraints.

"That would have been such a waste, though! You see… I've been following your career since you left my platoon after the war." Pulling out a thick file, he flips through the pages. "Looks like you've been quite busy. One of the Gambino capos, a founding father of Pakistan, a civil rights leader, and a senior member of the Ku Klux Klan—I like that, unbiased. Let's see, what else?" Skimming through the pages, he continues, "The leader of a labor union, even a soviet nuclear physicist. You're quite the accomplished assassin."

"I'm only what you made me, you piece of shit! You stepped all over and exploited me to become a cold-hearted killer!" Leo says with a huff, but takes a breath and rests his head against the gurney. "If only I hadn't let you torment me into being your own personal murderer…"

Bartram doesn't respond initially. Instead, he replaces the file in his satchel and sits in a seat alongside the gurney. "No. I couldn't have made a professional like you if I tried. Skills like yours are hard to come by, you know? There's something in you that makes you exceptionally good at ending others' lives. I want to find that something and isolate it."

"Isolate it? What the hell are you talking about?"

"I want you… but better. Specifically, I want only the part of you that makes you an astounding killer."

"You want to cut into my brain? Give me a lobotomy? Is that it? Why couldn't you just do that with my corpse?"

Bartram laughs. "Oh, no, no, no. I won't be cutting into your brain, that's far too precious of a resource to damage. No, I'm going to *perfect* you, then I'm going to sell you." Leo's brow furrows, and his stomach drops when Bartram goes silent. "For the record"—Bartram abruptly stands up to loom over Leo—"I wouldn't have found you if it wasn't for your little display at the hospital. That was a great letter you wrote, but unfortunately, the only story they told was one of a lunatic."

Frozen in horror, Leo looks Bartram in the eyes as he stands up and zips the body bag back up.

CHAPTER FIFTEEN

April 6th, 2020

Monday

Monday is testing day. Vincent wakes up early and feels jittery, but his hot shower calms his nerves. He wakes up early enough to grab a hearty breakfast at the cafeteria before heading to the lab. Mavis is already there, along with a team of the project's engineers, gathering equipment and loading everything in the motorized, gyroscopic carts designed specifically to transport sensitive equipment, including quantum computers. Despite being preoccupied, Mavis greets Vincent with her patented morning coffee. "Today's the day! It'll be a piece of cake!" she says, then goes back to loading up equipment.

Vincent packs up his own clipboards and pulls his lab coat off the wall. When Sarah and Grace come into the lab, he and Sarah make eye contact. She gives him a bright smile. Vincent doesn't reciprocate; instead, he averts his eyes and turns away. He can hear her and Grace exchanging confused, mumbled words, but he blocks them out. *If I'm going to help her mom, I'll need to focus. She'll understand.* The rest of the crew files into the lab over the next twenty minutes. Everyone except for Karl. Mavis steps in front of the crew for a last-minute pep talk.

"Good morning, everyone! I hope you are all excited for today's presentation! I'm sure you all have already noticed Karl's absence; unfortunately, he will not be joining us today. He had an urgent family matter and is currently on emergency leave."

What? I thought he said he was staying?

"But that aside, we have worked so hard over the past eight weeks to get this leg of the project up and running. This is still just a preliminary experiment; we're just testing out what we have ready at this time. Now let's all, in an orderly fashion, make our way down to the atrium."

It takes four elevator trips to ferry all twenty-nine members of the team down to the first floor, but upon making it to the atrium, Sergeant Martinez, Senior Airman Little, Sergeant Cesar, and Dolly are waiting for them at the entrance to the north wing in full tactical gear, including Dolly who wears her own little Kevlar vest.

"Alright, everybody, most of you know the drill already, but for the newbies, the testing facility is over ten miles away heading north along the mountain chain behind the base. We will be loading up on a subway car to make our way out there." Sergeant Martinez scans his ID, and the double doors open to reveal the hall of an art gallery. The floor and walls, carved from black opal, shimmer with the entire color spectrum as they enter; in-ground lights shine on framed artwork, creating a dim aura of light throughout the gallery.

The group slowly disperses to gawk at the art. Vincent hears Sarah and Grace squealing in excitement as Sergeant Martinez's voice echoes off the walls. "Obviously, don't touch anything. There's two exits at the end of the hall; we are going to the right." As he says this, Vincent notices the wall opposite the entrance—two works seem to be the centerpieces of the gallery. He walks to them and admires the juxtaposition of these two pieces. *Who chose these?* A landscape drip painting by Jackson Pollock is mounted just underneath the framed Leonardo Da Vinci drawing of *The Vitruvian Man* and Vincent stands in front of them, entranced. Individually, they speak to him in a beautiful way, but together, he is incapable of pulling his attention away. Mavis watches him from afar, smiling at him.

"Dr. Creighton!" Sergeant Martinez exclaims, "Giddyup, let's go!" Vincent shakes himself out of his stupor and follows the crowd as they funnel into the right corridor that leads to a small platform with a subway car.

They load the equipment cart in first, then the passengers. Making sure to be near Mavis during the trip, Vincent asks, "Why is the testing facility so far away from everything else?"

"Well, whenever it comes to experiments like ours, things can go… catastrophically wrong. Back during the space race, we were working on a light-speed engine. The project seemed to be going well enough, but then they did a test—off-site and away from Fort Chivington, thank God. When they fired up the drive for its initial test, for some reason, it accelerated much faster than they intended. They instantly lost control of its speed. It went faster and faster until it surpassed the runway they had made specifically for that test. It sped up to the point where the air molecules in front of it compressed together, leaving a wake behind it, and eventually—"

"It broke the Coulomb barrier?" Vincent cuts in.

"Yeah. It created an explosion that changed the very geography of the testing site. Since then, they moved the testing facility underground and far away from where we all live."

"That's incredible. I can't believe I'd never heard about this."

"Well, we are exceptionally good at keeping secrets."

"So I've heard." He looks out the window as they travel through the bedrock that supports the Wyoming Red Desert. Every couple hundred feet, Vincent notices that they pass through a ring of steel embedded into the rock. He looks at Mavis and asks, "What are those rings?"

"Those are blast doors. In case one of those aforementioned catastrophic events occurs, those doors are designed to shut, stopping—or at least slowing—anything that might make its way back to the Abaddon."

"Have you ever had to use them?"

"Just once. Last year, we had a machine failure that set off the blast doors, but there was no danger of damaging the Abaddon."

Vincent nods his head as the car's brakes activate, gradually slowing to a halt. Getting off the car, they gather in front of one of those large blast doors. One of the engineers behind him comments on how it looks like something straight out of *Star Trek,* which prompts an argument over design aesthetics of *Star Wars, Star Trek,* and *Battlestar Galactica.* Sergeant Martinez scans his ID, causing it to slowly split open.

Through the door, the crew finds a massive cylindrical room that extends about a hundred feet up and a hundred feet down. They step onto the grated floor suspended in the center of the facility. The walls around them are lined with various electronic equipment and wires that crawl up into a vented ceiling and down below the grate into the ground beneath them. The centerpiece of the facility is a large glass chamber attached to a three-foot metal box. Spreading out across the room, Mavis directs the engineers in setting up the equipment while Vincent ogles at the grandiosity of the space when Sarah and Grace approach.

"Hey, Vince." Sarah smiles, but Vincent doesn't return the gesture.

"Alright, everybody," Mavis's voice echoes loudly. "Dr. Smith will be joining us in an hour. Let's try to be set up before he gets here."

"Hey, Mavis, what's that box next to the teleportation chamber?" Vincent asks as Sarah turns to Grace, who shrugs.

"That's the power unit. It's very delicate and is the reason we'll be staying behind the glass."

"What kind of power does it generate?"

"I'm, uh, I'm not sure. Dr. Smith keeps that kind of info under lock and key." Her tone shifts to one of frustration when she mentions his name.

"Hm…" Vincent's curiosity is piqued, but he walks into the observation room and begins his part of the setup.

Forty-five minutes later, they turn on the glass chamber, which illuminates with a white light to display the round teleportation pad they have spent years developing. An array of sensor equipment, high-speed cameras, and—most importantly—the custom-designed quantum computer are all wired up to create a chaotic system of cabling that brings their creation to life.

The entrance door opens, and in walks a tall, Native American man, Armani-clad with long, silver hair pulled back in a ponytail. A polka dot tie is the center of attention for his elegant suit, but his oozing charisma is what overwhelms the room. "Such a pleasure to see you all on a gorgeous day like today, my friends." His voice is deep, and he speaks with a deliberate cadence that commands attention from those around him.

"Good morning, Dr. Smith! Welcome to today's test." Mavis walks over and shakes his hand. "You've met most of the team already, but we have had a handful of new folks show up since our last test."

"Yes, I have been looking forward to meeting them."

Mavis gestures to the sea of white coats and introduces the new team members. "Here we have Dr. Grace Medina, head of the computer science team. Her counterpart, as you know, is unable to join us today."

"Yes"—he squints furiously at her—"an unfortunate… scheduling conflict, of course."

"Indeed, but moving forward, we have Dr. Sarah Boyce, head of the astrophysics team. We have a couple of new engineers, Doctor Frank Johnson and Mister Randall Weaverly. And finally, our mathematics expert, Dr. Vincent Creighton."

"Ah, yes, Vincent, I have heard a lot about you. I am excited for our meeting today."

Vincent just nods shyly and retreats into the crowd.

"Well, Dr. Blackwell, if your team is ready, let us get this show on the road."

"We're ready, sir."

Everyone packs into the observation room, except for Sergeant Martinez who reaches for the last box still on the equipment cart. Mavis, operating the master-computer, presses a button and a section of the glass chamber detaches and opens on a hinge. Sergeant Martinez removes some kind of taxidermied cat from the box.

Grace is the first to ask, "Is that a stuffed cat?"

Mavis responds, "I figured it's only appropriate for Schrodinger's cat to be the first test subject." The entire room chuckles as Sergeant Martinez places the cat into the glass chamber. Mavis closes the chamber door, then Sergeant Martinez joins them in the observation room, closing the door behind him.

"Alright, everybody. History in the making right here, you ready?" Shouts of giddy excitement erupt from the crowd. Vincent, nearly pressing his nose against the blast shield, watches intently, but he is a bit startled to hear Mavis say, "Vincent, would you mind doing the honors?"

His eyes widen and his face flushes with embarrassment as the entire team looks on. "Me? Are you sure?"

"Absolutely, you've put more time and thought into this project than any of us. You've earned it."

His instinct is to withdraw in the light of everyone's attention, but he finds himself back in front of the press conference with Mark standing behind him, tongue-tied at the thought of real science questions. He remembers the reporter in the back of the room giving him a questioning look. *Demand their attention, Vincent.* He stands up straight and tall, then proudly states, "I'll do it."

"Great." Mavis smiles at him and steps aside for him to take the conn. "Do you mind giving a quick breakdown of our expectations for Dr. Smith before we start?"

Vincent turns to face everyone, and the first thing he sees is Grace in the back of the group with a scowl and her arms crossed. He grins, clears his throat, then addresses Dr. Smith.

"Sir, when my team from Marysworth first joined this project, I had already—" Vincent looks at Sarah standing next to Grace, a proud grin painted on her face as she watches him. "…*We* had already come up with a way to compress quantum data in a way that we could actually store it using a quantum computer. We just needed to make a computer that could do it. It turned out you already had that computer. I concluded it would take us two hours to teleport an object using your computer."

"Is that true? I was unaware of this," Dr. Smith says

"Well, as it was pointed out to me by a scientist who is no longer part of this team"—Vincent starts, but Mavis clears her throat before he continues—"the project is intended for a human to be teleported. If a human stepped into that machine, it would take two hours before they rematerialized on the other side."

"Ah! And the subject would die before rematerializing—a less than preferable outcome."

"Exactly. The brain can survive six minutes without oxygen. The system that Mavis and I created ensures the body will be rebuilt in a way that keeps it alive for the transport, but we need the computer to be able to process every qubit of data—"

"Within six minutes. That is a tall order."

Vincent nods. "Grace's team"—*with immense help from me*—"has managed to cut the computer's processing time down to ten minutes, which is impressive, but still needs improvement before we can test on humans."

"Naturally. Well, today is not a day of judgment, so please, fire it up."

"Right. The target destination is exactly one meter to the left. We're just going to put it back inside the cart." Vincent takes a deep breath. His finger hovers over the "Enter" button on the keyboard. "Teleportation in five… four… three… two… one…" As he presses down on the button, a green laser begins scanning the cat. Vincent's eye is fixed on the target location. Watching an object rematerialize during teleportation has been his dream since he was a child. Then, a catastrophic event occurs.

An invisible beam of atom-sized cat material shoots out from the intended location toward the observation room. The side of the cart cracks, then the blast shield shatters. Senior Airman Little begins choking and falls to the floor, followed by a line of scientists standing behind Little—every one of them falling to the floor, seizing, and shaking with violent convulsions until their bodies lie still. The entire crowd screams and presses against the walls. "Vincent!" Sergeant Martinez grabs Vincent by the shoulders and pulls him away from the line of destruction as Mavis takes his place at the helm to abort the experiment.

"What the fuck was that?!" Mavis shouts but gets drowned out by the screaming.

Sergeant Martinez kneels and begins first aid on Little while shouting instructions, but when his voice gets drowned out by the hysteria, he straightens his back to use his command voice. "ATTENTION!" This quiets them down. "Cesar, call for medical! Blackwell, grab the emergency supplies off the wall, and start first aid! Anyone else who can help, do so. Otherwise, get against the wall, and stay quiet!"

Twenty minutes pass, silent except for the sound of Martinez, Cesar, and Mavis performing CPR on Little and the four scientists who mysteriously fell, but they never wake back up. They die long before medical arrives on scene. When medical does arrive, their bodies are escorted away from the facility, and the survivors are treated for shock. It takes about two hours, but most of the team is evacuated back to the Abaddon, everyone except for Dr. Smith, Mavis, Vincent, and the team leads.

Dr. Smith initiates the line of questioning by asking, "What exactly just happened?"

Mavis starts, "Well, sir, all I can say for sure is the cat rematerialized incorrectly. It seemed to rematerialize in a line rather than stay in place. But I can't figure out what could have possibly caused something like this."

Grace, looking through the logs on the computer, adds on, "It doesn't look like it had anything to do with the teleporter itself. It was sending the data to the specified location correctly."

"I know what it was," Vincent chimes in.

"Quick on the draw. What are your thoughts?" Dr. Smith asks.

"The Earth. We didn't account for the movement of the Earth."

"What are you talking about?!" Mavis spits. "Of course, we did! You wrote a whole algorithm dedicated solely to adjusting for the rotation of the Earth."

"Right. The rotation of the Earth around its own axis. Not the revolution of Earth around the Sun."

"Oh my God, Vincent, you're absolutely right," Sarah says as it clicks in her head. "Grace, how long were we actively teleporting?"

Grace clicks around on the computer and answers, "About three and a half seconds."

"The Earth revolves around the sun at thirty kilometers per second. If we had that thing active for three and a half seconds, then we would find a line of cat particles shooting up through the ground to what? One hundred and five kilometers into the sky?"

"Conversely," Grace says, eyeing the glass chamber, "there will be particles of dirt and debris from the ground above us inside the chamber." Sure enough, when they all look inside, a miniscule, nearly invisible pile of dirt sits against the brightly lit chamber floor next to the remaining cat. Vincent knew that teleportation made particles swap places, but it was striking to see it happen in front of him.

"*Yeheihoo…*" Dr. Smith mutters while covering his mouth and shaking his head.

"What does that mean for us?" Mavis asks.

"That means I must return to quantify our loss and ensure there were no losses above the surface." Dr. Smith turns for the subway. "Vincent, our meeting will take place tomorrow; come see me after work. Tzofiya gave your badge north wing access; I will have her extend it until close of business tomorrow. In the meantime, Mavis, if anything comes up, you know where to find me." He takes off for the subway and leaves.

"Now what does it actually mean for *us*?" Grace asks.

Vincent says, "We have to find a way to account for the trajectory of Earth through space, which, unfortunately, is being pushed and pulled by every other object in the universe. It's constantly changing."

Grace makes a point of nodding to Sarah when she says, "But luckily for us, we have a chart that maps out every celestial object whose gravity makes a noticeable difference on Earth."

"Interesting," Mavis says, eyeing Sarah suspiciously. "Vincent, looks like you're going to have your hands full for a while." Mavis sighs and addresses the group. "We lost a few good friends today. If you need to talk to anyone, don't hesitate to find Delilah; she lives in the barracks next to yours. I'll have maintenance come up here and clean things up."

VINCENT RELUCTANTLY JOINS Sarah and Grace in having lunch in the cafeteria together for the first time in months. The more time he spends with Sarah, the harder it will be for him to focus on his work, but in light of recent events, they have much to discuss. Most of the project team members are finding comfort in food after the incident, causing an eerily quiet aura to overtake the cafeteria. As they pass by tables, Vincent hears people asking questions that nobody knows the answers to amongst each other.

"So what happened?"

"Did Stephanie make it? I thought I saw her breathing before they left."

"Do we get to take the week off?"

As they find a table, conversation doesn't pick up. Vincent has a few things he wants to say but hasn't seen others deal with grief before. *Are they not talking on purpose? I mean... I know it was my fault they died, but... that's on me, right?* Mixing his peas with his mashed potatoes, he takes a bite. *People die all the time... even in the name of science.* He sips his can of coke.

"I should have seen it coming," Sarah says in tears.

"No! Sarah, nobody could have seen that coming." Grace holds her hand. "It isn't your fault—it was an accident. Unprecedented science leads to unprecedented consequences. We couldn't have seen it coming." Her voice is more consoling than it usually is.

"But... astrophysics! The Earth moving is my whole field of study! How did I not consider the *revolution of the Earth*?!"

"Well, technically, it was my fault," Vincent says with a mouthful of mashed potatoes and peas. They both look at him confused.

"What are you talking about? Of course not!" Grace says again with a sympathetic scowl.

"No, it was. Technically, I pushed the button which initiated the machine. Plus, I neglected to do the math to adjust the subject's intended target location." He sips his soda again. "Algorithms are my department. It was technically my fault."

"That doesn't make it your fault. It really doesn't matter. Look, I'm going to see Delilah with some friends, you guys should come with me."

Sarah nods while drying her tears with a napkin. "Yeah… I-I should go."

"Do you want to come with us, Vincent?" Grace asks with her eyebrows raised at him.

"Um, no, wait, before you go, I need to talk to you about Karl." He scans the area for prying ears.

"Yeah," Grace says in an almost accusatory tone. "I actually was going to ask you about him too. Did you know he was leaving?"

"He told me that his sister was visited by a couple of Army folks who looked like Martinez and Little to inform her of their father's death, but he told me that he wasn't going to the funeral. He said it yesterday, but it's weird that he would turn around on his decision that quickly."

"He said he wasn't going? What a bastard! Why would he leave his sister alone at a time like that?"

"I hate to disagree, Grace," Sarah says. "Everyone grieves in different ways. Maybe not going was his way of grieving."

"No," Vincent asserts. "It wasn't grief. He said—"

"You know what, Vincent," Grace interrupts him. "Since you're such an expert on grief, what do you need us for? I mean, you must understand what Karl was going through far better than we would, right?"

"Grace! There's no need to bite his head off!" Sarah says defensively. "Sorry, Vince, I do want to talk about Karl, but… now just isn't a good time." She wipes her eyes and continues, "How about tomorrow? Are you sure you don't want to come with us?"

"Uh… okay… um, no. I-I'm good, thanks."

Grace rolls her eyes at him. "Well, I'm glad you feel so *good* about your coworkers dying!"

"Grace!" Sarah shouts back at her. "He's allowed to be okay! Don't shame him for feeling the way he feels!"

Grace blushes and squints at Vincent. "Fine. Let's go."

Chapter Sixteen

April 7th, 2020

Tuesday

Vincent and Mavis are the only two who come to work the next morning. The team was authorized two mental health days before returning to work. Vincent asked if it was mandatory, but Delilah said it was not. Mavis prepares her typical coffee for Vincent before they get to work figuring out how to deal with the Earth's revolution.

"I gotta tell you, Vincent, I really feel out of my depth here. Astrophysics and algorithms aren't exactly my bread and butter."

"That's okay, I know more than enough about both of them to make up for you."

They share a laugh, and Mavis jokes, "Well, let's hope you know more about astrophysics than your friend Sarah, right?"

"What's that?" Vincent chokes.

"I just mean to say, if you were in charge of the astrophysics team, we would have caught the issue before we got to the testing phase, right?"

"Maybe, but I was constantly checking everybody's work. I had plenty of opportunities to see the problem. It wasn't Sarah's fault." Mavis shrugs and digs her nose in some reading while Vincent writes out one of his ideas on the board. After a while, he looks back to see Mavis reading through an astrophysics textbook from the library. He thinks for a minute before catching a confidence high. "When did you join the military?"

"I'm sorry?"

"Yesterday, you jumped into action with the sergeants doing first aid. Sergeant Martinez called you Blackwell, and I noticed you jump in with the military like you were falling into formation with them. You looked like you fit in pretty well."

She chuckles. "You're good, Creighton. Um, yeah. I used to be military police in the Air Force. That's actually where I met Martinez, Little, and Cesar. Bartram requested that I join him out here. I recruited the others to join me, then I got out to get my doctorate and came back as a scientist. I recommended most of the military that works here to Colonel Bartram."

"Why did he request you specifically?"

"He'd heard of me through the MP grapevine, then he brought me back here so he could have a fellow vet bridge the communication gap between the scientists and military."

"Smart..." Vincent says. He thinks silently for a moment, then unpromptedly says, "He's got kind of an ego, doesn't he?"

She starts to clam up, but forces herself to answer, "Oh, yeah, but that's how he came to be so successful. He's really a sweet guy when you get to know him."

"Did you know Master Sergeant Kritzman while you were still in?"

"No, she's only been here for a few years, but she has earned herself a respectable reputation."

"You know a lot about this place... how long have you been here?"

"As a scientist? Oh, let's see... ten years? Maybe longer, I can never remember."

"That's a long time." *She looks very young to have been in the military, gotten a doctorate, AND been here for ten years.* "How old are you?"

"Vincent! You never ask a woman her age!"

He blushes, but she just laughs. They get back to work, but this proves to be unsuccessful as Vincent's mind is too preoccupied.

At lunch, the cafeteria is much quieter than usual. Apparently those who died yesterday were friends with people from every project. Nearly everybody is taking advantage of the mental health day. Come time for the end of the work day, Vincent becomes visibly upset at repeating the same steps over and over and coming up with no results.

"You should call it a day, Vincent. Take a breather, maybe get a drink before your meeting with Dr. Smith."

"Yeah, that's a good idea." He hangs up his lab coat and packs up.

"Vince." She catches his attention as he walks out the door, a somber look on her face. "Don't forget to take what he says with a grain of salt. He's a snake."

"Right… thanks."

Following her advice, he takes a break at the cafeteria, and though the bars don't open for a couple of hours, he does see Sarah and Grace talking over a cup of coffee. *I should go and talk to them about Karl… but… what if they don't want to?* Grace looks over Sarah's shoulder, sees him standing in the entrance, and gives him a dirty look. *Grace didn't think much of his leaving and definitely knows more about how people grieve than I do, so… I don't know.* He returns her glare and just steels himself before crossing through the garden toward the north wing. He notices an uptick in couples taking walks through the garden, bathing in the light of the artificial sun and breathing in the aroma from the cornucopia of floral arrangements across the flowerbeds.

Malingerers.

Passing the waterfall at the far end of the garden, he heads for the north wing entrance, breathes deep, and scans his ID, then the doors open. He sighs and marches on. Having more of a chance to appreciate the opalescent art gallery, he takes his time in admiring each piece. On the right side of the wall, a painting depicts an old man sitting at a desk piled high with open books and cauldrons. The old man diligently, desperately studies one of the open books. Vincent watches him study. *What could he be searching for?* Mounted on the wall next to it, a card labels the piece as "*The Alchemist,* Oil on Canvas, Mattheus van Hellemont." *Ah. Gold. Alchemy was all about creating gold and immortality. Born out of man's greed, people sought to turn magic into science and paved the way for chemistry as we know it today.*

Across from *The Alchemist,* another piece took up the left side of the wall. A painting depicts a gathering of five men at a table as they count money; next to the table, two men seem to approach the table while one of them points toward the money counters. At the table, one of the men has an astonished countenance, as if he was just called out by the popular kids in high school to join their clique. *"Who? Me?"* The man appears to say. Vincent peers at the label: *"The Calling of Saint Matthew,* Oil on Canvas, Caravaggio." *Saint Matthew? Why would they display this of all pieces in a science facility?*

Checking his watch, Vincent realizes he should get going, so he heads into the corridor on the left side of the gallery. Walking down a long, reverberant marble hallway, he comes to a spiral staircase that goes up or down. *Um... where do I go? Up, I guess?* He heads up the long staircase that winds up to a door labeled "Military Director of Operations, Colonel Henry Bartram." *Oops. Wrong way...* He turns to head back down, descending the staircase and seeing a door at the bottom that says: "Civilian Director of Operations, Dr. Russell Smith."

Vincent knocks on the doors and waits, but receives no response. The scanner turns green as he passes his ID across it. Opening the door, he steps into a marble foyer decorated with multi-colored geometric designs on the wall. Next to him is an oak armoire, and Vincent takes a peek inside to see several suit coats hanging on wooden hangers. *My god.* Feeling out of place, he keeps moving.

Exiting the foyer, each step is taken with extreme caution. *Does he still know I'm coming?* The foyer opens up and leads to a round, spacious living room filled with what feels like natural light pouring in from massive arched windows that overlook... *the Grand Canyon? Where am I?* He looks around the living room to see the walls are lined with hide tapestries, blankets, and other forms of decoration—all sporting similar yet unique geometric designs. The center of the room has an active campfire currently with a pot of stew simmering over the flames. *Is that a real fire?* Upon further inspection, it seems to be some kind of fancy heating device that is made to appear as a campfire.

"Vincent!" a deep voice calls out, and his stomach drops. He turns to see Dr. Smith with his arms open welcomingly, dressed in a comfortable looking Versace suit emblazoned with a paisley inlay.

"Sir, I… sorry, I knocked but—"

"Please, no apologies my friend, I was in my study. Welcome to my humble abode!"

"Thank you, sir. It's"—his attention is drawn to the Grand Canyon—"Is that some kind of—"

"It is." He smiles vivaciously at Vincent. " It is live feed from the South Rim viewing point." He pulls out a remote and clicks a button. The video fades to black, then returns on a dark, desert cityscape at the edge of a deep blue waterfront. The room around them reflects the night time darkness. "The top of the Burj Khalifa in Dubai. The time for them is about ten o'clock at night." He clicks the remote again and the scene fades. A dim light appears as it shines through murky waters, then a vile-looking creature comes into frame. It jolts in fear and swims off into the darkness. "This is our probe near the seabed of the Mariana Trench." He switches the scene back to Arizona and lays the remote on a nearby table.

"This is… incredible. I didn't know the government had the funds to sink into this kind of domicile," Vincent says in awe. Dr. Smith just shuffles uncomfortably in response.

"Yes… well, can I interest you in a cup of tea?"

"Um, sure."

"Delightful." He gestures for Vincent to follow him. "I myself am not much of a tea person, but I enjoy learning and practicing the traditions of others. I learned this recipe from a friend a long time ago."

Dr. Smith leads Vincent through the most immaculate condo he has ever seen. The Native American patterns and designs calm Vincent's mind as he walks, though he eyes Dr. Smith carefully. Mavis's warning streams through his mind. Moving into the most beautiful kitchen and dining room, Dr. Smith fills up a kettle of water and places it on the stove.

"This place is beautiful," Vincent says.

"*Hohou*, I designed it with my tribe in mind, hoping they would come here and enjoy it with me. But given the black site nature of the facility, this was not in the cards." He places a spoonful of tea leaves into an ornate teapot, then grabs two glass teacups from the cupboard.

"Was it Colonel Bartram's idea to make it a black site?"

"Yes. In fact, it was a good idea given the sensitive nature of our work; keeping secrets from your enemies is a smart practice. But I would have liked to let people come and see the things we do here." He spoons some sugar into each cup while Vincent stands uncomfortably near the island that separates the kitchen from the dining room.

"How long have you been here working with DARPA?"

Thinking carefully, he picks a few leaves off the potted mint plant he has on his island and places them atop the sugar in the teacups. "I have been here since the beginning. Right here for most of my career, alongside Henry. We used to have an understanding, but many years ago our paths split. He went down a road that I could not follow."

"What road was that?"

He shoots Vincent a knowing look and smiles. "He likes to control things." When the kettle whistles, Dr. Smith pours the boiling water into the teapot and waits a minute. "How are you feeling after yesterday's incident?"

Vincent looks at his feet. "Fine. It's not… good that people died, but bad things happen from time to time."

Dr. Smith lowers his head to meet his gaze. "Death is a natural part of life, yes. However, we must never forget the value of each and every life on Earth—be it the life of our friends and family, or the life of the redwoods in the atrium, or even the life of a single grain of sand." *Sand? Sand doesn't have life…* "If we could discover the greatest secret the universe holds, but learning it meant losing the value of a single life, would it be worth it?"

Vincent thinks for a moment and says, "Is knowledge more valuable than life? It depends on what you could do with the knowledge, I guess?"

A disappointed smile creeps across Dr. Smith's face. "You are a good scientist, Dr. Creighton." Grabbing the teapot, he pours tea into each cup, the mint leaves wilting slightly as he stirs. He places the tea cups onto a platter. "May I show you my study?"

Taking the platter in both hands, he walks down intricate corridors to a relatively small part of the home. Though it's about twice the size of the Marysworth research room back in California, it feels homey. Buckskin rugs bridge the gap between each wall, which are lined with huge bookshelves and wooden architecture. Dr. Smith sets the platter down on a table in front of the fireplace that sits at the center of the study, then he lights a fire and gestures to the armchairs that mark the reading area. "Please, take a seat. Make yourself comfortable."

Wary of what Dr. Smith might say, Vincent sits and takes the teacup he is offered. "Do you like music?"

"Not particularly."

"Well, let me change your mind." He smiles and pulls a vinyl record off a shelf, then walks over to a wooden table with an electronic record player sitting atop it. "You might like this." Laying the needle down, an electric guitar begins to squeal, ushering in a heavy metal song with loud, brash noises. *What the fuck is this?* Dr. Smith hastily returns to the chair next to Vincent and hurriedly says, "Listen to me, Vincent."

Woah. Dr. Smith's entire demeanor has shifted; he's no longer having a conversation with him. He's looking Vincent directly in the eyes as his tone turns into that of a command. "They are watching us, Vincent. They are listening to us. You need to find Trent and meet with him. Find a way to leave this base and come back without their knowledge. Do you understand?"

Vincent looks back at him completely unsure of how to respond. His eyes dart back and forth as he cranes his neck around the room, looking for some kind of Candid Camera crew or a one-way mirror, but it's just the two of them alone. Focusing back on Dr. Smith, he asks, "How do you know Trent?"

"Do you understand what I have said, Vincent? We do not have time to discuss."

Is… Is this a test? Am I supposed to say, "No! I'm loyal to the Colonel!" There isn't time for him to think about it much more. He's been staring at the Doctor for too long. "Yes. I understand, but who is 'they'?"

"Bartram, Mavis, and their cronies. They are not who you think they are. Trust no one but Trent, Vincent. You have unrestricted access to the north wing until midnight tonight. Tzofiya will cover your tracks. Get in, find whatever you need to learn the truth that I am telling you, then get out."

"W-Wait, what do you—"

"We will meet again in two months' time. The record player is about to shut down, pretend that you are turning down a job offer with Lockheed Martin." As he says this, the lights seem to flicker, and the music becomes distorted, slows down, and stops.

Dr. Smith returns to his natural tone. "Agh! It happened again." He walks over to the record player and kicks it a few times. "Oh well." He leaves it be and sits back down. "What do you say, Vincent? I can connect you with my friend at Lockheed. They would love to have a sharp mind like yours on their team."

"Um…" Vincent stutters as Dr. Smith widens his eyes at him. "No. Thank you, I like working here."

"Are you sure? The benefits are exemplary, and the pay is something to write home about."

"I'm sure. The work here is… rewarding."

"Well, in case you change your mind, my home is always open to you." He stands, flattens out his suit and finishes his tea. "Let me show you out."

As the door closes behind him, Vincent stands frozen for a while.

What. Just. Happened? He plays the hushed conversation over and over in his mind as he ascends the stairs. He steps toward the gallery, but stops. He looks up the spiral staircase, then goes to the top of the platform. Waiting a minute at the top, he looks down the spiral. He listens. Nothing. *What if he's inside?* Putting his ear to the door, he waits. Nothing. *Unrestricted access?* He scans his ID, and the door clicks; he turns the door knob. *It's now or never, I guess.* He steps through the door and gently closes it behind him.

The foyer is similar to Dr. Smith's in shape, but much different in design. Much more Greco-Roman architecture, the blue marble extends up nearly fifty feet in height around him. The corridor that leads to the living room is bordered by two rows of columns, at the top of which are individual gargoyles looking down at Vincent. As his footsteps echo around him walking through the corridor, he can't help but think that if there were rows of pews on either end, it would feel like he's walking through a cathedral. The end of the hallway opens to what is essentially a penthouse with a large tinted window that overlooks the canopy of the redwood garden in the atrium.

The penthouse is dim. A grand piano accompanies the living room set with leather couches encircling a glass coffee table, all overshadowed by a piece of modern art that acts as a chandelier. *What... the fuck...* Catching his jaw as it drops to the floor, he walks in silence to the window. Several couples walk through the garden and others sit at tables next to the waterfall directly below him, sipping on coffee and talking.

He explores the rest of the penthouse, navigating through a vast maze of corridors and hallways until he finds himself in some kind of a private chamber. It looks like an unnecessarily gorgeous home office containing a work desk with a computer and a series of oak filing cabinets. Next to the computer, several open cashboxes sit in a messy pile of paperwork. Vincent approaches the desk and begins looking through the pile. The paperwork seems to be mostly financial records; sales receipts, expense reports, and cash flow statements. *This must be the records room.*

Flipping through a hefty stack of papers inside one of the cashboxes, he finds what looks to be old sales receipts to several companies based around the world: Bo-An Security Group, Kong Zhi Security Professionals, Jam'iyat Alamman Al Islamiyah, and tons more. *What are they selling to these companies?* He reads through the records and finds that these companies have been buying technology from the Abaddon. *NLS Engines? Cuttlefish tech? A virus? These are all projects that we've worked on here. Is… is Bartram selling our technology to foreign companies? The military would never approve of that, how did he… oh no… He's not military, is he?*

Vincent starts to feel jittery but continues exploring the room until he finds an adjacent set of filing cabinets labeled "Negotiation Assets." He opens the drawers and pulls out a file that first appears to be one of the personal history records that they filled out during the hiring process, but when he looks closer, he finds it to be something far more sinister.

"Reid, Brian, Double Masters in Quantum Physics and Electrical Engineering." He scans through the folder to find information that has no place being in government records: "Emotional vulnerabilities: Girlfriend—Boyce, Sarah, PhD currently residing in the Abaddon, see pertinent file for more information; Mother—Reid, Lorraine (Home address: 153 Shadowmare Court, Ashford, OR. Work address: Same as home address. Occupation—Small business consultant. Allergies—None. Medical conditions—History of cardiovascular disease and arrhythmia); Father—Deceased."

Vincent cringes when he reads Sarah's name. *Emotional vulnerabilities? What the fuck?* Behind the other documents, a hospital record pops out to him, and he reads it over. "Certificate of Death. Name of Deceased: Brian Oliver Reid. Date: 2013-07-10." *What in the fuck is this? He's not dead, he's… oh my God…* He starts rifling through the other files in the cabinets and finds entries for everyone there in the Abaddon, but there were only death certificates for the scientists who'd been moved to the underground barracks: "Jeffery Goodman, 2017-06-15." "Chadrick Machen, 2015-12-10." "Lonny Silver, 2016-10-21."

Once we're here, they cut off our access to the outside world and… then what? We just—they just force us to work by threatening our families? And if we cause too much trouble or lose our value, they kill us off. This is… demented. Then he notices something interesting. There's another file, but this one's for Sergeant Kritzman who apparently died in 2018… and another one for Airman Little who died way back in 1990… and Sergeant Martinez who died in 1975… Mavis died in 1962. Then he reads a name that stops him in his tracks: Trent Carlisle. Died in 1985. *This is impossible. There's no way Trent worked here, especially not back in 1985! The dude is in his mid-thirties, tops. There's no way he was here thirty-five years ago. And Mavis can't be in her sixties or seventies.*

Once he continues his search, he notices a distinct lack of two names: Russell Smith and Henry Bartram. It dawns on him that if this is a database containing leverage over the workforce, the two guys running the whole show wouldn't need files on themselves. He can't help but wonder though, how old are they? *If Mavis has been here since the sixties, surely, they've been here longer, right?*

With his stomach tied tightly in knots, he sets the room back the way he found it and sneaks back through the maze of cathedral-like columns to return to the living room. He looks out of the window, and through the redwood canopy of trees, he can see Colonel Bartram, Master Sergeant Kritzman, Sergeant Martinez, and Dr. Blackwell strolling through the garden and heading his way. That's when it hits him.

The Abaddon is a plantation that grows weapons… and Colonel Bartram is the slave master.

SPRINTING DOWNSTAIRS TO THE GALLERY as fast as he can, he wonders what Bartram is going to say as they cross paths. *I still have to call him 'Colonel'… He can't know that I know. Nobody can.* Slowing to a casual walk when he enters the gallery, he tries to catch his breath as quickly as possible. The glass doors open as Bartram leads Tzofiya, Mavis, and Martinez to a halt in front of Vincent.

"You feeling alright, Dr. Creighton?" Bartram notices Vincent sweating. "You're looking a little red in the face."

"Um… yeah, yes… Colonel. It's just, I was nervous. For my meeting with Dr. Smith, I mean."

"Right. How did that go, by the way? Enlightening, to be sure."

With an intense gaze in Vincent's eyes, he says, "Yes. Very. Dr. Smith is a very… insightful man." Noticing Mavis squinting at him curiously, he continues, "He offered me a job with Lockheed-Martin, but I turned him down."

Mavis responds, "Oh, really? But that's such an amazing career opportunity. Why would you turn something like that down?"

"I, uh…" His eyes drop to the floor, unsure of whether or not to lie. "I love the work we do here; I'm excited to see my research come to life. Plus…" Mavis catches his attention. "I feel like I'm really protecting people."

"Well"—Mavis reaches out to shake his hand—"it's nice to hear we have such a loyal member on our team." Vincent hesitantly shakes her hand. "What do you say, Colonel? I think Vincent is going to make a great member of the team."

"Yes." Bartram approaches to shake Vincent's hand as well. "It's good to have someone of your talent so dedicated to the betterment of the world. However, I'm afraid we have some business to discuss so we must be on our way."

As the gaggle walks past Vincent, Tzofiya looks him up and down with a critical glance. With ice in his throat, he sighs deeply and leaves for the elevators to return to his barracks. He immediately picks up his phone to call Trent.

"Hey there, Vinny," Trent's voice answers.

"Hey… Sergeant Carlisle."

There's a pause on the other side of the line. "Congratulations. You've discovered the truth."

"When did you leave? How did you do it?"

"Over a year ago. As for how, that's a story for another time. First, we need to meet again."

"Why should I trust you?" Vincent's tone is direct, sure-footed. This is a new feeling for him.

"Why *should* you trust me? Why would you *not*? Think about it, who are the ones keeping you prisoner there in that godforsaken building?" A little bit of attitude sneaks into his voice, almost taken aback that Vincent would even ask this.

Prisoner? "I mean, they're bad guys, sure, but *prisoner?* Prisons are awful, scary places. This place is huge, comfortable, cozy. The work we do affects people's lives."

"They're selling your tech to war mongers, murderers, and criminals around the world. Whatever good it could be doing is negated by the hands that control it. Doesn't that bother you at all?"

Vincent hesitates. "Well… at least my discovery is going to get made. Some people out there *need* me to figure out this technology, and this place is my best bet at getting it made."

"Come on, Vincent! We chose you because you could have been better than the rest! You're smart, and you have scientific integrity, but you also have the balls to stand up to bullies when it counts."

Vincent thinks back to Leo standing up to the bartender for him while she was talking to Bobby. "Bartram might be a bully, but that doesn't necessarily mean he needs to be brought down, does it?"

"Is that really what you think? Or do you just want to see your discoveries make the headlines, no matter the cost?" Vincent doesn't respond. "I know you're just trying to make sense of everything. It's a lot to take in, I get it. But you're not driven by your greed and lust for glory like the others. You just want to see justice in the world." The line is quiet for a moment. "Listen, I have a plan. But I want you to meet my friends first. What do you say?"

Vincent considers this. *If I can manage to get off base and back on without Bartram noticing, then there's no harm in at least meeting with him. But if I get caught, Bartram will see me as his enemy and… I don't want that; I still want to be on his good side.*

"Sure," Vincent finally says. "But how do we do it?"

"I'm going to leave the how up to you and Dr. Smith since you're the smart ones. Let me know when you're ready, and I'll provide you with the when and where. Call again soon, Vinny." The line goes dead.

CHAPTER SEVENTEEN

April 9th, 2020

Thursday

Since his excursion in Colonel Bartram's records room, Vincent has taken up a hobby that is unfamiliar to him—people watching. He sits in the cafeteria, atrium, library, the above-deck gazebo—anywhere that people spend their time—and he makes a strange observation, one that he doesn't know whether it's true or just a projection. Those who live below deck are cynical. While people like Sarah, Grace, Megan, Beth, and many of the newer scientists step into the atrium with a sense of amazement, people like Brian, Lonny, and others who have been here long enough to have moved underground often walk with their heads down and with less pep in their step. They just seem tired more often than those who live above ground.

Are they all just going through the motions so their families don't get hurt?

"Good morning!" Mavis greets everyone as they gather for the first time since the mental health days were authorized. "Today is going to be a short day. I just want to address some things, then make sure we have a plan moving forward after Monday's… incident." She shoots a glare at Sarah. "Tomorrow we will get back into it full force." Vincent sits in the back of the room, unsure of how to carry himself around the two of them now. "First and foremost, Sarah." The room's attention falls on her, who is now red in the face sitting at her computer. "Another slip-up like that will be unacceptable. The revolution of the Earth around the sun? Really? Such an elementary oversight should have been noticed far before the test ever took off." Sarah shrinks into her chair.

"Ma'am"—Grace stands up—"don't you think you're coming down a bit hard on Sarah? She mapped out the whole goddamn galaxy, not to mention discovering geologic phenomena that have been impacting several of *your* other projects. We have a whole team here who failed to consider it; it's not just her fault." Some of the group begins murmuring.

"Do you think Senior Airman Little shares your forgiveness?" A hush falls over the gathering. "What about Stephanie? Robert? Those scientists were members of our team. We cannot allow for a fuck-up of that magnitude to occur again." Grace looks at Sarah, who is fighting back tears. Mavis stands powerfully over them, then continues. "It seems that our top priority will be finding a way to adjust for the Earth's revolution. Secondary to that, we still need to shave about four minutes off the quantum computer's processing time to make it suitable for human transport."

Sarah swallows hard. "I was"—she sniffles—"I was thinking if Vincent joined our team—"

"Actually," Mavis cuts her off, "I was thinking Vincent could take over as team lead for you, Sarah. Considering his track record so far, I think he would do a superb job as your direct supervisor. How does that sound, Vincent?" Sarah's eyes well up, but she brushes them away with her lab coat's sleeve.

Vincent's head pops up from the back. "Um… I actually think I would be better off working alone."

Sarah's posture wilts as he says this, which Mavis notices and remarks, "I completely understand, I sometimes work better alone too. Unfortunately, that is not a luxury I can afford to give you right now. The astrophysics team is in desperate need of a change in leadership, and you will be taking up that role. Is that clear?"

He glares at her for a while before acquiescing. "Yes, Dr. Blackwell." She brushes off his look, then dismisses the team for the day once they break for lunch. Vincent hides himself in the crowd to leave without having to talk to Sarah.

He returns to his room before getting lunch; he doesn't like fighting through crowds to get his food. Upon scanning his ID to enter his room, the scanner blinks red, and the door fails to unlock. *What?* He tries again, and it blinks red. *What's happening?* He tries several times but remains locked out of his own room. As he stands there confused, one of his neighbors walks by.

"Are you locked out? That happens from time to time. Just go talk to Master Sergeant Kritzman in her office. She'll be able to fix it up for you."

"Oh, thanks." Vincent gulps nervously and heads down to the admin building, where Murphy is standing watch and escorts him to Master Sergeant Kritzman's office.

"Thank you, Murphy," Tzofiya welcomes Vincent into her office, but her resting-bitch-face doesn't feel very welcoming. "What I can do for you, Vincent?"

"Um… yeah, I can't get into my room? Someone said I should talk to you."

"Ah, yes. Simple fix." She begins typing away at her computer, leaving a moment of silence. Vincent shuffles uncomfortably, awaiting some kind of criticism about his response to Bartram. She tries to fill this silence by saying, "Martinez tell me about your… how you call… episode, last week."

His face turns bright red. "Uh, yeah. I just got a little overwhelmed by… by the party."

"Many people in Abaddon feel same way sometimes. I wish I was there at time though—to help you. We have extra people work downstairs during party, so I must work gate guard duty." She looks him squarely in the eyes as she clearly states the following, "Every Friday from seventeen-hundred to zero-eight-hundred hours."

She turns back to her screen and clicks around. "Fifteen hours shift is hard work, but feels nice to be only one out there. Just watching stars in sky." Vincent looks at her curiously. "Only thing, sometimes camera breaks. Fixing cameras is not fun. Can I have your ID please?" He hands it over. She looks at the card, then types some information into the computer and hands it back. "All good. If you have problem, come back." Vincent pauses, confused, when she gets back to work, then timidly returns to his room.

Okay… Dr. Smith trusts Tzofiya. Was she like… does she want to cover for me? He picks up his phone, but just looks at it nervously. Eventually dialing Trent's number, he nearly throws the phone across the room when a knock at the door startles him. "Um, hold on a second!" He scrambles to put the phone away and rushes to answer the door. It's Sarah. "Uh, hi."

"Can we talk?" she asks softly. Vincent stammers but fails to find an excuse and lets her in. She sits on his bed and stares at the floor, arms crossed sadly. "Do you blame me for everyone dying?"

"What? Uh, why do you ask?" He eyes the drawer where he stowed his phone.

"I don't know, I feel… I feel like you've been ignoring me all week, and then when Mavis was"—she brushes a tear away—"when she was briefing us, you weren't looking at me at all, and I just feel like you don't want to have anything to do with me anymore." She looks up to him and worriedly spits out, "Not that I would blame you! I wouldn't! I just… what's going on?"

"I-I don't know what you mean. I never said I blamed you. It doesn't matter who did what."

"Really? You don't think that matters? I feel pretty… I don't know… guilty. I feel like it was my fault."

"I mean, astrophysics is your department, but who cares? Incidents happen, then we move on."

"So… you *do* blame me?" Her throat closes up, and she frowns.

"Why does it matter who's to blame? We learned what we learned, and next time, we'll do better."

Vincent sits next to her for nearly ten minutes while she processes, not sure if he should say anything. He takes a breath to speak several times but never utters a word. She swallows at a point, then asks, "If you don't care whose fault it was, then why didn't you want to be on my team? Are you…" she hesitates. "Are you still jealous of me and Brian?"

He feels a pang in his stomach when she says his name. "No! No, no, no. I just… I like working alone. That's all…" He stands up and paces around the room, eventually standing at the window to watch the desert. She remains seated on the bed, but turns to study him.

"Do you feel guilty about the incident?"

"No, like I said, incidents like that are just part of the job. Experiments go wrong. It happens." He looks at the drawer where his phone is and becomes engrossed in his own thoughts.

"Are you frustrated about the algorithm? We'll get it; it's just going to take some—"

"No, I already figured that out, don't worry about me! I just have something else on my mind."

"Wait, what? You already figured it out?" she asks, astonished. His eyes widen as he realizes he let it slip, then he turns and sits next to her again.

"I mean… no, I didn't like… *figure it out,* you know, I just—"

"C'mon, Vince." She looks at him sincerely, her green eyes somehow pulling the truth out of him.

"Okay, yes. I solved it last night. Mavis and I were working in the lab all day, then I came home and kept working through the night. I figured it out right before heading into work this morning. But listen, you can't tell anyone."

"Last night? You did it in a single night? That's… wait, why not? Why can't you tell anyone?"

He sits up with a slight stammer, "Th-There are some things I need to figure out first. I'm not sure if I'm ready to present it yet or not."

"Figure out? Like, with the math?"

"No, the math is fine. Perfect, actually."

"Then… what's so important that we have to lie"—she lowers her voice—"*lie to the government* about it? That's like… a crime or something, isn't it?" Her face twists, unsure how to feel.

It's not the government! "Well, not *lie* necessarily, just leave out one piece of information. For a little while."

"Vince, lying by omission is still lying."

"Okay, then, yes. I want to lie about it. But I promise, it's for good reason. I just can't tell you what it is."

She stares at him with her jaw agape. "I told you about my mom. Her life is on a ticking clock, you know what this project means to me. What reason could possibly be so good you'd risk my mother's life?"

I can't tell her what I found in Bartram's office; it'd put her in too much danger. I can't risk giving them the algorithm if they're going to sell it to shady organizations… but we need to get the tech up and running if her mom is going to survive…

"I-I can't say."

"You can't say? You don't trust me? Is that it?"

"No, that's not it, I swear, it's just…" He looks her in the eyes but can't find the right words. "I'm sorry."

She stares back at him, quivering. "You know what, Vince…" Her voice is stern and menacing. "It's fine. I'll trust you. That algorithm won't help my mom until Grace gets that computer up to speed anyway, so I'll keep your secret until she gets that up and running. But the second she figures that out, it's over. I'm going to Mavis. Is that understood?"

"I understand. Thank you, Sarah, I promise I'll come forward the second I figure it all out!"

"I know you will, because you wouldn't betray my trust, Vince." She stares at him hard and leaves.

Chapter Eighteen

April 10th, 2020

Friday

Sarah is impressed by the show Vincent puts on pretending to figure out the algorithm. Spending most of his time at the board writing, Sarah still essentially acts as the leader of the team; directing workflow, mentoring the less experienced scientists, and bridging communication gaps when fights break out. Every so often, she will look to Vincent writing away on the board, intermittently crossing out failed equations. She also notices Mavis hovering over her team more often—doing rounds with a clipboard, taking notes on what each person is doing, and analyzing how they are behaving.

"Dr. Creighton," Mavis approaches him. "I adore the amount of effort you put into your work. But a leader doesn't lead from afar. Here—" she hands him a clipboard with a bulleted list of chores. "Every hour, I want you to do rounds. They're your subordinates now, and you need to check up on them."

"Are you sure? They're pretty self-sufficient; Sarah was pretty good at leading her team without me."

"And look where it got us. Do you really think her leadership led to a better work environment?" With a disappointed scowl, she twists her voice to make him feel stupid, "You're smarter than that, Vincent. Smarter than her. And if you don't keep tabs on them, they'll never respect you as a peer or as a leader."

"Oh… okay, but what if they're working efficiently already?"

"Then they have nothing to worry about, do they?"

He takes the clipboard and freezes. Mavis pats him on the back and returns to her desk. He begins roaming around the room, afraid to get close to the others. Instead of actually talking to them, he ends up just watching them and pretending to take notes so that Mavis thinks he's doing something. After a couple hours switching from the board to uneasy roaming, people take notice of him. Whispers break out, and everyone intermittently looks at him with interest. Sarah stands up and approaches Vincent. "Hey, fearless leader," she says in a sarcastic tone and crosses her arms at him. "Would you mind easing up on the note-taking? My—*your* team is getting nervous and flustered."

"Uh—" his eyes flit to Mavis momentarily, and seeing her watching him intently, he clears his throat. "Well, uh, if they're being efficient… they have, well, they have nothing to worry about."

Taken aback, her eyebrows raise, and her hands fall on her hips. Following his eyes to Mavis, she shakes her head. "Really? That's the route you're gonna go? The 'nothing to hide, nothing to fear' tactic? Keeping track of our every move is bound to stunt creative output. Nobody wants to work when they're worried about what you're scribbling about them."

"Hey! Doctor Boyce," Mavis shouts, then crosses the room. "Do you have an idea for the algorithm? Or an update on your project?"

Sarah humphs. "No, Dr. Blackwell. Just giving Vincent a suggestion to improve workflow efficiency."

"Workflow efficiency? That's not your area of concern anymore, is it?" Mavis crosses her arms. "Vincent is very busy, so if you would please join the rest of his team in finding something that might help him do his work."

Sarah glowers at her, then returns to her team's section. Mavis sticks around and asks, "How are rounds going, Dr. Creighton?"

"They're… they're going well." The team's attention is collectively on them. She takes the clipboard and looks at the empty note sheet.

"Very good, I'll review this later. In the meantime, why don't we break for lunch?" Confused, Vincent nods silently and eyes the rest of the team with a flushed face. After the rest of the team takes off, the two of them are alone.

"So you did very well during your first experience with leadership, but what about your research? Is it moving along well enough?"

"As well as it can for the first day." He walks to the board and grabs a meter stick to point at various parts of his algorithm. "See, we need to transfer the data to a location, but that location is consistently dynamic, right? With the Earth constantly moving through space, we have to predict where the data needs to arrive in order to keep the subject… alive. But it's not a simple pattern recognition algorithm, is it? Luckily, thanks to Sarah's graphs, we can extrapolate the Earth's exact movement for the past year or so. This gives me enough data to get started on writing a supervised algorithm, but the input is so complex, there's so many dimensions that I'm going to need an ensemble, I've already got a bootstrap aggregate that'll—"

"Vincent… in English?"

"Oh, sorry, uh… it's going, but it'll be a long process."

"I'll have to take your word for it; this is some truly wondrous stuff you're making." She smiles at him, then walks off to get some lunch.

When the day comes to an end, Vincent returns to his barracks and calls up Trent.

"Hey there, Vinny."

"Tonight."

"Will you be ready by sunset?"

"Yes. I need to be back in the morning, though."

"Of course. Once you leave the gate, head due east for one mile, but avoid the road."

"What will I be looking for?"

"A black pickup truck. I'll be the one driving."

"Okay."

"I'll see you soon, Vinny." They both hang up the phone.

Vincent breathes for a moment. *God, I hope Dr. Smith is right to trust*

Tzofiya. He paces in his room for the hours leading up to departure time. *Should I get some dinner first? No, I already ate, I'm fine. Should I make face at the party? Maybe it'll trick people into thinking—no! It's fine. Just breathe.*

As eight o'clock rolls around, the grounds of Fort Chivington seem to be completely empty. The sun begins to hide behind the mountains as the red sky fades to purple, then to blue. The cool air becomes crisper, and the temperature drops a few degrees to an even fifty Fahrenheit. Most people are downstairs celebrating the lives of their deceased friends and the dawn of another weekend. Vincent watches the admin building, and Murphy is still posted up in the front of the building, but Vincent can't wait much longer if he is going to make it on time. Zipping up a black hoodie over a pair of jeans, he pulls the hood up and leaves his barracks to stealthily walk around to the backside of the building.

Vincent casually strolls along behind the barracks as if he is just clearing his mind with some fresh air, when in fact, this is as far from the truth as possible. He watches the gate security booth like a hawk, sweating bullets with heart beating out of his chest as he draws nearer. He's pulled the drawstrings on his hood, tightening it around his glasses, and though it's uncomfortable, the cloth absorbs his sweat and keeps it out of his eyes. Hiding against the wall of the building closest to the security booth, he watches carefully. *Do I... do I go now?* He can't see inside the booth, so he isn't sure if Tzofiya is inside, but then he hears a mechanical whirring overhead. A camera mounted on one of the corners dies. A pit in his stomach opens, and his hands shake with adrenaline. *Okay... okay... okay... it's time. Time to go.* He takes a step forward but nearly trips when he sees Tzofiya step out of the booth. He stumbles backward to hide behind the wall again.

Mumbling a few Russian curses under her breath, Tzofiya walks in his direction. *Uh... shit. Fuck. Shit. What do I do?* The closer she gets, the clearer her M4 carbine, sidearm pistol, and sheathed Ontario survival knife become through the darkness. So do her mumblings.

"Damn camera. Never working, always breaking." Vincent presses his back against the wall and holds his breath while Tzofiya rounds the corner. She mumbles more curses, never even looks in his direction, and then walks right past him. Sighing heavily, he realizes she blessed off on his exit and takes off, running toward the security booth and taking a peek inside to see several cameras displaying some kind of feedback loop. Staying low to the ground, he runs to the east, keeping his body low to the ground.

Oh my god, I did it. I did it! I DID IT! Briskly walking down the road for about fifteen minutes, he keeps track of exactly how far he is away from the base in his mind. *Five thousand two hundred seventy-eight point one seven five feet. Five thousand two hundred and eighty. Okay. One mile.* He pulls up his sleeve to check his watch. *They should arrive in one minute.* Just as the desert chill begins to settle in, he hears the faint rumble of an engine in the distance, then vaguely sees a truck pull out from behind some sage brush. With its headlights turned off, the truck pulls up next to Vincent. The door opens to Trent Carlisle in the driver's seat, greeting him in his black turtleneck.

"Hey there, Vinny. How did you get out?"

"Tzofiya. She was standing watch and looked the other way."

"Kritzman? Really? Do you trust her?"

"Dr. Smith does, so…"

"Well, then, so do I. Get in, we're going for a ride." Vincent obliges, buckles his seatbelt, and they take off into the darkness.

Trent's headlights only turn on once they reach a comfortable distance away from the base. LED lights irradiate the packed dirt and sand fields speckled with brush as they violently bounce over peaks and troughs to traverse the desert. Vincent holds the dashboard tightly as he tries to find whatever horizon there is to settle his stomach, but this proves to be of no use as he tucks his head between his knees and dispels his dinner all over the passenger side floor. In the chaos, Vincent fails to appreciate Trent's skilled maneuvering through the fields of brush and trees.

Through all the motion sickness, Vincent fails to realize that they have arrived at a small encampment with several military tents and a recreational vehicle that seem to be outfitted for long-term residence. He opens the door and nearly tumbles out of the truck, falling to the sandy ground. Trent walks around to his side with a hearty chuckle.

"Don't worry about the truck, Vinny. We'll get that cleaned up." He laughs.

"What the hell! That was the most insane driving I've ever seen!"

"You'll get used to it. You kind of have to if you want to travel through the desert with any sense of urgency."

Doubled over, Vincent takes a few breaths then straightens up. "Where are we?" As Vincent's stomach settles, he sees a variety of tents and vehicles strewn about around him. One of the tents seems to be a hangar-bay for their pickup trucks, workbenches, and sheets of metal. The others are standard issue, general purpose military tents with camouflage that fades into the sand-scape around them. The recreational vehicle has a trailer behind it and a generator running. At the center of the camp, a fire burns under a pot of stew, but from one of the RVs emerges an Indigenous person who immediately calls out to Trent, "Is that our man?"

Vincent instantly shrivels up with anxiety, but there's a strange vibe to the person that puts Vincent at ease. Trent smiles and responds, "In the flesh!"

"What a joyous day! Welcome to our camp, Vincent!" The man in the RV finishes drying a dish in the kitchen, walks over, and extends a calloused hand. "I'm Dallyn Smith." Vincent doesn't quite know how to interpret the long, flowy dress that he's wearing, nor the higher pitch of his voice, but those aren't the features that stand out to him.

"Smith? Are you related to Dr. Smith?"

"Dr. Creighton! How dare you! Smith is quite a common last name!" Vincent blushes, but Dallyn laughs it off. "I'm kidding, sorry... Yes, I grew up on the same rez that Russell came from, he's family."

Vincent's stomach feels queasy. *Is this guy trustworthy? Why does he want to help Trent?* But the question he decides to ask is, "How are you guys able to hide from the Abaddon? I mean, the generator alone produces a ton of noise, noise that carries *far* in the desert. And the vehicles, can't they track you?"

"That's what that bad boy is for," Trent says, gesturing to an antenna that protrudes from the RV roof. "Little bit of Abaddon tech I took with me. It emits an electromagnetic signal that cancels out all noise and soundwaves within a given area. It's our own little bubble of silence."

"As for being tracked, that's where I come in," Dallyn says. "My tribe still practices the same techniques that made our ancestors such successful nomads. Especially the techniques that kept us from getting caught by enemy tribes."

"Nomads? So… you two are traveling through the desert, bouncing from place to place to hide from Bartram?"

Trent answers, "And we're damn good at it. Between my experience working security for the Abaddon and Dallyn's knowledge of these lands, Bartram and his cronies haven't gained an inch on us." Vincent just stares at them with a mix of curiosity, anxiety, and fascination, but Trent helps him understand. "But… it's not just the two of us. I have something else to show you."

Trent walks him past the fire and into one of the tents that seems to have been arranged into a common room and meeting area. Vincent feels for a moment that he's been transported to a military base in Iraq, but that feeling fades as the warm lights come into focus. He sees three others loitering inside the tent and sipping on cheap beer. Right off the bat, he recognizes one of the residents sporting a big, bushy, silver moustache.

"Leo!" Vincent exclaims.

"Vinny! It's good to see you here, boy!" Leo replies excitedly.

"What are you doing here? How do you know Trent?" As he asks the question, he sees the others in the room.

"What's up, Einstein?" he hears a strangely familiar voice say. He looks over to see the bartender from the Ducky Luck standing next to the very man who stole her attention while he was trying to order a drink.

He pauses, doing several double takes between everyone in the room, then stammers, "B-Bobby? What are you doing here?"

"What's up, bud!" Bobby gives him a side smirk as Trent lays his hand on Vincent's shoulder.

"I know you must be confused right now, Vinny," Trent says in an attempt to calm him down.

"How do you… why…" Memories flash as he thinks back to that night at the Ducky Luck. Leo was waiting for him at the bar. The bartender ignored him on purpose. Bobby took advantage of Vincent's drunken friends. Trent was behind the scenes, orchestrating all of it. *They were working together. All of them.* "You were targeting me, weren't you?" Vincent stares Leo down. "You lied to me. Made me think my friends were ignoring me just so you could sweep in and be my savior, didn't you?"

"No, Vinny. They *were* ignoring you. You deserved better than the way they'd been treating you."

"How would you even know that? You don't even kn—" a disquieting thought settles in while Vincent figures it out. "Oh my God…" He sighs in embarrassment. "You were staking out the bar. Watching me and my friends for… how long?"

Trent answers, "A year."

"A year! You've been watching me for a year?!" Vincent sweats before pulling himself away from Trent. "Why? What do you want with me?"

"Vinny, just take a seat, we'll tell you whatever you want to know."

"Fuck you!" Vincent slowly backs up toward the tent entrance. "Who are you working for? Bartram? Smith? The government?"

"Listen, Vinny—" Leo tries soothing him.

"No!" He shoots a scared expression at Leo. "I've listened to you too much already."

Bobby draws his pistol, loads a magazine, and releases the slide. "If you don't want to chill out, we can take this conversation in a different direction." Vincent's stomach drops, and his muscles tense up.

"Oh my god, Bobby!" The bartender pulls his hand down. "The dude's world just got flipped upside down. He's scared, pissed off, and rightfully doesn't trust us, so what's your big idea? You point a gun at him? What the fuck is wrong with you?" Watching this interaction, Vincent senses the chemistry between them at the bar was at least partially fabricated.

"He doesn't want to be here, Becca! I've been saying this the whole time; he's not a real man! He's not gonna nut up and help us on his own, what else can we do?"

"Answer his damn questions!" Becca cracks open a beer and approaches him. "Here you go, Vince—" she offers him the drink, but he doesn't take it. "We're not working with Bartram or the government. Trent and Smith want to expose the Abaddon for what it is."

Trent says, "Take a seat, Vinny. We'll tell you every—."

Becca interrupts him, "Stop telling him what to do! You boys are always trying to control one another! Just let him be." This puts Vincent at ease, and he steps away from the exit before taking the beer she offered him. However, when he smells the alcohol, he winces and puts it back down.

"…Thanks… why have you been following me?"

"Because Bartram wants you," Trent says. "He and Mavis have been watching you since you were at M.I.T. You've been their number one target for years. They've just been biding their time until you figured out the teleportation thing to bring you to the Abaddon."

"And how the fuck do you know that?"

Trent sighs. "I was part of his inner circle while I was there. It was me, Martinez, and Mavis."

"Then you left. Why?"

Trent turns to Leo and suggests, "Why don't you take this one?"

Leo stands and paces around the tent. "Bartram and I go way back. He was my direct supervisor while I was in the Army Air Force." Vincent gives him a disbelieving look, remembering Karl mentioning once that the Air Force became an independent branch in 1947. This would mean that Leo was in the military during World War II. *He looks exactly the same age as Bartram.* "The man was a bulldozer, mowing through enemies on the battlefield and steamrolling every one of his own people—his inferiors, mostly—unless they were one of his handpicked, subservient yes-men."

Trent's face flushes at this point.

"He found out I did some… I'll call it *security consultation* work after the Army, so he coerced me into playing security guard for him. That's where I met Trent. We got sick of being part of his weapons trade, so we planned our escape. We were going to gather intel on him that could be used to bring the lab down, but our plan didn't work out perfectly. We managed to escape, but not quietly."

Vincent's critical gaze doesn't let up. "Army Air Force… I'm sure you can guess my next question."

Trent smirks. "How do we look so young? Well, Mavis is an incredible biomedical engineer. When CRISPR was discovered, she quickly figured out how to halt and even reverse the aging process."

Vincent's head begins to ache. "I-I need to get some air." As he stumbles out of the tent, Bobby tries to follow with his gun drawn, but Becca holds him back and scowls. Bobby responds by sticking his tongue out at her.

Vincent steps outside to hear Dallyn say, "I'll give you some space, bud." Then he heads inside the RV. Vincent shuts his eyes tightly and walks circles around the campfire. *So… Mavis is using CRISPR to keep people young. Bartram is probably staying about fifty years old so he can play the part of a colonel. Leo says he was a security guard at the Abaddon, but if that's true… why didn't I see his file in Bartram's office?* He takes a seat in the sand in front of the fire, staring deep into the embers. *He's lying about something, and Trent is going with it. What do Becca and Bobby know? What's in it for them?*

Vincent looks up at the pitch-black sky again, stippled with the Milky Way emerging over a distant sand dune. *Sarah would love this view.* He realizes that, given Bartram's security protocols, she'll probably never be able to leave the confines of Fort Chivington again. Neither will the rest of the scientists who live in the Abaddon if he doesn't stop Bartram's operation. *Bartram affects so many people, not just here but around the world… if he's the one selling weapons though, doesn't that mean he's also the one leveling the playing field?* Then he looks back into the fire. Leo exits the tent, closes the door behind him, and sits across from Vincent in the sand.

"I saw the press conference, you know. You did a damn fine job up there."

"Thanks."

"How are you liking the job?"

"Is it bad for me to say I really like it? The job itself, that is."

Leo grins. "Not at all. It feels good to be doing what you're best at." They sit in silence, listening to the crackle of the fire. "What do you think of everyone here?"

"I don't know who to trust. Everyone in that tent, including you, I met under false pretenses. As for Dallyn, just because he's from Dr. Smith's tribe—allegedly—all of a sudden, I'm supposed to trust him?"

"It would be unfair of me—or anyone—to tell you who to trust. What does your gut say?"

Vincent listens to his gut for a while. "It says I'm scared."

"Scared of what?"

"Of… I don't know. Scared of acting on incomplete information. Being lied to. Hurting anyone… hurting Sarah."

"Do you expect me or Trent to hurt anyone?"

"I mean, I met Trent after he broke into my place with a gun, but… no. I don't think he'd hurt anyone unless he had to. I don't know about that Dallyn guy though, what's his deal? What's with the weird dress?"

"It's not weird. He's what his people refer to as 'two-spirit.' His people believe that everything has a spirit—men, women, animals, the earth below our feet. But some people have two spirits living in their bodies— that of a man and that of a woman."

"Spirits? Spirits don't exist."

"You didn't ask about your own beliefs, you asked about his. His people hold two-spirits in high regard. They fill the traditional roles of men and women equally—just as they'll care for children, they'll defend the tribe from raiders."

"Okay… does that mean you trust him?"

"Not necessarily. I trust him because I've seen him lead us through these lands. He helps set up camp, hunts for food, cooks that food, and covers our tracks when we travel. He's been a reliable asset to this team. That's why I trust him."

"I haven't seen him do any of that…"

"Give him a chance. And while you're at it, give us a chance, too. We weren't lying to you back at the Ducky Luck." *Right, only inside the tent…* "Bartram targeted you because you are incredibly smart—the smartest person in that lab, in fact. But *we* targeted you because we saw the rage building in you. Trent said it best: you have scientific integrity, and you know what it's like to be bullied."

Vincent locks his eyes onto the fire and asks, "What do you want me to do?"

Leo shuffles in the sand before answering, "We, uh, we need your help to remove Bartram and his friends from power."

"*Remove* them from power, huh? How's that?" Vincent asks despite knowing the answer already.

"I do one thing very well, Vinny."

"What's that thing?"

"Something I'm not proud of anymore. Killing."

Vincent shuts his eyes as he sighs, almost disappointed. "Why do we have to kill them? Can't we just turn them over to the police? Tell the government?"

"I wish we could. I do. Unfortunately, Bartram still has influence in the government. Nobody would dare make a move against Bartram unless they had a death wish."

"He still has power in the government? Is he still actually in the Air Force?"

"Not exactly, but people fear him. The man should be well over a hundred years old, yet here he stands, defying death itself. Who would stand against that?" When Leo says this, Vincent can't help but think something to himself. *Nobody would. Nobody would bully a man who controls death itself.*

Vincent looks up through the fire, over Leo's silver moustache, and into his blue-grey eyes. He hears Dr. Smith's wisdom in his ears. "*If we could discover the greatest secret the universe holds, but learning it meant losing the value of a single life, would it be worth it?*" "I understand that people die sometimes. It happens. But… this is different. I can't go on a murder spree."

"Look, Vinny, I know it's hard for you to wrap your head around the idea of killing another person, but you have to understand that this man deserves it. I'm sure you've noticed the disappearances?"

Vincent nods. "Yeah. A friend of mine and an old coworker. Probably more but I don't really, like, know people."

"They didn't just go home. They were problem children that Bartram had to deal with."

Vincent's head drops. Deep down, he knew he would never see Karl again, but it felt like a punch in the gut to hear Leo say it aloud.

"I'm not asking you to do this lightly. I understand how it feels. But remember, Bartram is forcing our hands. We're only doing this to serve our purpose."

"What purpose is that?"

"Freedom. You'll be freeing your friends, the other scientists, and the service workers who are trapped there. Entire populations who are being killed by the tech coming out of the Abaddon."

"But what about the tech itself?! If we develop teleportation, it could be used for medical purposes, too. It could save lives that have no means of being saved otherwise!"

"Only if those who need it have the money to pay for it. If we take out Bartram, his monopoly would be dissolved."

I know it's the right thing to do… Bartram is a monster… but what if I can help Sarah's mom? Considering this for a while, he looks up. "I don't know how to fight."

Leo grins again. "That's what friends are for, Vinny. We'll teach you."

"Okay… but! We have to try and keep him alive. Sarah wouldn't want to see me actively trying to murder someone, no matter how bad he was."

"Capture is always plan A. If we can turn him over to the authorities, we will. We have to be ready to kill if necessary though, is that fair?"

Vincent doesn't like it, but he nods. Dallyn steps outside just in time for Leo to shoot him a grin. "He's in."

"Brave man. I knew you'd step up to the plate. Come on, let's go tell Trent." He and Leo help him up, and they step into the meeting tent. Dallyn looks at everyone and announces, "Game on, guys."

Trent sighs in relief. Behind him Becca punches Bobby in the shoulder and shouts, "I told you so!"

"I do have a few ground rules and a couple questions though. Firstly, our plan A is to not kill. Capture if possible, kill if needed. Understood?"

Everyone nods in agreement; Dallyn almost seems impressed.

"Second, no more lying. If I find out I've been lied to again, I'm walking away. Is that clear?"

Dallyn nods right away, but everybody else seems to hesitate before agreeing. Leo and Trent lock eyes, but Trent subtly shakes his head. When Vincent catches onto this, he takes note and moves on. "Good. Question one: there are tons of smart and capable people in the Abaddon; why does Bartram want me specifically?"

"Because you're not just smart, you have an eidetic memory—"

"It's not eidetic," Vincent cuts him off. "I just have a higher-than-average ability to encode and recall information through practice and study."

"Whatever it is your brain does, that's the thing that they want to"—Trent stops and chooses his next word carefully—"exploit. You're different. They want the thing that makes you different."

"Interesting. Second question: why do you guys need my help? You've worked for Bartram; you were on the inside. You must know enough about his operations to easily take him down. So why take on a weakling who doesn't know the first thing about combat?"

"Many reasons. Leo and I have been disconnected for over a year. Bartram wants you and might make mistakes in order to get you. We need someone on the inside to coordinate with Dr. Smith. Auxiliary to that, you're just a smart dude who has a good idea of right and wrong. We need that."

Vincent nods. "Wow. Okay… last question before we start: what's in it for you three?" He points at Becca, Bobby, and Dallyn.

Becca says, "To the victor go the spoils."

"From what we've heard," Bobby continues, "there's quite a treasure trove of valuable shit down there, and that's a cause worth fighting for as far as I'm concerned."

"Save for the dangerous tech we're keeping off the street," Trent reminds him. "Remember?"

"Right, of course." Bobby winks and smirks at Trent.

Becca rolls her eyes. "No. We're not going to take the tech—that would defeat the whole purpose of this thing. Just a portion of the cash that Bartram uses to fund the joint."

Vincent paces uneasily around the room. "Alright. What's the plan?"

"Tell you what…" Trent exhales. "It's been a stressful meet-and-greet. Let's cover the plan next weekend. Tonight, we do something fun."

"Something fun?" Vincent asks nervously. "Like what?"

He smirks at the rest of the group, who smile excitedly in return. "Let's teach you to shoot a gun."

Vincent gulps.

CHAPTER NINETEEN

October 31st, 2000

Tuesday

"What's up, four-eyes?" One of Vincent's *best friends*, Charlie, greets him in the cafeteria at lunch along with a small posse of three adolescent children behind him.

"H-Hey, guys… where's y-your costumes?" Vincent asks, wearing a blue lab coat, white-collared shirt, and bow tie.

"I can't believe you're still dressing up for this baby-ass bullshit holiday." Charlie looks at his friends, prompting them to laugh. "But if you are gonna dress up, might as well do it right, huh? You got the coat and bow tie, but those glasses seem wrong. Johnny, does Bill Nye wear glasses?"

"Uh, he's one of those nerdy science guys, so yeah," Johnny says while breathing through his mouth.

"No, you idiot, he doesn't." He looks back at Vincent. "So if you really want to dress up like Bill Nye, you'll have to ditch the glasses."

"But…" Vincent says weakly. "I can't see without them."

"You should have thought about that before dressing up like a *normal* person." He extends his open palm. "Hand 'em over, I'll get rid of them for you."

"But—"

"Hand 'em over, pussy!" Charlie shouts.

Vincent trembles as his *friends* loom over him. After a minute of being stared at by the much larger boys, he reaches up to his face and hands his glasses over.

"Good boy." Charlie passes them off to Johnny for safe-keeping. "Now you look normal. But! You did make me raise my voice, and you know I don't like that. So we're gonna have to play a game of capture-the-fag."

"Uh…" Vincent's face turns beet-red, and his stomach drops. "I-I don't know, guys. I can't see… and I'm still kind of sore from yesterday's game."

"Sounds like he just needs more practice, huh boys?" Charlie's friends chuckle in agreement. "You have a five-second head start. Five…"

Vincent's eyes widen in fear, and he throws on his oversized backpack that he carries with him everywhere, then takes off running through the halls away from the cafeteria. He could hear the footsteps of his four best friends trailing behind him. Sprinting is difficult as he has to hunch under his backpack, which lurches from side to side. He runs into lockers and closed doors all along the way until finally managing to duck into the boys' bathroom. He locks one of the stalls and puts his feet up to hide. Jar-headed laughter comes bursting through the door as Charlie opens each stall until he reaches Vincent's.

"We found you, pussy! Come on ouuuuut!"

Vincent holds his breath until they start pounding on the stall door, then he shouts, "You got me, guys! Good game, let's go do something else now."

"You know the rules, pussy! When the fag gets captured, the fag gets punished. Now, get out here before we start huffing and puffing."

"Come on… just let me go… just this once!" Vincent halfheartedly shouts as they pound harder and harder on the stall door until the lock breaks off. Charlie grabs him by the scruff and backpack, then removes him from the stall. Johnny and his other two friends unzip his backpack and begin ripping his books and flushing papers down the toilets until they clog and overflow. Charlie shoves a urinal cake in his mouth and treats him as the urinal itself. The four of them take turns kicking him until the whole floor is flooded.

"We gotta go, pussy, but good game! Don't forget to tell your mom I said 'hey' when you tell her about how much of a pathetic little weakling you are." The whole posse laugh and high-five each other as they leave Vincent lying on the floor, feeling pathetic and violated.

CHAPTER TWENTY

April 11th, 2020

Saturday

The midnight moon shines bright over the desert while Vincent follows his band of combat experts to a makeshift shooting range set up against the base of a sand dune. Bobby turns on a stand-up work light, then sets up a poker table while Becca and Trent carry a large chest full of weapons and begin unloading the armament. Leo stands back with Vincent as they set up.

"If you're going to join the team, you'll need to know how to handle a variety of weapons. Hopefully, you'll have to never fire a single round inside the Abaddon, but you need to know how. Just in case." Leo explains what the others are doing as Vincent nervously watches them prepare the range. "We're going to familiarize you with firing the Glock 19." Trent removes a compact pistol from the chest and pulls the slide back to make sure it's empty before placing it on the table. "The AR15 carbine." Bobby shoulders a tactical looking rifle, pulls the charging handle back and inspects the chamber before placing it beside the pistol. "The Benelli M4 shotgun." Becca clears the beast of a weapon and places it next to the rifle. "And last but not least—"

Dallyn approaches from behind Leo and unsheathes a knife with a seven-inch blade. "The KA-BAR. An invaluable, versatile tool for survival."

The whites of Vincent's eyes expand as he watches on, thoroughly intimidated by the idea of having to use any of these weapons against another human being.

"I-I-I've never been in a fight before, guys. I don't th-think I can do this."

Becca smiles at him. "That's what we're here for; we're going to teach you."

Bobby yells, "Range is cold!" Then he walks downrange and sets up twenty empty beer bottles in a little divot in the sand dune before returning.

"You ready, Vinny?" Trent shoots him a confident smirk as Vincent reluctantly approaches the poker table. "First things first, before you pick up the Glock, we need to teach you some basics."

Looking down at the weapons, Vincent's knees shake. Trent draws his own pistol, unloads it, and clears the chamber.

"All weapons are loaded. Despite the fact that I ejected the magazine, the chamber is clear, and the safety is engaged, I will treat this weapon as though it is fully loaded and ready to kill. Is that understood, Vinny?"

"Uh-huh…" Vincent's voice trembles.

"You will not point this weapon at another person unless you intend to kill that person, is that clear?"

Vincent swallows, then he nods his head.

"I need you to say it, Vinny."

"No pointing the gun at people. Got it."

"Unless you want to kill them," Trent repeats. "Say it."

"Unless…" He takes a wispy breath and repeats his words, "I want to kill them."

"That's right. Third, your finger will not touch this trigger until you are ready to fire. Is that clear?"

Vincent nods but remembers to say aloud, "Yes."

"Okay, then I think we're ready to start practicing."

Leo passes out ear protection to everyone and takes a seat on the weapons chest. Everyone else pulls up lawn chairs to hunker in like they're all about to watch a blockbuster movie.

Bobby leans over. "We don't have any popcorn, do we, Bec?"

Vincent's hands shake as Trent shows him how to handle the weapon—loading, unloading, clearing, aiming, everything he can possibly teach before actually shooting. Due to his nerves, Vincent accidentally points the gun away from the range a few times, prompting Trent to aggressively correct him.

"Alright, Vinny. You have your gun and a full magazine. Load it up, take it off safety, and fire away."

With trembling fingers, Vincent follows Trent's instructions and gets into the ready position. He takes several deep breaths before finally lining up his sights, inhaling, and then… he squeezes the trigger. The sound is louder than anything Vincent has ever experienced before in his life; a percussive bang rings inside his head as he nearly drops the gun, but he gasps and catches his breath before looking to Trent with a wide grin lighting up his face.

"That… was… AWESOME!" Everyone laughs as he fires off the rest of his magazine, managing to miss all twenty targets that are lined up for him. "You're sure none of this noise is getting back to the Abaddon?"

"Positive. You leave the radius of our bubble, and you won't hear a peep."

Everyone takes turns firing off round after round deep into the night, talking and laughing with the shared excitement that comes from shooting things. Dallyn only shoots his own hunting rifle but nails every single target he aims at. After the first magazine, Vincent focuses on getting a feel for how the bullets exit the barrel and travel through the air. Studying and adjusting for their trajectory, he attempts to hit a single target but always comes up just a bit short.

"It's alright, bud," Bobby says condescendingly. "Not everyone's a natural like me."

Becca chuckles. "And how well did you do your first time?" She then teaches Vincent how to fire the carbine, but he learns some respect when the Benelli kicks back much harder than he was anticipating. His shoulder bruises up quite nicely, so he decides to wait a while longer before returning to it.

Several hours of target practice later, Vincent is having an amazing time studying, but Trent finally says, "Alright, Vinny, we gotta get you back home. Next week, we'll go over our game plan. We're relying on you to be our eyes and ears inside the base, so pay attention to everything. Don't let anyone know that we're out here."

"Of course." He removes his hearing protection with the most jovial grin Trent has ever seen.

"After covering the game plan, we'll get into close quarter combat."

Vincent's excitement keeps him from getting carsick on the bumpy road back to base. Trent drops him off at the same spot he was picked up from and says, "I'll meet you back here next Friday, same time. Sound good?"

Vincent agrees, then he watches Trent leave with his headlights turned off. Making his way back, he sneaks through the gate, hoping against hope that Tzofiya is still the only person guarding the gate. Fortunately, she is and just remarks on how old and crappy the security screens are while Vincent walks past her to return to his room. Everybody is still passed out and hungover in their rooms from the previous night's party, so sneaking back into his room is a simple task. Getting to sleep, however, is not as simple. He lies restlessly on his bed until the rising sun shines through his window, bathing him in blood orange light while he reflects on what an exciting night he just had.

CHAPTER TWENTY-ONE

April 15th, 2020

Wednesday

The week passes quickly as Vincent spends most of his energy pretending to research the teleportation algorithm. In his off-time, he researches every caliber of bullet and their muzzle velocities with respect to every type of firearm he can find, specifically the ones he saw and trained with over the weekend.

"Dr. Blackwell!" Vincent waits until everybody filters out of the lab at the end of the day to approach her.

"When are you going to end it with the last name? For the last time, you can call me Mavis."

"Oh. Okay, I, uh, Mavis?"

"See, that's not too hard, is it? What can I do for you?" She hangs up her lab coat and lets down her hair.

Vincent looks away. "I was wondering…" *What am I doing? This is a terrible idea.* "You're a scientist… I'm a scientist. And…" *Stop. Cease. Leave.* "You like the same things as I do… and, like, since you were in the military, I was wondering if maybe you could…"

Mavis gives a knowing smile. "Vincent, you don't need to be nervous. Just say it."

Continuing to look down, he finishes his thought by saying, "Well, you have a commanding presence. Attention just tends to radiate toward you. And I think that since you were a soldier, you could maybe teach me CPR?"

Mavis's eyes shoot open. "Oh. CPR? Well, that's not what I expected."

She chuckles and paces around the room. "First off, I wasn't a soldier; I was an airman. Secondly, is this because of what happened at the test?"

"Kind of," he says with a shrug. "But it doesn't have to be CPR, maybe just some self-defense moves. Or how to handle a gun. It's just"—he stumbles over his own words for several minutes until finally managing to get them out—"I've always been the victim, you know? Things always happen *to* me, but I never get to be the guy who stands up to save the others. When I saw you guys jump into action to help those who… those who died, I just felt… useless." Choking up, his eyes begin to well up. "What if something had happened to Sarah? All I could do is just stand there and be helpless."

Mavis frowns. "Vincent, it was our job to help the others. Martinez and Cesar, their whole job is to protect everyone around here."

"Right, but it shouldn't have to be just *their* responsibility. I should be able to help, too, shouldn't I?" A tear drips down his cheek as he imagines Sarah seizing up on the observation room floor.

Mavis walks over to him and wraps him up in an unprecedented hug. "Vincent, you don't need to blame yourself for what happened. You really don't."

Vincent's chin rests on her shoulder with his arms pinned to his side. "Well, you don't seem to have any issue blaming Sarah… even though algorithms are my department."

"Exactly, it's your job to come up with equations and algorithms that solve whatever issues we give you. Sarah neglected to find this incredibly important issue to bring to your attention. You aren't to blame one bit."

Vincent sighs. "I guess that makes sense."

"That's why I put you in charge of the team, Vincent." She pulls away from him and holds his shoulders at arm's length. "That's how you can help others. You're the smartest, most observant member of this team. When it's your job to bring the important things to the table, you will."

Will I?

"Vincent, did I ever tell you why I became a scientist?" He shakes his head. "I loved being a security guard; protecting my people was dutiful, honorable work. But when I went to sleep every night, I felt like I could've been extending my reach. I felt like I had the potential to protect people by doing more than just shooting a gun. It was a crazy thought, but I felt like I could cure death itself."

"Cure death? Like keep people from dying?" *That explains the anti-aging serum.*

"When I became a scientist, I gained knowledge that was bigger than anything I did in the military. I learned things that could potentially lead to reversing the aging process or even advancing human evolution past the point of needing to die. My mind is a far more dangerous weapon than any soldier's kit."

As she talks, Vincent wipes his eyes with his white coat's sleeve and asks, "What does this have to do with me?"

"At the same time, a scientist's discovery isn't very meaningful if somebody doesn't use it properly. Soldier-scientists are invaluable to this world, someone who can fight like a soldier but think like a scientist. Vincent, your mind is a work of art, far more than mine or Dr. Smith's will ever be. As long as you're using your mind to create things to be used by the rest of the world, you are fulfilling your purpose."

They share a moment of quiet. "Thanks… that really helps," Vincent says with a grin.

"It is my genuine pleasure." Mavis brushes her hair away. "We'd better get going."

She shuffles off, and Vincent leaves for the cafeteria. He grabs a chicken sandwich and a bowl of green beans for dinner. It's nothing fancy, but it's become one of his favorite combinations. Sitting at a table in the quiet room, he finds time to think to himself.

That… was unexpected. They definitely recruited me to exploit my mind, but she was making a lot of sense. What's the point of creating if no one ever gets to use it?

After dinner, he immediately heads for the library, but as he leaves the south wing doors, his eyes fall on the garden. A patio set in the garden is lit by a romantic glow from the sunset breaking between the tree trunks. Sarah, Grace, and Brian seem to be enjoying an elegant dinner in the atrium. He and Sarah make eye contact, but Vincent breaks the connection and heads for the west wing.

"He's going to the library again," Sarah comments to Grace and Brian. "He's been in there every day since this weekend."

"What do you think he's doing?" Grace asks.

Brian sips on his beer and tears into his half-rack of ribs. His mouth covered in barbecue sauce, he crassly says, "Probably watching porn. You know they have a private section in the back where you can do that now? There's like… an online Library of Congress but for porn."

Sarah and Grace look at him in disgust, and Sarah says, "That's… gross. Doesn't sound like the Vincent I know."

"I don't think that's what he's up to, Brian," Grace says. "He's probably trying to see if he can read through the entire library during his tenure here."

"Which includes the erotic section," Brian chimes in. "Just saying."

"Do you think he's okay?" Sarah asks Grace. "He's been withdrawn recently; I hope he isn't spiraling into some kind of depression."

Grace catches her eye. "Hey, I'm sure he's fine, okay? The dude's a robot. There isn't an emotion or piece of datum in existence that he can't process more efficiently than the rest of us. That's probably what he's reading up on. *Human Psychology for Dummies*."

Sarah returns a half-hearted smile. "Yeah, you're probably right. If anything, he's reading up on leadership and management. He's not used to being in charge of people. He wasn't too bad today though, despite Mavis constantly telling him to do those stupid rounds. She's really been getting in his head, I think."

Grace studies her best friend for a moment, sensing her concern. "How about we go check in on him?"

"I don't think he'd want me around; I don't want him to feel like I'm following him or anything."

"Come on, we'll just go say 'hi' and see what he's up to, then we'll leave."

"No, really, he wouldn't want me in there. But you should go because I am kind of worried about him. It would be nice to know that he's got someone looking out for him. Brian wanted to go, uh"—she clears her throat—"watch a movie for a bit, anyway."

Grace protests for a few minutes but eventually says, "Fine. I'll go talk to him by myself."

She heads for the library and starts browsing the aisles between the bookshelves. Not seeing him anywhere, she searches one of the reading nooks and sees him with a stack of books. Quietly, she tries to sneak up on him, but the floorboard squeaks under her feet, and Vincent looks over in a panic. He covers the stack with his backpack, then shovels them all in as quickly as he can.

"What do you got there?" Grace asks suspiciously.

"Uh, nothing. Just studying for a little side project."

"Side project? Got a lot of time on your hands?"

"You know how it is." He slyly puts the backpack on and makes to leave, but Grace blocks the doorway.

"Right. Sarah said 'hi' to you yesterday, but you ignored her. What's up with that?"

Recalling exactly the moment she's referencing, he lies to her. "Oh, did she? I didn't hear her. I was, uh, busy at the time."

"So you do remember that? What's been keeping you so busy?"

"Oh, you know, work. I'm just trying to figure out the algorithm, you know," he says dismissively.

"Uh-huh," she grunts. "Well, the atrium's safe now. She and Brian left for a date night."

He winces. "Date night? You mean, like…"

"Yeah. That's what I mean. Does that bug you?"

He chokes on his own spit. "W-why would it? She's… she can do whatever makes her happy."

"You know what doesn't make her happy?"

"What?"

"Being ignored. If you're her friend, and if you ever want to have a chance with her, you can't be ignoring her like you have been."

He looks at the ground and asks under his breath, "Can I go now?"

She hesitates, then moves out of the way, allowing him to scurry off back to his room.

CHAPTER TWENTY-TWO

April 17th, 2020

Friday

As Trent picks Vincent up on Friday night, he notices that they take a different route than last weekend.

"Where are we going?"

"To the camp. One of Martinez's patrols got a little too close for comfort the other day, so we moved."

"Do they get that close often?"

"Not really, but I bet the longer we're out here, the closer they'll get to finding us." Upon arrival, Vincent insists on setting up the shooting range again before they get started. "Are you sure, Vinny? We kind of need to tell you the game plan."

"I'm positive, it won't take long." Vincent helps carry the weapons chest out, not realizing how heavy they were.

They spend a few minutes setting up the range, but with Vincent's determined single-mindedness it goes by much faster than last week. Trent starts to review the basic firearm safety with Vincent, and though he's memorized each step, the gun looks to weigh a hundred pounds in his hands as he awkwardly handles it. "You ready, Vinny?" They all don their hearing protection and watch closely as Vincent fires the gun. Emptying the first magazine, he fails to hit a single target.

Bobby chuckles as everyone sighs. "Hey, bud, I know it's fun… but we got work to do."

Without pulling his attention from the range, Vincent slowly reloads. "I'm just training my muscles to remember the weapon's weight." Bobby laughs out loud, then flashes Becca a skeptical face. Stiffly, Vincent loads the magazine into the weapon, slides the action back, steadies his grip, comes to the ready, disengages the safety… then numbers and calculations fly through his head before he squeezes the trigger fifteen times. Fifteen of the twenty beer bottles shatter.

A collective gasp lets out as everyone stands up out of their seats. Vincent loads another magazine, does a ton of quick calculations, and finishes off the targets downrange before clearing the weapon and reengaging the safety.

Becca punches Bobby in the arm and exclaims, "Holy crap, Vincent! How did you do that?"

Vincent turns to address them, "I've been studying. I read everything I could find in the library on guns. *The Physics of Firearms, Encyclopedia of Handguns and Rifles, A Complete Reference for Ammunition,* and a few others. Once I learned the physics behind ballistics and firearms, doing the math was the easy part. Accounting for gravity, wind speed, air density, and everything else, getting the bullet to go where I want it to go is a simple matter. Loading it and, like, handling it is still clumsy, though."

"Wait, Vinny." Trent reaches inside the weapons chest and pulls out ten clay pigeons. "Reload and safety off. Let me know when you're ready."

Vincent nods and takes a significant amount of time to fully come to the ready.

Trent throws one of the clay pigeons. Numbers fly, and Vincent points the gun, then he squeezes the trigger. Shards of clay fall to the ground. Everyone watches Vincent's performance like he's an acrobat in the circus. Trent throws pigeon after pigeon with only broken shards returning to the ground. Throwing the last three pigeons at the same time, Vincent keeps up with them, getting all three within two seconds.

"It's *a simple matter* he says," Dallyn remarks while being blown away by the performance.

Leo smiles from underneath his silver moustache. "That was some damn fine work, Vinny." Vincent smiles proudly back at him.

They repeat the process with the AR15 and M4 shotgun. His handling is awful, and he misses the first few shots, but once he gets a feel for the weight of the weapon, he nails every single round he fires. Once he's satisfied with his ability, he helps to clean up and stow the chest. Inside the common room tent, Trent lays out a set of blueprints on the center table. A map of Fort Chivington shows the above-ground part of the base; the perimeter gate, the buildings, each barracks room, vehicles, more than what Vincent has actually seen while living on base. Another map displays the Abaddon in its entirety. Each wing branching out from the atrium, every lab, barrack, and broom closet the Abaddon has to offer, including the north wing, is all displayed on the map.

"Holy fuck. Bartram's room is more massive than I realized," Vincent comments.

"Yes, he has his own recreation room he shares with the guards, the records rooms, his own viewing room, a bowling alley, bar, kitchen, everything—including prisons and interrogation rooms."

The six of them study the map. Leo pours everyone a glass of fine whiskey before they begin, and Vincent gladly accepts his offer this time. Trent starts off with a serious tone.

"Alright, so our goal is to gain positive control of the Abaddon."

Vincent asks, "First things first—how are you getting on base?"

"Well, you don't have too much trouble getting on and off base with Tzofiya watching your back, so we figure that would be our best bet."

"Makes sense. I don't see why she couldn't let a few extra people slip by, plus most of security's attention would be on the party downstairs."

"Which brings me to my next point: containment. If we want to control the Abaddon, we'll first need to manipulate the movement of all the players on the battlefield. A high percentage of the total personnel—service staff, science staff, security personnel—would be in the south wing and atrium on a Friday night. So if we can lock down those two sections and keep anyone from leaving them, we'd eliminate the biggest threats and liabilities."

"Wait, wait, wait, you want to lock almost all of the civilians in a room with the very people we're fighting against?"

Leo nods. "Yes. I understand your worries, but… that's where you and Tzofiya come in."

"Me and Tzofiya?"

"Yes. Once she lets us on base, you and she will go into the atrium together while Trent and I make our way into the security office and lock the place down. Tzofiya will tell everyone to shelter in place due to an earthquake or something. If all goes well, the security team there won't get too up in arms."

"And if they do?"

Trent says, "You guys will handle the situation."

"*Handle* it? Like, put them down?"

"No! Like, use your words first, but if it comes to it, then you hit the room with these." Trent reaches into a weapons case and shows him a grenade. "Another Abaddon recipe I pocketed. These guys will render an enemy completely helpless for about an hour or so."

"Oh, so gas the place, then? *Much* better."

"Only if it comes to it; hopefully you won't have to pull these out."

"Hm… I don't like it, but it's something. What about Bartram?"

Becca answers, "That'll be our job. According to Trent, the big man spends his time during the party watching over the staff from the window in his office. Likes to think he's a big man with a big office. So Bobby and I will take the service elevator down into his office and scout ahead."

Trent continues, "Once we finish up in security, Leo and I will join them. Even if he has a small team with him in his office, the four of us should have no trouble catching him off guard."

Vincent's brow furrows. "And the plan is still to capture him, right? No killing?"

"Absolutely." Trent nods. "Capture, only kill if absolutely necessary."

"Okay… what's Dallyn's role?"

"Oh, I'm not part of the strike team. I'm on team 'camp defense force.' I'll watch over the campsite and stand by with a radio, ready to rush in to provide medical support or evac if needed."

"That's good to know. This sounds like a good enough plan… but what if it fails?"

"That's plan A," Trent says. "Plan B: once we all make it to our positions, Dr. Smith cuts power to the whole place, and we negotiate with Bartram."

"Wait, he can do that?" Vincent asks. "Why isn't that plan A?"

"In order to time it right, he'd have to be in there with us, but we'd rather not take that risk. Also, if Bartram doesn't agree to our terms, then our options would be to turn the power back on and fight or to keep the power off until everyone starves to death. Not great options."

Dallyn nods. "Not to mention the mass panic that would take place when everyone freaks out at losing power."

"Hold on…" Vincent tries to wrap his head around this ability of Dr. Smith's. "If he can just shut the place down, why doesn't he just do it?"

Leo says, "There's hundreds of people living down there. Letting the place die would mean letting everyone who lives there die."

"Wait… so to gain positive control of the place, we just need to get everyone above ground?"

"That's actually a taller order than it seems," Trent says. "That security checkpoint is there to keep track of how many residents are above ground at one time. If we have a mass exodus of staff, Bartram would quickly shut down the elevators, and the rest would be trapped."

"Oh… that makes sense…" Vincent thinks about it further for a minute but moves on. "What kind of time frame are we looking at? When do we want to kick this thing off?"

"The sooner the better," Trent says. "But we need to do some recon. You need to talk to Smith and Tzofiya to loop them in on the plan, which I understand isn't the easiest task under Bartram's watchful eye." *So we won't kick it off until I talk to Smith and Tzofiya… I wonder if I can time it right so I can have my cake and eat it too…* "And you'll need to be combat-ready in the unlikely event that all else fails, and we go in guns blazing. So in the meantime, how about some sparring?"

After discussing the plan, they go outside and clear out a small circle in the sand. Vincent's nerves unravel again when Bobby taunts him about his gangly form. Becca straps a sheathed dummy knife into the small of her back, then she and Trent step into the circle.

Trent turns to Vincent and says, "Vinny, we're going to teach you some basic self-defense techniques. Becca is armed with a knife. I am not. We're going to do a bit of sparring, then Bobby will teach you what we just showed you."

Vincent feels impotent as they attempt to teach him what they refer to as Krav Maga. His spindly arms and legs react awkwardly to his attempts at redirecting attack after attack. After a few hours of straining his muscles and mind to keep up with Bobby's scrappy fighting style, his muscles finally give out, and he collapses on the sand.

"This is what we're bringing into the fight with us?" Bobby asks before kicking sand in Vincent's face.

"Don't do that!" Becca shouts. "Just because you won doesn't mean you get to be a dick! Help him up."

Bobby reluctantly helps Vincent to his feet. "Look, bud, you're gonna need to hit the gym." He pokes at Vincent's scrawny arms. "Your arms shouldn't be *al dente*." Vincent feels ashamed of himself when he eventually returns to the base, despite the rest of the group's efforts to help him ignore Bobby's comments.

CHAPTER TWENTY-THREE

April 20th, 2020

Monday

fter work, Vincent doesn't go to his room, the cafeteria, or even the library. Instead, he takes his backpack to the east wing and finds the indoor gym that Karl used to go to with his volleyball friends. Walking through the lobby is strange for him. Sweaty, muscular people walk around in revealing clothing and wrapped in towels, the reception desk has a protein shake bar that serves dietary supplements and energizing food and drink, and he can see and hear a mix of hulking brutes and lean runner-types grunting as they lift a variety of weights and operate cord machines.

Walking with a hunch in his back, he steps into the humid locker room where several different guys are showering and joking with each other. Vincent counts the tiles on the floor as he walks around to find an empty locker in which he can stow his backpack, then he timidly changes into his pajama pants and white sneakers. Sitting on the bench between the lockers, he notices a few guys looking over at him before turning to their group and erupting into a roar of laughter.

As he rushes to leave the locker room, the doors close behind him. He then heads to the first open machine he can find. Standing in front of a complicated piece of metal equipment, he tries to make sense of the cushion placement to figure out how he is supposed to mount the machine. *Where do I sit? Am I supposed to sit at all?* He leans in to study an image of a human body with part of its muscular system highlighted red on one of the machine's metal faces. *So I sit on this piece here, but… my legs go there? What is this piece up here?*

"Hey, buddy," Lonny Silver says, startling him. "Are you using this machine?"

"Oh, no, just finished. All yours." Vincent blushes and walks away, looking around the metal jungle for something that seems a bit more intuitive. He finds a row of punching bags along the back wall. *It's hard to fuck up punching a bag.* He walks to the back and sees a few people practicing their martial arts and boxing training. *Perfect. Just do what they do.* He takes some time observing the boxer, but she seems to be using different punch combinations, jabs, and explosive hooks. Vincent shrinks a little when he sees her, so he switches focus to the martial artist, but not only is he throwing complicated punch combinations, he's also involving kicks and elbows into his technique.

I'm just going to punch the thing. Squaring up to the bag, Vincent puts his bare fists in front of his face and leans forward, trying to mimic the boxer. Throwing a single punch, Vincent recoils in pain when his knuckles scrape against the nylon fibers, and his wrist buckles. Withdrawing from the bag, he holds his wrist and cradles it while cursing aloud.

"Vincent?" a familiar voice asks from across the room. He looks up to see the last face he wants to see.

Fuck… "Oh. Hi, Brian."

"What are you doing in here, little buddy?"

"You know, just hittin' the gym… liftin' the weights… and… and the like."

"Oh really? You come down here all the time I bet, huh?"

"This is kinda my first time." Vincent veils a look of absolute disdain.

"Ah!" Brian smirks. "You don't say."

"What do you mean?"

"What made you suddenly decide to be a gym rat? Girl trouble got you feeling self-conscious?"

Vincent's face flushes, and his gaze focuses on one of the empty machines behind Brian. "No. Just… I…"

"I get it man! Why do you think most of these people are here? I'd wager at least half of these people only come here to get more ripped than the dude that their girl went down on in high school." Vincent looks at his sneakers, face ablaze. "There's nothing wrong with it, man! Tell you what, I'm about to hit the bench. You mind spotting me?"

"Uh…" *Fuck straight off.* "I gotta… get out of here."

"Really?" Brian looks him up and down, and Vincent suddenly feels ashamed of his pajama pants, cotton T-shirt, and sneakers. "From the looks of it, you haven't worked up much of a sweat yet. Come on, I'll show you how to do it." He leads Vincent to a bench press and loads up weights on the bar. "Alright, all you're gonna do is stand over me and make sure I don't drop the bar on myself."

Yeah, right. I'd rather let you choke on it. "Okay." Vincent hovers over Brian's supine form as he lays down on the bench and begins doing his reps. From across the gym, however, his attention falls on a group of people gathered up in the lobby. It's the same guys that were laughing while he was in the locker room. They're just loitering in the lobby, talking, and laughing amongst themselves. He watches them for a while as Brian pumps the bar up and down. When one of them points in Vincent's direction, the rest of them look over and giggle before leaving as a group.

"VINCENT!" Brian's breathy voice grunts, then Vincent looks down to see him red-faced, struggling to hold the bar a few inches above his chest. Vincent panics, grabs the bar and accidentally pushes down against Brian's throat before pulling it up to the bench's saddle. Brian sits up and sighs. "Thanks for that. Next time though, when you're spotting someone… spot them." Vincent apologizes under his breath.

While Brian cools down from nearly choking on the bar, Vincent wonders something to himself before blurting out, "Can I ask you something?"

"She's a solid ten. She keeps it tight."

"Uh, wait, what do you mean?"

"Never mind, what's up?"

Vincent thinks for a moment and looks around the noise-filled room. *If they're recording, they won't be able to hear us.* He bites his lip before asking, "How did they tell you about your mom?"

Brian flinches. "What did you just say?" His tone is direct but careful.

"Your mom. When did they tell you about her? Like, how did they do it?"

He squints. "What about her? What do you know?"

Does he not know? "Um… Bar-Bartram. He… do you not… not know about… the death certificate?"

"How do *you* know about that?" Worry starts to grow in his voice, and he twitchily whispers, "You're still above ground, you're not supposed to know yet. Who told you?"

"Nobody told me. I found—" Vincent hesitates. *Don't tell him you went snooping around Bartram's office.* "I figured it out on my own. You know, deductive reasoning, patterns of movement… math."

Brian shifts into a panicked whisper, "Listen, you can't tell anyone else what you know, do you understand? They'll come after you, your family, anyone they can just to silence you, got it?"

"I know, I know, but… is it everyone who lives below ground?"

"It's *everyone*. The science staff, the service staff, even Dr. Smith is trapped here! Before they bring anyone to the Abaddon, they make sure to have some kind of leverage over them. They make sure we're willing to work on any project for as long as they deem necessary."

"Do they tell you to keep it from the newcomers?"

"Yes. It's part of the deal. In fact, I'm risking my mother's *life* just telling you any of this. They try to keep the newcomers as facile as possible, just to keep them motivated to work. But the minute you lose motivation—boom! They show you your death certificate, prove that you're dead to the world, tell you exactly how your loved ones will meet their fate unless you keep working, then move you underground until you lose your value."

"And by that point, there's nothing you can do about it…" Vincent realizes that the hundreds of other scientists who are here aren't just scientists. They're people. They have friends and families whose lives are at stake. As long as these people are down here… they're slaves to Colonel Bartram. *I have to help these people… but… if we remove Bartram, what happens to the facility? I might not get to create anymore, and Sarah might lose her mom…*

"Exactly. Listen, Vincent, you cannot let this get out, okay? It will get back to me—or somebody else—and people will die. You understand?"

"Yes. I understand."

"Good." Brian looks around suspiciously and sighs deeply. "Because the sooner you accept the nature of our… captivity… the sooner you can forget about it." Vincent stares at him and sees the heavy burden that the rest of the Abaddon carries with them. After a few moments of quiet, he says, "We play Dungeons and Dragons on Saturday mornings. The party needs a wizard, if you want to join us."

"Isn't… Sarah goes to those, doesn't she?"

"Yeah, but… I think she'd like to see you there."

"I-I don't think that's really my thing."

"It's no one's thing until they do it, and… it's good to escape this… hellhole every now and then, even if it's just in your imagination. What do you say?"

"I appreciate the offer, but I don't think I can do that."

"Alright, man, it's your loss. Anyway, you ready?"

"Ready for what?"

Brian looks down at the bench. "You spotted me; now, it's your turn."

"Oh, no, no, I'm pretty tired. I think I'm just gonna go to my room."

"Nah, nah, nah, you came here to train, you're gonna train. Get on the bench. We'll start with just the bar to teach you proper form."

Vincent tentatively lies on the bench and looks up at Brian from a perspective he never wanted to see. Brian goes through the motions of teaching him how to properly pump the bar up and down without dropping it or hurting himself. They spend an hour or so working out, and Vincent works up quite a sweat before getting ready to leave. Feeling dehydrated and hot, they head back to the locker room. Passing through the lobby, Brian says, "Next time, get yourself some proper gym shorts, shoes, and maybe a water bottle. You can put in a request through your project supervisor for the next resupply run."

Vincent nods in embarrassment. "Will those work for running outside?"

"Oh yeah, those will work much better than those pajama pants of yours." Brian laughs. "I'll see you back here on Wednesday."

"Wednesday?"

"Monday, Wednesday, Friday. Gotta set a routine if you want to see results."

Vincent nods, then goes back to the locker room feeling more confident, but his heart weighs heavy in his chest.

Chapter Twenty-Four

October 5th, 1967

Thursday

Desert sands blowing in the wind cross the only paved road in the Red Desert of Wyoming as the sun reaches its height. The roar of a V8 engine reverberating throughout the desert emanates from Henry Bartram's 1967 Plymouth Barracuda Formula S as he screams through the desert. The road ahead of him reflects off his aviator sunglasses. Reaching for his pack of cigarettes, he pulls one out and turns to his guest sitting in the passenger seat.

"Can I get a light?"

Dr. Russell Smith, sporting a flamboyant three-piece suit stitched with lavender plaid, pulls out his lighter and helps with Bartram's cigarette before lighting his own. After a few drags, Bartram reaches for something to talk about.

"So… Berkeley. A lot different than Wyoming, huh? How did you like leading the physics department?"

Without looking in his direction, Dr. Smith puffs his cigarette. "Rewarding."

"Okay…" He lays on the gas pedal a little harder. "Are you excited to transition into government work?"

"*Hee.*"

"He? He who?"

"I said, *'hee'* which means 'yes' in Arapaho."

"Oh, well that's… confusing." Bartram forces a few laughs. Receiving none in response, he clears his throat and continues, "Well, you're quite the welcomed asset to the team. I got a whole squadron full of scientists who are just too eager to start work in our new facility."

Dr. Smith looks out the window, intently staring at the horizon, but sees an old, tattered Bible on the dashboard. He reaches for it and opens to the bookmarked page.

"That thing's been in my family for a long time," Bartram says. "Does your family have any religious texts?"

"The Book of Mormon."

Bartram flinches. "Oh. Really? Well, that's good to hear! Any follower of Christ is a friend of mine!"

Dr. Smith scans through the book and remarks, "Atheist, actually. Mormon family."

"Oh."

Dr. Smith reads from a passage off the page: "Blessed are the peace-makers, for they shall be called the Children of God."

"That's a good one, right? Every good soldier should be a peacemaker at heart."

"It is ironic, yes."

Bartram doesn't quite understand what that comment was supposed to mean, so he shifts focus to the endless road in front of them until they reach the base a few hours later.

As they approach the gate, Bartram points to a couple of run-down old shacks. "You see those old buildings? They've been standing since our ancestors were travelling the Oregon Trail." Dr. Smith seems dis-interested, but Bartram continues, "Um, the small one was an armory where they held weapons. The big one used to be a general store; they would protect emigrants against the Shoshone Indians here."

Dr. Smith purses his lips and simply raises his eyebrows in acknowledgement.

Bartram takes what he can get and produces his ID for the gate guard. As they pull through, Bartram can tell that Dr. Smith isn't entirely sure of what he's looking at. *The aboveground section is fairly underwhelming at first glance, but once he sees the facility... then he won't be able to stop talking.* When they park, Bartram puts his flight cap on and gets out of the car. He is greeted by a security guard wearing an Air Force uniform, slightly out of breath and seemingly flustered. He addresses Bartram.

"Sir, things are getting out of hand. The project supervisor forbade the scientists from working in the Abaddon."

"*The facility*, Airman. Aboveground we call it the facility," Bartram corrects him.

"Right, my apologies, sir. The scientists are getting antsy now. We had one of them try running off yesterday."

"Running off? They know it's a desert out there, right?" Bartram turns to Dr. Smith and sighs. "This is exactly why I need someone like you, Doctor. You ready to get to work?"

Dr. Smith asks the guard, "Where is the team right now?"

"In their barracks. I think they're in the second-floor common room."

Dr. Smith nods. "I will talk to them." Bartram walks by his side as he heads to the building, but Dr. Smith stops in front of the door. "Sorry, Henry, you will not come with me."

"Excuse me? This is my base. My building. My project. I'm coming inside to talk to my people."

Dr. Smith cocks his head and says, "This may be your project, but those are not your people." Bartram grunts, but Dr. Smith continues, "The guys capable of doing the extraordinary things you are hoping to accomplish have a different mindset than you. The military yes-men working for you might murder a village of 'Charlies' just to make sure you get your warm cup of coffee in the morning, but those guys up there—" he gestures to the third floor of the barracks building. "They are the same people who protested at Berkeley by my side. If they think you would have them build weapons used for carpet-bombing more innocent families, they would rather die in the harsh desert."

Bartram glares at him. "They aren't building weapons, Doctor. Our goal here is to develop tools that can be utilized to usher in peace."

"Save your rhetoric, Henry. I'm not here to halt your operations—quite the contrary, actually. Between your resources and their minds, we can create something truly beautiful here; I simply want to help guide it in the right direction."

Bartram is unsure of how to feel about this assertion, so he simply nods and takes a step away from the door. Dr. Smith enters the asbestos-ridden building and ascends the staircase to the second floor. The halls are reminiscent of the college dorms that his university students stayed in. He navigates the halls until he finds a common room occupied by just over a dozen scientists sitting in the sofas and loitering all around the room. The buzz of concerned conversation goes dull as he makes himself visible. One man sitting on a sofa stands up.

"Professor Smith?"

"Ah!" Dr. Smith smiles at his former student. "Mario! Why am I not surprised to see you here?"

Mario steps through the team and reaches out to shake hands with Dr. Smith. "I cannot express to you how relieved I am to see you here. These government guys are wanting to shove us underground and build weapons for them. When we told them we wouldn't do it, they... they *reminded* us of the family information we gave them. What does that even mean? Why are they doing this?"

"They are manipulating you. What did they tell you you would be doing when they brought you here?"

"They said we'd be building peacekeeping tools to prevent the wars of the future. They said we would keep World War III from having a chance to kick off."

"What did they actually have you do?"

"At first, it was great. Our first project was a weather machine. They wanted to be able to replicate the effects that caused D-Day to get delayed. The colonel suggested that a strategically placed thunderstorm could prevent the invasion of a country or the assassination of an Archduke."

"For your first project, they assigned you to control the weather?" Dr. Smith asked incredulously.

Mario chuckled, followed by the rest of the project. "Yeah, I guess they did. But we did it! We made a weather balloon that affects the water vapor in the air, effectively accelerating the condensation rate in order to form clouds within an hour or so. From there, the balloon is also able to supercharge the electrons in the clouds to form lightning on demand."

"Wow…" Dr. Smith's face reflects how proud he is but cannot hide his horror. "That is quite a feat, Mario."

Mario blushes and says, "Thank you, professor. We learned from the best." He gestures to the rest of the team, and Dr. Smith recognizes most of the other faces in the group as his former students. "But after that… things got weird. The next project is something like a missile that requires no explosives. Then they moved the lab to this underground facility, and now they want *us* to move down there to do our research. Tony heard from one of the guards that they are building barracks *inside* the facility. Bartram wants to have us live and work down there. We don't trust him, professor."

"Good. You should not trust him." The group of scientists look slightly relieved at his affirmation. "His people use power as a weapon, not as a tool. Does that mean, though, that we should not create the things he wants to create?"

One of the scientists in the back of the room immediately answers, "Of course we shouldn't!"

Dr. Smith asks, "Why not, exactly?"

"Because we'd be fueling the war machine! Any bloodshed that comes from our science will be on our hands."

"Would it?" Dr. Smith asks. "Our ancestors evolved into the people we are today by learning to use rocks as hammers, but some used those same tools as weapons to harm their brothers and sisters."

Mario squints. "What are you saying, professor?"

"Tools have never been the problem. Those who use tools as weapons are the problem." Everybody in the room listens with bated breath to each of his words. "We should work with the colonel. I have been hired to act as liaison between the scientific workforce and the military leadership. With my position I will use my power to guide Bartram in the proper application of our tools. This means that as long as you are willing to create, we will accomplish great things."

Mario looks back approvingly, but there is still doubt in his eyes. "Professor, I agree with you. Completely. But… do you really think you can keep these guys on a leash? What makes you think they won't just ignore your guidance and do whatever they want? Like… I don't know, sell our tech or use it against the American people?"

Dr. Smith grins. "Because I know something about this facility that they do not."

"What do you know?"

"I have leverage against them."

"What do you have?"

"Information. If they want what you have to offer, they'll have to play ball with me." Dr. Smith spends the next few minutes answering their questions as vaguely as possible, then shortly thereafter goes back outside where Bartram is waiting for him leaned up against the hood of his Barracuda. Dr. Smith walks over, looks at him, and says nothing.

"Well?" Bartram asks, continuing to lean against the hood of his car. "How did it go?"

"They will work with me."

"With *you*? You're not the boss, though, you understand that?"

"If you want them to create, then I am their boss. Think of me as your counterpart."

"My counterpart? No, no, no. You're the liaison. You're the guy I hired to convince these eggheads to keep working for me, not become co-manager of the entire facility."

"They do not need a manager, just a leader. You supply them with what they need, and they will create. What they need is trust in you.

And the only way you will earn that is by trusting me to guide you in post-development deployment of all technology created in the facility."

"Post-development deployment? You want a say on what we use the tech for? That's not how the military works; you know that. We don't sit around a drum circle deciding as a group what we all think is best. I'm the C.O. of this site, so what I say goes."

"Then we walk." Dr. Smith turns on his heel and steps toward the barracks building.

"Wait!" Bartram shouts, and Dr. Smith halts. Bartram looks around the small fort, then paces around his car. "I can give you Civilian Scientific Advisor. You'll have creative control over R&D, but final say over project goals resides with me."

"Advisor? An advisor is only useful when the advice he gives is considered." Dr. Smith doesn't turn around. "You do not strike me as the type to consider advice given by others."

Bartram adjusts his flight cap and takes off his aviators. "Fine. Throw in hiring and recruitment authority over the scientific body. We're going to expand this operation, and we'll need a keen eye for scientific minds. I can't give you control of what we do with the tech once it's created, but control of those who make it is just as powerful."

Dr. Smith ponders this for a minute, then turns around. Stepping up to Bartram in his lavender plaid suit, he squints, then looks toward the old buildings. He lights a cigarette and leans against the car. "You know, the Shoshone in this area were peaceful with the white man."

Bartram flicks his cigarette butt. "Is that so?"

"It is. The Mormons moved in on the lands that we thrived upon, and sure, they declared the land as their own by divine right, but they kept open trade relations with us. They helped us survive in the white man's world, and we helped them survive in unfamiliar territory. It was not until the federal government moved in, with forts just like this one, that those relations were strained. We began to struggle. We hungered.

Our hunting grounds were dried up by trappers. We had no means of survival. Only *then* did we fight back."

Bartram gives him a disinterested gaze.

"I come from the Eastern Shoshone and Northern Arapaho tribes. My people were nomadic—incredibly efficient nomads to boot. But after all the massacres were finished, and the Shoshone's connection to these lands was tarnished, many of them converted to Mormonism and other forms of Christianity. They settled in Utah and Wyoming on reservations. Inspiring, is it not?"

"Quite inspiring, yes. What's your point?"

"The Shoshone and their culture were all but destroyed." His tone shifts; he looks Bartram in the eyes more intensely and says, "Your military constantly justifies genocide and oppression in the name of maintaining freedom. I won't contribute to that government, which is why I am here."

"You want to coerce me into doing what you want. How? Threatening me with a walk-out? Even if the other eggheads agreed to follow you, how far do you think you would get in the desert without me?"

"You should be more concerned with how far you would get without me, Colonel."

"Without *you*? What do I need you for?"

"What do you know about your new facility, Henry? Where do you think all the power comes from?"

Bartram's pupils dilate. "I was informed it was self-sustaining; the power source would indefinitely generate new energy."

Dr. Smith laughs. "No. It will not indefinitely generate new energy, although it is a rather ingenious piece of technology. What happens is it converts a wide variety of forms of energy into thermal energy. A lot of it."

"How do you know that?"

"Well… I designed it, Colonel. I built it. I'm the world's leading expert on thermal energy conversion… and the only person in the world who knows how it works, how to fix it if it breaks… and more importantly—where to find it."

"Wait… what do you—"

"You see, Colonel, I may know science better than you, but that is not where my power lies. I understand the importance of others and the value of friendship. I have friends, Colonel, and one of those friends was an architect. He was contracted by the government to design a facility… and then killed off when he completed the work."

"Look, Dr. Smith, I didn't—"

"I am known to my tribe as Runs With Fire. And yes, you did. You ordered his murder. What you were unaware of at the time, though, was the blueprints he provided were falsified."

Colonel Bartram glares at him with disdain but says nothing.

"It works remotely. You will not find it unless you play ball with me, Colonel."

Bartram tries to mask his horrified expression, but Dr. Smith can see through it. He extends a hand, which Bartram simply stares at for a few minutes before finally reaching out to grab it. "I look forward to our partnership."

CHAPTER TWENTY-FIVE

May 4th, 2020

Monday

Th_here is no try._ The phrase becomes Vincent's mantra over the next few weeks as he pushes himself further and further past his limit. He memorizes every grain of sand in Fort Chivington after running so many laps around the border fence. The strain in his muscles almost starts to feel refreshing after spending hours upon hours pumping iron in the gym. He feels a strange craving for sweat dripping down his face throughout the day. When he sleeps, he sleeps harder. When he eats, he feels hungrier. When he thinks, his mind is clearer. It becomes clear to him why so many people become fitness buffs; you feel better. It's more than that though; as nice as it is to feel more physically fit, he starts sizing up those around him, and while there's only so much progress he could make in such a short time, he feels cockier.

BREAKFAST IS FILLING after his regular hot shower before the others wake. He always finishes eating just as the rest of workforce begins filing into the cafeteria; he's boiled down the timing to a science so that he leaves the showers as the others are waking up, finishes his breakfast as the others begin, and cleans the lab alongside Mavis with enough time to enjoy a cup of hot coffee before work begins. Mavis knows how to warm him up in the morning so that by the time actual work begins as a group, he doesn't become upset by the others' time wasting and relative incompetence.

"How was your weekend, Vincent?"

"My weekend? It was… uh, good. I guess."

"Did you read any good books? I notice you've been hitting the gym with Brian a lot lately."

She's really the only person, other than Sarah, who has asked about how he spends his weekends. He's become accustomed to answering her questions with as little information as possible. "Um, yeah. You noticed that?"

"Of course! I keep an eye on all my staff members. I think it's good for you to make friends and establish yourself here."

"Why do you think that?"

"It's healthy! It makes for a more productive work environment, you feel happier, and—honestly—Brian is a good scientist. I think he could be a good influence on you."

"Okay… that's, uh, interesting."

"All I'm saying is I'm proud of you, Vince. Spend more time with people like him and avoid people like his girlfriend, and I think you'll do just fine here." Vincent looks deep into the void of black coffee in his cup; the thought of not having Sarah in his life lingers at the forefront of his mind. He frowns. Mavis pats him on the shoulder as the door opens to a flood of scientists starting their work week.

As the team gathers up for the morning brief, Mavis's expression hardens. The warmth in her voice grows cold, especially when she sees Grace and Sarah leading their teams. Vincent sits at his computer, contemplating what she had just told him. "Since Sarah's work on the revolution correction issue hasn't made much progress"—she eyes Sarah, who looks embarrassed—"we will just continue focusing our efforts on the computer science aspect of the project. Grace, how's the computer's processing speed coming?"

"Uh, we're kind of at a standstill as well," Grace sheepishly states. Mavis's nostrils flare up, and Grace stutters, "B-But we still have a few avenues that we're exploring." Hearing Grace stutter is unusual to Vincent, but Mavis rolls her eyes in disillusionment and gives Vincent a look suggesting, *"Can you believe this?"* Shifting in his chair, he notices Sarah's expectant glare from across the room and sinks.

"How is the algorithm coming, Vincent?" Mavis asks warmly.

"Oh, it's going steady. I just did some calculations regarding…" Vincent has become adept at stringing together mathematical sounding words in a convincing way to make everyone think he is indeed moving forward with his work. He's made a game of it to see how long he can go before being stopped. Sarah always seems less amused by this game than he is. Today, he went on for one minute and twelve seconds before Mavis stopped him and had everyone break into their teams.

Since becoming supervisor of Sarah's team, he has been forced to interact with the others more than he is used to. Today, one of the astrophysicists wants to run some of her hypotheses by him, which means he has to review her mediocre report filled with grammar errors and shoddy research then physically tell her how inadequate her writing is; he doesn't like being the guy who has to tell her how inadequate she is, but it's his job now.

Lunch is where he gets to do the things he really wants to do; he usually grabs a submarine sandwich from the cafeteria and returns to the lab to get some alone time to work on his computer. Unfortunately, every now and then, he'll get a few stragglers who spend their lunch in the lab gossiping and laughing at each other's unfunny jokes.

"Oh my god, did you hear about Matt and Riley?"

"No, what happened?"

"I heard Riley ditched him the other night, something about their project manager keeping them late. Matt got all pissed, but Riley said they were just knee-deep in cephalopodic research and couldn't get out."

"Matt just doesn't give a shit about the job. If he did, he would totally get that Riley is just doing their work. If he's not careful, he might end up getting *'fired'* like those Chad and Karl guys. Poof. Never to be seen again."

"For real, although, it's better than being like…" They lower their voices, but Vincent can still clearly hear them say, "This job is Dr. Creighton's whole life. Just wait until he gets brought into the underground barracks; I bet he'll be *happy* to slave away for Bartram."

"I heard that Sarah only got with Brian to get back at Vincent since he's so in love with Dr. Blackwell."

"Good, he's a jerk. Did you hear what he said about Erin's report today? Such an ass." Vincent swallows hard and closes the document he was working on, then tries to quietly leave the lab without them noticing.

After work, he and Brian go to the gym for their Monday upper body routine. They spend the afternoon working out, but about halfway through their time on the bench, Brian breaks off to go chat with some of his friends—friends that Vincent has been actively avoiding for the past several weeks. They were Chad's old volleyball friends. Brian beckons for Vincent to join them, and though he protests at first, Vincent gives in when everyone calls him together.

"Do my eyes deceive me? Vincent Creighton working out? Hell must be freezing over," one of the bulkier guys comments.

Brian answers for him, "Have you not been paying attention? Vincent's out here running laps every day!"

The bulky friend says, "It's good to see friends of Karl hanging out around here. This place just hasn't been the same since he and Chad… uh, well, *went home.*"

Everyone coughs at the awkward moment of mutual understanding, and Vincent simply mumbles, "Yeah."

Brian breaks the silence. "Alright guys, we have to get back to our workout, but how does a game of volleyball sometime this week sound?"

"Sure, man," one of the skinnier guys says. "As long as your new buddy comes with. What do you say, Creighton?"

Vincent looks at him with confusion, then to Brian who gives him a nod. *The last two guys who were associated with you people wound up dead…* "Uh, I don't know guys. I'm not really a sports kind of guy."

"Ah, c'mon bud! It'll be fun!"

Vincent shakes his head. "Sorry, guys…" After much fruitless goading, Brian and Vincent finish their workout and turn in for the night.

Vincent settles into his room and burns the last few hours before bed reading his most recent book obsession—*Frankenstein; or, The Modern Prometheus*. As he reads Mary Shelley's famous story, he can't help feeling that she mischaracterized Doctor Frankenstein as a modern Prometheus. *A scientist who creates, then quickly abandons his creation is no respectable Titan-hero. Prometheus stole fire from the gods and gifted it to humanity with pride; upon seeing humans burn their neighbors' villages to the ground and creating weapons capable of lighting the air itself ablaze, Prometheus never felt regret for his actions. Frankenstein took no such responsibility.*

A scientist who turns his back on his discoveries is no scientist, but a scared child at play. As a man of science, Frankenstein could have replicated his creation to build cities, amass an army, or create monuments that would dwarf the pyramids. The gods looked upon humanity as if we were their playthings, but Prometheus knew we deserved better and were capable of more than what the gods would allow. Doctor Frankenstein created something great, but bowed to the fear of superstitious beliefs; he is no scientist, just a child playing with things he refuses to understand.

The more he reads of Frankenstein's failed efforts at following through with his discovery, the more steam rises in him.

If you can create, you must do so despite how the rest of the world perceives your creation. The village chasing that which they don't understand is the monster, it's the job of the creator to facilitate understanding. The true modern Prometheus showed us how to harness electricity; Ben Franklin never patented his inventions. He never hid science from the people, and he was never afraid of sharing knowledge. I don't want my legacy to be that of Victor Frankenstein: a scared child playing with magic. I want to be a post-modern Prometheus, gifting humanity with my truly awesome power of teleportation.

That night, Vincent's mind swims with images of himself accepting the Nobel Prize, news headlines praising his name, and the scientific community going wild for him. After earning the respect of the world, he will turn the page and begin unraveling the next chapter of secrets the universe is hiding. As he closes his book and tucks into bed for the night, a fleeting thought occurs to him before drifting off.

Humanity will see what I am capable of.

Chapter Twenty-Six

July 10th, 2020

Friday

Blood and sweat drip down his brow as Vincent is thrust to the sand below him. It's been a few months since he started really focusing on his regimen. Bobby takes a taunting lap around the ring. "That all you got, Creighton?" Struggling to his feet, Vincent stumbles to the center of the fighting pit and readies his stance.

"C'mon, Vinny! You got this piece of shit!" Becca shouts from outside of the ring while Trent and Leo cheer and jeer alongside her.

"Ready for another beating? Alright, let's do this!" Bobby steps into a better practiced, more solid fighting stance and swiftly lunges. Vincent blocks the first jab and parries the cross-body punch with his forward hand, then attempts to rush Bobby's chin with his back elbow but completely misses as Bobby ducks out of the way and slides behind Vincent to get him in a rear naked choke hold. Bobby destabilizes his center of balance and tosses him across the pit.

"Get back up, Vinny!" Trent yells out. Vincent stumbles around, failing to see as Leo tosses a training knife to Bobby, who grabs it in a reverse grip and does another lap around the ring.

Giving him only a second or two to stand back up, Bobby begins to lunge again. The light from the fire and the work lights blurs as Vincent spins back to his feet, focusing on where he expects Bobby to come from. He looks up just in time to see Bobby charging him with an overhand strike when he notices a glint of light shining in his hand. Vincent's instincts take over as he bursts forward, propelling his forearms up to halt Bobby's momentum, then hooking Bobby's knife arm with his left and holding him stable with his right, Vincent knees Bobby in the groin before shoving him to the ground and disengaging.

Trent, Leo, and Becca all hoot and holler as Vincent successfully conducts his first take down. Vincent helps Bobby to his feet; the latter congratulates him sportingly. Leo passes them a couple of dry towels and pats Vincent on the back as they clean up. Retiring to the meeting room, Becca turns on the dim interior lights, and Trent lays out the Abaddon maps.

Vincent dreads this part of the weekend. Trent has been riding him for weeks about talking to Dr. Smith and Tzofiya about the plan, but week after week Vincent returns to camp with the same excuse: "I couldn't find a chance to talk to them." *Sorry, guys... I just... I need that machine to be built.*

"Alright, let's review the plan again," Trent says. "So Friday night, whatever date we choose, we drive both pickups—which will have been loaded up with our gear the night before—over to Fort Chivington, arriving at midnight. By that time the party should be in full swing and security sufficiently distracted."

Leo says, "Vincent, that gear on those trucks might become incredibly important if things go south. You need to get in contact with Tzofiya and make sure she'll be able to get vehicles in, too. If not, we'll be limited to what we can carry on our backs."

"Right..." Vincent gulps.

"So..." Trent raises his eyebrows at Vincent and finishes his thought, "So you're going to talk to her, right?"

Vincent nervously nods. "Definitely."

"Good... because her response will heavily impact our strategy."

"I got it, yeah."

"Alright," Becca says. "So assuming she *will* be able to get the vehicles on base, we'll pull right up to the armory and unload our equipment into the service elevator, then ride it down to Bartram's office."

"At the same time," Trent says, "Tzofiya and Vincent will be *en route* to the atrium to take care of crowd control. Leo and I will lock the atrium down before joining Becca and Bobby in Bartram's office, where, hopefully, we will catch Bartram with his pants down. Once we get him subdued, Dr. Smith will take over, we can evacuate the Abaddon, then finally shut the place down."

"However," Becca continues his thought, "if he's waiting for us with a combat unit, we'll have a full armament with us and be ready to fight back."

"But worst-case scenario," Leo says, "if we can't take our trucks with us *and* Bartram is waiting for us with a combat unit, then Dr. Smith shuts the whole place down, and we open negotiations."

Bobby says, "I still don't understand how we can get a signal to Smith for him to shut the place down."

Leo answers by looking at Vincent, "Yeah, that's where it gets dicey. If we can't bring the trucks on base, Trent and I would allot a bit of extra time for Vincent to enter the north wing before initiating lockdown. He'll find Dr. Smith and let him know we couldn't bring the trucks; then, if we don't knock on his office door within ten minutes, Dr. Smith shuts the place down."

Bobby shakes his head. "So… hopefully we manage to survive a full-frontal assault from a fully prepared combat unit for ten minutes? That's a long time to survive a firefight."

Leo asks, "Aren't you a professional?"

"Yeah, but I'm still *mortal*."

Everyone ignores Bobby's comment, and Trent says, "Vinny, once Tzofiya and Dr. Smith are in the loop, all we'll need to do is pick a date, which should be sooner rather than later; Bartram's patrols have been getting more tenacious. I'm pretty sure they know we're out here."

Leo says, "I think they've been onto us for a while. Fortunately, we know all their moves so we've been able to stay one step ahead of them, but they will catch up if we wait too much longer."

"So what I'm hearing is… next weekend?" Bobby says gleefully.

Leo notices Vincent tensing up and says, "I don't know, even if Vincent is able to tell Dr. Smith and Tzofiya about the plan, I'm not sure he's combat ready."

Vincent looks at his feet, trembling in shame. "I-I mean… If we could just w-wait like…"

Becca says, "Einstein, I'm usually in your corner on things like this, but we have to get moving. Your buddy Martinez is going to catch up to us soon."

"I hate to say this"—Trent looks at Leo apologetically—"but she's right. We've gotta move. If all goes well, Vincent won't even be in combat. It's been three months, and he's only had one job." Trent looks back to Vincent and adds, "You gotta do your part, Vinny."

But… I'm not done yet. Vincent's apprehension seems to be visible only to Leo.

"Do you really want to go into battle when one of our fighters isn't ready yet?"

"He's ready, Leo," Trent says. "His skills are sharp, and his instincts are honed. He knows what he's doing. Again, he won't even be in combat."

"You all know as well as I do, no plan survives contact with the enemy." Everyone rolls their eyes and nods when Leo says this.

"Murphy's Law," Vincent backs him up. "Everything that can go wrong, will go wrong."

"Exactly. We're bringing a civilian into a warzone; we have the moral obligation to ensure that he is capable of taking care of himself before we bring him with us. Three weeks. We go in three weeks. That'll give us a bit of extra time to get our shit together, which works out because we needed to acquire a few extra gas masks anyway. That'll give Vincent three more final sessions to wrap up his training, then we go."

Trent looks at him skeptically but gives in. "Three weeks. We move on"—he looks at the calendar posted on the wall with several red Xs leading up to today's date—"July 31st. It's a Friday; we move that night at midnight. But Vinny… you have a job to do. You better get it done."

CHAPTER TWENTY-SEVEN

July 11th, 2020

Saturday

Vincent's body aches when he wakes up after returning from his desert excursion to Trent's camp. Working out three times a week has put a strain on Vincent's muscles that he hasn't felt since P.E. class in high school. He struggles out of bed, takes a much-needed shower, then gets dressed for whatever he decides to spend his day doing, which winds up being another night at the theatre.

Finding his usual seat in the back row of the theatre that night, Vincent settles in for the acting guild's stage adaptation of *Dr. Horrible's Sing Along Blog*. Most of the bleachers are filled tonight; it seems the work they put into advertising their show this week is paying off. Vincent wears his black hoodie and puts his hood up to hide in the darkness of the back seats. He's found that people like to talk while the play is going on, so he makes a point of looking uninterested in conversation.

"Oh my God, did you hear Piper's voice just crack?"

"Ugh! Chad would have played a great Captain Hammer, wouldn't he? Speaking of, where has he been?"

"Really? They used blue construction paper over a flashlight for the freeze ray? *That's* creative."

The show goes by relatively smoothly, despite Johnathan accidentally cracking the lenses of Dr. Horrible's prop goggles and James's oversized Captain Hammer gloves being tossed into the audience. The crowd gives a standing ovation when the cast takes a bow, then Vincent waits for the rest of the audience to clear out before departing. As he leaves, however, he is stopped by a familiar voice calling his name. He turns to find someone he didn't expect.

"Dr. Smith?" Vincent asks.

"Good evening, Vincent. I was not aware you were a fan of the arts."

"I'm not really."

Dr. Smith chuckles. "Well, it is good to try new things. Hey, you should join me in my office for a cup of tea? We can catch up a bit."

"Um, sure. Why not?"

Dr. Smith leads Vincent back to his office, where he sets up his living room window to overlook the Manhattan skyline. Dr. Smith goes into the kitchen to make some tea, leaving Vincent to admire the living room. Standing in the middle of the open, round space, he doesn't know what to do or where to look. *It would be weird if he came back, and I was still standing in the same spot...* He tentatively walks around the room, passively examining the various objects displayed. An intricately woven basket sits upon one of many podiums displaying artwork; he looks at the basket closely but doesn't know if it should impress him or not. On the opposite side of the circular room, an old painting depicts traditional Arapaho dances being performed at some kind of public event. It looks like a powwow. He had learned about them in an elective that he took as an undergrad but doesn't remember much.

Shifting his attention to one of the bookshelves, he notices two columns of books containing dozens of advanced readings on history, ethics, biology, nuclear energy conversion, in vitro fertilization, computer coding, and so much more. *Wow... Is this what he's spent the decades doing? Just reading?*

"Looks like you found my current fascinations." Dr. Smith returns with a platter of tea and cookies in hand.

Vincent gasps in response, "Sorry! Uh... yeah. Sorry, I was just looking around."

"No, no, please, art is meant to be admired, and books are meant to be read. Tell me, do you know much about energy conversion?"

"Of course! I've read every book you've ever written on it. One of my professors had us read your book discussing biochemical to thermal energy conversion. It was genius!"

Dr. Smith blushes. "That is a high compliment coming from you, thank you. Please, have some tea." He pours two cups from the kettle, along with some sugar and herbs, then hands it to Vincent. They sit at the low couches against the walls and drink. "Have you given more thought to the Lockheed Martin job?"

Vincent chokes on his tea, then mumbles, "Uh… the job offer. Yes."

"You contacted the recruiter, I presume?"

"The… the what now?"

"You called him, right? What did he say?"

"Well…" *Did I call someone? Trent?* "Yeah?"

"Did he tell you about the job fair? He and I have been planning an event, but I have not heard from him in some time."

What event? "Uh…" Vincent's throat is dry, so he finishes his tea. "Can you jog my memory?"

Dr. Smith's patience seems to be wearing thin. "Well, we were hoping to help others like yourself—other scientists trapped in situations like yours—to find employment elsewhere. You know, escape the humdrum lives they find themselves in here. Working for Colonel Bartram. In the Abaddon."

"Right…" *Is he talking about the attack? How does he know?* "I… haven't heard anything. No." He immediately feels ashamed of himself as he tells the lie, but he buries that feeling down.

"You haven't?" Dr. Smith looks at him suspiciously. "Are you sure?"

Vincent avoids Dr. Smith's glare. *The moment I tell him the details of the plan… it becomes real. I won't be able to work on the project anymore… The Abaddon itself might get destroyed… If I can just push it out a little longer.* "I'm sure."

"Well, please keep me apprised of any updates, yes? I would like nothing more than to see this event come to fruition." Dr. Smith abruptly takes Vincent's cup and leads him to the front door. "You better get going. Time is slipping away from us quickly."

CHAPTER TWENTY-EIGHT

July 17th, 2020

Friday

Bullets ping as steel targets fall to the ground with each squeeze of Vincent's trigger; he's grown to quite enjoy the aroma of gunpowder lingering in the air. Each bullet strikes exactly in the center of the bullseye with record time, but then Trent, Becca, and Bobby circle around him with bated breath when his magazine runs dry. Beads of sweat drip down Vincent's forehead as he ejects the magazine and picks up a new one. Hand shaking, he shoves the magazine into the well, but it stops abruptly against the metal. Turning the gun to see what happened, he sees he twisted his wrist and pushed it at the wrong angle. Fiddling with it in his hand, he manages to slide it in, but he doesn't hear the click. He struggles to get the magazine to click, but eventually just punches it into place causing the barrel to swing out wildly. Everyone behind him collectively yells, "Woah!" and ducks. Once he timidly pulls back the slide, he takes a deep breath and resumes firing at the targets, hitting the bullseye on each of them.

"That… was a bit better," Leo stutters. "You could still use some practice on the reload." Vincent clears the weapon, then steps away as Becca goes downrange to inspect his work.

"At least your aim is still spot on. You're already surpassing Leo's accuracy," she says almost proudly.

"A well-placed shot is great," Bobby interjects, "but if you take fifteen minutes to reload every time you run out, all of this will be for nothing."

A pit opens in Vincent's stomach at the thought of being in an actual fight. He knows the whole point of this is to stand up to Bartram and his army, but training with everyone has been so fun that he doesn't want to think about it coming to an end. Envisioning himself being shot at nearly brings him to tears, but he pulls himself back into the moment when Becca says, "He's right, Vince."

As a tear drops down his cheek, he responds, "I know. I just—when it comes to handling the gun itself, I get nervous. Pulling the trigger is easy, putting the bullet where I want it is simple math, but my arms and fingers turn to spaghetti when I have to do anything else with it."

"You know what you need?" Dallyn asks rhetorically. "Trial by fire. I had this idea a while back, and we've all been working on it. I think you'll enjoy it." Dallyn winks at Trent before leading Vincent into the RV to hang out while everyone sets something up outside.

Vincent takes a seat at the folding dinette table adjacent to the kitchen to gather his nerves, which go haywire at the sound of drills and hammers clanging against metal. *What could they possibly be making?* Dallyn gathers up his colorful gown and gingerly sits across from him. "Don't worry, you're going to love it."

"What makes you think that?"

"You're a brave guy, even if you don't think you are."

"Oh… thanks?" That doesn't really calm his nerves though, since now he's wondering what's going to require him to be brave.

"There's one thing I've been wondering about, though. Do you mind if I ask?"

"Um, sure?"

"You've had plenty of opportunities to tell Dr. Smith and Tzofiya about the plan, haven't you?"

Vincent blushes. "Uh, I don't know what you mean."

"It's okay." His smile is disarming but genuine. "I won't tell the others. Your secrets are safe with me. It's just… I can tell there's something keeping you from getting them involved. At first, I thought it was a matter of safety, but I don't think that's it. You say Tzofiya is the one who lets you off base every week, so you could easily approach her. So… what is it?"

"I… it's nothing. I'm not keeping anything from anyone."

Dallyn chuckles. "You don't know me. I get it. You don't trust me, and that's okay. But Trent does trust me. He thinks very highly of you, and I don't want a misunderstanding to cause a rift between you guys."

"What kind of misunderstanding are you talking about?"

Dallyn shifts in his chair and says, "The kind that could jeopardize this whole operation. If he thinks you're a double agent due to you withholding information, or delaying the op, or even if he just thinks your judgment has been compromised, then he might try and circumvent you. Cut you out."

"He wouldn't do that. He said he needed me on this, why would he do that?"

"We do need you. But if he thinks you've become a liability, then he might move in another direction. I don't want that. And I don't think you do either because you also want Bartram to be taken in, don't you?"

"Of course, I do! He's a power-hungry bully, and we need to get rid of people like him at all costs!"

"*All* costs?"

Vincent stops to reconsider his words. "Well… no. Not *all* costs…"

"Right. I think—" Dallyn reaches out and touches Vincent's hand— "you just don't want to see anyone get hurt. Even Bartram." Vincent nods. "I respect that about you, but we have already promised to keep him from getting hurt if we can help it. So… Vincent, who's going to get hurt if Bartram is removed from power?"

Vincent pulls his hand away from him and stands, pacing in the few feet of runway inside the RV. "Look, say what you will about Bartram, but the man's track record is incredible. Under his control, we've made developments that would take other facilities decades or even centuries to make. If we remove him and return to doing things"—he has a word on the tip of his tongue that he doesn't want to use, but he can't think of a better one, so he just says it—"*ethically*… then we may not be able to make the great strides that we have been."

"Ah." Dallyn raises his head in understanding. "So you want to use the power that Bartram has accrued? To do what?"

Vincent looks at him with trepidation. "I want to save someone's life."

"A loved one's?"

"Sarah's mother."

Dallyn nods and smiles. "Okay. So you're buying time?"

"Basically, yeah."

"Well, far be it for us to stop you," Dallyn says, which makes Vincent do a double take. "However, the longer you wait, the harder it will be to evade Martinez's patrols. I know these lands well, but Martinez and that dog of theirs are good hunters."

"Okay."

"Make sure saving Sarah's mom doesn't sacrifice our lives, okay?"

"You're… you're not going to tell Trent about this?"

"No. And I'll do what I can to keep him off your back. I trust you to do the right thing."

Vincent cocks his head, but Dallyn quickly changes subjects by offering him some food. They chitchat for a while, anxiously listening in on the construction site outside for nearly an hour until Becca pokes her head in to ask, "You ready?"

"As I'll ever be."

She leads him outside, and opposite the campfire, he finds a hastily constructed maze with sheet metal walls. As they approach, he notices a table with an array of M16 rifles, M1911 pistols, and knives, but they all look different.

"What's with the orange tips?" Vincent asks.

"Have you ever played paintball before, Vincent?" Trent asks excitedly while he straps on a Kevlar vest, gloves, and knee pads.

"N-no. Do I look like a paintball shooter?"

"Let me guess," Bobby says, "you were a mathlete, not an athlete?"

"Uh, yeah. Mathlete. I *definitely* joined a social group in high school."

Everyone chuckles at his sarcastic comment, which momentarily makes him feel like a part of the group. Trent holds a magazine in his hand and says, "We got the guns that would most closely resemble our own and marked them with an orange tip. Unfortunately, the weight of the paintballs is slightly different than the rounds we use. If you want to get a feel for the new weight, go ahead and fire off a couple mags." Vincent takes him up on this offer and finds that the paintballs are much lighter but easily manages to adjust his math.

Everyone gears up, but Vincent changes his clothes before getting started to avoid getting paint on his regular clothes. Bobby pulls up a crate of helmets and rubber gas masks.

"What are those?" Vincent asks with concern in his voice.

"The bastards we're going to fight like to play dirty. Since we'll be in his domain, we need to be prepared for anything that Bartram might throw at us. Don't worry though, I got some prescription lens inserts for yours."

Vincent swallows nervously, then looks on as the others don their masks, create a seal, and strap on their helmet. *What the fuck have I gotten myself into?* Taking his glasses off, he fumbles around with the mask and tries tightening the straps for a few minutes before Trent approaches and teaches him how to handle it. Without his peripheral vision, he needs to crane his neck to see his friends around him. His hot breath condensing on his face and lenses, he can feel his lungs laboring more and more until he pulls the mask off in a fit, gasping for fresh air.

"There's no fucking way! I can't fight in this thing!"

"I know it's uncomfortable." Trent's voice is muffled under the mask. "But you're going to have to make it work. Otherwise, you'll end up writhing on the ground, struggling to breathe in the middle of combat. Obviously, we can't have that. We'll do one run-through, then you can take it off."

Vincent holds it in his hand anxiously but ends up sliding it on and strapping it in. Feeling clunky and top heavy, he feels around the table for his weapons. Clumsily loading them and fastening his belt with extra magazines, it takes him several minutes before he is finally ready to run the course. The five of them gather around in front of one of the maze entrances exchanging idle chitchat through muffled voices.

"Alright, Vince, it's time. You ready?"

"How does this work? Are we all running through at the same time?"

"We will all be in the maze at the same time, yes. We're basically playing team deathmatch. You choose your partner, then face the other three as a team. Each team will enter through opposite sides of the maze. If you get shot, you hit the deck, and you're out. Last team with a member standing wins."

"That puts my team at a severe disadvantage though."

Bobby grins and pats him on his shoulder. "Then you better put up a hell of a fight." Vincent gulps.

"Don't worry," Trent tries reassuring him. "Let's just do it bad once, then do it better the next time. Sound good?"

"Uh… I… I guess."

"Who do you want on your team?"

Vincent looks on at the rest of the team, fully equipped in their combat gear and gas masks. "Leo, do you want to be my partner?"

"It would be my honor, Vinny." Leo nods, and Vincent can see his cheeks through the visor pushing up into a smile.

The two of them stand in front of the maze entrance, waiting as Trent leads the other two to the opposite entrance. Leo pulls back the slide on his rifle and inspects the chamber, making sure his weapons are ready for the fight. Vincent pretends to look at the same things alongside him, nervously awaiting the onslaught they're about to receive. Leo notices his mimicry and grins.

"I never asked, but how was that whiskey?"

Vincent pauses and grins back. "It was sweeter than I expected." They share a laugh. "I've found it tastes better with friends though."

"I've noticed the same thing." Their muffled voices make it difficult to understand each other, but they hear Trent's voice from the other entrance.

"You guys ready?!" Trent shouts from the opposite end of the maze.

"Ready!" Leo answers him, then winks at Vincent before getting into his ready position. Vincent looks at the shaking gun in his hands through the lens of his gas mask, then approaches as well.

"Three! Two! One! Go!" Trent shouts, then Leo takes off into the maze, Vincent hesitantly trailing behind him as quickly as he can.

Vincent struggles to keep up as Leo skillfully maneuvers through the sand, carefully clears corners, and directs Vincent as they pass by multiple forks in the path until he comes to a sudden stop at a corner. Holding up his arm, Leo signals for Vincent to halt; instead, Vincent runs into the arm and stumbles. Leo grabs him by the collar as he trips to stabilize him. Gesturing with a shushing motion, Leo indicates to turn, then signals for them to stay low. Gradually, Leo leads Vincent around the bend until a sudden burst of paintballs are fired.

All Vincent notices are the three paintballs that crash into the metal wall in front of him, but a second later he realizes they had gone right over Leo's head while shooting at his target. Leo had popped off three shots of his own, then pushed forward to attack others who might be firing, gesturing for Vincent to follow. Nearly hyperventilating, Vincent gathers himself and brings his gun up, accidentally smacking the lens of his mask. Stepping past Bobby's prone body, Vincent sees two paintballs splattered against his chest and one between his eyes.

Together they move forward down a couple of corridors until Vincent gets into the groove of mirroring Leo. His own breath echoing in his ears, he has to squint slightly to see through the corrective lens inserts. Leo signals for Vincent to take the lead, and Vincent then steps forward without thinking about it until they reach the next corner. Sweating profusely, he mimics the motions Leo had made but feels that something is off. Slowing down, he takes caution and his eyes catch some motion before, instinctively, his muscles retract, ducking back behind the corner as two paintballs smack the wall behind him. Leo gives him a subtle nod.

Vincent takes a deep breath. He gets low, pulls his gun up to his mask, then, making sure to keep his barrel from peeking out, he sweeps the corner until he is completely exposed. Leo, covering him, signals to move on, and Vincent follows the order, but halfway through the corridor, Vincent's gut speaks to him. Swiftly coming to a halt, he faces about and sees a short figure rounding the corner. *Becca.* Vincent's trigger finger itches as the math is calculated instantly in his head before firing two in the chest and one between the eyes. Behind him, more paintballs are fired, and Vincent turns just in time to see Leo jump in front of him and shout, "Retreat!" Leo's body takes the shots fired by Trent from his position of cover, but Vincent fires back at Trent, then his heart stops when the most terrifying thing that Vincent can imagine happens. His gun jams.

Paintballs flying at him, he narrowly dodges the projectiles and ducks around the corner. He clumsily inspects his rifle through his bulky mask, then fiddles around with it, but his fingers never find the right parts. Then he hears Trent sprinting down the corridor. *Fuck it, I'm out.* He lets the rifle drop on its strap around his neck and bolts down the corridor, weaving his way back to one of the forks they had passed.

Running through the sand reminded him of running around the base every day for the past few months. Adrenaline coursing through his veins, he barely thinks as he swiftly ejects his magazine, throws his rifle down the corridor that he and Leo had already trekked through, runs down the opposite path, and drops his ejected magazine. *That should at least buy me some time.* Taking cover around the next corner, Vincent fiddles with his pistol to make sure that it's ready. Blood pumping echoes through his ears, he exhales, then stands up in the ready position, listening carefully. Footsteps approach, come to a halt, then back up and fade away down the other corridor. Vincent sweeps around and returns to the fork, but as soon as he rounds the corner, his blood freezes.

Trent's eyes are staring at him behind the gas mask not four feet from him. Both of them fire, simultaneously ducking out of each other's line of sight. Using the wall as a barrier, they shoot back and forth until they both hear an ominous click, which means one thing to Vincent. *I need to keep him from drawing his pistol.* He rushes forward, throwing his body at Trent, who is halfway through his draw when Vincent's hand halts his, then twists his wrist to force the gun out of his grip. Trent, taken aback by the brazenness, hesitates for a moment before breaking free of the grip and bringing Vincent to the ground in a grapple.

Fighting in full gear like this is a new experience for Vincent, but his instincts are sharp. The sound of various materials rubbing against each other is muffled and disorienting, but Vincent can think of something else that would be equally as disorienting. As the two of them hit the deck, Vincent does his best to roll out of the grapple. Though he has been spending a lot of time at the gym, he still can't break free of Trent's grip; he does, however, manage to find just enough traction to free his right hand. Reaching straight up, Vincent slips his fingers under Trent's mask and forcefully shoves it up and over his eyes. Trent recoils and drops the grapple. Vincent rolls away, grabs the pistol, and fiddles with the trigger for a moment only to realize the safety was on. Thinking for only the second that he needs while Trent struggles to fix his mask, he disables the safety and fires three rounds—two to the chest and one between the eyes just as Trent fixes his gear.

Vincent's chest heaves for several moments before he hears Bobby's deadpan voice say, "Damn, dude." Vincent looks up and sees the rest of the group watching him, Leo beaming with pride after taking his mask and helmet off.

"Congratulations, Vinny." Trent also removes his mask, now splattered with a single paintball. "That was some of the finest work I've ever seen." He reaches up with a hand and says, "Little help?"

Vincent, still coming down from the rush, exhales a deep breath, then carefully places the gun on the ground and helps Trent to his feet. Trent helps him remove his headgear as well while they all exit the maze.

"Vincent! That was incredible! You did so well!" Becca squeals as Trent serves a round of whiskey around the campfire. Vincent takes a sip of the sweet nectar and blushes at her compliment.

"Seriously, Vinny. You really fought with your head in there. When we got to the fork with the two sets of prints, and you threw the rifle, I figured you ejected the magazine first and *then* your rifle. If you hadn't switched it up on me, I might have gotten to you sooner." Trent takes a seat in the last empty folding chair in the circle. "Not to mention pulling my mask, that was good! If there had been smoke, I'd have been done for."

"Thanks… Leo's leading me at the beginning really helped out a lot. I would have just been too anxious if you hadn't let me lead."

"That was the whole point, right? Get you comfortable doing the real deal."

"Well… he *did* fail to clear the jam in his rifle. He totally froze up on that," Bobby says without really addressing Vincent. "He's gotta practice that shit more."

"True, but he used his head to outthink me," Trent undercuts his comment. "I gotta say, when I left the gun on safe, I thought I had you. But you handled it like a champ."

"Thanks, guys," Vincent yawns, then looks at his watch. "Oh shit, I have to get back. Thank you, guys, this was really fun and helpful."

"It's our pleasure, Vinny," Leo says.

"Don't forget though," Trent says assertively, "you've still got a job to do. We're relying on you." Vincent's buzz is killed, but he nods solemnly.

Chapter Twenty-Nine

July 23rd, 2020

Thursday

After lunch, Mavis has Vincent check up on Sarah's work as she quietly helps one of the team members when a loud ruckus of cheering and applause breaks out from inside the workshop. Everyone looks over curiously before exiting the back doors to see what the hubbub is about. Grace rushes them with a wide grin, shouting, "We did it! Three minutes! We got the computer's time down to three minutes!" The entire crew congratulates her and the rest of the computer science team, but Vincent begins to sweat nervously. *Now it's all on me.*

During a celebratory soirée in the lab, Vincent hangs his head in the corner while everyone else enjoys idle chitchat and pizza. Vincent sits in the corner by himself until Sarah walks over with a slice of pepperoni on a paper plate. She hands it to him and quietly declares, "You have twenty-four hours." She pats him on the shoulder, then walks away. *It's time, Vinny. You have your cake—can you eat it too?* He looks up to see Mavis observing him from across the room. She pushes through the crowd to reach him, but he swiftly ducks out of the lab before she can find him.

Narrowly escaping the party, he heads straight to his room, lies on his bed, and closes his eyes for a few minutes before hearing a knock on the door. His eyes pop wide open. *Did Mavis follow me?* He waits a beat, but the banging continues. He gets up and stands by the door. "Who is it?" There is no answer, but the banging continues. He opens it slightly, but whoever is on the other side pushes hard. Vincent can tell that his time spent at the gym is paying off because he manages to keep them from pushing all the way. "Who the hell are you?! You can't come in!"

"Let me in, Vincent!" Grace's voice shouts.

"Grace?" He calms down slightly.

"Let me in!"

He opens the door so she can storm through the room, searching through drawers, under his pillow, blankets, mattress, and inside his wall locker.

"What are you looking for?"

After tearing his room apart, she stands, faces him, and crosses her arms. "Close the door."

Despite his confusion, he obliges. "Why aren't you down at your party?"

"You're scaring me. Letting Mavis push you around, being mean to Sarah, going to the gym every day, and spending your whole weekend asleep; you're not being yourself anymore. What's up?"

Vincent blushes. "I have no idea what you're talking about—who else would I be?"

"Don't you bullshit me, Creighton! I know that you've been lying to everyone about the algorithm, but you better not lie to *me*! Just tell the truth!"

"Lying about the algorithm?" He starts sweating and becomes defensive. "What exactly am I lying about?"

"I don't know, but for weeks now, you've just been saying nonsensical bullshit to everyone. You might be able to fool the rest of them, but Sarah and I can tell when you're just spewing nonsense and mathematical jargon."

"Oh, do you?" His nervousness suddenly turns to rage. "So all of a sudden you know me so well that you can tell when I'm lying? How convenient."

"Convenience has nothing to do with it. We've been working together for years! I'd like to think I know you pretty damn well. And I think I've earned the right to not be lied to!"

"You've *earned the right* to not be lied to, huh?" Vincent's anger flares up. "What about me then? Have I earned the same right?"

"Of course, you have, Vince. I would never lie to you."

"Then please explain why the fuck you spent years lying to Mark about *my* work. Every day, every presentation for three fucking years, you lied about my work to that motherfucker. What happened there, huh?"

Grace pauses. She steps backward and tilts her head. "What are you talking about?"

"You spent years taking credit for *my* work. Telling Mark that it's a *group effort* whenever *I* made a breakthrough. I would come into the office every day and listen to you talk shit about Mark and Karl while gossiping with Sarah, then in between it all, I would do double or triple the amount of work that all three of you would do in a week!" He inches closer to her, pointing in her face and accidentally spitting as he speaks. "Before I showed up, you guys couldn't do shit without getting at each other's throats. But once you had some geek from M.I.T. to do all your work for you, listen to your sob stories about how hard it is to work for a sleazeball like Mark, and unload about Karl's dude-bro attitude, suddenly all four of us are *best friends!* Not anymore, Grace! I'm done being your homework-jockey."

Grace's breath gets caught in her throat, and she stumbles onto his bed. This is the first time that he's known her to be utterly speechless. Vincent's scowl burns in her direction, and she studies him. "I had no idea you felt that way."

"Of course, you didn't. That's the best part: to you, I was just the weird little bug you stepped on and forgot to scrape off the bottom of your shoe. And yet you still come here expecting me to trust you with a secret. I wouldn't trust you to write a simple recursive algorithm, much less a clandestine operation!" Vincent's rage starts spewing from him without thinking. "I'm glad you managed to shave the last seven minutes off the computer's processing time, but you never thanked me for the other hour and fifty-three minutes that *I* cut *for* you!" Vincent hovers over her, seething.

Grace furrows her brow. "You don't get it, do you, Vince?" She looks at him with disgust. "Do you know why I said everyone contributed to the project equally? Because we're a team. And that's what teammates do."

Vincent scoffs. "Steal credit from each other?"

"We look out for each other. Do you know how many times I saw men like Mark and Karl take credit for the work that my girlfriends and I did? You don't understand what it's like to be a woman in science! People try to walk all over you! I hated seeing credit get stolen from me and other women, so I took the reins as team lead to make sure everyone got an equal piece of the pie."

"You know where you fucked up? You did exactly what those misogynists did to you, except you forgot to take out the most important part—the exploitation. You exploited the quiet one, the one who wouldn't stand up for himself. You took so much away from me just to make yourself feel better. Well, guess what, Grace!" He looks at her sitting on the edge of his bed with tears welling up in his eyes. "I'm strong now. I won't be bullied anymore. I'm not a pushover."

Grace's breathing is labored as she wipes the tears from her own eyes. Digging her finger into his chest with aggressive vigor, she bursts out, "You're an asshole, Vincent!"

"I have years of being stepped on by people like you to thank for that!"

She steps closer to him so she can shout directly in his face, "NO! You don't get to blame me for that! It's your OWN fault that you never stood up for yourself!"

"You don't *get* to say who I can blame! It's people like you, Bartram, and Trent! You all just *use* me to get what you want! It's *your* fault, and I blame *you*!"

"It's not my *fault*!" In this last rush of energy, Grace reaches out with both arms and tries to shove him onto Karl's old bed. But Vincent's newfound reflexes kick in, and he takes hold of her arms, places his right foot behind hers, shoves his elbow into her throat, and thrusts her to the floor. Vincent's glasses fling from his face as he knocks the wind out of her, then she gasps for breath and rolls over. Popping back into his fighting stance, he realizes that he may have overreacted a little bit. Catching her breath, Grace squirms on the floor for a few moments before Vincent fully calms down.

"Oh, fuck! A-Are you okay?" he asks timidly, reaching a hand out to help her up.

"What the *fuck* was that?!" she cries out, swiping his hands away.

"You attacked me!" he says defensively. "What was I supposed to do?"

"I don't know—*not* pin me to the fucking ground!" She slowly sits up without his help.

"First off, I didn't pin you to the ground; it was a takedown. Secondly, if you don't want me to take you down, don't lunge at me."

They sit across the room from each other on either bed while catching their breath. There's a moment of quiet while neither of them wants to be the first to say something. Vincent picks up his glasses, cleans them, and puts them back on.

"I'm sorry," Grace finally says.

"Me, too."

"I didn't know you felt like I was stealing credit from you. If I'd known that, I would have done something."

"I didn't know you were just trying to be equal. I thought you were just using me, like everyone else does."

Neither of them speaks for a while. Grace rubs her throat, and her voice is hoarse. "Where did you learn that move?"

Vincent looks at his feet and mutters, "It's, um… a long story."

"I'd like to hear it." She looks at him, her eyes glistening in the sunlight that's shining through the window. Cautiously, he returns a meaningful gaze of his own.

"It's not that I don't want to tell you; I do. It's just… it's too dangerous."

"More dangerous than you throwing me to the ground?" She gives him a playful grin.

"Yes. A lot more dangerous." He returns a much more serious look, and her grin disappears.

"At least tell me what you told Sarah."

That's right… Sarah. He thinks for a moment and acquiesces. "Okay. The day of the failed experiment, I figured out the correct algorithm to fix the problem. I decided not to tell anyone but Sarah. She said she'd keep the secret safe until you figured out the computer processing issue. That was three months ago. And then today… you did it. Sarah's giving me twenty-four hours before she tells Mavis."

"Oh my God, that's huge! Why'd you keep it a secret?"

"That's the thing that I can't tell you."

They fall quiet for a while, but it doesn't last long. "I don't trust her either, Vincent." He starts to say something but stops to let her continue, "I don't trust Mavis."

"Why not?"

"Aside from her just being a two-faced, micromanaging bitch? I don't know; I feel like she's hiding something. Her and Colonel Bartram, they always seem like they're up to something."

He bites his tongue, not wanting to say anything. *I have to tell her. She's going to find out in a couple weeks anyway.* Taking a choppy breath, he reaches into his drawer for his phone and removes the battery. "It's because they are." She gives him an interested look, and he lowers his voice and continues, "Bartram isn't in the military. None of them are. This base—the Abaddon—it's not DARPA. It's an unsanctioned black site."

"What do you mean? They wear the uniforms, they have the guns, they have the money to pay for all this."

"They *used* to be in the military. They haven't been for a long, long time. Now they're security contractors who sell the weapons tech that we develop to shady organizations and governments around the world for profit and power. They move us downstairs and blackmail us into working until we become a liability, then they kill us off."

She shoots him a skeptical look. "How do you know this?"

"I saw it. With my own eyes. In Bartram's office, he has cabinets full of financial records and documents detailing our vulnerabilities—stuff that no government organization has any business maintaining. They have the names—and death certificates—of every person who lives here. When we no longer contribute to the mission, we disappear, and those death certificates are issued. That's how they *fire* us." She looks at him critically, so he adds, "They have information on our families, friends, whoever matters most to you. Once you move downstairs, they tell you everything and forbid you from telling the newcomers."

She considers this for a while. "I have to say, I have a hard time believing you, but… I kind of forced this out of you. It's a wild thing to make up."

"It's all true. You can ask anyone—Brian or anyone else who lives downstairs. But… it's not hopeless. I have friends who want to help."

"Friends named Trent?"

He gets nervous for a moment. "Yeah, how did you know that name?"

"You said it earlier—I just assumed. Who is he?"

"He used to be a guard here. But he escaped and has been working against Bartram for the last year and a half. That's why I've been sneaking out every weekend—he's been training me. We've been planning… something."

Her eyebrows rise like a mom who knows her child is hiding something. "Planning *something*?"

"Yeah, uh… a coup."

She perks up. "A coup?"

Vincent chuckles. "I know how it sounds, but yeah. I'm supposed to help him and the rest of our team break in, and… well… we're going to put Bartram out of business. Put an end to it."

"*Put an end to it?!* To what exactly?"

"All of it. Bartram's management, the security forces here, the weapons trading. Everything." He sighs. "The Abaddon itself will crumble."

She laughs at his funny joke out loud until she realizes that it isn't a joke. "You're not kidding. How?"

"The plan is to break into Bartram's office and arrest him, leaving Dr. Smith to take control and release everybody. However, if it doesn't pan out that way, there are other… more violent means to take him out of power. We all want to avoid those options though."

"So you, some guy named Trent, and your *'friends'* are going to storm a highly secured facility? There's like thirty guards here."

"More than that, but… there's five of us in total."

"Who?"

"You don't know them." *Well, technically you met them at the Ducky Luck but… that's a different story for another time.*

Seemingly unconvinced, she asks, "Why don't we just steal the documents and leak them to the public? Someone would come asking questions at some point, right?"

"Bartram still has power in the government. As long as he's alive, no one is coming near this place. And even if the public gets ahold of this information, do you think Bartram would just give up? No. He would burn this place to the ground with us inside to destroy the evidence. Then he would move the Abaddon somewhere else and start again. Our way, everyone still gets to live."

Thinking deeply, she continues her questions. "When?"

"One week."

"How long have you been planning this?"

"A few months."

"Why is it taking so long?"

Vincent blushes before answering. "Um… well… a few reasons. I needed to get combat ready. They had to train me in a lot of stuff."

"Like takedowns?"

"Among other things, yes. But also…" He hesitates. "I've been lying to them as well."

Grace shuts her eyes and lets out a breath. "You just can't help yourself, can you? What about?"

"Well… has Sarah told you about her mom?"

"What about her?"

"She has brain cancer."

"Wait, what? Really? Why hasn't she told me?"

"I think the more she talks about it, the more real it becomes for her, and… I don't know. But what matters is that's the reason she joined the project in the first place. She wants to save her mom by teleporting the brain cancer away."

"That's genius, but what's that got to do with anything?"

"Well… just think about how far we've come in developing this technology. We went from hypothesis to an actual, working teleportation machine in a matter of months. If we're going to save her mom, we need this place."

"But… what about the warmongering, the selling weapons to shady governments, the murdering of our coworkers, all the crazy shit you just mentioned?"

"Don't get me wrong, I want to stop that stuff too. It's monstrous what Bartram's doing… but if it's the price we have to pay to help Sarah save her mom… wouldn't it be worth it?"

Grace contemplates this for a long time. Vincent's stomach bubbles while she paces around the room until she finally says, "We have to tell Sarah."

"No. No, no, no. No. It's far too dangerous for her. If she tells someone about it, or if they find out that she knows… they'll hurt her. I can't let that happen."

"Just because you're willing to pay the price, doesn't mean Sarah is. Or her mom for that matter. They should get a choice."

"I agree, they *should* get a say in this, but it's too dangerous to tell her!"

"If she tells Mavis that you've had the algorithm this whole time, that's it. Your whole operation is over. They'll know you're withholding information from them and assume you've been working against them this whole time. They might even hurt Sarah for obstructing the project alongside you."

"I'm not telling Sarah. She needs plausible deniability. I'll let them kill me before they think she had anything to do with it."

"Okay," she says with a hint of respect in her voice, then she thinks for another moment. "But we need to get her off your back. You should tell Mavis you figured out the algorithm—"

"I can't do th—"

"BUT! You bring her a fake one. If these guys are as dangerous as you say, we can't risk giving them the power of teleportation, despite whatever good can come from it. We can at least buy ourselves some time if we make even just a little progress."

"I've thought about that, but they'll never buy it. As soon as we run it through a test, they'll know we lied."

"No way, you've strung them along this far. They'll forgive one algorithm needing a bit of extra work."

He thinks on it until asking one last question, "Are you sure they'll buy it?"

"Honestly. No." Grace smiles proudly. "But if nothing else, it'll buy us some time to let your friends come and… put an end to it."

He sighs in exhaustion. "Thank you for listening to me and… understanding. I know I've made some stupid decisions—"

"Hey, you're the smartest person I know. I know that you wouldn't make any decisions without having some kind of reason behind them. I trust you."

They look into each other's eyes and smile. "Thank you, Grace." She pulls him in for an awkward yet much needed hug.

They spend the rest of the day in his room, catching up on all of his excursions for the past few months. Grace accompanies him while he writes an algorithm that will just turn the subject into a ball of hot plasma post-teleportation. She listens attentively as he tells her about how he's been learning to fight and shoot guns like an action hero.

Chapter Thirty

July 24th, 2020

Friday

The next afternoon, Sarah gives Vincent a death glare from across the lab. He writes on the board throughout the morning, pretending to be entranced by the math. The morning was a little strange, however, as he felt Mavis's negative attitude toward the rest of the shop spilling over to him as well. After working through lunch, he comes to have a "miraculous breakthrough."

"Guys, I think I got it."

Mavis approaches, reads over the board, and shrugs. "You think this is it?"

He replaces the cap on his marker and steps back to admire his work. "No… I know it is." Sarah rolls her eyes. Mavis tries to have the rest of the lab check his work, but it's so far above everybody else's heads that they just smile, nod, and agree.

"Splendid. As long as you're confident, Vincent, we can go ahead and schedule our next test for Monday." She smiles at him, then dismisses everybody for the day.

Vincent packs up and leaves as quickly as possible. He takes the first elevator down to the west wing entrance and sees Sarah hurrying to catch the same elevator, but he lets the door close in front of her. As he gets out, he tries to hide in the cafeteria, but Sarah eventually finds him in the Quiet Room. Taking a seat across from him, she says nothing.

"What do you want?" Vincent finally asks.

"I'm proud of you."

"Okay." He shrugs and watches the bowl of macaroni and cheese that he hastily picked up from the food carts.

"I just wanted to say thank you. For telling her the truth."

"Well, you did." It pains him to shut her out like this, but he can't have her asking more questions. She frowns at him, then quietly leaves.

THAT NIGHT, Vincent dons his usual black hoodie and sneaks behind his barracks building. He waits around the corner nearest to the front gate, but when Tzofiya passes by him to "check on the cameras," she doesn't ignore him. Instead, she stops in front of him.

Her heavily accented voice is louder than usual, "Doing midnight jog instead of going to party?"

Vincent stammers, "Uh… um… y-yeah?"

"You exercise too much. Today, you should go to party," she says curtly before turning on her heel and returning to her booth.

Vincent looks around, confused. *Do I… I guess I should go back to my room? Trent's going to freak though when I don't show up.* He returns to his room to change back into his regular clothes. *Let me just call and tell him that Tzofiya is keeping me here.* He pulls out his phone and dials Trent's number, but an automated voice immediately answers, "We're sorry. The number you are trying to reach is unavailable. Goodbye." Perplexed, Vincent tries a few more times to no avail, then looks out his window to see if he can find Trent's truck off in the distance somewhere. Nothing. *This is weird. This isn't good. Should I go to the party?* Leaving his barracks for the admin building, he notices Malkovich is standing watch outside the doors. *Strange, Malkovich doesn't usually work Fridays.*

Another guard who doesn't usually work Fridays is manning the checkpoint as Vincent walks through the metal detector. *What's going on?* He gets into an elevator and takes the long trip down into the Abaddon. The beat of the music vibrates the elevator floor as he descends. It's been months since he's been to one of these parties. He exits to the characteristic roaring party in the atrium, but he notices Murphy keeping watch alongside Ashley, Miller, Jones, and a slew of other B-team guards that don't usually supervise the party. *Martinez must be pretty busy if he's having Murphy work the party.* Through the crowd, Vincent sees his friends dancing and laughing, but he reverts to being a wallflower in the background. *What could Martinez be doing? Why did Tzofiya want me to see this instead of leaving base?*

Then it hits him. Vincent's jaw drops. *Martinez's patrol. They found the camp. Fuck… fuck, fuck, fuck. What do I do? Do I do anything?* He looks around the atrium for some kind of inspiration as to what he should do. Realizing that Grace comes down here every Friday night, he sighs and detaches from the wall, then begins pushing toward the center of the crowd.

The thumping of the beat presses in on him as he pushes through, and people fight back as he slides in between sweaty bodies and drunken coworkers. Everybody's rhythm pulses into him, along with elbows and knees bruising him all over. Surprisingly, he finds it easier to push through the crowd after having spent a few months in the gym. On the other hand, every little irritant, every sensation, every drip of sweat, and each brush against his skin still feels overwhelming. His skin starts to itch as he pushes further. Suddenly, being shoved into a group of girls on his right, he nearly trips, stumbles into someone, and spills their drink. He recognizes the person as Riley from the invisibility project. In a drunken stupor, Riley throws a punch in Vincent's direction, but with his mind in overdrive, Vincent's instincts take over, and he reacts in kind, bringing Riley down to the floor.

The party-goers take this as an invitation to start a mosh, but Vincent can sense another episode sneaking its way in and thinks to himself, *Why did I think this was a good idea?* He climbs atop those around him and gasps a deep breath of air as he stares up into the tree-covered night sky. Getting a chance to breathe, he looks around to find a red-haired Sarah dancing next to Grace. Swimming in their direction, he gets pulled every which way until finally arriving at his stop.

"GRACE!"

Grace's glazed over eyes see him and smile. "Hey! "Wait. Aren't you supposed to be at—"

"Shh!" He covers her mouth, afraid others will hear her over the pounding music. "We have a problem."

"You're damn right we do!" She passes him a beer. "You're not drunk!"

He ignores her and shouts, "We need to get out of—"

"Vince!" Sarah shouts. *Oh no…* "Vince! Vinaaaaay! What are you doing down here?!"

They're too drunk… Even if I could get them out of here, they won't be of much use. "Leaving!"

Turning away from them is no task, and they forget about him the moment he leaves. Fighting his way to the nearest wall, he skirts the edges until he can get inside one of the elevators to return to the surface. As he passes through the checkpoint again to leave the building, his ears are still ringing in the quiet desert night. That's when he sees a truck drive through the gate. When it parks, Bartram and Martinez jump out of the cab while Cesar and Dolly hop out of the bed. They all rush to the back seat of the cab to help a fourth person out; Vincent recognizes her as Peterson, one of Martinez's most trusted soldiers after Little had passed away.

"Malkovich!" Bartram's booming voice shouts. "Get help! We found Peterson!"

"Peterson, did you see how many there were?" Martinez asks as he applies pressure to a bloody bandage around her ribcage.

"N-No…" Her voice is weak. "They… Bell, Shaw, Laurier… they killed them."

"I know, Peterson. I know."

"No, you don't get it. They were… they were terrifying." She coughs, and a gush of blood spurts from her wound. "Nothing… nothing worked. They were always one step ahead…"

"Not always, Peterson. We got one of them. We're gonna get some answers, I promise."

Bolting out of the admin building, Mavis carries a box of medical supplies to the truck and begins triage on her wounds. Martinez steps back to give her some space, then kneels down to pet Dolly.

"Good girl, Dolly!" He looks up at Cesar to say, "For real man, thank you. She would have died out there if you guys couldn't track her down."

I… should… go… Vincent starts scurrying away, but is stopped dead in his tracks.

"Hey, Creighton!" Martinez shouts. Vincent gasps before turning around and seeing Mavis whisper in Martinez's ear. *Oh no.* Martinez jogs over to him, his uniform soaked with blood all over. "I know that was kind of a crazy thing for you to see, but would you mind using some discretion before you talk about it with others? If Peterson pulls through this, I don't want her to wake up to a handful of rumors about how she nearly died."

"Oh, yeah. Sure. Lips are sealed."

"Thanks, if you need to go talk to Delilah, feel free. You know, keep your mind healthy and whatnot. Thanks bud." He makes to leave, but stops and turns back around. "By the way, have you seen any suspicious vehicles around lately? There's been some—well—security concerns."

"Uh…" Vincent hesitates. "N-No. Never. I've never seen any trucks or anything driving around here." Heart pounding out of his chest, he stands stone-still. "D-Did… did I hear you say that you, uh, you got one of them?"

Martinez raises an eyebrow and shuffles before answering, "You heard me say that, huh? Yeah, we, uh, we caught one of the bastards after the skirmish. But don't worry, they were turned over to the authorities immediately." *You lying son of a bitch.* "Anyway, I gotta get back. Let us know if you see or hear anything." He returns to help out with the scene, leaving Vincent to book it for his barracks where he watches attentively through his window. Martinez and Cesar clean up briskly before disappearing into the armory service elevator.

Back against the wall, he slides to the floor and buries his face in his knees. *I'm dead. They attacked the camp and took one of them prisoner. What if they find out I've been visiting them? Who'd they get? Leo wouldn't break. Neither would Trent. Dallyn's loyalty lies with Dr. Smith... Becca and Bobby, though? What if Bartram makes them a better offer? I just have to lay low until... until when? Just get through the next test and... hope for the best.*

Chapter Thirty-One

July 27th, 2020

Monday

Testing day number two. Mavis addresses the team before they leave for the atrium. "Good morning, ladies and gentlemen. In light of our previous test's unfortunate failure, we are going to cut down on the number of attendees allowed inside the testing facility. Only myself, Vincent, Sarah, Grace, Kevin, security, and management will be observing. The rest of you can take an early day. We'll reconvene tomorrow, assess the results, and discuss our path moving forward."

Mavis leads everyone to the north wing entrance where they meet with Dr. Smith, Bartram, and Martinez. Vincent glowers at Bartram as they approach. *Who the fuck did you kidnap?* Bartram's boisterous voice bellows out, "Dr. Blackwell! Is everything prepared for today's live subject test?"

"Affirmative, sir. The computer is up to speed, and Dr. Creighton has assured me of his confidence in his new algorithm, so we are good to go."

Vincent's eyes widen. "Wait, did you say 'live subject'?"

Mavis turns and gives him a wicked grin. "Yes. Your confidence was inspiring to me, so I figured there's no reason to delay any further. Sergeant Martinez will meet us there with the volunteer after we get the equipment set up."

"Right." Vincent begins to sweat and makes eye contact with Grace, who appears just as worried.

During the subway trip up to the testing facility, Grace makes a point of sitting right next to Vincent. In a hushed tone, she whispers to him as subtly as possible, "We have to tell them. A living person will die if we let them follow through with this experiment."

"Relax, experiments like this are usually done with just a mouse or rabbit. Probably another cat if Mavis had anything to say about it. Let me find out." Vincent finds an empty seat next to Mavis.

"So did you get a regular old Algernon for the test, or did you spring for a cat?" He gives a fake laugh but receives nothing in return.

"Neither, actually," she says coyly. "Considering our work is designed for human anatomy, we are going to use a human subject."

"A human?" Vincent's voice cracks. *Oh, no… they wouldn't waste a valuable prisoner on a test, would they?*

"Don't worry." She shoots him a knowing look. "The man is pure evil. He's a convicted mass murderer. He forfeited his life when he shot up a hospital, killing over a dozen people using military grade weapons. A real psycho. We 'rescued' him from death row a while back and have been using him as a guinea pig for different experiments." Vincent watches the floor, trying to maintain his cool. "It's okay, Vince! Don't be nervous about your algorithm. I would trust nobody else with the task."

He looks at her from behind frozen eyes. "Uh-huh."

Moving back to his seat next to Grace, he tells her about the human subject and says, "We can't go through with this. We specifically took this job to keep shit like this from happening."

"It's too late though." Vincent's voice is grim. "We can't tell them it's a fake algorithm. They'll know we lied and ask questions that I don't want to answer." Grace scowls, but he continues, "If Bartram finds out, he'll kill us."

"So what do we do? Trade this jerk's life for our own?"

"Yes." He looks at her sternly. "Our lives and the lives of the hundreds of scientists who are trapped here with us."

Grace doesn't say anything after that. When they arrive at the testing facility, Bartram scans his ID to let them through the doors. An hour later, all the equipment is set up, and the test is ready. Vincent hides out in the observation room while Grace and Kevin do most of the legwork with the computer and teleportation pad, then Sarah enters the room.

"This is exciting!" she tells him enthusiastically. "I think they're jumping the gun a bit, bringing in a live subject, but the sooner we get this tested, the sooner my mom might get the treatment she needs."

With guilt eating away at him, Vincent has very little to say, "Yeah. Exciting." As everyone files into the observation room, they see the subway car pull up. Martinez exits the car holding a chain, attached to which walks an emaciated man wearing handcuffs, an orange jumpsuit, and a large, bushy, brown moustache. Vincent sees him through the observation room window and can't believe what his eyes are showing him. It's Leo. But he looks to be at least twenty years younger than when he last saw him, and he appears to have some kind of tattoo on his neck. He looks at Grace, who is on the verge of tears.

Oh God. His lips part as if to say something but fails. *Leo...* He looks around the room to see Mavis watching him studiously. Examining Leo further, he realizes something doesn't add up. *Why would she reverse his age? And... why is he so skinny? He wasn't that skinny last weekend.*

"Are you alright, Dr. Creighton?" Mavis asks.

Vincent takes a beat before whispering, "No." Bartram's attention snaps to him, then he and Mavis stare intently as Vincent's posture strengthens.

"You're not alright, Vincent?" Mavis asks.

"No. Let him go."

"Let who go?"

"Let... the prisoner... go." As he utters the words, Mavis and Bartram exchange interested glances.

"Go where? He's got nowhere else to go... no home, no one to call a friend... or does he?" She cocks her head to better see Vincent's wince.

Sarah's voice pops up, "Who is this guy? Why is he wearing cuffs?" She then looks to see Grace's stoic countenance.

"Let him go, Mavis," Vincent repeats.

"Why would I let him go? You're so confident that your algorithm is going to work; nothing bad can possibly happen to him, right?" She presses a button on the master computer, and the glass chamber door opens. Martinez drags Leo across the room and shoves him inside. Leo looks around the chamber, scared and confused. "Or… is there something we should know?"

"We're not doing the test, Mavis."

"Yes, Vincent. We are."

Martinez enters the room and senses the confrontation. "What's going on here?"

"Vincent is having second thoughts about testing his algorithm on this particular subject."

Martinez scoffs. "Don't worry, Vince. The dude was a mass murdering sicko."

"Exactly," Mavis continues. "He's a criminal, Vincent. You don't care about a violent criminal like him, do you?" *It's not him. It can't be him. If that's really him, why would she reverse his age?* "Do you, Vincent?" she asks again.

Vincent looks at Bartram, then at Leo. *I can't do this… I can't show my cards.* He softens his face and quietly submits. "No. I don't care about him."

Bartram says, "On the other hand, Dr. Creighton, we'd prefer not to waste precious resources—especially biological resources—on experiments we know are going to fail. Your algorithm won't fail, will it?"

Needing to crane his neck up to meet Bartram's eyes, Vincent steels himself. "Not to my knowledge, Colonel."

"Well, good!" Mavis says cheerily. "Would you like to do the honors?" She presents the keyboard of the master computer to him.

He takes a deep breath, and his hand hovers over the keyboard, eyes glued to the teleportation chamber. The scared man inside looks all around the chamber until his eyes fall on Vincent, whose throat tightens.

Vincent shuts his eyes and swallows. As he opens his eyes again, a tear sheds down his cheek, and he presses the "Enter" key.

As the quantum computer begins humming, numbers and symbols scroll across the screen, and Leo looks down at the teleportation pad below his feet. He looks back to the observation room while yelling *"No!"* over and over again and punching the glass walls. As his punching gets weaker and weaker, Leo backs up and doubles over as if he is about to vomit. When he stumbles to the ground, his body almost appears to be absorbed by the teleportation pad and disappears. Next to the chamber, a stream of plasma-like sludge begins to materialize and drip through the grated floor and splatters against the concrete floor a hundred feet below them. Sarah screams and backs into the wall behind her. Grace is horrified, but tries to comfort her while Kevin regurgitates his breakfast in the corner.

"Dr. Creighton," Bartram sighs while addressing him. "I'd like to have a word with you in my office." He gestures to Martinez, who grabs Vincent by the arm and leads him to the subway car at Bartram's side. Dr. Smith catches Vincent's eye as they leave and nods confidently at him.

AFTER BEING LED PAST BARTRAM'S OFFICE WINDOW overlooking the atrium, Vincent is dragged through a labyrinth of halls and corridors before being shoved into a small, concrete room with only two chairs that sit on either side of a metal table. The chamber feels like that of a police interrogation room, yet somehow less welcoming. Martinez locks the door behind him, leaving Vincent alone in the chamber.

He stumbles into one of the chairs and lets his head fall into his hands. *I killed him. I… I killed Leo.* His eyes are shut tightly as he grips his greasy black hair between his fingers. *I shouldn't have done it… I should have just given them the real algorithm; Leo would still be alive and… and… and then they'd be able to sell it… and ultimately cause damage on a global scale…*

Pounding the table, he lets out a loud cry that echoes off the walls and pierces his own ears until he finds himself looking down at his own clenched fists through teary eyes and a heaving chest. As Bartram opens the door, Vincent swallows hard and quickly wipes his face clean before straightening his back to right himself. Bartram puffs his chest out and approaches the table, then he looks down his nose at Vincent. Removing his blues uniform coat and draping it over the back of the opposite chair, he unbuttons the wrist cuffs on his long-sleeved shirt, rolls them up, then takes a seat.

Bartram calmly leans his elbows on the table and interlaces his fingers. He stares curiously past the glare in Vincent's glasses and into his furious eyes. Taking deep, choppy breaths, Vincent fails to wipe the snarl off of his face, and Bartram watches him try to repress the anger for several minutes before breaking the silence.

"I'm sorry about what happened to your friend, Dr. Creighton."

Vincent winces slightly. "I… I don't know what you're talking about. I had never seen that man before in my life."

Bartram laughs. "Of course not. You're just a kind soul who gets upset at mass murderers getting their just desserts. Don't worry, though, that's not what we're here to discuss." Vincent doesn't look at him, so he continues, "We're here to talk about the future of your career."

"My career?"

"Correct. I've been keeping tabs on you. You've done great things in the short time that you've spent here; the teleportation project has been pushed forward by leaps and bounds, and Dr. Blackwell has told me about the potential you possess in this lab." Bartram shifts in his chair. "There is only one problem, Dr. Creighton."

Vincent looks over the frames of his glasses. "What problem is that?"

"I don't tolerate dishonesty." Vincent holds back a scoff at the irony. "I need to trust my employees. I need to know that the scientists working in my labs won't waste my time by withholding major discoveries. If you and I can't be honest about the research you're doing, then I'm afraid there isn't a future for you here in the Abaddon."

"What would I possibly lie to you about? I want to do good just like everyone else here."

"See, I don't think you're interested in the 'good' that you can do; you aren't an altruist. I think your eyes are set more on the legacy—the satisfaction of seeing your discoveries come to life. Isn't that right?"

"Isn't that what all scientists want? To be the greatest minds of their generation?"

"Maybe some people, but with you, it's a possibility. You might actually *be* the greatest mind of your generation. Unfortunately, nobody will know it unless you *work with me*. You understand this, don't you, Dr. Creighton?"

Vincent doesn't respond, he simply stares Bartram down while hunched over in his chair with his hands limp in his lap.

"Of course, you do! You're a smart kid! So why would you lie to me about your research? Why would you halt the advancement of this project? I just don't understand it—could you help me see your point of view?" Bartram leans in sarcastically as if to hear better, but Vincent just continues to stare him down. "Fair enough. If I was involved in a rogue, terrorist organization, I wouldn't talk either."

"Terrorist organization? What are you talking about?"

"That man wasn't just a criminal; he was a known terrorist. You can deny your affiliation with him all you'd like, but you just refused to perform an experiment on a volunteer upon identification of who they were. You then proceeded to have an *emotional* reaction *prior* to the experiment occurring—suggesting two things to me. One: you knew the man. And two: you were aware that the experiment would fail. How did you know the experiment would fail, Dr. Creighton?"

Vincent remains stark silent, breathing heavily to calm himself down.

"The Fifth Amendment won't help you here. You gave us an algorithm that wouldn't work but would cause minimal damage. You have the real algorithm, Dr. Creighton."

Vincent perks his ears up. "Why won't it?"

"He speaks!"

"Cut the shit! You said the Fifth Amendment won't help me here; why not? You claim that I'm involved in criminal activity, so wouldn't the Constitution grant me the right to freedom from self-incrimination? This *is* U.S. soil, isn't it? The Constitution *does* apply here, right?"

Colonel Bartram smiles. "Ah. So you know then?"

"Know what?"

Bartram smirks. "Well, if you won't show your cards, I will. I want you to work for me. Not just as a staff member, not just as a project supervisor, I want you by my side, Vincent."

Vincent scoffs. "You want me to work for you? By your side? Like, in Dr. Smith's role? You can't be serious."

"Dead serious. But not in Dr. Smith's role. That one's all his. I want you to be the mastermind behind every project we have. Think about it, Vincent; you know what we do here! We make massive strides in scientific research and sell them to the world to secure our spot as gods among men! Don't pretend that that doesn't speak to you! Vincent, with a mind like yours driving the Abaddon's engine, there is nothing we can't accomplish."

"You only make those strides by exploiting your staff and working them into their graves! At the first sign of dissent or laziness, you go straight to murder!"

"The world runs on exploitation, Vincent. If we're not benefiting from it, someone else is. This way, we get to control the production line and do it *our* way."

"Your way gets people killed. A lot."

"Death is a part of life, Vincent. Only the strong, only those willing to kill will be able to conquer it. Be my Azrael, Vincent. Be my own personal Angel of Death." Vincent doesn't say anything, instead he just looks at the table in contemplation. "Oppenheimer quoted the Gita when he said, 'Now I am become Death, Destroyer of Worlds.' But he was wrong, Vincent. Death doesn't destroy worlds. It's just part of the cycle."

Their eyes finally find each other on equal terms. Vincent suddenly finds himself back in the elementary school bathroom with his feet against the stall door. *We found you, pussy! Come on ouuuuut!* He remembers being left alone in that flooded bathroom as though it was still happening; he's had many moments of humiliation and shame, but one memory stands above it all: Sarah's green eyes looking up at him in the Marysworth parking lot.

"So is life. And I'd rather protect life than use death as a weapon."

"All life? Or… just the one?"

Vincent furrows his brow. "What do you mean?"

The interrogation room door opens, and Sergeant Martinez walks in to hand a Manila folder to Colonel Bartram. "Thank you, Sergeant, I'll call if we need you again." Martinez leaves, and Bartram opens the folder and drops it on the table for the contents to spill out. Vincent rifles through a few photographs, medical records, and doctors' notes that he doesn't recognize until he sees the patient's name atop every document: Fiona Boyce. *Oh no…*

"Your friend, Sarah, came here under very noble pretenses. Her mother's brain cancer is terminal, and they're just waiting for her to croak. Dr. Boyce decided to sacrifice what little remaining time she has left with her mother to hopefully create a way to cure cancer. Selfless."

A pit opens in Vincent's stomach. With his heart beating lead through his veins, he looks into Bartram's bright, azure eyes. His lips part to speak, but nothing comes out of his mouth for several seconds until he mumbles incoherent syllables. "W-why are y-you showing m-me these?"

"Like I said, you're not an altruist. Don't pretend to care about the good of all mankind. You love Sarah, and you want to help her mom. Fair enough. I propose a trade: you give us the correct algorithm—*become* the Grim Reaper… and Dr. Boyce's mother will survive, continuing to fight her losing battle against cancer. Keep the algorithm for yourself, and she will accidentally overdose on a few choice medications."

Vincent looks at the photographs of Sarah's mom, unsure of whether he really cares about her life or Sarah's happiness… or his own selfish desires to call Sarah his own. *Regardless of why I want her to live… I discovered this thing. I should see it through to the end.* Vincent looks up at him with a renewed sense of vigor. "That's your trade? Really? You have one piece of leverage over me, and you threaten to get rid of it in favor of a single algorithm?" Vincent straightens his back and looks Bartram dead in the eyes. "You want me. You *need* me to work with you, so can't you do a little better than *'give it to me or else'*?"

Bartram sighs with frustration. "I'm giving you a chance to become something great. A chance to seize the power that you have earned. Don't get too big for your britches now." Vincent holds his gaze, which Bartram returns in kind before resigning with a nod. "Fine. The hard way it is."

He slides his chair out and opens the door. Martinez appears again, standing next to a man in a grey jumpsuit with a cloth bag over his head and his hands and ankles cuffed. Bartram pushes him into the room. Leading the man to the metal table, Bartram punches him in the stomach, causing him to double over, then grabs him by the back of the neck and slams his face on the table. Vincent gasps and slides his chair back. The man lets out a weak groan.

Martinez closes the door behind him as he steps inside, posting up in the corner with his full tactical gear, his hand on the grip of a carbine. Bartram watches Vincent's face intently as he grabs the cloth bag over the man's head and rips it off. Vincent fails to conceal the shock of seeing Bobby's beaten and battered face bleeding on the table in front of him.

Bartram looks at Vincent and casually says, "I'll give you three chances to give me the algorithm." He reaches behind him and pulls out the M1911 pistol he had tucked into his belt, then points it at Bobby's head. "Or you'll have the blood of your girlfriend's mom, your buddy Leo, *and* your friend Bobby on your hands."

Vincent jumps out of his seat and shouts, "No!"

Bartram grins at him smugly. "I don't want to do this, Vincent. But you're forcing my hand. By not giving me the real algorithm, you're sentencing your friends—and your girlfriend's mom—to death."

"No! You can't just execute him like that! I won't let you!" Vincent steps forward, but he stops when Martinez clears his throat to remind him of his presence.

"I hope that's true, Vincent, because it's not Bobby's time to die. According to the report, Fiona also might have a good six more months left in her, but who knows?"

"I'm not trading the algorithm for the life of a human being."

"Three," Bartram says curtly, and Vincent snarls. "Two." Vincent looks Bobby in his swollen-over eyes to see that while his body is in severe pain, not an ounce of fear has infiltrated him. "One." Bartram moves his finger to the trigger and begins to pull.

"Wait!" Vincent shouts. "If I give you the algorithm, what *exactly* will you give me in exchange?"

Through his peripherals, Vincent can see Bobby's face shifting, his brow raising, and his body tensing up. Bartram grins again. "Power."

"The ability to murder isn't power. Controlling death is. Doling it out to those who deserve it *and* protecting the innocent from it… that's power. If I give you the algorithm, we will use it to help Sarah's mom—and others who deserve help. Then we will reunite Sarah's family."

"I can't let her go home. You know that."

"Then you'll have to kill me. Because there is no way I will do any work for you until I know Sarah and her family are safe."

Bartram snarls at him and points the gun at Vincent; his hand is steady, but Vincent can tell that the safety is on. "You need me. The teleportation project is impossible without me." Vincent slides his chair under the table. "And efficiency will skyrocket in the other projects too. We both know how valuable I am. I'll do your work, but under my conditions. I'll never be your lapdog, like Martinez over there."

Vincent carefully steps around Bobby and moves toward the door. Martinez waits for a command from Bartram that never comes. "I'm leaving now. And I don't know who this man on the table is"—Vincent opens the door—"but when you have a job offer ready, have Mavis pass it to me in the lab. Only then will I consider giving you the algorithm."

As Vincent crosses the threshold of the door, Bartram says, "Dr. Creighton." Vincent stops in his tracks. "You just killed this man."

Bobby shouts, "NO! VINCENT, YOU TRAITOROUS SON OF A BI—"

Bartram's pistol lets off a single pop, which electrifies Vincent's spine. Then he hears a thud as Bobby's limp form slides to the concrete floor. Vincent closes the door softly behind him and chokes on his breath. He nearly falls to his shaky knees before the adrenaline kicks in, and he books it for the exit. Walking through Bartram's office, down the staircase, and across the art gallery, he sees Dr. Smith enter the north wing. He comes to a stop in front of Dr. Smith and gasps for breath.

"Woah! Vinny, is everything alright?" Dr. Smith asks.

"Uh, yeah—I just—I don't know," he tries to gather himself.

"It has been a rough day, I understand. But listen, I would like to talk sometime. Catch up with you a bit, what do you say?"

"Y-Yeah…" Vincent nods his head uncontrollably. "That would be great."

"*Wohei.* How does tomorrow sound?" Vincent, still out of breath, nods profusely and tries to leave, but Dr. Smith grabs him by the shoulder. "Listen, you did well today." Vincent squints at him, confused. *I did well? But Leo died! Isn't the secret to the universe less valuable than a single human life?* Dr. Smith nods. "You look hungry. Your friends are waiting for you in the south wing."

Vincent agrees and tries to walk casually through the atrium, looking up through the canopy to where Bartram's office window is set. Still quivering, he goes to the cafeteria and immediately finds Sarah and Grace at a table by themselves, Sarah still distraught over the second failure. Approaching their table, Sarah is the first to see him, and her shock swiftly turns to fury. She power walks over to him and slaps him across the face; Vincent doesn't try dodging out of the way.

Her voice is almost a hiss as she says, "You! What did you do?!" The entire cafeteria falls silent to watch.

His hands are still shaking from hearing Bobby's body slump to the ground. "I-I know. I'm… I'm sorry, can we—"

"Sarah!" Grace gets up to join them. "There's something Vincent needs to tell you. Right now."

The fire in her eyes is unrelenting. "You're goddamn right, there is." She steps off, allowing the cafeteria to again roar with conversation.

It's a long, painfully silent elevator ride back up above ground. As they exit the elevator, Cesar and Dolly are standing watch at the security checkpoint.

"Hey, Creighton," Cesar says abruptly. "How did things go today?"

"Uh…" Vincent rubs the back of his neck. "Not well."

"I'm sorry to hear that. You'll get it next time though."

"Yeah…" Vincent utters as they pass through security and leave. Sarah leads the three of them across to their barracks building, and as they enter Vincent's bedroom, Sarah closes the door and crosses her arms.

"Talk."

CHAPTER THIRTY-TWO

November 20th, 1987

Friday

"Subject two-seven-six: the embryo has remained stable through the sixth week of development. We expect him to be carried to full term. I think I'll name him Xerxes," Dr. Blackwell tells Colonel Bartram while taking notes on a clipboard. They are examining a small cell filled with a green fluid and a nugget of organic tissue about half-an-inch long that's attached to a small tube.

"Incredible work, Mavis," Bartram praises her. "This kind of development is unprecedented!"

"Thank you, sir. It's the result of thousands of man hours of grueling, painstaking research."

"Well, let's get some more samples from the prime subject and get rolling on a cool dozen for observation."

"Will do, sir. You do realize what this means though, right? I'm not sure we'll be able to keep this a secret from Dr. Smith for too much longer."

"I've been thinking about that myself. Don't worry, I'll figure something out. Oh, and uh, tell the prime subject that the samples are for a bioweapon. I want him to think that we're using his DNA to make some kind of mustard gas or something."

She chuckles. "Oh, he'll love that, sir."

Mavis walks through a small bay stacked with shelves upon shelves of fetal development chambers. All of them are wired up with various equipment pumping that same green fluid through a vast network of veins and arteries that seem to feed the cells. She exits the lab and takes an elevator down to the large blue marble staircase that surrounds the library. Exiting the west wing, she crosses the atrium and dodges hordes of party-preppers to admire several young redwood trees beginning to climb up the walls of a domed roof.

Inside the cafeteria, she sees one of the newer security hires that she recommended to Bartram. "Sergeant Carlisle! Follow me; I want you to see something."

Trent follows her into the north wing, through the cathedral foyer of Bartram's office, and past the grand piano next to a circular seating arrangement in his living room. She always loves coming here; the view of the atrium is busy but beautiful, and she's enjoyed watching the redwoods grow. But now is not the time for sentimentality. Now is the time for work.

She leads him into a small office and wheels out a cart of medical equipment, and they take Bartram's service elevator to the lower levels. The door opens to the low-hanging ceiling of an unfinished blue marble corridor lined with tiny, barred prison cells, several of which are populated with emaciated husks of people chained to the wall. A horrific stench emanates from the cells, making Trent gag almost immediately. The corridor ends in a simple, wooden interior door.

"Where are we?" Trent asks.

"This is the holding facility where we hold our test subjects. I know it looks grotesque, but it's a necessary part of the job. You remember Airman Declan?"

"Wasn't he the guy who got '*reassigned*'?"

"I brought him down here for the first time a few months ago, and his stomach was as steady as it needed to be. A few weeks later, however, he decided to come down here in an attempt to *rescue* one of the prisoners. Bartram had to… well… fire him.

His jaw slightly agape, Trent says, "Oh… Understood."

At the end of the hall, Trent opens the door to let Mavis push the cart through. A glass wall separates the room into two parts. Trent and Mavis find themselves in some kind of observation room and looking in on a cramped cell with flickering, fluorescent lights, white walls, a white floor, and a white ceiling. A skinny man wearing a white jumpsuit sits upon a bed with white sheets; he's kneeling and doing breathing exercises. Trent gathers that they must be looking through a one-way mirror.

"Is he meditating?"

"He says that it 'keeps the demons at bay,' but the hallucinations are inescapable."

"Hallucinations? Do you pump him with LSD or something?"

"Better. The White Room depletes nearly all sensory input for him. He survives on a diet of white rice and water, the walls are soundproof, and those flickering lights hum constantly which practically guarantees he never sleeps restfully. After a while, the brain starts hallucinating on its own."

"Jesus Christ…"

"Pretty cool, right? Let me do the talking, Trent." She presses down on an intercom and briskly says, "Get up, Sideris, I need a sample for a bioweapon test."

Leo jumps out of his trance, which Mavis gets a kick out of. "A bioweapon? What kind of bioweapon?!" Leo's mannerisms are twitchy, but he seems to be actively trying to keep that twitchiness under control.

"We think we found a compound that reacts with your blood in a way that could be toxic to others. Just get over here." She prepares a syringe with a glass vial and opens a small window for him to slide his arm through.

"No, thank you."

"You really want to play it that way?" she asks threateningly.

"Why not?" Leo cracks his knuckles. "You sending a couple of goons in here to subdue me? I've been itching for a fight!"

"No need for that, we actually just completed a project I think you might like."

"A project, huh? What is it?!"

"I'd rather just show you." Closing the window, she moves to a panel on the wall that resembles an automated teller machine. She presses a few buttons, then a hissing sound in the ceiling prompts Leo to look at one of the air vents. He notices white smoke filtering into the room.

Hiding panic in his voice, he asks, "What is that?"

"You've heard of CS gas, right? We gave it a younger, meaner brother. This guy attacks the central nervous *and* the respiratory systems simultaneously. So not only will you stop breathing, but you'll also lose the ability to struggle."

"If you're trying to scare me into giving you a sample, just stop."

Mavis watches him interestedly as the gas slowly permeates the room while Leo cautiously eyes the mirror. Trent eyes Mavis from his peripheral vision. Leo knows the gas reaches him when his sinuses are invaded by an intense burning sensation that runs down his throat. His eyes, nose, and lungs begin seizing up and expelling every fluid they can produce to keep the gas from getting in. Falling out of his bed, Leo coughs, cries, wheezes, spits, and vomits until he lies still, prostrating on the tiled floor.

"Aaaand the paralysis should be kicking in… now."

The back of his head feels as though it has caught fire, splitting from his skull all the way down his spinal cord. Every square centimeter of his head, inside and out, tries to rip itself away from the sinking ship of his body, but the more he fights, the less his limbs respond to his brain's commands. Then finally, sweet release comes when Mavis presses another button on the panel to stop the gas from filling the room. Another button vacuums out the gas and replaces it with fresh, clean air. She enters a code into the panel, revealing a door in the glass, and gathers her equipment.

Opening the door, she kneels over his body. "You have this to look forward to each time you fight us for a test. Carlisle, get in here." Trent tentatively steps inside and stands behind her. "Take this. We need to get a sample from right here." She hands him the syringe and points to a vein that is protruding from Leo's arm. Trent steadies his shaking hand and plunges the large needle into the target area. Leo's bloodshot and teary eyes are unable to react when his blood is crudely drawn. As they finish up their work and leave, Mavis closes the glass door behind them and seals the White Room back up.

"Are we just leaving him like that? Doesn't he need medical attention?" Trent asks frantically.

"Oh, don't worry. The paralysis only lasts for a couple hours." Trent stands frozen at the glass wall, mouth agape. As Mavis leaves, she beckons for him to follow her. Trent just stares down at Leo's agonizing face, body slumped to one side and eyes looking to the mirrored wall.

"Carlisle!" Mavis calls him one last time, prompting him to break eye contact and run after her.

CHAPTER THIRTY-THREE

July 27th, 2020

Monday

"Talk." Sarah's arms are crossed as she stands in front of the closed door.

Vincent stands at his window and tries to center himself, but his body is still trembling. He looks out of his window, staring out across the desert, and sighs. "Do you remember our last night at the Ducky Luck?" She nods impatiently. "Well, I met a man named Leo at the bar that night. He helped me order a drink and said a lot of nice things to me. Things that made sense and made me feel good. He made me feel confident. Confident enough to stand up to that reporter at the press conference." He sits at the foot of his bed and starts rubbing his eyes from under his glasses. "The night after the conference, I met another guy who said he wanted me to meet his friends and gave me his phone number. Just in case I… well… in case I needed some new friends."

"Some *new friends*?" Sarah asks angrily. "Were you planning on abandoning your old, used up friends?"

"I mean I wasn't *planning* on anything!" Vincent snaps at her but reels himself back. "But… it felt nice to have someone *want* to be friends with me rather than, I don't know, having to *deal* with me."

"Do you not understand how hurtful that is to me, Vince?" Sarah asks. "I have been so patient with you and put so much time and effort into being your friend! Your BEST friend, might I add!"

"I know! I know exactly how hard it is to be friends with me! I always feel so guilty for making you TRY to be friends with me!" His voice cracks. "It was so easy with Leo… He understood what it was like to be in my head without trying. Without the constant trial and error. Without the maze of social customs and having to figure out what I'm supposed to say in a given situation."

Sarah frowns as her throat closes up. "I… I didn't know I made you feel that way, Vince."

He looks at her and realizes that he just hurt her feelings. "See, this is what I mean. Just saying how I feel hurts others. You feel sad right now because of *how I feel,* and that's not fair. To you or me. But with Leo, everything I said was validated. He understood me…" None of them speak for a while, then Grace breaks the silence.

"Go on, Vincent."

Vincent nods. "So… when we got here, the project was going great. Mavis and I were making a ton of progress while you guys were making a bunch of new friends and having a good time." He fails to notice both of them inhale sharply. "And eventually, Dr. Smith wanted to meet with me, so we did. But… he told me something that I didn't want to believe at first. Then I checked it out, and he was right."

"What did he tell you?" Sarah asks.

Vincent stands and lowers his voice, "He said that Bartram and the guards aren't military. That the Abaddon isn't even a DARPA lab."

"What? That's crazy. That doesn't even make sense," Sarah says, rolling her eyes.

Grace says, "Think about it, Sarah. Think about all of the weird stuff they do here."

"No way. We signed those papers that Colonel Bartram gave us, and… I mean, look at this place! How would this place even exist if the government wasn't funding it?"

"They sell the tech that we make for them." Vincent keeps his voice low. "I went snooping around Bartram's office and found one of his records rooms. It had financial documents from a bunch of shady companies and foreign governments. They also have entire files on every individual who works here—*'Emotional vulnerabilities'* they call it. Once we've proven our worth to Bartram, he moves us downstairs and blackmails us into working for him."

She crosses her arms and looks from Vincent to Grace and back. "You are kidding, right? You can't expect me to believe that all of my coworkers—Brian included—are only working here because they're being blackmailed… and that they've all been *lying* to me about it this whole time!"

"You don't have to believe me. It's the truth. You can ask Brian yourself; they have his mom: Lorraine Reid. She works from home—at 153 Shadowmare Court, Ashford, Oregon—as a small business consultant and has a history of cardiovascular disease and arrhythmia."

Sarah looks at him in horror. "How do you know all that, Vince?"

"I read it. All of it; it's all there in his file."

"Woah, woah, woah, you're fucking serious right now, aren't you?" Sarah shakes her head and paces around the room. "Is that why you withheld the algorithm from Mavis? Because Smith told you not to give it to them?"

Vincent blushes. "No, Smith didn't tell me to do anything, but he does know I've been working with Trent. Sarah, teleportation is a powerful tool. In the wrong hands, it can be more dangerous than any nuclear bomb."

"Don't you dare talk to me about what this technology could do! I staked my mom's life on this project!"

"I know you did, and ever since you told me that, my number one priority has been getting your mom the treatment that she needs."

"You've been sitting on the correct algorithm for months! How could *withholding* that knowledge be *helping* the cause?!"

Grace cuts in, "Knowing what you know now—what Vincent has known for months—would you trust Colonel Bartram with that algorithm?"

Sarah huffs. "I don't know… no! But what was it you were trying to figure out this whole time?"

Vincent sighs. "Well… knowing about your mom, the right way forward has been hazy. I couldn't trust Bartram with my algorithm, but I couldn't just let the project die because then you might lose your mom unnecessarily." Vincent looks at his feet as talks. "Leo, Trent, and everyone—we had a plan."

"What kind of plan?"

"A coup. We were going to dethrone Bartram and have Dr. Smith take over. Free all of the scientists and take this operation above board. But… I was being selfish."

"You? Selfish? Never." Sarah laughs sarcastically.

"Hey, I know you're mad at me, but I was trying to save *your* mom!"

"Did you never think to loop *me* in on this? Maybe *I* would have some opinions about how to move forward with my own mother's treatment? Did that ever even occur to you?"

"Of course, it did! I wanted to tell you so bad, but I couldn't risk you knowing about everything. If Bartram found out you knew any of this and didn't report it, he'd have your head."

Sarah looks away from him and paces around the room. "Okay. So what? You've been buying time—time that my mom doesn't have, I might add—until Grace got the computer up to speed, then what? You gave them a fake algorithm?"

"Yeah."

"Knowing full well it could kill someone if they tested it on a human?"

"Hey," Grace cuts in again. "Don't get mad at him for it. That was my idea."

"We didn't know they'd test it on a human!" Vincent stands up. "They only did that to test me. They recently raided Leo's camp and… they took prisoners."

"Wait, really?" Grace says in shock. "Who'd they take?"

"That's kind of the thing. That 'volunteer' was Leo. It was a younger version of him—oh, Mavis has anti-aging technology, by the way. She's been keeping Bartram, herself, and probably Dr. Smith young for a long time."

"She has what now?"

"An anti-aging serum, but that's not important. What's important is"—Grace and Sarah look at each other in shock but shrug it off—"that volunteer was Leo. I assume that she de-aged him for some reason, but it was definitely him. They used him as the test subject to see if I would react to his presence."

"And you did."

"Yeah. When Bartram took me away, he brought me into this interrogation room in his office, and… and a lot happened. He asked me to work for him. But when I refused, he showed me pictures and medical files of your mom."

"What?! Are you serious? He knows about her?"

"Sarah," Grace says, "that's what he's been saying. They know everything, especially how to manipulate you."

Vincent continues, "He said… if I don't give him the algorithm, then he's going to kill your mom."

"Oh my God…" Sarah clasps her hands over her mouth and backs up against Karl's old bed. "Did you give it to him?"

Vincent looks off for a second. "No." Sarah nearly bursts out in tears, but Vincent tries to reassure her, "He won't do it though. He knows that I won't cooperate if he hurts your mom. So… he brought in another prisoner."

"Who?"

"It was Bobby. He was part of our team."

"Did they take more than one prisoner?"

"Apparently. I only heard Martinez mention one, but they must have taken them both, because it was definitely him. Bartram put a gun to his head and told me to give the algorithm over."

Grace's jaw drops as he recounts the event. "What did you do?"

"I told him I won't work with him unless I know Sarah and her family are safe and brought back together. He said he couldn't let that happen, but…"

"But what?!"

"But I wasn't willing to budge. I told him my demands, then I walked away."

"*You walked away?!*"

"Yeah. He knows what I want; I told him if he wants me to work for him, then he needs to have Mavis give me a job offer in the lab."

"What happened to Bobby when you walked away?"

Vincent shuts his eyes and swallows hard, "I told him that I didn't know who Bobby was, so… he shot him."

The air goes still. Sarah and Grace have no idea what to say; Sarah simply stands up, walks over to him, and wraps her arms around him. Vincent's stomach erupts with a hurricane of feelings, though he isn't quite sure what most of them are. Sarah whispers in his ear, "Thank you for standing up for me."

Grace gives them a moment to themselves, but eventually joins in the hug. "I'm sorry you had to go through that, Vince."

"Thanks." Vincent pulls away from the hug and looks out the window. "But now what?"

"Are you really going to work for him?" Grace asks.

"What other option do I have? Bobby and Leo are dead. We were already short stacked on manning, so I don't see how we could continue with half of our people missing. Even if we could, their phones are dead. I have no way to reach them."

"Can we talk to Dr. Smith?" Sarah asks. "He might know what to do or have some other way to contact them."

"No, he's constantly being monitored. I mean, I have a meeting with him tomorrow because he wants to discuss the experiment, but we can't get any messages sent back and forth. He was relying on me for contact with them, but… I haven't told him anything…" His head falls into his hands. "God, I'm such an idiot…"

Sarah stands next to him. "No, you're not. You're… selfish… but you're not an idiot. If anything, you're too smart for your own good." This makes him smile for the first time in several hours. Grace joins them in watching the Fort Chivington grounds, and Sarah says, "I don't know what comes next, but… from now on, we're in it together, right?"

Grace looks at Vincent and smiles, "Equal partners?"

Vincent grins, "Yeah, equal."

CHAPTER THIRTY-FOUR

Tuesday

Knocking at Dr. Smith's door, Vincent is relieved to see him answer immediately. Dr. Smith is dressed in his usual fine leisure suit and invites him in. They enjoy a nice cup of tea in the circular living room that overlooks Paris from the top of the Eiffel Tower.

Dr. Smith begins with, "Yesterday's incident was quite… unexpected, yes?"

"Yeah, it was something."

"How did your meeting with Colonel Bartram turn out?"

Vincent's eyes fall. "Um, it was okay. He said I have a lot of potential and wants to see me do great things in the lab here." Lowering his voice, he continues, "I heard he's going to offer me a promotion."

Cautiously, Dr. Smith asks, "I heard the same, I think he said Friday is going to be the day. Do you think you will accept his offer?"

"Well… I don't know." Not knowing what to say, he ends up going with, "Through his resources here, I've managed to get the teleportation machine essentially up and running… save, of course, for the last piece of the puzzle, which I'm… still figuring out…" Dr. Smith nods in agreement. "I could really see myself doing… amazing things here—alongside Mavis and the colonel. Depending on the offer, you know, I might"—he almost feels ashamed of himself to finish the thought—"I might have to take him up on it."

Dr. Smith purses his lips, and his eye twitches as he places his teacup on an end table. "Of course." His cadence is deliberate as he says, "You would be a fool to turn him down. We accomplish quite the variety of achievements down here in the Abaddon. Wonderful things. Things like what happened during yesterday's test. You really took our scientific prowess to its limit."

Vincent's face flushes as the image of Leo's body—coagulating into a slime and dripping through the grated floor of the testing facility—flashes in his mind. He doesn't respond.

"Do you ever read the news, Dr. Creighton?" Confused by this question, Vincent shrugs. "Of course not. The moderators are careful about what they let you see down in the labs and library." Dr. Smith retrieves a tablet from the entertainment center and begins poking around on it, eventually passing it over. Vincent scans through several articles from different websites.

"Mental health professionals baffled as suicide rates in political leaders around the world skyrocket. Experts say recent victims suffered from rapid onset paranoid schizophrenia."

"Russia, the United States, China usher in modern Space Race by testing Near-Lightspeed Engines in the coming months. Sources refuse to provide details on the technology's development."

"North Korea deploys new stealth technology on aircraft and tanks, claiming to use a method that improves on the cuttlefish's adaptive camouflage."

"Pandemic sees no end in sight as recent test results suggest multiple variants of the virus have been detected. Experts suggest these mutations were synthetic in nature."

Vincent reads through article after article, all of which describe technology coming out of the Abaddon's labs. One that grabs his attention describes a terrorist organization using an advanced tear gas that paralyzes its victims to raid an embassy, then proceeding to torture and behead the embassy staff while they were still paralyzed.

"We do amazing things here, do we not, Vincent?"

Vincent looks at him from over the frames of his glasses. "Yeah," his voice takes a dark tone, "we actually do…"

Dr. Smith lets him take in the news articles for a while longer. "Have you heard anything about when that *event* might be kicking off?"

The attack? "You don't think that's still happening, do you? In light of recent events?"

"Do you not?"

"I mean, we lost half our people, what do you expect?"

"I expect a tenacious team that gets the job done, even if the going gets tough. Now tell me, when was the job fair planned for?"

Vincent blushes with shame in his eyes. "Friday."

"Fri—what?! That soon?!" Dr. Smith tries to hide his frustration. "Why was I unaware—you know what, the why is unimportant at this time…" He stands up and paces around the room. Vincent looks on nervously while Dr. Smith works some things out until he seems to have been struck by an idea. "You might be right, Vinny. You may as well accept the job, right? I mean, just in case the event does not pan out as we intend, it might be good for you to have some job security."

"Wait, really? You think so?" Vincent stands and poorly attempts to veil his excitement. "You don't think it's a bit… defeatist?"

"You do not want to keep him in suspense for too long, do you? I mean, Bartram is an eager beaver. If you accept that job, I am sure you will see some upward mobility faster than you might expect."

Vincent has gotten completely lost in Dr. Smith's double speak. "Right… I'm totally with you. But just so there's no confusion…"

"The sooner you jump on this wonderful opportunity he is offering you, the sooner you get to do some real good—maybe even figure out the correct algorithm to make teleportation a reality. If they make you a satisfactory job offer on Friday, you should take it."

Vincent, puzzled by the sudden shift in attitude, stares at him long and hard while trying to dismiss his shameful exuberance before finally agreeing. "Yeah… okay…" Dr. Smith just gives him a knowing smile and collects his teacup. After cleaning up, he ushers Vincent out the door and says, "By the way, would you mind relaying a message to our team?"

"Uh… I don't have any way of contacting them… "

"That is okay, just whenever you see them next, tell them, '*Honoʼooneni-itowoo*,'" Dr. Smith then proceeds to string together a strange combination of syllables in a language that Vincent has never heard of before. When Dr. Smith finishes, he asks, "Will you be able to remember that?"

Vincent gives him a confused nod, muttering, "Sure…"

He then bids Vincent good night and leaves him to enjoy the rest of his strange evening.

AS DR. SMITH CLOSES THE DOOR behind Vincent, he revels in a renewed sense of determination. *This weekend.* He sighs, then walks through his living room, past the view from the Eiffel Tower, through his kitchen, and into his study. Stoking the fireplace, he takes a seat at his computer and turns on a custom virtual private network that he designed to gain limited access to the rest of the Abaddon.

Opening a read-only file from a folder buried deep inside the network, a 3-D image appears depicting a man floating inside a green fluid and attached to several tubes, wires, and IV apparatuses—one of which is labeled "Intravenous CRISPR receptacle" and has the image of a bacteriophage next to it. A wire attached to the man's temples labeled "Electro-Neural Stimulation Connector" has a symbol that resembles a lightning bolt. Next to the image, a long list of chemicals is titled "Chemical Composition of Artificial Amniotic Fluid" and contains far more volatile chemicals than what would typically comprise this fluid, due to the need for carrying the embryo through to early adulthood.

Dr. Smith then opens a code writing program and reviews his work. *Once I plug this virus into just a single clone maturation chamber, it will spread to the main computer, then into every single one of the other chambers.* Scrolling down to a specific part toward the middle of the code, he ensures that the nitroglycerin transition phage is written properly.

The virus will have CRISPR rewrite their DNA to flood their systems with highly explosive nitroglycerin.

At the bottom of the code, he reviews the ignition sequence. *We will have thirty minutes before the main computer sends an electrical pulse to every chamber, triggering a shockwave that will propagate through the Artificial Amniotic Fluid and crush the clones' bodies. Then… boom. The nitroglycerin will ignite… destroying the entire Abaddon.*

Reaching into one of his desk drawers, he opens a small, secret compartment and retrieves an empty USB drive. He uploads the virus to the drive, then pockets it. *Kookoos, Trent better still make it.*

Chapter Thirty-Five

October 31st, 1988

Monday

The cafeteria is alive with colorfully costumed scientists when the labs break for lunch. The room is abuzz with rumors about the haunted house that the acting guild is building in the atrium tonight. A table staffed with a robotic xenomorph, Freddy Krueger, a *Thriller* zombie version of Michael Jackson, a gender-bent Jareth the Goblin King, and two realistic Darth Vaders are bouncing gossip that they've heard off of each other.

"I heard they replaced one of the sprinklers with pig's blood, so that when they announce the 'best-dressed' awards, the winners all get *Carrie*-d."

"No way! What if there's a fire? Dr. Smith would never sign off on that."

"Why not? It'd be just as effective at putting out a fire, wouldn't it? I mean it *is* ninety percent water. What I don't understand is how would they keep it from coagulating in the pipes?"

"That's literally, like, literally the definition of what blood thinners are for."

"Didn't Amanda say her boyfriend went to clown college? What if there's an actual, real-life clown there, guys? Gag me with a spoon!"

"You do realize that if he went to clown college, he is an actual, real-life clown. Like, all the time, right?"

"EW! David, don't say that!"

The cafeteria doors open and in walks an outraged Dr. Smith living up to his Arapaho name—Runs With Fire. He tears through the cafeteria until he reaches Colonel Bartram sitting at a table with his new favorite scientific staffer, Dr. Blackwell. Dr. Smith plants himself in front of Bartram and leans into his personal space. The rest of the cafeteria quiets down to listen in on what is probably the only outburst any of them will see Dr. Smith have. "My office. Now." He turns on his heel and starts to leave, but Bartram doesn't budge.

"Your office? I'm sure whatever you have to say can be discussed in front of everyone, can't it?" Bartram's smug face infuriates him.

"This is not the way we will handle this matter. We will discuss this in private. My office."

"No, I don't think we will, Dr. Smith."

Dr. Smith squints at him. "You want to do this here? We will do this here. I vetoed those cloning program contracts! They present too many ethical problems for us to go along with; what in the hell do you think you are doing by accepting them?"

"We are a military supplier. We supply weapons to the military." Bartram's tongue is decidedly *not* in his cheek when he says 'the military.' "And armies are the most important aspect to a military's arsenal."

"People are not weapons, Colonel! We will not breed clones to be soldier-scientists! You will refuse those contracts, end of story."

"End of story, huh?" Bartram sits up straight in his chair. "You sure about that?"

"Positive."

"Okay… it's just that I was reviewing Mr. Jeffery's file recently, and his performance seems to be dropping. I'm not sure if we can afford to keep such a low-performing member on this team."

"Are you really threatening Dr. Jeffery's life in front of the entire staff?" The air becomes a shade tenser as he asks this, and a few of the newer staffers look around, thoroughly flabbergasted by Bartram's behavior. Bartram's response doesn't help the tension.

"That depends. Are you vetoing the cloning contracts?"

"Yes." There's no hesitation in Smith's voice.

"Well, then…" Bartram finally stands up and calls out, "Mr. David Jeffery, front and center!" One of the Darth Vaders starts trembling in his cheap, plastic boots but doesn't move.

"Stay where you are, David," Smith calls. "You will not be going anywhere."

"Sergeant Carlisle," Bartram calls for Mavis's newest confidant. "Please bring Mr. Jeffery to my table."

"Trent, you do not have to follow his orders."

"I'm sorry, sir, but…" Trent's voice cracks, "he's got my daughter." Dr. Smith closes his eyes in defeat, and Trent proceeds to take David by the arm to usher him toward Bartram's table.

"Dr. Jeffery, we can—" Smith takes a step forward, but Trent points a gun at him.

"Don't move, sir… please."

Dr. Jeffery nods. "It's okay, Dr. Smith. He's got my brother and his kid, so… I'd rather it be me than them."

Trent bends David over the table and holds him steady, then Bartram pulls a gun out from under his belt. He cocks the slide back and presses the barrel to David's temple. "I'm going to ask one more time, Dr. Smith: are you vetoing the cloning contract?"

Dr. Smith stands steadfastly opposite Colonel Bartram as though they were facing each other down outside the OK Corral. "Alright, Colonel, you have forced my hand." Without warning or any sort of gesture from Dr. Smith, the lights turn off. A constant hum of electricity that nobody seemed to realize was surrounding them falls silent. Neon green emergency lighting illuminates overhead, and everyone gasps. Bartram keeps his eyes locked on Dr. Smith, which gives Smith a window to see the panic that's setting within him.

"What did you do?"

"The Abaddon has lost its power."

"What? How did you… turn it back on! Now!" He brandishes his gun wildly about David's head.

"Let us not be hasty. You wanted to discuss the matter here; we will discuss the matter here."

"I will shoot this motherfucker dead! Turn it back on!"

"You can shoot every single one of us if you'd like. But you will not leave this room until we discuss the matter."

Bartram's rage persists for some time while shouting obscenities at Dr. Smith, but it ultimately subsides when he realizes he currently has no more power than the others in the room. He keeps his gun ready, but pulls it away from David's head, who then gets back to his feet, considerably shaken. "We're already well underway with the clones. We have a whole lab filled with them that you had no idea existed! Your veto means nothing. You have no power!"

Dr. Smith snidely remarks,. "So they are currently surviving off the Abaddon's resources?"

Mavis gasps and engages for the first time during this entire exchange, "Colonel, the clones are fragile this early into their development. They'll drown within a minute or two without power to the system!"

Bartram points the gun at Smith and tries to give him an order. "Turn the power back on, now."

"You pull that trigger, not only will you never learn the location of the Abaddon's power source or how to work it, you will die in this room—probably at the hands of your very own prisoners."

Bartram watches the others from his peripheral and lowers his gun. "What do you want?"

"Drop the cloning program. The ones you have already made will not survive, so there is no need to concern yourself with them."

Mavis's jaw drops, so she covers her mouth with her hand. "No..." Her voice is small, "Please, turn it back on. They don't deserve to die."

"You have Colonel Bartram to blame for their deaths. His failure to recognize the value of my opinion led you directly into participating in this ethical minefield of a project."

"No… please, please, please, they'll have already suffered brain damage! Turn it back on, please!"

"Colonel," Dr. Smith continues, "you will drop this project, and the next time I hear about someone's life being threatened, I will immediately shut this place down." Colonel Bartram grinds his teeth at him but eventually nods contemptuously. "Good. It pains me to do this"—he gives Mavis a sincere look—"it truly does… but we will wait a few more minutes to ensure the clones… will not suffer another day."

Mavis's stare grows more and more hateful as the seconds pass. In the tense silence, many of the scientists cover their mouths in horror while others admire Dr. Smith's resolve. Nobody moves an inch for the five minutes that Dr. Smith holds them there until finally, again without a gesture of any kind, the lights turn back on and the hum of electricity in the walls resumes. It's an awkward few minutes until Dr. Smith breaks the tension by saying, "Happy Halloween, Colonel." Then he walks away, coolly striding toward the north wing.

Nobody moves until Colonel Bartram proclaims, "Anyone who currently lives in the above ground barracks is not to return to the surface until your phones have been confiscated. Everyone else, LEAVE." After a mass exodus of terrified scientists, he continues barking orders. "Sergeant Carlisle, find Martinez. We have work to do."

Trent hesitates but acknowledges and takes off.

Bartram turns to Mavis, who is a sniveling mess at this point, and says, "Effective immediately, he's on a short leash—his accesses are restricted, and his every move is watched. Your top priority is creating a facility with its own power source to create an army of clones. Understood?"

Mavis is too distraught to respond to him, but he knows she understands.

Dr. Smith retreats to his study to brew a cup of tea and recuperate from the trauma. He knows they're going to continue the clone project—if they can manage to pull it off, then it would certainly be their most profitable project ever. He needs to be ready. The fireplace crackling, he searches through his library for a book to distract himself when he comes across a particular shelf that he doesn't typically pull from. Finding a book he hasn't read in some time, he settles into his reading chair, takes a sip of tea and cracks it open. *The Fire Within, A Complete Reference to Biochemical and Thermal Energy Dynamics. By Russell "Runs With Fire" Smith, PhD.* A terrible idea sparks in his mind's eye, then he gets to reading his old work.

CHAPTER THIRTY-SIX

July 31st, 2020

Friday

Mavis awaits Vincent in the lab early on Friday morning. He is rarely beaten to work by anyone, even her. *It's time.* They exchange glances as he steps inside, but he first reaches for his white lab coat and sanitizes the workstations. She watches him through narrow eyes and crossed arms, eventually being the one to break the silence.

"This is the only offer you are going to be given. Consider your response wisely."

Vincent says simply, "Okay."

From her back pocket, she pulls out a folded, typed note, then reads off the page: "Senior Scientific Advisor. You will have access to all projects and will be responsible for contributing to each one as needed. If any project supervisor needs you to solve a problem for them, you will do so in a timely manner. You will be moved to the underground barracks, along with Doctors Medina and Boyce."

"Wait," Vincent cuts her off. "Sarah was supposed to be released and reunited with her mother."

"We cannot afford to release her, Vincent. I think you know that."

"If you can't help her, then the deal is off!"

"Stand by, let me finish." She continues to read: "Upon completion of the teleportation project, one machine will be supplied to Garden City Hospital, free of charge, where Fiona Boyce will receive proper treatment to extricate the tumors from her brain. Her insurance company will cover the complete cost of the operation. No harm will come to her." Mavis folds up the paper. "Vince, this is the best offer you're going to get. If you want Sarah's mom to survive, this is your chance."

Vincent contemplates the offer carefully. "Will you guys continue to censor my use of information systems? News websites, obituary columns, contact with the outside world?"

"Your network usage will be monitored but… we can turn off the censorship."

Vincent walks over to the coffee machine and makes himself a cup. "And what exactly will the nature of our relationship be?"

"My hopes are that you and I will remain close, personal friends. I think you and I make great partners. I would hate to ruin that."

Vincent looks into his coffee cup and asks, "Mavis… how are you okay with everything Bartram does in his conquest for power? The man wants to be a god among men."

"His ego is… boundless, sure. But look at what he built here; we can accomplish anything inside these walls, Vincent."

"By exploiting your fellow scientists and murdering friends. How do you justify that?"

"Vincent, there are eight billion people alive today. There have been over a hundred billion people alive throughout the history of our species. Every one of them has suffered and died. We can keep that from happening. If protecting the human race from death—saving hundreds of billions of innocent lives from oblivion means causing a few hundred people to suffer… that's a price I'm willing to pay."

"What if they're not? What if Karl wasn't willing to pay that price?"

Mavis looks at him grimly. "Then he should have buckled down. I'm sorry, Vincent. That's just how it needs to be."

It takes him a few minutes to process her statement before saying, "Well, if the best I can do is save Sarah's mom, I'll settle for that. I'll take the job."

Mavis smiles at him. "I'm proud of you for this, Vince." She shakes his hand, and a sense of dread looms over him until Sarah and Grace file in with the rest of the team. After he finishes his coffee, he goes to the whiteboard and picks up a marker. As he writes his algorithm on the board, Sarah approaches him and whispers in his ear.

"That's a fake, right?" Vincent looks her in the eye and says nothing. She bites her lip and searches his eyes for more answers, but there are none. "You're giving up?"

Mavis's voice perks up from across the room, "What are you guys talking about over there?"

Vincent shakes his head at Sarah, then turns to Mavis to say, "I've made a breakthrough." Vincent's deadpan voice matches his expression.

"Wonderful. You just took a major step forward in your career, Dr. Creighton." Mavis grabs a phone and calls Bartram.

Sarah grabs his shoulder and spins him to face her. "What are you doing?"

"I had to do it, but your mom is going to be okay." He caps the marker and goes to sit at his computer. Dumbstruck, Sarah walks over to Grace, and they exchange terrified glances.

"Great news, everybody!" Mavis shouts over the team's conversation. "Vincent has made another breakthrough! I just called Colonel Bartram, and he's agreed to a test this afternoon. Let's get packing!"

During lunch, Sarah and Grace grab Vincent and drag him to the cafeteria.

"What the hell were you thinking back there?!" Sarah shouts furiously at him.

"That better not have been the real fucking thing," Grace says. "And it damn well better not be another fake one! We can't be responsible for another person being killed!"

"I talked to Smith about it." Vincent understands their confusion and tries to quell their feelings. "He told me to give them the algorithm. He wants me to take the job. And… I don't know. If I work *with* them, they might trust me more. Maybe I'll even get a say in what projects we take on eventually."

Sarah says, "No. Look, I get what you're saying. It's easier to change the system from within. But that's not how it's going to shake out."

"Alright, well what's your suggestion? Karl, Mark, and Chad are all gone; Leo and Bobby are dead; and Trent and Becca are missing. These guys are really good at making people disappear. It's kill or be killed right now, Sarah! We need to play our cards right." Both of them stare at him with no answers to give. "I'm open to suggestions, but… for now, this is our play."

Everyone meets in front of the north wing after lunch where Martinez is poised to escort them to the testing facility. Vincent finds it odd that Bartram showed up for the test, but Dr. Smith isn't present. They take the ten-minute subway ride up there and begin setting up their equipment. Nearly an hour later, everything is set up and ready for launch. Vincent wrestles to keep his lunch down as he watches Martinez take the subway back to retrieve the live subject. To his surprise, however, when the subway car returns, Martinez is only accompanied by Dr. Smith in his pinstripe suit and red tie.

There's a look of dismay on his face as he shouts, "What exactly is going on here? I did *not* authorize any test to be conducted today!"

Colonel Bartram comes bounding out in his uniform. "It's okay, Doctor. We have new data to test; the customer has been on us about this project for long enough."

"The customer can kiss my ass! We had a failed test earlier this week that ended in a fatality. We are not conducting a second test in the same week that we lost one of our live subjects. We will not be testing another one of Dr. Creighton's algorithms until I personally review it. This test is postponed until *I* sign off on the data!" Colonel Bartram looks like he is about to rip Dr. Smith's head off.

What is he doing? He's the one who said they'd want to test early. Vincent watches silently.

266

Mavis looks distraught. "Why… I understand your concerns, sir. I have been assured by Dr. Creighton himself that this test will be a successful one."

"With all due respect to Dr. Creighton, how has that turned out for us in the past?" Vincent blushes. *What the hell, Dr. Smith?* "Just leave everything in its place. Once I am convinced Dr. Creighton's work *will not* result in *another* fatality, we will proceed with the test."

"You want us to tear everything down?" Kevin, the head of the engineering team, asks, sounding exhausted.

"Tearing it down and transporting it presents unnecessary risk to the equipment; there is no need to risk potential damage. Just power it down and leave it all where it is at. I will take the weekend to review Dr. Creighton's work, then we will pick it up fresh on Monday."

Mavis begins whipping herself up into a frenzy, but Colonel Bartram holds his hand up to silence her. She obeys. He and Dr. Smith square off in front of the glass chamber, then Colonel Bartram quietly asks, "You're really going to put your foot down on this? If you try to pull another Halloween stunt, you can kiss Vincent and his friends goodbye."

Dr. Smith leans in and whispers in his ear, "Shall we find out together?"

Bartram freezes up, but paints on a confident smile before backing down. "Sergeant Martinez, make sure to lock the blast doors behind us."

"Thank you, Colonel," Dr. Smith says begrudgingly. "I appreciate your sensitivity regarding this touchy subject."

After a tense moment of quiet, the group breaks. Kevin turns off the power converter, they secure the facility, and then everyone returns to the main part of the Abaddon before breaking for the weekend.

CHAPTER THIRTY-SEVEN

November 23rd, 2018

Friday

"**S**ergeant Carlisle!" Mavis shouts to the medical bay's waiting area. Trent sees Martinez leaving the patient room while covering up his *Dora the Explorer* Band-Aid with his uniform sleeves. Trent closes his magazine to follow Mavis. While preparing a shot for him labeled "Telomere Regeneration Formula #3", she asks, "Are you ready for tonight's feast? Working double-time with Martinez and Little during Thanksgiving must not be terribly fun."

He laughs and says, "Nah, they're good dudes. But I'm actually working guard duty at the Cultivation Center tonight."

"Oh, really? But you love Thanksgiving dinner, don't you?"

"I mean, who doesn't? But work is work. Somebody's gotta make sure nobody raids that place."

"Don't Malkovich and Ashley usually work the Cultivation Center?"

"Which is why I figured they deserve a night off. They haven't been to Thanksgiving dinner in years."

"Well, that's awfully sweet of you." She wipes his skin with an alcohol pad. "This is going to sting a bit." He winces as the needle goes in, and he is injected with the serum. She gives him a flowery pink Band-Aid and says, "That should tide you over for about five years. So I'll pencil you in for November 2023—" she stops for a second. "Wow. 2023. Time is going by so fast. It feels like just yesterday Bartram hired you."

"I'll tell you what's weird: you're a doctor! You spent decades guarding gates and dropping bodies, but look at you now!"

"Me? Look at you! You're *leading* this group of ruffians! You moved through the ranks faster than I ever thought possible. I couldn't be prouder of you."

"I can say the same about you."

They share a moment of catharsis and smile. Trent looks at his feet. "You know, you've been an influential person in my life. You've done a lot of good for me. I want to thank you for that."

Mavis, looking confused, responds, "It's my pleasure, Trent. Where'd that come from?" She looks in his eyes and can tell his thoughts are a million miles away, then he makes eye contact again.

"I mean, it *is* Thanksgiving, right? You just taught me how to properly shoot a gun, clear a room, and how to use my hands to incapacitate somebody in no less than fifty ways. But… you also cared for me. You showed me what it meant to protect people. You showed me how to distinguish right from wrong." Not knowing how to respond, Mavis just smiles and gives him a strange look.

That night, Trent dons his tactical gear and sets off for the Cultivation Center. Entering the atrium, he pushes through hundreds of people gathering in the cafeteria for the feast. Cutting through the garden, he passes by Bartram and Dr. Smith under the redwood trunk pathway. Bartram looks slightly buzzed already as the two of them walk in opposite directions, but when he sees Trent, he smiles broadly.

"Carlisle! What are you so dressed up for?! It's dinner time!"

"Evening, sir. I'm actually on my way to"—he looks around at all the passersby and clears his throat—"well, take my post. I'll see you in the morning though, sir."

"You'll do no such thing! Join us!"

"Now, now, Colonel," Dr. Smith saves him, "you understand better than anyone the importance of duty. The man has work to do." Dr. Smith turns and extends a cupped palm to shake Trent's hand. "Thank you for your diligence and sacrifice, Sergeant." Dr. Smith then pats Bartram on the back and urges Trent along, who smiles and pockets the USB drive that Dr. Smith just handed him. *A little parting gift.*

Through Bartram's office, Trent finds the service elevator, skips over the "Holding Cell" level, and presses the "Basement" button. When the doors part, he steps into a massive bay that's stacked high with rectangular containers atop one another. Each box is exactly seven feet tall and four feet wide and attached to a computer displaying the contents of the box. As he passes by each container, Trent checks the screens to see human figures attached to hoses and wires floating inside some kind of green fluid. He can see each of their serial numbers tattooed to the left side of their necks through the video feed. Stacks upon stacks of these boxes are organized five hundred feet deep and five hundred feet high into the warehouse.

As he conducts his rove, each aisle features a different stage in development: Adulthood, Early Adulthood, Adolescence, Late, Middle, and Early Childhood, Infancy, and Prenatal Development. Stepping through each aisle and inspecting each computer, he starts his rove again, but stops at subject zero-one-seven. Looking at the screen, he watches the thirty-one-year-old man float in his chamber. *This man is older than I was by the time I started working here.* His heart wrenches as he notices the man's eyelids wriggling from side to side. *What does a fully grown man who's never been awake dream about?* He shuffles uncomfortably in his steel-toe boots and adjusts his M16.

Trent is stirred from his wonderings by his watch as an alarm begins beeping wildly. *Eighteen thirty. It's time.* As he types on the keyboard, the container's fluid begins to drain; Trent reaches into a small drawer set into the box and retrieves an orange jumpsuit. As the tubes and wires detach from the man's body, the fluid drains from the container. The container's door opens, and Trent watches as subject zero-one-seven awakens, opening his blue-grey eyes and standing in his cell, naked as any other newborn is on their birthday.

"Who am I?" the subject asks.

Trent knows the answer is supposed to be "Alpha-Zero-One-Seven" but can't bring himself to say it. Instead, he tells the truth. "Your name is Leonard Sideris. Your friends call you Leo."

Leo looks around at the other cells and asks, "Where are we?"

"Somewhere dangerous. I need to get you out of here, and then we'll talk. Okay?"

Leo notices another cell and sees the screen displaying himself. Trent expects him to ask another question, however, all he says is, "Okay. Tell me what you need me to do."

"Just follow me and do what I say," Trent says, giving him the orange jumpsuit and leading him to the elevator that returns them to the north wing. Leading him through the labyrinth of corridors, they end up in Bartram's living room. Leo stops at the window overlooking the atrium garden, staring in awe at its grandiosity, along with the hundreds of feast-goers littering the grounds.

"I'll give you a few seconds, but we're on a time crunch." They both admire the redwoods for a few moments. He places his hand on Leo's shoulder and says, "Alright. Let's go." Leo immediately follows the order. They head down the north wing gallery, and Trent pokes his head around the corner to make sure the coast is clear. Right on cue, Dr. Smith starts a speech that guarantees no attention is being paid to the north wing gallery. They seize this moment to sprint across the gallery and into the subway station. Trent lets Leo into the conductor's car. "Alright, Leo, see this lever?" He points to a lever on the control panel, and Leo nods. "You're going to push that all the way forward, okay? Don't pull it back no matter what."

Leo nods with a shiver. "O-Okay… what is it going to do?"

"It's going to—" he shudders. "It's going to help us escape. So push that lever, and don't let it go. But first, you have to count down from thirty, okay?"

Leo nods and says nervously, "I'm scared."

Tears well up in Trent's eyes, but he says, "I know. Me, too. But it's all going to be okay in just a few minutes." He swallows hard before Leo starts counting down, and the doors close. Trent takes the stairs back up to the gallery, hesitating for only a second. *I'm sorry, Leo.* Eyes shut tight, he crosses back through the gallery and sprints to Bartram's office. Readying his rifle, he looks down through the spiral staircase until he hears a faint whooshing of air from the subway speeding along its track. Trent feels his heart sink. *Eight minutes and forty-five seconds.*

Finding the service elevator again, this time he takes it to the "Holding Cell" level, and the door opens to a long, dungeon-like hall that ends in a simple, interior door. Passing by the currently empty prison cells, he enters the chamber belonging to Leonard-Sideris-Prime. The glass wall looking into the White Room shows an exhausted, worn-down, depleted Leo meditating atop his mattress. Leo doesn't notice his presence until Trent presses down on the intercom to get Leo's attention.

"You ready, friend?"

Leo's head weakly turns. "What? Oh. Trent, it's… is it you?" His tone is less manic than when Trent had first met him, and he carries himself much differently.

"It's time, buddy." Sighing deeply, Leo gets off his bed, and Trent lets the glass door open for him. "C'mon, we don't have much time." Leo's not used to moving this fast anymore, so he slows their pace down to a near crawl.

They exit and head down the corridor, but before he calls the elevator to open, he hears it already moving. It's descending. *Where did it go?* Then he realizes his biggest fear has come true. *Nobody was supposed to be here! Who the hell is coming down here?!* Then the door opens to a woman wearing a flowy, black dress decorated with yellow sunflowers.

"This isn't the Cultivation Center," Mavis's cold voice says coyly, then she cocks the gun she's holding and points it at Trent.

Shoving Leo out of the way, he bum-rushes Mavis, pushing her gun away. He shoves her against the back wall of the elevator and starts punching at the side of her head, but she proves to be a little more resilient than he anticipated. She gets the upper hand on him and kicks him off, but Leo slides in between them to deal three swift strikes to her various pressure points, then he kicks her out of the elevator. Trent quickly presses the button to close the door, and they begin their ascent, away from a temporarily incapacitated Mavis.

As they catch their breath, Trent takes inventory and realizes something awful. "Shit. She's got my radio."

"So our escape is going to be louder than expected?" Leo asks.

"Yeah…" They sit in silence for a moment as the elevator ascends until Trent says, "How'd you do that back there?"

"I may have been confined to the White Room for sixty-four years, but I wasn't just sitting there the whole time. Meditation and working out. It kept the demons at bay by clearing my mind and strengthening my body." He has a determined look on his face.

Trent is thoroughly impressed, yet slightly intimidated. "Shit, well, just in case, here, you'll want this." He reloads his pistol and hands it to Leo, along with two extra magazines. As they approach the surface, a discordant crashing sound resonates through the walls. Trent sighs heavily.

"What the fuck was that?" Leo asks.

"That was our distraction. Whatever backup she sent will, hopefully, go to check that out instead."

"Hopefully."

As the elevator comes to a stop, they give each other a look, then nod. They raise their weapons just as the door opens, but fortunately, there's no one returning the favor. Softly, they step into the armory, masking the sound of their footsteps as much as possible. Trent gestures for Leo to avoid the front door, then reaches into his belt and pulls out a multitool. As quietly as he can, he begins to remove a few nails from the wooden planks that make up the back wall. Leo helps by keeping watch until he manages to remove two planks, leaving a hole in the wall large enough to fit through.

Leading the way, Trent ensures the path is clear for them to crouch between the armory and the perimeter fence. They need to cross the alley between the armory and the general store; after that, they will be able to hoof it through the front gate. Trent peers down the alley to see two of the security guards posted up and pointing guns at the armory's entrance. He looks back to gesture their next move to Leo, but as he looks back, Leo's eyes are glistening with the reflection of the moonlight in his tears.

Lighter than a feather, Leo whispers, "I never… thought I would see it again. I thought I would die down there." He takes a deep breath of fresh air, then falls to his knees and drinks it in. Trent taps on his ankle to get his attention, then Leo breaks his trance in favor of a determination to survive. Trent points at the gate to show him their goal, then gestures for them to cross the alley and sprint for the end of the store. Leo nods, and Trent swiftly crosses the gap, but they hear shouting from the barracks on the opposite side of the base, followed by gunshots in their direction.

Both of them hit the deck; Leo gets Trent's attention and gestures for him to provide cover fire, then counts down with his fingers. *Three… two… one…* Trent rounds the corner and begins firing wildly while Leo sprints across the alley. Back-to-back, they sprint along behind the store until they reach the end.

A full-on firefight breaks out when the rest of the security team joins in on the game. Trent reloads and shouts, "I'll hold them off, you break for the booth! The guard should have been relieved before we came up!"

Leo nods while Trent sidles up to the corner and begins laying down fire on his own teammates. Leo sprints at top speed to the booth, but to his surprise, a helmeted guard appears and raises his rifle. Denying him the opportunity to pull the trigger, Leo puts a bullet through each of his knees, and he drops. *Please don't be dead…* As he slides into the booth, he first feels for a pulse, and when he finds one, he replaces his own pistol for the guard's M16 to return cover for Trent. Once they both cross the gap, Leo shouts, "Now what?!"

Trent looks at his watch and impatiently says, "They should be here by now!" Then he looks down the street to find a pair of headlights breaching a hill. A black Humvee speeds into view, and the whir of a Browning machine gun blasts across the desert valley, then the vehicle screeches to a halt in front of them, prompting Trent and Leo to cover each other while sprinting into the truck before shutting the door and speeding off.

"You boys friends with Russell?" Becca asks from the passenger seat, manning the machine gun that's hanging out of the window.

"Yeah! You Becca and Bobby?" Trent replies.

"Would you get out if we weren't?" Bobby asks from the driver's seat.

Trent chuckles and hands Becca the USB drive that Dr. Smith handed him. "Here, this is a little gift from Dr. Smith."

"What is it?"

"Blueprints for some survival equipment we'll need."

"Fun stuff." Becca puts it in the glove compartment.

Bobby turns over his shoulder and asks, "Where we heading, guys?"

"Once we lose our tail—the Wind River Reservation. We have a friend to meet up with."

"Sounds good."

Leo looks up at the moon while resting his head against the window until finally passing out to the most restful sleep of his life.

CHAPTER THIRTY-EIGHT

August 1st, 2020

Saturday

The gatehouse clock strikes midnight on yet another quiet Friday night watch for Tzofiya. Staying awake for long hours isn't a chore for her; it's become second nature after years of training and shift work, but the uncertainty of her tenure here at the Abaddon makes it unbearable. Will she ever return to the real world? Will she die here? Not knowing is what kills her. She looks over the computer's bright, blue lights to see into the desert in front of her. The stars overhead are pleasant to watch, but having spent the past couple decades earning herself a reputation that would land her a spot as Bartram's head of security, she wasn't so sure anymore if she'd ever see a city again.

The starlight makes it quite easy to survey the desert landscape at night, but in the desert, the first indication of trouble is usually a strange sound. A distant rumble perks her head up, causing her to scan the horizon. *That is not animal. Not plane. Maybe vehicle?* On the horizon, a shifting of dark shapes catches her eye. *Black truck with no headlights. Trent?* She immediately sets a loop on the cameras and watches him come to a stop just inside her visual range. Trent's truck just sits there for a while, and she watches patiently. *What is plan?* After a few minutes of inaction, she draws her pistol and removes the laser sight from underneath her barrel. *As long as I stay inside gatehouse, Murphy will not see light.* She points it at the truck and flashes the light twice, then waits until she sees two short bursts of a flashlight back.

I hope you remember Abaddon optical signals… She starts flashing the laser in intervals reminiscent of Morse code, but in a dialect that she created and taught to the other security officers. She starts by passing the message: "What. You. Need. Question."

Trent uses the same dialect, but needs to spell Vincent's name out using proper Morse code: "Where. V-I-N-C-E-N-T. Question."

"In. Barracks."

"Why. Question."

"V. In. Barracks. Asleep."

She can sense the rage bubbling from inside the distant vehicle before she sees him say, "Plan. A. Happen. Now."

"What. Plan. A. Question."

There is a pause. "Repeat. Last."

"V. No. Communicate. Plan."

Another pause followed by more distant outrage. "What. F-U-C-K. Question."

Shit. Well… time to improvise. "New. Plan."

"Ready."

"Approach. Gate. No. Lights. Stand by."

"Acknowledge. Out."

She responds simply, "Out," then raises the barrier to block the gate and steps out of the gatehouse to take a stroll over to Murphy at the administration building entrance.

"Ma'am, what's going on? You alright?"

"Yes. We have vehicle inbound, ready for covert resupply op?"

"Covert op? What are you talking about? Resupply happens on Sunday."

"Right, which is what makes this covert. Did you forget to check email again? Bartram sent PDF of operation details to you, me, and Cullen on Wednesday."

"Did I read my email? Uh… yeah… definitely."

"Good, tune radio to channel four, and keep quiet." She pushes past him to enter the checkpoint where Cullen is manning the metal detector.

"Cullen, vehicle inbound in support of covert operation. Tune to channel four, and remain quiet. Understood?"

"Uh, ma'am? Covert resupply?" Cullen asks.

Tzofiya groans at him. "I swear you two will be death of me. You must read emails! Just stand by, I will go to office and return after few moments. Remain here and speak to no one, understood?"

"Yes, ma'am!"Cullen's face burns red as she slips past him to rush into her office where she quickly disables all elevators except Bartram's service elevator and locks all doors to every room in the guards' barracks, then books it back through the checkpoint, but the moment she steps outside she notices something terrible. *Wait, where's Murphy?* She looks across the grounds to see him greeting Trent's truck, and her heart stops. *Fuck.*

Tzofiya sprints across the grounds to find Murphy at the gatehouse staring into the black truck that has pulled up to a stop in front of him. "Murphy!"

The moment she calls out his name, he raises his rifle at the driver and shouts, "Step out of the vehicle!"

Tzofiya quickly reaches him at the gatehouse and pushes his rifle down before Trent, Leo, and Becca need to retaliate. "Murphy, shut your fucking mouth!" she whispers to him, then watches the barracks building windows to see if she can see any lights turning on, but there is no change. "What do you not understand about *covert*?!"

"Ma'am, it's Carlisle!" he whispers back and tries to raise his gun again. "He's a traitor!"

"No, idiot! This is reason you must check fucking emails!" She pushes his gun back down and points in his face. "If you read email, you would know he returns from secret mission to spy on government!"

Murphy's hands are shaking as she lowers his rifle, but he's not sure whether to believe her or not. "Wh-what are you talking about?"

"He has been on mission with Leo Prime to spy on government. We had to make show of his escape couple years ago so people would believe he was traitor."

"W-Why didn't you say anything at the beginning of our shift?"

"Why didn't you read fucking email?!"

He blushes and lets his rifle waver. Tzofiya continues, "You weren't even supposed to see them! If you stay at post as I instructed, there would be no problem."

"So…" Murphy slowly calms down and switches his stare from Tzofiya to Trent and Leo, then back again. "They were on a mission? And he's back now… to do what?"

Trent answers for her, "Delivery. See that crate in the back?" Murphy looks at the bed of the truck to see an unmarked weapons crate, the same type that they use during resupply. "Special delivery for Bartram. I got next gen weapons tech, intelligence, all sorts of useful stuff back there that our boys down in R&D will just go nuts over." Murphy gives a discerning eye to them all and backs off. "Sorry we had to lie to you, Murph. It was a sensitive op—bit of a long con that needed to have eyes only clearance."

"Sure… Sergeant Kritzman, I'm just going to check in with Martinez. Bartram runs all security matters through him, and I'd feel a lot better if—" He tunes back to the general frequency, but Tzofiya grabs his wrist.

"Martinez not have need-to-know. Just you, me, and Cullen. Clear?" She glares at him hard for quite some time until he finally relents. "Your job is to guard entrance."

"Okay… I'll just… go back to my post."

"Good," she says with a sigh of relief. They all watch Murphy slowly return to the admin building entrance until he is out of earshot. "Fuck, that was close. He is suspicious. What is plan?"

"Vincent really didn't tell you anything about the plan? What the fuck has that kid been doing?!"

"I think when Bobby was clinched, he got spooked and lose his nerve. I heard he took job offer from Bartram today."

"*Job offer?* What the fu—you know what? Doesn't matter. Do you know if Bartram is in his office?"

"Should be, yes."

"Good. The plan is a simple ambush. Does he have a security detail with him?"

"Should be alone, but I cannot confirm."

Trent considers this carefully and says, "I'd rather be over prepared than under. Let's get these guns loaded up in the service elevator; we'll take it down to his office and light him up. You make sure Martinez doesn't use the partygoers as hostages or whatever in case the lights go out."

"And Vincent? Should I wake him?"

"Do we even need him for the rest of this op? He had one job to do and failed to pull through! I don't know if he's up for this task."

Leo comes to his defense by interjecting, "The boy is scared, Trent. He has something worth fighting for, but he's afraid to lose it in the fight."

"Oh, and I didn't? I haven't heard from my daughter in decades; I don't even know if she's still alive because I'm committed to taking Bartram off the map. I don't care what his reasons are; his judgment is compromised."

"Trent, you're wrong. Removing Bartram is still his priority. We need him by our side."

"For what?! We *needed* him to be our liaison with the Abaddon, but he failed to do that. We got in without him, so let's finish the job without him."

"We aren't inside yet." Leo eyes Murphy, who is glaring at them suspiciously. "Sorry Trent, my gut says we're going to need him. Tzofiya, wake him up and get him down here."

Tzofiya nods and lowers the barrier, then leads them into their parking spot. Murphy's eyes are fixed on them, but it's clear he is internally wrestling with what he should do. She walks over to him and says, "I have matter to attend in barracks building, please help Carlisle unload crate."

"I thought my job was to guard the entrance?" he asks with a dirty, suspicious look.

"Your job is what I say. Now *please*, help unload crate."

"What matter do you have to attend to?"

"Dr. Creighton's presence is required for Carlisle's meeting with Bartram. As new Senior Scientific Advisor, he needs to review material that Carlisle has recovered."

"Sure…" he says while continuing to glare.

"Do you have problem, Sergeant Murphy?"

"No problem… ma'am…"

"Good. Now, go help them. I will be back shortly."

He watches her walk off to the scientists' barracks, then joins his old coworker—and his former prisoner—in unloading the truck. Becca can taste the tension and suspicion in the air but goes about her job anyway.

"SHH…" VINCENT'S EYES OPEN to the sight of Tzofiya's hand covering his mouth. "We must be quiet. It is time for operation."

"What… wait, what?" It takes him a second to rouse from his sleep. "It's still happening?" His heart immediately starts pounding, and though he is still groggy, he excitedly jumps out of bed.

"Yes, now get dressed."

Vincent quickly throws on his running shoes, jeans, and black hoodie and asks, "What about Leo and Bobby? We don't have the manpower."

She shushes him and quietly escorts him through the barracks building, but before they step outside, she cautions him, "You are about to be surprised, but you must remain silent, understood?"

"Okay?" He isn't sure what to make of her warning, but when she opens the door, they see a tired-looking man with a bushy, silver moustache hoisting a crate out of the back of a pickup. Vincent has to cover his mouth to keep from yelping, then rushes over to the truck exclaiming, "Leo! You-you're alive! Oh my God, I-I can't believe you're still alive!"

"Of course, I'm alive, bud! You didn't think I'd let some punk ass rent-a-cops take me out, did you?"

"No, but… I-I-I saw you die. I pushed the button; how are you still alive?"

"What are you talking about? I've been kicking this whole time, buddy. Must have been a bad dream. C'mon, let's get this crate on the service elevator." They start moving, but Vincent stops them.

"No, it wasn't a dream. I *saw* you die. It was you but thirty years younger!" Trent and Tzofiya nervously eye each other.

During this entire interaction, Vincent—in his groggy, single-minded state—seems to be unaware of Murphy's presence, who has been listening intently. Tzofiya knows where the conversation is heading, so she intervenes, "Whatever it was can be discussed on elevator. Come, let's get move on."

"I thought you and I were on crowd control in the atrium?" Vincent asks, but the moment he utters these words, Tzofiya and Murphy lock eyes, then Becca slowly positions herself behind Murphy. "What? What happened?"

"Vincent," Murphy's shaky voice says, "what do you mean by 'crowd control'?"

Once it dawns on him that Murphy wasn't supposed to be here, he looks around to see everyone's hands on the grips of their guns. "Oh, uh…" His veins flood with adrenaline as he realizes what's about to happen. Murphy gradually moves his hand up to his radio but stops when Trent raises his rifle at him. Vincent's heart beats in his ears, and he says, "They'll kill you before you can get your message out. You'll die for nothing."

"I have to, Vincent. Carlisle's a traitor; Sideris is supposed to be in lockup, and Kritzman just lied to me. Whatever you're doing is treason."

Trent says, "Only if we lose."

"And *when* you lose, Bartram will have my family's heads."

"Then help us win."

"You can't."

"Not without your help."

"Not even with my help."

Becca goes into stealth mode and quietly approaches him. Murphy doesn't hear her, so Trent keeps talking, "Please. Everyone here wants to be free. That's all we want."

"It doesn't matter. Bartram is always one step ahead; you won't succeed."

"We certainly won't if you give him a heads-up that we're here."

"Sorry, Carlisle, I can't risk it." He snaps his hand up to his radio, but Becca swiftly twists his wrist and kicks out his knees.

Trent liberates him from his radio and says, "Sorry, man." He then pistol-whips him, knocking him out on the spot.

"Shit," Vincent says bluntly. "Sorry, guys…"

Trent grabs him by the zipper of his hoodie and hisses, "That was *your* fault! He almost blew our whole op, which could have been avoided if you had done your fucking job in the first place!"

"Hey, I thought we had lost half our team! What do you expect?"

"I expected you not to give up at the first sign of trouble!"

Their argument is broken up by the opening of the admin building entrance and a voice reporting, "All units topside! Officer down!"

"Fuck me!" Trent exclaims before every rifle in the courtyard is raised. Vincent instinctively hits the deck and arms himself with Murphy's rifle. Trent shouts, "You don't know what you're doing, Cullen! Just put the gun down, and we can all go home!"

"What happened to Murphy?"

Tzofiya thinks quickly, "Cullen, thank God you came. Carlisle's back!"

"I saw you talking to him at the gate. What's going on, Kritzman?"

"He had gun on me; he coerced me into letting him on base. We must arrest them!"

Leo starts playing along and grabs Tzofiya. He puts his pistol to her head. "Drop your gun, or I swear you'll be cleaning her brain out the dirt!"

"Woah, woah, woah!" Cullen shouts, "Let her go! There's no need to threaten her. Just let Kritzman go, and we'll talk."

Trent gives Leo an overly enthusiastic nod, and Leo lets Tzofiya go. She quickly closes the gap, and when she gets behind Cullen, she puts her own rifle to the back of his head, "Sorry, Cullen."

"What the fuck? Kritzman, what are you doing?!"

"Just drop your gun, and all will be well."

"Goddamn it, you fucking traitor!"

"There is lot of that going around right now," she says as she takes his rifle from him. Trent and Becca come to help strip him of anything else he can use against them, then handcuff him and Murphy inside her office. Tzofiya tosses their radios to Trent and Vincent. "Channel six, go! I will be your eye in sky."

"What about the party?" Vincent asks. "What's keeping Martinez from using them as hostages or killing one of them as a gesture to 'keep the peace' if Smith turns the lights off?"

"I will take care of this—just go!"

Trent nods and leads the others loading the crate onto the service elevator. "Gear up, Vinny; we might be heading into a warzone."

"This is still a capture mission, right?" Vincent asks, while clipping on his utility belt that carries spare magazines, his gas mask, and various other pockets and holsters.

Leo raises his eyebrows at Trent, who sighs. "Yep. That's our goal."

"Good." He straps his Kevlar on, readies his weapons, and looks up to Leo, "Where did I leave off? Leo, I saw you die. I watched it happen with my own eyes. What happened?"

Trent cuts in, "Vinny, let's talk about this later, okay? Now's not the time."

"When the hell *will* it be the right time?"

"When we get out of this alive."

Leo looks at him curiously and asks, "Do you know something about this, Trent?"

"Like I said, Leo: another time."

Leo shares a skeptical glance with Vincent before Trent leans into his radio. "Eagle Eye, this is Badger One, comms check. Over." Vincent's radio crackles at the same time, but they wait for Tzofiya's response.

"Good copy, Badger One. I secure north wing entrance. Nobody will be joining you for party. Over."

"Roger, what's the situation in the atrium? Over."

"Party still going… wait, disregard. Look like guards have stopped music, and panic is setting in. There are *a lot* of guards. Why are so many guards assigned to party? I think it is time for my announcement. Over."

"Keep your mic hot. Over."

She keeps her radio transmitting while she makes an announcement to the atrium: "Attention residents of Abaddon. There has been security breach. Please file into east wing and shelter in place. Guards remain in atrium for further instruction." A few seconds later, she says, "Badger One, this is Eagle Eye. I do not see Martinez in atrium. Over."

"Roger Eagle Eye, we'll keep our heads on a swivel. Badger squad is about to dismount. Going dark. Over."

"Roger. Good luck, Badger squad. Out."

Leo chuckles at him and snidely asks, "Badger squad?"

"What? Badgers are badass! And we're going into an underground base! They're burrowers!"

Becca says, "Is Leo's callsign Snake? Can me and Vinny both be callsign Mushroom?"

"We've been over this, Becca—nobody gets your internet references!"

Becca sighs with a sad grin and says, "Bobby would have gotten it… or said you were more like a mole-person." Vincent assumes this is some kind of pop culture reference he doesn't understand, but he laughs along with Becca anyway, which she appreciates. "See! Vinny gets it!"

When the elevator starts to slow, Trent says, "Alright people, eyes up. I've got point." The four of them assume a practiced formation, and when the elevator door opens, they gradually spread out into the hallway. Trent whispers, "Clear." Becca and Vincent watch their backs while Trent and Leo unload the equipment.

"What exactly did you guys bring?" Vincent asks.

"It's actually their own stuff. That's an Abaddon crate that we nicked during a resupply once," Becca explains. "They carry everything: Browning machine guns, boxes of all sorts of illegal grenades, different types of rifles, battering rams, explosive charges—you know, just in case."

"In case of what?"

"In case of anything."

"Jesus Christ…"

"We brought him, too." She shows him a hand grenade with a mini golden cross duct taped to it.

After hoisting the crate, Trent says, "Alright, we got it off the elevator. Let's fan out and find this son of a bitch. Vinny and Becca take the north, Leo and I take the south. Vinny, radio me and rendezvous back here if you run into trouble."

The four of them split up and explore the labyrinth that is Bartram's office. Becca and Vincent cover each other as they traverse the corridors and scan unoccupied rooms, including the same records room he had investigated many months ago, until they wind up back at the crate.

"Check with Trent. See if they found anything yet," she instructs him, but before he can try calling them, they hear a crackle on their radio.

"Badger Two, this is Badger One, come in. Over."

"Badger One, this is, uh, Badger Two, I guess?" Vincent stops talking, but Becca mouths something at him until he remembers to say, "Over."

"Looks like the place is empty, but come find us in the living room. Over."

"Roger." Vincent stops the transmission and remembers to finish with, "Over and out?"

Becca chuckles. "You're doing great, bud. Come on." They navigate the halls until they reach the living room. Trent and Leo stand at the large window overlooking the atrium, and their jaws are agape. Vincent and Becca join them. "What's going on? What are you guys—Oh, no!"

Vincent looks through the window to find what they were hoping to avoid: panic. The partygoers have completely ceased their revelry and tried to evacuate the atrium into the east wing, but a platoon of armed guards have formed a barrier. Half of the group has even taken to trying to escape through the elevators, but when they find them to be disabled, the group starts getting rowdier. Vincent scans the crowd to find Sarah and Grace bobbing back and forth, struggling to keep their footing. Just outside of the crowd, a fully geared up Mavis Blackwell is pacing and calling out commands to what looks like approximately thirty security guards.

Trent leans into his radio again. "Uh, Eagle Eye, you seeing this? Over."

"Affirm, Badger One. I reactivate elevators, but someone circumvent me and disable them again. Over."

"Wait, someone re-disabled the elevators?"

"Affirm, I am locked out of elevator controls. Over."

Trent thinks for a moment, then says to Vincent and the others, "Bartram's trying to keep the staff inside the atrium. He knows it's us and wants bargaining chips. Goddamn it!"

"We have to get them out of there!" as Vincent shouts this, the crowd forms into more of a mosh, but Mavis isn't having it. She shouts a few commands and fires her shotgun in the air, causing a wave of shock and awe to befall both the crowd of partygoers and Vincent and his team.

Trent shouts into his radio, "Eagle Eye, is there anything you can do?!"

"Negative, Badger One!" Her voice is breathy, as if she's sprinting while talking. "Few guards escape barracks and found me!" Vincent can vaguely hear gunshots on the other side of the transmission.

Trent rushes the group back to the crate and pulls out a battering ram. "Vinny, you and Becca, go find Dr. Smith. Leo and I will get set up here. Come back as soon as possible. Go!"

He takes the ram, and they book it for the spiral staircase and descend to Dr. Smith's office, but Vincent hesitates when they reach the gallery. He looks through the hall to see Sarah in the middle of the crowd as they are being corralled onto their knees. "Vinny! Let's go!" Becca pulls him by the sleeve and continues down the stairs.

Dr. Smith's door is locked, so they start trying to beat it down, but it's a heavy-duty door. Becca has to show him what "put your back into it" means, but they eventually manage to crack the door jam and make their way inside. "Dr Smith!" Vincent calls out while trying to catch his breath. The two of them explore his room until they find him staring at a mirror. His appearance is striking. He's wearing his typically bold suit, but his long, silver hair is braided, beaded, and woven with a leather strap holding two eagle feathers straight up on the back of his head.

"Dr. Smith? What are you doing? We have to move."

Dr. Smith turns around, and Vincent can see his face; it's painted black, but over his right eye and covering nearly half his face, he's used red and gold paint to make a symbol that looks to Vincent like a large circle with petals surrounding it. "Is that a sun?"

"It is. The Mississippian Fire symbol. To the Mississippi civilization, it was a symbol of change. Purification. Cleansing."

While Vincent is caught off guard by Dr. Smith's appearance, Becca is still moving with a sense of urgency. She says, "While that's fascinating, sir, there's a bit of an emergency upstairs. They've taken the staff hostage, and Trent says you're needed."

"Indeed I am. Let me just grab something from my office, and we will be on our way." Dr. Smith looks at himself one last time in the mirror, then disappears for a moment and drops something in his coat pocket. "It is time."

When the three of them return to Bartram's living room, Dr. Smith contemplates the grandiose architecture of Bartram's cathedral inspired foyer until they reach the window where Trent and Leo have been busy setting up a small arsenal. Becca quickly grabs a few explosives and races back to the door to set a trap. "Just in case they decide to head our way."

"Good call, Becca," Trent says before addressing Dr. Smith. "Sir, it's good to see you again. Is that war paint?"

"Indeed, something to discuss at another time."

Leo approaches and pats Trent on the shoulder. "So this is him? The man who arranged for my freedom?" He then extends a rough hand, which Dr. Smith takes with pride.

"In the flesh. And you choose to repay me by returning to the belly of the beast? Perhaps not my wisest investment."

"I just missed this place *so* much. I couldn't stay away." Leo chuckles, then turns to the window where hundreds of civilians are being held hostage. "I believe we have some business to attend to. What's the plan? Is it time to turn the lights out?"

"It is not. You will need the power on in order to escort these fine people to the surface. My hope is for everyone to flee without a single shot being fired… However, I understand that that is more of a dream than a plan."

"Unfortunately," Trent agrees, "I think the only way anyone's getting out of here without a shot fired would be through negotiations. Do you think that's possible?"

"We are past the point of negotiations," Dr. Smith says calmly. "These hostages are in a precarious position, but they are not his priority."

Leo asks, "What's his priority?"

Vincent cuts in again, "Are we just going to breeze past his comment about negotiations? Wasn't that the whole plan?"

Trent doesn't acknowledge the question. Instead, he asks a question of his own. "They're definitely his most valuable project, but don't you think his worker bees would be top of his list?"

"I wish that were the case, but alas, the colonel's priorities are not in order."

"If that's the case, you need protection. I'll go with you."

"No. He has the tactical advantage; if I arrive with company, then we will be done. Stay here and do what you can to keep our people safe. You need to get them above ground."

Vincent watches on as if he were a child watching his parents spell out words to keep him from understanding, then Leo asks, "Where's he going? What's happening?"

Trent retrieves a pistol from the crate, loads it, and hands it to Dr. Smith, "You know how to handle this?"

"I have spent almost a century on this Earth. I was seventeen years old when the Second World War broke out. I am one of the world's foremost leaders in the study of thermodynamics—you better believe I have fired a gun before."

Trent chuckles. "Fair enough. Don't forget the safety."

Dr. Smith tucks the pistol into his belt and turns to Vincent. "Dr. Creighton, do you remember that message I asked you to remember?"

"Of course, but what is going on here?"

"Verbatim?"

"Yes, what does that matter right now?"

"It matters more than you can possibly know. Please pass it along to Dallyn for me, would you?"

Vincent isn't satisfied with the lack of information he's being given, but Dr. Smith moves with a purpose. He reaches into the box of grenades and pulls out an M84 stun grenade. "Mind if I borrow this?" Trent nods. "Good luck, my friends. I will see you on the other side. Oh, Vincent and I have arranged for your exfil by the way, just in case things do not go exactly as planned." Then he walks off, disappearing into the corridors.

Leo grabs Trent's shoulder and asks, "What's going on, Trent?"

Trent sighs and looks deep into Leo's eyes. "Dr. Smith has the most important role in this operation. But we need to keep our people safe. Do you guys understand that?"

Leo maintains eye contact with him and thinks for a moment. He asks simply, "Can I still trust you, Trent?"

Unblinking, Trent responds, "Of course, you can." Leo waits a beat, then turns to the crate and retrieves a bolt-action hunting rifle. He hands it to Vincent and says, "Gear up, soldier. We showed you how to shoot this thing, right?"

"Soldier? I'm not a fucking soldier! Tell me what the fuck is happening here!" Vincent stands steadfastly, but nobody pays attention to him. Instead, Becca, Trent, and Leo all prepare for some kind of assault. Eventually realizing that a fight might be coming for him whether he gets his way or not, he huffs and tightens the straps on his Kevlar vest, then checks his weapons: pistol, loaded; M4 Carbine, loaded; hunting rifle, loaded.; Ka-Bar, strapped. Standing against the window, he can see the reflection of a warrior overlooking the atrium.

Mavis patrols the crowd of half-drunken scientists, waiting for someone to misbehave; she sics her guards on anyone who starts whispering or looks like they might cause trouble. A quick slap or cold-cock is quite sobering when properly applied, but when that doesn't work, the pump action of a twelve-gauge does the trick.

Trent says, "Stay vigilant, guys. If anything happens, our priority is to take out their leader—Mavis—and to give the hostages somewhere to run. Vinny and Leo, you two are our snipers. Vinny, you're on Mavis duty. The second she pulls any shit, you drop her. Understood?"

"Drop her, like…"

"Kill her, Vincent. We are past the capture mission here; if she threatens someone's life, you end hers."

"Uh… oh, um, o-okay…"

"Becca and I are on the Brownings; we are the pathfinders. Where there is room to fire, we will take out the glass doors to the east wing. Give the hostages somewhere to escape to. Are your jobs clear?"

Becca grins. "Clear as mud."

"Good."

Once Trent establishes their roles, they watch on as the crowd grows restless. A few people start to fidget and get testy with Mavis. Sarah, Grace, and Brian are seated next to each other, and Grace has a face of absolute disdain in her eyes. Vincent can practically hear what she keeps whispering to Sarah and Brian. *They can't get us all! Let's rise up and take their guns! Fuck these guys!* Sarah's eyes are more concerned as she constantly scans the crowd looking for him, intermittently shushing Grace's whispers.

Brian, however, doesn't stifle Grace's whispers. In fact, in his drunken state, he whispers back in a voice that is probably much louder than just a whisper. This causes a chain reaction in the rest of the captives; dozens of hushed conversations grow subtly into a dull roar. Mavis doesn't like this, so she walks over and grabs Grace by the back of the neck, but Brian stands up to her by throwing a punch across her chin.

"Here we go," Trent whispers. "Do you have a shot, Vinny?"

He looks down the sights and does as much math as he can manage, but seeing Sarah's head so close, he gets nervous and says, "N-No, there's too many people." His heart is beating in his ears as he watches the interaction; Mavis drops Grace to the floor but strikes Brian upside the head, then drags him out in front of the group. She puts him on his knees in front of her.

"You got it now, Vin?"

Mavis places the barrel of her shotgun against the back of his head and shouts at the crowd. Brian's eye swells up, but he retorts to her calls with a likely smart-ass comment, and Mavis angrily shouts again with her finger on the trigger.

"Vinny?"

Four.

Brian gets to his feet and turns around, proudly raising his chin to Mavis. Sarah's jaw drops as tears stream down her cheeks, and Grace is practically bursting at the seams to stand up too.

Three.

Mavis fires a warning shot, and the entire atrium flinches. Then she pumps the action and points it back at his head, but Brian fails to heed the warning. He seems to be goading his peers into rising up with him, but they remain frozen.

Two.

"Vinny, do you have the shot?!" Numbers fly through his head as he lines up the perfect shot, adjusting for the refraction of the bullet's path when it breaks the surface tension of the window. He has it.

292

One.

Vincent's finger wraps around the trigger and tries to squeeze… but his muscles seize up. Mavis's familiar face hardens as she makes the decision to use Brian as an example, but Vincent's body refuses to pull the trigger. *Boom.* A dull blast is audible through the window as she ends Brian's life. His body goes limp, and the husk of his torso thuds to the floor. Sarah's scream pierces the air throughout the entire Abaddon.

"FIRE!" Trent shouts, and everyone but Vincent manages to fire their weapons. Leo gets the first shot off, trying to help Vincent by taking Mavis himself, but he fails to calculate for the bullet's refraction through the window, and his shot glances off her helmet. Her head whips back, and she falls on her ass.

Chaos erupts. Thirty-five guards rally, spreading out across the atrium; some of them sidle up against the walls, some of them trail through the gardens for cover, and some of them even take cover amongst the hostages. Mavis ignores the whiplash until she manages to sprint behind the trees for cover.

"Oh, for fuck's sake, Einstein!" Becca starts unloading her machine gun at the east wing entrance, while Trent suppresses fire from the guards. The two of them rain down lead through the redwood canopy, spraying blood into the flower beds and dropping guards left and right. Most of the guards struggle to hide, but the ones who are brazen enough to return fire have to shoot up through the canopy and wind up just damaging Bartram's chandelier. With an unobstructed view, Leo fires round after round at the guards using scientists as human shields, and he doesn't miss a shot.

"VINCENT!" Trent shouts. "They're using human shields! Get your head in the game!" Trent's voice is muffled by the deafening sound of bullets whirring in every direction and screams reverberating off the walls. He struggles to find his breath when the smell of gunpowder invades his sinuses, but then a hissing that comes from overhead replaces that scent with something vile. "Gas! Gas! Gas!" Trent's voice is still distant and slow, but a hand gripping him by the back of his neck snaps him back to reality. Trent basically forces Vincent's gas mask onto his face and slaps his helmet. "Pull yourself together, son!"

Vincent shakes his head and looks down at the stream of scientists fleeing into the east wing. Near the entrance and between intermittent muzzle flashes, he recognizes Peterson's face hiding behind Sarah. His heart stops. Instantly raising his rifle to his shoulder, he looks down the sights. Scratches on the visor of his gas mask throw off his aim. He tries to focus, but the rubber irritates the skin on his cheeks and temples. Each individual pop he hears from the battlefield draws his attention. He shuts his eyes and takes deep breaths while his muscles twitch. The smell of smoke and silicone creeps down his throat as he breathes. *I can't deal with this thing!* He loosens the straps on his gas mask and pushes it atop his head so he can breathe. Instead of fresh air, however, he gets a sinus full of rank-smelling smoke and replaces the mask. He moves to the couch to hack up a lung.

"We don't have time for you to die, Einstein!" Becca shouts at him.

As he catches his breath, his blood pressure manages to stabilize, and he steps back up to the window, bringing his rifle to his shoulder yet again. Lining up his shot, numbers fly through his brain. Though the smoke obstructs his vision, he can sense where Peterson is holding Sarah. Calculating the shot, he feels a burst of bullets whiz past his ear, one of which brushes against his helmet. He falls to the ground and gets the wind knocked out of him.

With most of the scientists having fled the immediate area, Trent throws a grenade that illuminates the garden with white light and a wet fire that sticks to the trunks and canopy of the redwoods. Several guards spread out from the garden like scattering insects, but most of them are burning from head to toe and keel over before they can get far.

Smoke starts to rise to the atrium ceiling, and the artificial sky glitches out temporarily. The sprinkler system kicks on with the sound of thunder and a few flashes of lightning across the sky. Vincent stands back up in time to see the smoke breaking in the rain, but he's lost Peterson and Sarah in the crowd. *Where the fuck did you go?* He scans the atrium until he finds Sarah's red hair being dragged into the east wing corridor. He lines up his shot, but his hand starts to tremble again. He wants to pull the trigger, but… he can't. Then a pop from over his shoulder places a bullet between Peterson's eyes, leaving Sarah to disappear into the stream of scientists.

Leo says something to him, but Vincent can't hear anything over the chaos, so he simply stares back at him with fear in his heart.

DR. SMITH NAVIGATES THE CORRIDORS of Bartram's office for the first time, but the service elevator stands out to him. He steps inside and notices the button that leads to the surface is illuminated with a red light, but the lower levels and basement are still available. Pressing the button for the basement, he descends. With his eyes closed, he slows his breathing and feels his surroundings. The metal walls of the elevator warble as he is pulled deeper and deeper into the underbelly of the Abaddon. *Mother… father… ancestors and descendants… please forgive me for the act of darkness which I am about to commit.* He takes a deep breath of stale air and checks to make sure that his pistol is still in his belt and that the USB drive is in his breast pocket, then he holds the stun grenade behind his back with both hands and waits.

The elevator slows to a halt, and the doors slide open. Before him, Dr. Smith sees the cavernous, one-and-a-half million square foot warehouse stacked floor to ceiling with clone maturation chambers. Ten feet from him, Bartram and Martinez stand on either side of one of the chambers, Bartram in his dress blues holding out his pistol and Martinez in full gear, pointing his M4 at Dr. Smith. They can hear rumbling coming from the elevator shaft as a battle breaks out above them. Periodic explosions and a consistent hum of machine guns vibrate through the walls.

"Welcome to the Cultivation Center, Russell." Bartram and Martinez step out from their cover, as he has shown up unaccompanied. "I like your war paint. I'm shaking in my boots."

"Thank you for the… warm welcome," Dr. Smith replies and steps out of the elevator. "I hope you do not mind my friends crashing the party upstairs."

"I can't be too mad. I saw something like this coming a long time ago. I'm actually more surprised that there's still power to the rest of the Abaddon. I thought you'd have shut it all down by now."

"It would not matter if I had, would it?"

"Not at all. I can get a new team in a matter of days, but these guys? They take a lifetime to grow."

Dr. Smith turns his focus on the fields of maturation chambers. "This place is far more expansive than I anticipated. I want to be impressed, but then I remember that you intend to sell these human beings into slavery."

Bartram lowers his weapon to get more comfortable while Martinez remains steadfast. "Slavery is a strong word; let's call it… 'serving their function.' They've been designed to carry out orders without question— be it warfare, or if we can get our hands on Vincent's brain, scientific discovery."

"And thanks to Mavis, they would not even be liberated by old age catching up to them."

"You always fail to see the true scope of our creations, Dr. Smith. We create the perfect soldier, and all you can focus on is the question of ethics. Leonard Sideris was the greatest assassin this world has seen in at least a millennium; just one of him was capable of changing the world's political and civil landscape. Imagine what an army of him could accomplish."

"They could finally solve 'the Indian problem' by simply eliminating the rest of my people. They could settle the immigration debate by murdering every immigrant to this country. They could topple countries by killing off heads of state."

"Or prevent World War III. Or end a holocaust. Or bring about world peace. You see? Your mind is too narrow to see the possibilities around you."

"Not narrow, just distracted by the potential of your unchecked power," Dr Smith replies.

"*Unchecked?* What exactly qualifies someone to check power? Are *you* qualified? If anything, your hippy-dippy Berkeley protesters would be thanking me right now; I'm redistributing power to everyone equally across the board!"

"By selling weapons, not tools," Dr Smith retorts.

"Don't give me your bullshit *'I understand what it's like to be marginalized'* fake wisdom. I sell technology so people can use it, whether it's called a weapon or a tool is up to whoever writes the history book."

Dr. Smith gives a sad smile. "Unfortunately, you are correct."

"Speaking of history… your little friends up there won't last long. Even if they eliminate my entire security team, you are their only chance of surviving through the night; my people have orders to take as many prisoners as possible. Once their little firefight is over, we can begin our exchange."

"What exchange would that be?"

"Their lives for that information in your head."

"You see, that is the difference between me and you. My people are not assets. They are not something to be traded based on their value to me but warriors who will fight to their dying breath against tyranny." He pulls the pin on his grenade and tosses it, shielding his eyes and ducking.

"Grenade!" Bartram and Martinez both shout just as it lets off a blinding burst of white light. They stagger backwards while Dr. Smith pulls his gun and fires at Martinez in his center mass. He then sprints forward into the grid of cloning chambers, ducking and weaving through the aisles as he moves to throw Bartram off his trail. Dr. Smith stops at a computer and pulls the USB drive out. He plugs it in and types on the keyboard as fast as he can until a message window pops up: "Downloading…"

After a few seconds, Bartram gathers himself, and the after images dissipate. Instead of following Dr. Smith, he goes to the head of the front row of cloning chambers and types on the computer. "Draining Sequence Initiated" and "Detachment Sequence Initiated" message windows pop up. Then a few seconds later, ten of the chamber doors open. Out of the chambers step ten thirty-year-old, naked men. Their scrappy builds are identical to that of Leo when he was first abducted by Bartram.

Bartram's bold voice calls out, "Subjects zero-two-zero through zero-three-zero!" All ten of them look over. "Your mission is to take that elevator upstairs and kill the prime subject, along with anyone else who tries to stop you." They look at each other, nod, and step toward the elevator. "Wait! Look inside the closet next to your chambers. There should be gear and weapons. Equip yourself, then go." They proceed with their instructions. Bartram turns back to his computer, logs into his office security systems, and activates a protocol called "Riot Control" across the entire north wing. Once this protocol has been activated, he sees a pop-up message appear: "Download Complete." *Download? What download?*

The Leo clones gear up and take the elevator upstairs. Bartram checks on Martinez and finds the bullet lodged in his Kevlar vest. He slaps Martinez on the cheek and says, "Get up soldier, you still got work to do." They both get up and infiltrate the grid of cloning chambers.

BECCA AND TRENT FIRE OFF the last of their ammunition belts. Vincent recollects that he last saw Mavis trying to take Becca out of commission before disappearing into the chaos. The sprinklers manage to put out some of the fire that has started spreading through the garden, but Trent's white-phosphorous-napalm grenades stick to the flowerbeds, bushes, and tree trunks, persisting through the downpour.

Vincent's attention fixates on the silvery smoke descending on the black mask strapped to Trent's face, barely making out the color in his irises as muffled yells vibrate in Vincent's ear. Trent taps Vincent on the helmet, presses the rifle to his chest, and points toward the atrium. *They've… we've slaughtered more than half of the guards… we're winning, but… oh my God…* Trent starts picking off a few of the stragglers when the fog behind them lights up with golden flashes, then sparks shoot off the marble floors and walls around them.

"INCOMING SIX O'CLOCK!" Trent shouts, then he and Becca dismount their machine guns and switch to their carbines. They fire into the void, standing their ground. "We need to find a way out of here. Vincent, what's our exfil?"

"Me? How should I know?!"

"Smith said you have exfil covered!"

"I don't fucking kn—" as he says it, he realizes that wherever Dr. Smith ended up going was a one-way trip. "Downstairs! To the testing facility!"

They retreat into the cathedral foyer and take cover behind the columns; Trent lights a flare and throws it in the direction of their ambushers. The light from the flare illuminates the smoke as if they were fog lights, but they can make out half a dozen silhouettes with assault rifles, along with even more filling in from the corridor.

Leo asks, "Who the fuck is that? They have no masks!"

Becca opts to not debate the issue. Instead, she says, "They're targets! Shoot them!"

The three of them return fire, with Vincent fumbling to take the safety off his M4. He has to deliberately search for the switch, but he accidentally turns it to semi-automatic then back to safety. He looks up just in time for one of the silhouettes to sprint toward him. Emerging from the cover of smoke, Vincent can see a thirty-year-old Leo toss his empty rifle aside, draw a knife, and lunge toward him with an overhand strike. Instincts kicking in, Vincent's hands let his rifle hang by its strap, then he bursts forward to stop Leo's momentum, hooks the knife arm, and knees the groin. Leo's body shudders but maintains its posture. Vincent knees a few more times with as much might as he can muster, then throws the limp body away from him. Immediately grabbing his rifle again, he switches to fully automatic, and pulls the trigger until Leo's body stops moving.

Trent pats him on the shoulder as he retreats, then says, "Good job, kid. Let's move!" He starts to fall back with Becca, then directs her to disassemble the trap at the door. Leo and Vincent kneel behind their columns staring down at the Leo-clone's corpse. They look at each other with horror, then feel more gunfire scrape the column.

Leo says to Vincent, "Survival now. Questions later." Vincent nods shakily. They take up arms and retreat with Trent and Becca, providing suppressive fire while she disables the explosive.

Trent yells, "They must have raided our weapons cache. They're firing our own guns at us; we have to get out before they find the grenades. Becca, move it!"

"I'm moving as fast as I can! Setting it up is easier than tearing it do—" she screeches as a bullet rips through her shoulder.

"Becca!" Trent shouts, then drags her away from the door. "Fuck it! I'm blowing the door!" He throws a frag grenade, and everyone gets in front of the columns. As it goes off, the trap intensifies the explosion, blowing the door off its hinges and down the spiral staircase. "GO! GO! GO!" Vincent and Leo sprint into the staircase platform, covering Trent and Becca as they slowly make their way down the spiral, dodging high caliber rounds that rain down from above them until finally reaching the bottom.

Vincent and Leo survey the art gallery. Apparently, Tzofiya's last-ditch effort to defend them worked—Mavis and the guards who hadn't succumbed to phosphorus inhalation are struggling to break down the glass door. *Interesting... the north wing's entrance is reinforced, but the other wings' entrances were a lot easier to break down.* "Straight across, we're taking the subway." Trent and Becca limp across while Vincent and Leo stay back to cover them. A few stray bullets manage to crack the glass door, whizzing past Trent's head and ripping a hole into the

Jackson Pollock painting. From above them, Vincent can hear footsteps descending the staircase, followed by a *clink* directly behind them. *What is that?*

Vincent's center of gravity is thrust into the art gallery, hitting the floor with Leo's arm covering him. A blast from behind the wall flashes an incredibly bright white before liquid flames spew into the gallery, but when Vincent raises his head, he finds the wall had protected them from the majority of the explosion. He looks down to see Leo's helmet, mask, and Kevlar vest on fire. *Shit!* Acting fast, he uses his KA-BAR to cut Leo's vest and helmet off, but then he sees the mask and hesitates. A split-second passes, and Leo lets out a blood-curdling scream as he regains consciousness, which causes Vincent to recoil violently. Leo reaches up to pull the mask off, but Vincent puts his knee on his wrist to keep him from touching the phosphorus-napalm, then he finally decides to cut the mask off.

More gunfire breaks through the glass, then he hears Trent shout, "Vincent! Grab him, and go!" Vincent takes Leo's weight and channels Brian's lifting techniques to shoulder his limp body, then pushes through to the subway car. Trent drops Becca in the passenger car and shouts, "Cover them!" He gets in the conductor's car and starts up the engine. Vincent sets Leo in the center of the car and posts up at the door. The squadron of clones closing in, Vincent begins to unload his magazine, eventually emptying his rifle and switching to his pistol. As he makes the switch, the doors begin to close, but a single clone manages to slide in just as the subway car starts moving.

As Vincent struggles to find the safety on his pistol, he notices the clone focus his attention on the unconscious Leo. Becca pulls her pistol and immediately fires at the clone. He takes a few bullets to the chest before lunging on her with his knife. She throws both legs and her one good arm up to stop him, but the clone's blade shanks her thigh. Vincent finally readies his gun and empties his magazine into the clone's head until it collapses atop Becca's blood-covered body.

"FIND HIM. KILL HIM IF YOU NEED TO. I'll find out what this download is," Bartram whispers to Martinez as they spread out into the cloning chamber grid. Martinez nods and brings his rifle to his shoulder. Bartram scans the rows of computers, not knowing what he's looking for. "Dr. Smith," his bold voice echoes throughout the warehouse. "I've been considering making a change in management here at the Abaddon."

Dr. Smith ducks from row to row, getting as far away from them as he can and not daring to speak. Bartram continues, "I believe our esteemed colleague, Dr. Blackwell, has established herself as quite a competent leader amongst her scientific peers. I believe she may even be ready for the position of 'Civilian Director of Operations' here. What do you think?"

Dr. Smith rips one of the cufflinks off his suit and tosses it, then he hides a few rows down and waits with his gun drawn.

"I'm hearing you disagree? On what grounds, Dr. Smith?" Bartram asks facetiously, sweeping through an army of sleeping computers until he finds one that's awake. Dr. Smith can hear Martinez's gear rattle as he moves, staying just out of sight until hearing him stop. He points the barrel of his pistol at where he's expecting to see Martinez kneel down, checking the safety one more time.

"I suppose you think she's too eager to please me? Too willing to be a team player, to bend over backwards to accomplish my goals." He approaches the computer and sees the screen displaying some kind of list. "She is exactly the type I was looking for. She bridges the gap between an obedient soldier and a brilliant scientist. If you combine her, Leo, and Vincent into the same brain, who knows what kind of demon we'd create?" He scans through the list of gibberish, including an analysis of the Artificial Amniotic Fluid, the clones' wiring, IV tubes, and a computer code. He scrolls through the code trying to glean anything that resembles English. "I see you've been doing some coding, huh? Always learning new skills. Perhaps it's simply that you're not ready to retire." Hearing Martinez stop in his tracks, Bartram looks up from the computer.

An ear-splitting pop reverberates through the warehouse, followed by a back and forth between pistol and rifle shots—then a grunt and a thud. "Do you want him alive, sir?" Martinez asks.

Bartram smiles. "Good work, soldier. Alive, row six." Dr. Smith groans as Martinez cuffs him, drags him to row six, and drops him at Bartram's feet, who looks down to see just a flesh wound, then continues to scroll through the code. Dr. Smith nurses his wound, but remains as silent as possible. "I could really use your help figuring out what you've uploaded here."

Dr. Smith shakes his head. "I am sure you could."

"Rude." Bartram scrolls through the code as quickly as he can, looking for anything remotely familiar. The code itself proves to be wholly useless, but he reviews the chemical list, knowing that he has no idea what any of these are. Except for one: "Nitroglycerin? Isn't that—"

Martinez finishes his thought, "Dynamite."

Bartram notices an obscene volumetric measurement that causes his heart to sink. Thirty liters per unit. Thirty-one liters. Thirty-two liters. The number continues to rise with no apparent limit in sight. Bartram gasps and immediately sprints to the main computer at the head of the row, logs in, and navigates back to his office security system. He finds the initiative titled: "Project Locust: Master Shutdown (Do Not Press This Button!)." His hand hovers over the mouse as he fights the urge to press the button. Shutting his eyes tightly, he inhales and activates the initiative. A loading bar appears on-screen, and as it progresses, Bartram sighs heavily.

Five hundred feet above him, the fluorescent lights flicker and black out. The electrical hum of lights failing and the whir of thousands of computers simultaneously powering down echo across the grid. When his eyes open, he is met with darkness. Bartram's hand-polished leather dress shoes clicking across the floor reflect the powering on of the neon green glow of emergency lights overhead. When he returns to Martinez chaperoning Dr. Smith, he looks down at the doctor leaning against a computer with his hands cuffed behind his back. Dr. Smith's face paint glows, and the Mississippian sun shines back at Bartram. With fire in his eyes, Dr. Smith smiles before uttering, "Blessed are the meek, right Henry?"

Bartram reaches over, takes the pistol that Martinez recovered, and fires a single round between Dr. Smith's eyes.

Martinez doesn't flinch when the gun goes off, but when Dr. Smith's body slumps over, he asks, "Sir, what about the Abaddon's power source?"

Bartram stares him down with a snarl. "Just get him out of my sight."

BECCA SHOVES THE CLONE AWAY and sits up against the subway car's seat, bleeding profusely from the shoulder and thigh. "C'mere, Einstein… you have to… hafta… I'm just gonna…"

"No! Becca, you have to stay awake! We're gonna get you out of here; take you to a hospital and fix you up. Okay?"

"Tour… tourn… turn a…"

"Turn a what?" he asks, then looks down at the blood gushing from her thigh. "Oh! Tourniquet! Yes!" He looks around the car for something to use as a tourniquet, then realizes that she probably won't need her belt anymore. Acting quickly, he slides her belt off and slips it around her upper thigh, then pulls it as tightly as he can manage. Blood splattering on his hands and face and soaking into his hoodie, the smell of iron wafts across his nose and nearly makes him vomit. He ties off the belt, then leans back against the opposite seat, watching to see what she does. Her head droops off to the side.

Is… she alive? He pokes her elbow. Nothing. Pokes her again. Nothing. He gently taps her cheek with his bloody fingers. She inhales sharply, as if waking from a light nap. "I'm okay. I'm… just tired."

"Stay awake, okay? We have, just, like, five more minutes until we're there." He watches her struggle to stay awake, considering whether or not to look at Leo—that grenade burned him pretty seriously. Finally managing to turn his head, he sees Leo sprawled out on the floor. He's barely stirring. Vincent crawls over to him, a pit opening in his stomach, his throat dry as a desert, and his arms shaking.

Leo's long-sleeved shirt that he wore under his vest seems to have stayed intact after Vincent cut the vest off, but he's just now noticing that after removing the mask, the phosphorus-napalm streaked across Leo's left eye. *He must have passed out from the pain... but at least his moustache was untouched.* Vincent jumps nearly ten feet back when Leo's right eye opens. His head thuds against the metal floor, then it dawns on Vincent that he isn't unconscious. He's paralyzed. The subway car comes to a stop, and Trent circles around as the doors open. They drag the other two out of the subway, and as soon as the door closes, the car is called back to the north wing. *That doesn't bode well.*

Standing in front of the blast door, Vincent scans his ID, and the door slowly opens to reveal the cylindrical testing facility. *Thank you, Tzofiya.* They hurry into the observation chamber, then Vincent turns on the power converter and gets to typing on the master computer. "It should only take three minutes per person to transport, however, I do have to type in the correct revolution adjustment algorithm. That'll take about ten minutes."

"Just hurry as fast as you can!" Trent shouts, slapping Becca to keep her awake. "Those guys are going to be here in less than sixteen now."

"Do you have coordinates for your camp?"

"I have coordinates that are close, but not exact." He pulls out a GPS device from his cargo pants' pocket and tosses it to him. "We don't record the exact location, just in case it's ever recovered by Bartram."

"That'll work." Vincent takes the GPS and inputs the coordinates, then opens the glass chamber door and begins typing in the algorithm. Trent drags Leo out to the chamber and props him against the glass. Vincent watches from inside the observation room, and though he can't hear what they're saying, he can see Trent giving some kind of speech to Leo's paralyzed body.

After ten minutes, Vincent calls out to Trent, "Get back here! We need to close the blast doors!" Trent returns, teary-eyed, to the observation room, and Vincent uses the master computer to close both the main blast door and the observation chamber door.

Vincent closes the door and takes the deepest breath of his life. *Please, please fucking work.* He then hits "Enter" on the master computer. Leo sits propped against the glass, and Vincent can see his chest rising and falling faster than the computer is humming. The pad beneath him lights up, and his chest stops moving. *Oh no… What's happening?* Leo's eyes widen… then… Vincent blinks. Leo's gone.

Trent lets out a breath. "Did it work?"

"I… I don't know. I don't really have a way to find out."

"We don't have the time anyway. It's your turn, get in there."

"Me? What about Becca?" Vincent asks, flustered.

"You're next, Vinny. Go."

Vincent looks at Trent, whose expression has turned bleak. He looks over Trent's shoulder and sees Becca slouched in the corner, struggling to keep her eyes open. Vincent's jaw slowly falls as he realizes the fault of this plan. Vincent's stomach melts, dripping out of him as tears well up in his eyes. "What did you tell Leo?"

"Uh… I was just getting some things off my chest. And uh, I asked if he could find my daughter."

"Your *daughter*?!"

"Yeah, don't worry about it. Just get the job done." Trent opens the observation room and glass chamber doors, but he practically has to push Vincent to get him inside the chamber. "Listen. I made my choices. You two need to survive." Vincent's mind is reeling, but once he sees out from inside the chamber, he realizes something. *I get to see what Leo's clone saw before I…* Vincent prefers not to finish that thought. The teleportation pad illuminates and begins to glow, then, before long, he starts feeling queasy. Leaning against the glass, he feels vibrations from the ground. He looks over to see the main blast door beginning to crack open. Vincent watches in terror as several Leo clones come bursting into the facility and firing at him. The glass chips, but doesn't shatter. Vincent feels grateful for the engineers being overly cautious.

Vincent stumbles to his knees as he slowly dissipates on a quantum level. He watches bullets fly through the air, and time seems to move slower. He looks inside the observation chamber, where Trent is screaming silently and trying to open the blast door. Then his eyes fall on the silver box next to the teleportation pad sitting just outside the glass. A stray bullet ricochets off the glass and lodges itself into the power converter. Another bullet. And another.

The glass cracks as Vincent feels himself fall to the pad. Inside the observation chamber, Trent ducks, and the blast door starts closing again. Vincent somehow watches the trajectory of one last bullet traveling through the air until it penetrates the converter. With a spark of electricity and a deep, guttural grinding sound, the converter releases a concussive blast and a blinding fireball that expands to fill the entire room.

Vincent doesn't feel any heat though, nor does he feel the force of an explosion. Instead, he feels a tug behind his navel, and his entire body implodes in on itself. Once the darkness sets in, he hears what sounds like a crack, and then… nothing.

CHAPTER THIRTY-NINE

March 17th, 2019

Sunday

"**V**incent!" Karl's shouting and snapping in front of Vincent's face tears his mind away from the algorithm that he's been formulating. The noisy drunkards around him make the bar an even more unpleasant experience than usual. "Bud! The bottle's pointing at you. It's your buy." Looking at the table, Vincent sees the empty bottle pointing at him. *Wait, again? I bought the last round!*

He sighs begrudgingly and slides out of the booth. Pushing his way through the crowd of plastic, green bowler hats, green bow ties, and green T-shirts proves to be more painful than he would have expected, as drunkards take the liberty of pinching him harder than necessary. Each pinch stinging more than the last, he just pushes through the crowd as fast as he can.

When he finally makes his way to the front of the line, the bartender doesn't give him the time of day. Not only does she fail to notice him trying to place an order, she almost seems to ignore him to instead serve the bigger, more attractive customers that are placing orders. As he waits patiently to order, he suddenly feels somebody ram into him from behind, pushing him into the bar. *That's gonna leave a bruise.* He looks back to see just a group of rowdy dudes laughing and joking.

Bobby ducks behind the rest of his friends so that Vincent doesn't see him.

"What do you want, skinny?"

Vincent looks over to see the bartender crossing her arms and impatiently chewing bubble gum, waiting for him to speak. "Uh… can I, uh, get four, like, beers?"

"Uh, like, um, like, whatever." She sighs and reaches under the bar to crack four bottles, then places them on the counter. After handing her a twenty-dollar bill, she says, "You're eight short." He reluctantly reaches into his wallet and pulls out another twenty. She breaks it and drops the change into the tip jar. "Bye." She blows a bubble in his face, then turns to serve the rest of the crowd. *Oh… okay… you're welcome.*

As he struggles to grab all four drinks and leave, Becca eyes him wistfully.

Balancing the drinks has always been a challenge for him, but even more so during St. Patrick's Day in an Irish pub. When he approaches the table, somebody bumps into him, and he accidentally spills a significant amount onto his chest.

"Aw, Vince! Way to go!" Karl shouts disappointedly. Vincent passes out the beers to his friends… and Mark, who's invited them out for a "holiday team-bonding opportunity." He does this every time a holiday comes up: invites all four of them out, but spends most of the night hovering close to the girls while Karl ends up disappearing with some group or another that he's met that night.

"Here, take these, Vince." Sarah passes him some napkins to dry off his shirt. She moves to sit next to him as he cleans up, offering him help with a bright smile. She notices his attention diverting to her eyes instead of trying to clean himself up, and both of them blush slightly. She lets her hand linger on his, trying to interlace fingers before she senses his discomfort and retracts, feeling embarrassed.

"I gotta hit the john," Mark says, ungracefully shoving himself out of the booth. "Give me a few minutes—that corned beef hash isn't agreeing with the stomach." With a gross laugh, he pats his belly and leaves.

Grace groans loudly, "What a pig!" She grabs Sarah by the shoulders and practically shouts in a drunken slur, "It's like he *only* invites us out to these things to flirt! Such a creep…" She pouts before taking another sip of the beer Vincent bought her. "Don't you guys, just, like, don't you feel like he doesn't give a *fuck* about the project? It's like he's always distra—" she stops mid-sentence as a Dropkick Murphys song turns on; she squeals, grabs Sarah by the wrists, and pulls her out to the dance floor.

Mark carefully makes his way to the bathroom, but instead of opening the door, he looks back to make sure his employees didn't follow him. When the coast is clear, he walks to a nearby booth hidden near the back of the bar. Sliding into the booth, a woman wearing a black suit sits opposite him.

"You appear to be having a grand old time," the suit says sarcastically.

"I'm being friendly, isn't that the goal? Acting natural?" Mark responds. His sweaty comb-over falls in front of his face, but he licks his palm and slides it back.

"You ought to reconsider what 'natural' means."

"Are we here to talk about my personal life or conduct some business?"

"Right," she says with a smarmy look. "How's their progress?"

"Good, they're getting close. I think Vincent pretty much has it, but the others are distracting him."

"Bartram will be on him like a vulture once he gets that algorithm figured out. What about correspondence with the Abaddon?"

"We just got a check from 'the government' last week, so we're still getting paid. Smith has been calling every month or so for a report—it sounds like Bartram's been breathing down his neck."

"He still trusts you then?"

"I'm fairly certain, yes."

"Good," the suit nods solemnly. "Now, once Vincent does figure it out—"

"I'll schedule the press conference as quickly as I can." He swallows hard. "I'll schedule it about a *week* out to buy us some time. Your team better be ready though, because—"

Mark hesitates at the end of the sentence. The suit finishes it for him,

"Because once Bartram has Vincent and friends in tow… he's going to want a 'meeting' with you."

"Yeah…" Mark sighs and shakes himself out of a stupor. "But by then, the ball will be rolling, and I won't be able to help out anyway."

"Don't worry about it. I've already arranged a detail for you. You've got nothing to worry about."

Elsewhere in the bar, at a booth catercorner to Vincent's table, Trent joins Leo in bending an elbow while conducting surveillance on their target.

"Good of you to join me," Leo says. "Haven't seen you in a while."

"Yeah," Trent says. "I figured St. Patrick's Day would provide me enough cover to keep from getting spotted. How long has the… interaction between him and that red-head been going on?"

"Sarah? At least as long as we've been watching. It's been bubbling under the surface since they've met, it sounds like. It's never going to happen though. He's too cowardly to make a move, and she's too respectful to push his boundaries."

"What do you make of it?"

"Hmm," Leo considers his response thoughtfully. "Well, for starters, it'll be a good 'in' when it comes time to make contact with him. It also might be helpful for him later on. He'll need an anchor to ground himself against once Bartram starts clawing at him."

Trent nods. "Hopefully she won't weigh him down too much; he'll need to grow out of his shell some time."

"We have to be careful though," Leo says cautiously. "He's a good egg, but he's unstable as all hell. I get that he'll need some self-confidence to stand up against Bartram, but we'll be dancing on a razor's edge. We push him just a hair too far, and he'll end up just like me—clawing at more power however he can get it. The difference is he's smart enough to actually get it."

"Uh oh, the girls are dancing this way. Cover." They both cover their faces with newspapers, pretending to be minding their own business.

Vincent sits at his booth as awkwardly as he usually does when it ends up being just him and Karl alone. Despite his best efforts, Karl has given up trying to get Vincent to binge drink like the rest of the people around them. Offering shot after shot, he winds up taking every drink that Vincent refuses, reaching the level that he usually does in order to enjoy this particular coworker's presence.

"Vin-Vin-Vincent," his words slosh around, and he wraps his arm around Vincent's shoulder. "You gotta make your moooove, man. She-She's not gonna make it for you, bro—" he lets out a burp. "Sarah is like—she's, like, such a hottie man. Like… let's just look at her!" He grabs Vincent by the chin and points his face toward Sarah while she's dancing alongside Grace. Still well-coordinated in her heels and flowy dress, Vincent admires her infectious laughter as Grace gets her to do more and more intricate dance moves in time with the music. A smile begins to creep across his face, and he pulls away from Karl's forceful grasp. After another moment of adoration, Karl says to him, "You're gonna lose her."

Vincent turns his head in shock and asks, "What?"

Karl takes another shot, and strangely, his speech clears up, "You're gonna lose her. You've got to make your move, or she's gonna move… on."

"Move on from what?"

"C'mon! You're not *that* stupid, are you?" Vincent's face flushes, and Karl laughs aloud in his face. "She likes you, dude! And you like her, but if you don't move on it, she's gonna find some other guy. I can only do so much to keep the fucking hyenas in this bar off of her for you; you're gonna have to move on her yourself."

"You said the word 'move' way too much—what are you even talking about?" Vincent asks.

"This!" Karl abruptly stands up and stumbles toward Sarah and Grace. Walking right past them, however, he wraps his arms around a couple of guys trying to dance their way toward the girl. Karl successfully redirects their attention to another couple of pretty ladies.

A sudden slump lands in the adjacent booth. Mark's taken his spot back and lets out a loud burp. "Why aren't you out there with them? They're making some new friends; you could do with some new friends, couldn't you?"

Vincent ignores Mark and his brow instinctively furrows. *Karl doesn't know what he's talking about. He's just drunk, and… there's no way. Sarah and I are… just friends.* Mark strikes up a one-way conversation with him while Vincent thinks about Sarah. *Should I… what is a move? What move would be good enough for Sarah?* She turns and notices him watching her; Vincent's heart sinks for a moment until she smiles at him, brushes a lock of her hair behind her ear, and turns back to the group. Eyes widening, he abruptly stands and feels every millimeter of his nervous system urging him to join them in dancing. Instead, he turns on his heel and bolts for the exit. Mark looks up from the booth, confused, trying to say goodbye as Vincent quickly escapes. Surveying the bar to find what prompted this strange behavior, he finds Sarah looking back with disappointment painted on her face.

"Poor guy's gonna lose her."

CHAPTER FORTY

August 1st, 2020

Saturday

"**T**his is for your protection!" Mavis calls out to the crowd of nervous scientists while scaring them into a kneeling position. *Where is he?* Sarah's knees ache as she scans the group, yet again, for any sign of Vincent's greasy black hair, but she can't find anything. *Was he the security breach? He better know what's going on…* Grace's whispering goes in one ear and out the other, and even Brian's drunken indignation at the guards' disrespect is hard to listen to, knowing Vincent could be anywhere. Or dead. *Oh God… is he dead? Did they kill him?* Her thoughts escalate in her mind until she sees Mavis charging through the crowd in front of her and grabbing Grace by the back of the neck.

"No! Don't you touch her!" Sarah cries out, but it's Brian who takes action—he launches himself to his feet and throws a haymaker at Mavis's chin. While this causes her to forget about Grace, Brian just painted a target on himself. With a swift strike to the eye, Brain nearly trips over his feet, but Mavis drags him in front of the crowd, puts him on his knees, and puts the barrel of her shotgun to the back of his head. "Brian! No, let him go!" Sarah shrieks but dares not move from her spot.

"Silence, you little shits!" Mavis is nearly unrecognizable as she shouts at the group, "You are not *guests* here at the Abaddon! This is not a *home*! It's not a *party*! You are our prisoners, and we have spoiled you rotten!" The whispers come to a complete stop. The newer generation of scientists still living above ground are shocked; they almost seem to be under the impression this is some kind of performance art or drill or something.

Brian's eye starts to swell, but he retorts with, "You know what happens to the barrel when you have one rotten apple, right?" His words are still slightly slurred.

"Shut your fucking mouth, Reid! We have been very gracious hosts to you. Don't force me to make an example of you!"

Brian slowly gets to his feet, turns around, and raises his chin at her. "You can kill me, but you won't kill us all, will you?" Mavis fires a round off to the side, causing the room to jump, but she cocks her gun and points it back at him. "Go on!" Brian shouts and turns to his friends. "We got them outnumbered! They can't get us all!" Sarah can feel Grace practically jumping in her boots to leap at Mavis, but she manages to sit still.

Mavis gives the crowd a moment to respond. Nobody does. Her face hardens. "Brian, you know the consequences for insubordination." Sarah's heart skips a beat as Mavis moves her finger to the trigger again… then she pulls. A powerful blast reverberates off the atrium walls, then Brian's head whips back with a spray of blood spattering across the floor behind him. Sarah screams at the top of her lungs and collapses into Grace, whose rage takes a backseat to her trauma.

The second Mavis pulls the trigger, however, the blast initiates a sequence of events that ends in a chaotic free-for-all: Brian's body thuds to the floor, then a gunshot shatters glass from above them, then Mavis grunts as her own head whips back, then flurries of machine gun fire rain down on them and up through the trees. She feels Grace grab her shoulders and push them both to the floor, but the scores of other scientists around her rock them apart. Sarah tries to gain a foothold, but she loses Grace in the scuffle.

Amidst the others' mad dashes for survival, Sarah can't keep up with the stimulation as she perceives it. One instant, she sees Mavis leaning against a tree with blood streaming down her face—the next, her claustrophobia kicks in with people pushing and shoving her like she's in some kind of tug-of-war game. She sees a camouflage sleeve wrap around her throat before a black assault rifle appears in her peripheral vision. Several ear-shattering pops disorient her while being pulled toward the east wing entrance, and she screams even more, but her own voice sounds slow and muffled.

Her struggles accomplish very little, but Sarah manages to jab her elbow into the rib of whoever has her wrangled. She tries to run away, but the stampede of scientists seems to push her back into her captor's grip. A few more gunshots are fired next to her ear just as a flash of white light illuminates the garden. A wave of crying, terrified scientists pushes them away from the east wing entrance. She can feel the sleeved arm accidentally crushing her windpipe until another earsplitting blast causes her to flinch and gasp, which might be the first breath she's taken in several minutes—but when that happens, the arm goes limp. She turns around to see a hole in Peterson's forehead as she crumbles under the feet of the stampede. Sarah then lets the stream of escapees carry her into the east wing.

"Grace! Grace!"

"Sarah?!"

The two call each other's names until finally finding each other somewhere just outside the barracks entrance. They go with the flow of the crowd until they can link arms, then push their way to Brian's room and step inside, but they're joined by a handful of newer scientists who don't have a room of their own to take refuge in. Sarah shuts the door and immediately starts trembling and gasping to catch her breath. Grace approaches from behind her and pulls her in for a shaky hug so Sarah can break down in her arms. They slide against the door to sit down and process what just happened.

"What... what was that?" one of the new scientists asks.

Grace looks at them and grimly says, "A paradigm shift."

"Wh-What does that mean?"

"I don't know… I just hope we win."

The gathering of new scientists isn't satisfied with this answer, but they don't know what to ask to understand better. So they all sit in silence. Grace maintains a strong countenance to comfort Sarah and the others, but it slowly turns into a thousand-yard stare.

EVERY ROOM AND HALLWAY WITHIN THE ABADDON is stark silent, save for the vehement footfalls of Colonel Bartram leading his bodyguard through his war-torn living room. Marble walls are scarred with bullet holes and small, charred craters blown into them from various types of explosives. He stops in front of the completely shattered window of his living room, looking down on the handful of remaining guards collecting the dead and piling bodies into the elevator. Mavis looks up at him from the heart of a destroyed atrium amongst the security corps that allowed this to happen with shame in her eyes.

Meeting in the north wing art gallery, Mavis starts by ripping off the Band-Aid, "Sir… Kritzman is missing." The colonel's steady countenance intensifies. "I called for a few guards who were in the barracks at the time to investigate the security office. They found Cullen and Murphy tied up. They said she helped Carlisle and Sideris break in, then took their truck and disappeared into the desert." A slight snarl twitches on his face as he stares Mavis into submission; his quiet, seething rage is palpable in the air, alongside the aftertaste of paralytic gas. Shifting his attention to the walls, he takes stock of the hundreds of millions of dollars' worth of seared paintings and the body armor left behind in his enemy's wake.

Heading for the subway, he calls the train only to realize the blast doors have been shut. He inhales sharply and types on the console to reopen them. "Sir, we could take the maintenance cart," Martinez suggests, only to see Bartram already heading for the maintenance tunnel. Loading up into the utility vehicle, the three of them spend a long and quiet ride through ten miles of dimly lit tunnel until the flaming carcass of the subway car lights the way up ahead. Drawing their weapons, the three of them investigate the train, finding a trail of half a dozen burnt corpses splattered against the tunnel walls and the train car.

Inside the testing facility, they find the walls crackling with electrical fires; the center of the room seems to have been the epicenter of an explosion. Every piece of equipment vaporized and scattered across the room, and the grated floor appears torn and warped, barely able to take weight. Martinez takes point as he steps across the floor, dodging the ripped metal and weak spots while Mavis inspects the remains of their equipment. "Sir, there's nothing salvageable here." The observation chamber's window seems to have only spider-webbed in the blast, and the door completely withstood the force. Martinez approaches with his rifle drawn, then he peers through the window but can't make out any details of what's inside.

Mavis comes to help him manually open the door, and once they get it cracked enough, Martinez draws his rifle to let Mavis open it the rest of the way. The first thing he sees is a trail of blood leading from one corner of the room to the opposite. Martinez gestures to Mavis that they may have a survivor. Removing his compromised vest, he tosses it into the room and hears two bullets being fired followed by the locking of a Glock's slide as it runs out of ammunition. Martinez rushes in and tries to fire his rifle, but Trent is too fast and manages to halt him from raising the barrel while throwing his full weight straight at him. Martinez stumbles backward, but Mavis intervenes. Through much struggle, Trent is overtaken, grounded, and held at gunpoint inside the room.

His steps reverberating through the grated floor, Colonel Bartram approaches the three former friends. Martinez and Mavis move to make way for Bartram, who stands over Trent as he sits with a snarky face. Bartram surveys the room and sees Becca's bloodied body and tourniqueted leg slumped against the master computer's console, which Trent seems to have violently destroyed. Bartram looks down on Trent's vulnerable position, and his rage filled demeanor gradually shifts to a wicked smile.

SEVERAL INTERMINABLE HOURS PASS QUIETLY, then several more until all sense of time has dissipated. Grace and Sarah anxiously lie awake in Brian's bed when more commotion starts making its way through the east wing. A pounding at the door prompts Grace to answer it, but their hearts sink when they see Mavis standing there in front of them. In a strange look for her, Mavis is wearing full tactical gear—minus a helmet—and is covered in blood, viscera, and gore from head to toe. Her hair is matted with sweat, and her eyes are blood-shot. She looks as though she just performed surgery on a dozen patients who may or may not have made it through the night. "You're being relocated. I will escort you to your new home." Sarah and Grace share a hopeless gaze and follow her.

Dread looms through the halls of the Abaddon. When they emerge from the east wing corridor, they enter a war-torn battlefield. Sarah gasps, and Grace's jaw drops. Blood splatter, bullet holes, and scorch marks decorate the atrium. The scent of iron and sulfur hangs in the air. The redwood trunks are charred and crumbling, the garden beds are ashened, and the waterfall has been halted. Through the lack of tree canopy, they can see a hole in the wall that leads into some sort of room that overlooks the atrium. The entrance to the north wing seems to have been mostly shattered, displaying the destruction of priceless art and beautiful architecture. The most heart-wrenching image, however, is the only corpse not wearing a uniform. Sarah nearly vomits at the sight of her former boyfriend lying in ruin.

"We don't have time for that." Mavis hurries her along.

Approaching the north wing, they have to watch their step in order to avoid stepping in blood, broken glass, and flaming tree branches. The door having been shattered across the floor makes it easy for them to cross the threshold. Sarah takes note of the char and soot lining that the marble walls have accrued and wonders about the possibility of Vincent managing to escape safely, but she realizes the chances of that are quite slim. They are led up a spiral staircase and into a gaudy office where an exhausted Martinez awaits them. Sarah looks out across the chaos, but she doesn't have much time as Martinez escorts the three of them through several corridors until they reach an elevator.

Mavis announces, "The teleportation project is being dissolved. You two will be reassigned."

Sarah's throat is too tight to speak, but Grace asks, "What about Vince—"

"Dr. Creighton is dead." She looks Sarah dead in the eyes to say, "He was conspiring against the government with a terrorist organization to steal classified technology. Dr. Smith was trying to talk him out of it, but Vincent murdered him with the help of Master Sergeant Kritzman. Kritzman managed to escape, but Vincent and the rest of the organization did not." Sarah swallows hard and tears drip down her cheeks as her knees give out. Grace joins her on the floor, failing to notice that Mavis is speaking as though she doesn't believe the things she's saying. "When they realized their escape plan had been compromised by Colonel Bartram, they started a firefight and fled to the testing facility to destroy the teleportation equipment."

"I don't believe you!" Sarah shouts.

"You don't have to." Mavis's expression is deadpan.

"Where are you taking us?" Grace asks.

Martinez still says nothing, but Mavis answers, "We received a phone call from your old friend, Mark. He says you are needed back in California for a project that he and Karl have been working on." Their blood freezes in their veins.

Nobody speaks while the elevator goes down to the next level. Sarah and Grace exchange terrified glances, but Grace holds her chin up as she is walked to the presumed gallows. She insists on keeping an air of confidence to help Sarah from completely breaking down again. When the elevator door opens, Sarah covers her mouth when she sees a hallway full of dirty, dingy jail cells, two of which contain bloody bodies crumpled up in chains, and one of which looks to have a recently amputated leg.

"Oh my God! Please! No, don't throw us away down here, please! We didn't do anything wrong! I swear!" She shrivels up into the corner, but Martinez takes her by the wrist and drags her through the corridor. They all enter the room at the end where they find a one-way mirror looking into something they've never seen before.

"Don't worry, before you 'depart', we just need to debrief you. One of our old jail cells will be your new home until you can provide every ounce of information that we need from you regarding the attack that took place this morning." Sarah looks through the mirror to find a completely concrete room that has been painted bright white from floor to ceiling. In one corner of the room, a single bed has been set up with a white metal frame, white sheets, white pillow cases, and white covers with nothing else populating the space. Mavis taps on a console mounted on the wall, and a door emerges from the glass.

"We don't know anything!" Sarah bursts out, but Martinez grabs her and forces her into the cell. She fights and scratches at him as much as possible, but gains no ground. Grace doesn't offer such a struggle, instead glowering at their captors until she is led in at gunpoint.

"Then you're useless to us... and you don't want to be useless to us. Take some time, Dr. Boyce. You may realize you know more than you're letting on. You'll have plenty of time to rack your brain for the answers to our questions. Colonel Bartram will be paying you a visit at his earliest convenience to debrief you." Mavis shuts the door and makes it disappear into the rest of the glass, then they leave with the hum of flickering fluorescent lights buzzing away.

CHAPTER FORTY-ONE

August 2nd, 2020

Sunday

Stirring to the sound of sandy winds blowing around him, the hot summer sun beats down on Vincent's pale face. The heat is exacerbated by the black hoodie, heavy Kevlar vest, and combat helmet strapped to his body. Slowly rousing from his sleep, a rough tickle in the back of his throat causes his stomach to contract, prompting him to lurch forward and choke up a mouthful of sand and spit. The glaring sun stings the back of his corneas, so he covers his eyes to carefully survey his surroundings.

Desert. Mountains. Joshua trees. Sand dunes. *What is that?* Fifty yards off, he can see what looks like tents. Trucks. A campfire. A body. *A body?* Struggling to his feet, his muscles give out, and he stumbles, crashing to the sand below. Crawling forward inch by inch, he looks up to make out a blurry, sand-covered body sprawled out on the ground.

I'm coming, Leo. I just have to… keep… going… Crawling is too slow, so he tries pushing himself to his feet, which proves to be painful, but he keeps his eyes focused on Leo. He just has to put one foot in front of the other.

More sandy wind stings against the sweat on the back of his neck. He manages a meager three steps before rolling his ankle and begins to trip again, but this time he feels another tug behind his navel. He falls but doesn't meet the ground. He falls farther and farther until the sandy breeze escalates to gale force winds pushing up on him. Through the gusts of air assaulting his senses, he struggles to catch his breath.

Reaching down to break his fall, he opens his eyes to see the ground rushing up to him from hundreds of feet below. The horizon seems to have formed a circle on all sides of him, and he realizes he's free-falling without a parachute.

Fuck! Fuck! Fuck! Flailing his arms around to grab at the nothing around him, he instinctively closes his eyes. Remembering the scan of the area that he had done moments ago, numbers race through his mind's eye. With another tug behind the navel, Vincent's eyes open to see not the entire desert rushing up at him, but just a single sand dune. Covering his face with his arms, he grabs his helmet, exhales the deepest breath he can muster, and lets his body go limp.

Twenty seconds of physical agony follow as he bounces down the dune like a skipping stone against sandpaper. Gradually rolling to a full stop, he can only manage quick, shallow breaths as he takes in his first experience with road rash. His hands, arms, shoulders, the back of his neck, and most of his legs are covered in bloody abrasions obscured by shredded clothing and combat gear, all the while trembling involuntarily with the burn from the sun's persistent glare.

Once he regains his wits, he pushes through intense pain to sit up. *What… the fuck… was that?* Resting his arms on his knees, he watches the blood dripping from his fingertips curdle in the sand. *Did I just… teleport? Without the machine? Is it still locked onto me and just sending my quantum state to random locations?* He thinks for a minute and just lets his body process the journey he took. His eyes close for a bit, but when they open back up, he sees a small mesa off in the distance and wonders how far away it is, then—*boom*. He's pulled through space and arrives atop the mesa. *This is really happening.*

When he considers each of the other instances of teleportation, he realizes each time he did so, he was focusing on a location with the intent to be there. *Focusing on the location triggered the teleportation, but why did it send me into the sky at first?* Numbers fly through his head, and he arrives back at the base of the sand dune. *Wait, that's my algorithm.*

The first time, I didn't do the math, I just kind of went. The second time, my instincts took over and did the math automatically. Looking around, he only sees desert stretching out for miles, but then finds the top of the sand dune. Closing his eyes, he focuses, and numbers shoot through his head. *The top of the dune is approximately three hundred and fifty-four point four seven one five feet above where I'm sitting now, adjusting for the inclination and offset, which looks to be thirty-five point eight two degrees should be about...* Then another tug behind his navel prompts the familiar feeling of his body collapsing in on itself.

He opens his eyes to find himself in the same seated position he was just in, except he isn't in the same place. *I'm on the top of the dune.* Below him, a trail of blood and shredded clothing leads to a small depression. He delicately shifts his weight to begin standing up, and though this proves to be a slow and arduous process, he eventually rises above the desert. *Woah. This is... I need to collect a sampling of evidence.* Close to the northern horizon, he sees the camp where Leo was passed out. He closes his eyes, does the math, then butterflies erupt from his stomach when he opens them again to see the tents surrounding him on all sides. *Holy fucking shit.*

Bringing himself back to the moment, he sprints to Leo's unconscious body. Assessing the damage, he sees that most of the left side of Leo's face is melted, his left eye is missing, and he has severe sunburn. Vincent knows he needs to get him inside the tent and reaches to lift him up but feels the weakness in his muscles and the sun's harshness on his open wounds. *We're both too burnt for me to pick him up... how do I...* Then he realizes his new discovery might be able to come in handy.

Putting his hand on Leo's vest, he closes his eyes and begins doing math when he realizes the math has become less of an activity and more an extension of his sense of touch. Coordinates, headings, quantum positions, everything—he feels it all in his muscles, in his bloodstream, in his mind. This feeling extends into the vest through his palm; the numbers fly, and an instant later, he appears inside the tent. Opening his eyes, however, he finds only the Kevlar vest in his hands. He finds a bed next to a box of medical supplies, several crates of weapons, and a single case containing various alcoholic beverages.

Vincent peers out of the tent to see Leo still lying there. Slowly limping back across the camp, he kneels down and grunts as his severely abraded skin stretches at the joints. Taking time to regain his center, he breathes deeply and realizes for the first time just how dehydrated he is; the inside of his mouth feels like cotton and the headache that he's been ignoring creeps back into his consciousness.

He places his hand back on Leo's chest. *Focus. Take your time.* Feeling the fibers of his shirt, the movement of his skin cells, the flow of his blood as his heart beats, Vincent finds every individual piece of information that he needs. All of it compresses and integrates into the cloud of mathematics he's processing; it feels different than when he teleports himself. He doesn't have to think so much about his own positioning because it feels more intuitive. But with Leo's body, it's a slower process. About five minutes pass with his eyes closed, muttering the formulas and algorithms that he invented until he feels that familiar tug and opens his eyes. Leo lies on the bed of the tent; Vincent lifts his hand and watches it tremble. *Oh my God… oh my fucking God… I did it.*

The sputtering of an engine outside replaces Vincent's feeling of pride with a state of alertness. His headache spikes slightly, but his abrasions dull. *What now? How could they have possibly found us already?* He searches the weapons crate to find a rifle and quickly loads a few rounds. He approaches the entrance to the tent and peers around the corner to look for the intruding vehicle and sees a black truck pulling up. *Is that ours, or did they steal our truck?* Retracting into the room, he tries to remember every bit of training Trent and Leo had given him, but their training was mostly offensive and less focused on defending a position. *Fuck, fuck, fuck… what do I do?*

He sidles up to the tent's entrance and shoulders his weapon, then he takes a few quick breaths to psych himself up before rounding the corner, ready to shoot. Peering out, he sees the car come to a stop. Both of the cab doors open; adrenaline pumping through his veins, his trigger finger itches. Taking quick, choppy breaths, his head hurts, and he watches the silhouetted driver and passenger lift their hands out of the cab. His trembling hands contract as he involuntarily closes his eyes. He accidentally pulls the trigger and gasps when the rifle goes off. But when he opens his eyes, he's standing in the bed of the truck, and a puff of sand kicks up in the distance. *Fuck! I teleported!* His muscles tensing up, he's nearly hyperventilating as he hears a voice underneath him. He turns around as fast as he can to realize the driver and passenger are still inside the truck.

"Don't shoot!"

"Tzofiya?" Vincent reflexively asks, keeping the rifle shouldered

"Yes! It is me and Dallyn!"

He sighs in relief but forgets to lower his gun. "Y-Yeah, come on out. Where were you?"

Dallyn says, "When Tzofiya came back, we went out looking for you guys. When did you get here? And how-how did you get up there?" As Dallyn asks the question, Vincent's muscles relax, and his headache spikes again. His dry mouth returns, and exhaustion overtakes him. He drops his gun, and his head splits behind his eyes until his vision goes black; the next thing he feels is Tzofiya catching him as he falls out of the truck bed.

THE BLACKNESS IS SUDDENLY INTERRUPTED as Vincent jerks awake, sitting straight up in a sleeping bag and choking on sand and dried saliva. He turns to reach for a canteen of water beside him and drinks nearly all of it before he realizes his arms are wrapped in gauze, along with the rest of his road rash injuries. He looks around the gloomy tent that he's in, lit only by a red, low-light lantern, and finds Tzofiya and Leo sitting in a pair of fold-out chairs.

"Well, well," Leo says with a hoarse cough. "Welcome back to the realm of the living."

"Thanks. Same to you." Vincent's rough throat fights back when he tries to speak. After his blurry vision comes into focus, he can see a large bandage covering Leo's left eye and gauze covering a few third-degree burns.

Beside him, an uncharacteristically dressed-down Tzofiya is sitting with her head in her hands. Whenever Vincent saw her off-duty at the Abaddon, she would maintain her military bearing as much as possible, wearing her physical training gear when not in uniform and only lifting the veil to make the other security guards feel comfortable with her. Now she's wearing a set of Trent's sleeping attire and attempting to decompress.

"I cleaned and wrapped your wounds." Dallyn's voice startles him. "But Leo's injuries took more work."

"Thanks." He struggles to stand up, but Dallyn rushes over to hold him down.

"No, no. You need to rest. Your injuries may have been simple to clean, but they'll take time to heal."

Vincent waves him off. "I don't care. We have to go back and save the others."

From his chair, Leo sips a glass of water. "Neither of us is in any condition to be fighting, Vinny. We'll rest up, make a game plan, and head back."

"Not good enough! We need to get over there now! If anything happens to Sarah—"

"Then she's already dead, and there'd be nothing you could do. If she's still alive, you need to be at your best in order to help."

He tries to stand, but his muscles give out on him, and he falls into his sleeping bag, feeling defeated. "What if they followed us?" He cranes his neck to look outside the tent and sees the Milky Way overhead in the dark sky.

"I cover tracks. Nobody follow me," Tzofiya says.

He squints at her but reluctantly trusts her judgment over his own. "How did you know to come here, Tzofiya?"

"I track Martinez's patrols and plan my own escape route. Trent and I are of similar mind. When I got close to camp, I heard Dallyn on radio."

Vincent is impressed with her ability, but Dallyn asks him a question. "Vince, what do you remember about when we pulled up to the camp?"

"What do I remember?" He furrows his brow and tries to recall what feels like a distant, bad dream. "I had just gotten Leo inside the tent when I heard your car. I looked out and saw the black truck. I wasn't sure who was in it, but"—his headache returns, so he drinks some water—"I think the dehydration was taking a toll. I blacked out for a second, and the gun went off."

"Did you hit anything? When your gun went off, I mean."

"No, it just hit some sand because—" then his eyes widen as it all begins to flood back. "I was in the bed of your truck! I had teleported!" Tzofiya and Leo raise an eyebrow at him. "Yeah, I teleported from the tent. I must have been so exhausted that I just instinctively beamed over to where I was looking." They stare back at him in disbelief. "That sounds crazy, doesn't it?" They nod in unison. "It's true though. I'm not lying!"

Leo supportively says, "We don't think you are, son. Just… go back to our escape. Tell us how we got out."

It's not often that he has to struggle to recall his memories, but he has to close his eyes to recall, "We were in the art gallery. You had just tackled me after a phosphorus grenade went off. You saved me, but parts of you had caught on fire… I had to pull your mask off." His throat closes up. "I am so sorry, Leo. I had to do it; you kept bringing your hands to your face and—"

Leo cuts him off, "It's okay, Vinny. You did what you had to do. I'm proud of you. Because of you, I'm still alive. Just keep telling the story."

Vincent swallows hard and continues, "Yeah, I guess so. Anyway, I had to carry you to the train, and we fought off those… things. They looked like you, Leo. What the fuck were they?"

Tzofiya sighs sadly. "I can answer this." She turns to Leo with the most sincere look Vincent has ever seen on her face. "The colonel… years ago, he abduct you because…he want army. You were perfect soldier." Her face turns red as she speaks. "Never ask questions, not stand up to Bartram when he bully you, but you kill like machine. He want make *more* of you. Splice your genes with scientist to make… super-soldier-scientist hybrid."

"More of me? Like… did he…"

"He clone you. Hundreds. Thousands of clones."

Leo's face twists and looks like he is about to throw up. "Is that—Did Trent know about this? Is that what he and Smith were talking about?"

"Dr. Smith find out about project in eighties; he try to force Bartram's hand by shutting down Abaddon just long enough to kill infant clones. Bartram make threat to him—if he didn't turn Abaddon back on, he would murder a scientist. When Bartram move cloning project to facility on different power source, he spend decades figuring out way to destroy clones without risking lives of everyone else in Abaddon."

"Why the fuck didn't Trent tell me? He had a whole fucking year to let me know there was a goddamn army of myself sitting under the Abaddon. He never found it fucking *pertinent* that I learn about this?!"

"Dr. Smith tell him not to tell you."

Shaking with anger, Leo rises to his feet, ignoring the searing pain from his burnt skin, and exclaims, "And why the fuck not?"

"He say… he worry you become emotionally unstable." Leo, visibly offended, is taken aback and paces around the tent. "He want make sure you don't relapse. You don't lose yourself."

"He thought I might feel some form of responsibility for them?! Or maybe he thought I would find it morally dubious to murder *thousands* of people for the sake of removing one dictator from power?! I spent sixty-five years in a hole as retribution for crimes that I committed—" Vincent's expression changes when he says this. *Crimes that he committed? He actually did do those things?* "Have I not earned the right to determine whether I want to let… whether I want to let *thousands* of people die just to assassinate one man?" They both know that Tzofiya isn't to blame and that yelling at her won't help; she hasn't earned his fury, but she is the one who's there. Tzofiya looks him in the eyes and willingly accepts his rage.

Tzofiya says softly, "If it helps—we don't know if he succeeded."

"Attempted murder is still a crime," Leo's tone is biting.

Vincent sits up in his sleeping bag entirely unsure what he is supposed to do in a situation like this. *What do I do with my hands?* He twiddles his thumbs until Leo storms out of the tent, then he watches Tzofiya and Dallyn exhale. *Was this my fault? Should I not have agreed to work with Trent in the first place?* He silently picks at his nails, waiting for someone else to say something.

After a few moments, Tzofiya asks, "They tell you story of how Bartram capture Leo in first place?" Vincent shakes his head. He realizes he never got around to confronting Leo for lying to him.

"Leo was… troubled young man. He saw horrible, horrible things in World War II. Colonel Bartram was commanding officer and made him do… awful things. When Leo left military, he worked for security contractor and became assassin. People use him, treat him same way people treated you. He became weapon; he was best assassin world never saw coming. After few years, he lose control."

"He lost control? Like he—he snapped?"

"Yes. He was sick of doing murder for other people. He wanted to do it for himself. He wanted to have fun. So… he went to hospital with bag of guns." As she says this, Vincent almost stops believing her. "He go to emergency room, and… he slaughter everyone."

"Hold on now—"

"He threw grenade, killed most survivors. All but three. Used three survivors as hostages but—"

"No, you're lying. This isn't true—"

"He make hostage read note to news crew, kill hostages and police, then surrender. He tell news crew that he demand their attention."

"Now hold the fuck on, Tzofiya!" Vincent arduously sits up in his sleeping bag, "What the fuck are you saying to me? Leo's a murderer? He's an evil guy who *deserves* to be locked up in an institution?"

"Not for me to say," Tzofiya responds bluntly. "They send him to death row, but Bartram kidnap him instead. Leo serve life sentence. He learn what suffering is. He wish for death, but death never come. After sixty-five years, Leo learn value of life."

Vincent's head is spinning. He sits silently for several minutes while Leo paces outside. *What… what do I… there's no way…* Though he tells himself that she is lying, somehow he knows that she isn't. After a tense fifteen minutes or so, Leo returns to the tent, looking somewhat more disheveled than before. Tzofiya watches him for a moment as he calms himself and sits in his chair again.

"Sorry about that. What happened next?" he asks Vincent, who looks to Tzofiya for affirmation. She nods subtly.

"Oh… uh… we were fighting off the clones, but one of them snuck on board and attacked Becca. We managed to kill him, but… once we got to the testing facility and teleported you out, Trent started teleporting me out"—his memories appear to him in fractured images—"I was in the chamber… but the clones caught up to us. They started shooting. They shot the glass… over and over until it started cracking, shattering… but it wasn't just the glass. They were shooting the converter, and it—it exploded."

"It exploded? Then how did you—"

"I don't know. It must have pulled me out at just the right time…"

"Tzofiya," Dallyn pipes up, "we saw him do it."

"I don't know what I saw…" Tzofiya says.

"Yes, you do," Vincent says. "That's how I got Leo into the medical tent. I took him with me." Tzofiya and Leo are choosing their next words carefully. Vincent notices this and says, "I can prove it." He starts to stand, but his muscles have settled in, and they fight back.

"No, Vincent, rest. In morning, we can—"

"No!" He struggles through the pain and comes to a full stand. "I'm not crazy. Watch." He closes his eyes and lets the numbers fly through his head before feeling the tug behind his navel. Then he appears in the tent entrance. Opening his eyes, everyone is standing with their jaws agape, stuttering as they try to respond. "I think when they destroyed the machine mid-teleportation, something happened. Maybe the technology grafted with me on a quantum level or something, or… I don't know, something sci-fi like that. The bottom line is: I can do it." They stare in disbelief. "Leo, I'm not strong enough to pick you up. How else could I have gotten you inside? I sat down, took a few minutes to do the math, and I was able to teleport you with me."

Tzofiya stands and approaches him, walking circles around him and extending a cautious hand to make sure what she's seeing is real. She gives Leo a look of amazement and asks, "You also see this?"

He nods slowly, sits down, and says, "Let's… it's been a long day. We need to get some rest and—" he looks over Vincent's body to see if he can find any detail out of place—if his nose was a little off, if his shirt was a different color, if he was shorter, maybe. Nothing seems to be out of place, but he knows something isn't right when their eyes meet.

Vincent stares, for the first time, into the eyes of a murderer. Exhausted, blue-grey eyes. *You shot up a hospital?* Leo turns away and grunts as he lies in his bed, looking like less of a human than he did a moment ago. *Who are you?* Vincent lies back in his own bed and stares into the dark, hearing Mavis's voice say, *"The man is pure evil." They were telling the truth. "He forfeited his life when he shot up a hospital. A real psycho."*

Just as Vincent starts to drift off, he feels a tapping on his shoulder. His eyes open to Dallyn signaling for him to keep quiet. "Come with me." The two of them step out of the tent and sit around the ashes of the now extinguished fire. "I'm so sorry for waking you. I know it's been a long day, and you need your rest… but I have something very important to ask."

"What?"

"In all of your correspondence with Dr. Smith, did he ever tell you anything or give you anything in the event of his death? Something to pass on, by chance?"

"Um, actually yeah, he gave me a message—how did you know that?"

"It's kind of a long story." He chuckles. "Part of the reason I agreed to help Trent with this mission was that Dr. Smith had something to pass down; I was supposed to receive it from him in case he passed away."

"Well, I don't have anything to give you. All he said was to pass along a message, then he started speaking in some kind of language I couldn't understand."

"Did it sound like this?" Dallyn then starts to speak in a language that sounds very similar to the way Dr. Smith spoke. Vincent even hears a few words he recognizes.

"Yeah, what is that?"

"It's the Arapaho language. It's passed down to us by our tribe as we grow up; there are few who understand it today. Do you think you could recreate his message?"

"Sure." Vincent closes his eyes and pictures the words as Dr. Smith said his message. "*Hono'ooneniitowoo*," he says, then continues to relay the message that Dr. Smith had given him in perfect detail.

Dallyn simply nods and grins. "Thank you for the message."

"Should I ask what it was?"

"Nothing important—yet…"

CHAPTER FORTY-TWO

August 10th, 2020

Monday

With repairs to the Abaddon underway, business has resumed under the new definition of normal that Bartram has established. Since the incident, a "temporary" travel ban to the surface has been enacted, and morale has taken a nosedive. Mavis, however, is proud to hear that the invisibility project is on the verge of being completed. A win like this right on the heels of the catastrophic failure that was the teleportation project might be just what it takes to make her people forget about her… overzealous attempts at preventing a riot.

Today, she has a little extra work to do. Instead of hanging up her lab coat at the end of the day, she keeps it on and leaves the lab. She steps through the construction zone-filled atrium and socializes with a few scientists while avoiding the scaffolding and plastic sheeting hung everywhere. She skirts around the gardeners who are beginning to regrow plants and flowers—unfortunately the arborists have determined that the redwoods have suffered extensive damage from the fires and are unlikely to recover.

As she enters the north wing, she passes through a now-empty gallery and descends to her office, which is still ornamented with Dr. Smith's tribal furniture and artwork. She only has a few minutes to replace the bandages on her head wound before her meeting with the colonel.

Bartram answers her knock fairly quickly and silently leads her back to the service elevator. It's been quite some time since she's had to do any work in the Cultivation Center; the method of cloning she developed had become largely self-sufficient, so any hiccups in the system could be easily managed by the guards with minimal training. "Dr. Smith must have mucked the system up something fierce to necessitate a house call," she jokes to the colonel, but he remains stark silent. As the elevator door closes, she gears up to ask what the issue is, but he cuts her off.

"I've been thinking about the best way to break this to you, but I think the best thing to do is to just show you."

"Show me what?" she asks, concern rising in her as the doors part at the bottom. She looks out into the warehouse, which is totally dark except for the green emergency lights overhead. "What happened to the lights? …Why are the computers turned off?" They step inside the Cultivation Center, and Mavis quickly lunges toward the main computer, furiously trying to get it to turn on. "Where's the power?!" She looks back at Bartram with desperation.

"Dr. Smith had—"

"Dr. Smith nothing! He had no control of this facility! What did *you* do?!"

"*Dr. Smith* plugged a USB drive into one of the chambers, which must have uploaded some kind of virus or something because the bodies' chemical compositions changed."

"How could he have possibly plugged anything into anything? He had no access to this facility!" She purses her lips and closes her eyes. "Just… tell me about the virus."

"Their systems were being flooded with nitroglycerin. If I hadn't cut the power, the computer would have sent an electrical shock to their pods and blown the place up. It might have made the entire Abaddon collapse in on itself." Mavis, seething with rage, ignores him to stare at the decades of hard work floating dead in the water. Her children, her monuments, her ticket to immortality just… dead. "Blackwell, I know this hurts. I'm sorry that it had to go down this way, but is there anything you can do to bring them back?"

"Had to? No, no, no. You wanted this to happen. This facility was off limits to him. His little backdoor trick got him inside the network, but that was it. All he could do was look. How… how could he have gotten this far?"

"He came prepared. Martinez and I were waiting for him down here when the battle kicked off, but he was armed."

"SO WERE YOU! You had him outnumbered and outgunned! As soon as the elevator door opened, you could have blasted him to kingdom come. Why didn't you?"

"Listen, Blackwell, you're upset. I understand. It's not that simple though. You know what Dr. Smith had. I couldn't just kill him."

"You and I had a deal; I provided the science, and you provided the facility. That was it. I even kept the staff motivated despite your threats to their families, but you couldn't manage to handle one guy? Dr. Smith had one thing going for him, and you couldn't handle it?" She points at him menacingly and digs her bony fingers into his chest. "You could have tortured that information out of him, or hell, you probably could have found the damn thing by now if you'd bothered to look! But you didn't, did you?"

"Dr. Blackwell," Bartram's tone is calculated and reserved, "you better consider your words before you say something you might regret."

"No, you didn't do it because you couldn't deal with the idea of some-one holding something over you, so what did you do?" She pushes him back against a cultivation chamber. "You went under his nose and did the one thing he didn't want you to do just so you could bring him down here and show it off like a goddamn toddler… Well, look where show-and-tell got you—" she gestures to the warehouse of corpses around them. "You lost everything. Again. All because you let your ego blind you to the smarter options."

Colonel Bartram places his hand on her shoulder. "It's not over yet. You can still fix them! We have all the time in the world, thanks to your brilliant technology."

She throws his hand off and bursts out, "No! This isn't fixable! You could have prevented this, but you didn't. *You* ended it when *you* failed to take action against Dr. Smith. My clones are dead, thanks to you! Vincent is dead, thanks to you! My dream is dead… thanks to you."

"We can start again! Build the army from the ground up like we've done before."

"Which we only had to do because you fucked it up, twice now. I made a mistake trusting you for as long as I have; I'm not wasting more time by trusting you yet again." Colonel Bartram's face twists with rage, and he swiftly grips her throat and shoves her against the chamber, staring her in the eyes. "You won't hurt me," she says. Her voice is strained through his choking, yet there isn't an ounce of fear in her. "You need me. You always will."

He flinches. Then he throws her aside, causing her to double over in a coughing fit. He looms over her and calmly says, "You're right." He pulls a USB drive out of his pocket, pushes her back against the clone chamber's wall, and forces the USB into her hand. "You're going to make me another army."

Mavis looks up at him in confusion, unsure of what he means, but she is just met with a smile.

"MARTINEZ, THIS IS GETTING OUT OF HAND." Mavis is standing in his barracks room doorway.

"I know, but the repairs were fairly extensive. It should only be a few more weeks."

"That's not what I'm talking about. It's…" She looks around, checking the hallways for any prying ears. "Can I come in? We have something to discuss. Privately."

Apprehensively, he lets her in and shuts the door behind them. "What's up?"

She closes the curtains and asks, "Did he tell you what he wants me to do with Smith's virus?"

"The nanobodies? Yeah, think you can do it?"

"Of course, I *can* do it, but don't you think it's a bit… I don't know—" she looks into his unblinking eyes. "Irresponsible?"

"As in… what? You think he's gonna use them on us?"

"Well… I mean now that you say it, maybe, but that's not what I mean. He had every advantage over Smith and still managed to lose. He's losing his edge. If we put a dormant, biological version of the virus into the scientists' bloodstream, I just… I just wonder if we can trust Bartram with the trigger."

"Why would you wonder that? Smith was a traitor who lost Bartram's trust long ago. He deserved every millimeter of that bullet." The more she stares at him, the less she sees of Martinez and more of Bartram bubbles to the surface.

"Yeah." She paints on a façade of compliance and turns around. "You're right. I-I'm acting irrationally. I must still be shaken from the fight."

Martinez sighs. "Look, you were a good security guard, the best we ever had. But you're a scientist now. You know your new role in this place, right?"

She stares at her feet for a while, then looks up at him and agrees, "Right. I'll just shut up and do my job."

"Good."

CHAPTER FORTY-THREE

October 10th, 2020

Saturday

Mavis leans against the back wall of the dim observation section of the prison cells beneath Bartram's office standing next to a medical cart. With crossed arms, she stands in front of the cell and sighs a disenchanted breath. Through the glass, she observes Sarah and Grace rubbing their temples while trying to maintain a conversation. *The hum from the lights must be piercing.* She imagines the destruction in the testing facility on that day and constantly wonders why there was no evidence of Vincent or Leo Prime's deaths. *If there's even a chance he made it out of there alive, they're my best bet at finding him.*

The squeak of the door opening startles her, causing her to jump a little. Colonel Bartram steps inside and asks, "Have you done it yet?"

"Not yet. I was waiting for you to get here."

"What for?"

"Well, the rest of the work force took kindly to the hypodermic needle injections, but I'm not sure if the spray will cause any unexpected results. I'd rather you be here, just in case."

"Then let's get on with it."

Mavis stares into their cells again and bites her lip. "Sure." She reaches into a plastic bin and removes a spray injector labeled "Nanobody Treatment #1" then moves to the console on the wall. She taps on the keyboard and opens a screen displaying each of their vital readings, then moves the injector up to the console, hesitates, and turns over her shoulder to ask, "Are you sure this is a good idea? In the event Vincent or Leo Prime survived, it might be in our best interest to have them on our side. I don't think shooting them up with a virus is going to earn their favor."

Bartram reaches into his inner coat pocket and pulls out a small, handheld device with a single button. "When Carlisle and Sideris broke out of here, they created a terrorist organization that caused heavy damage to our operations. If, at the time, I had a self-destruct button that I could press at any time to kill everyone they cared about"—he gestures to a button on his device—"then they would have thought twice about leaving in the first place."

"I don't know, sir, it seems…" In her head, she thinks, *like your ego's going on a power trip.* But she thinks better of it and finishes by saying, "Unnecessary to me."

"First you tell me that I let my ego get in the way of success, now you're telling me I'm being too cautious. How am I *supposed* to be treating my prisoners? Would you like me to pull up the Geneva Conventions?"

Mavis shakes her head and turns back to the console. "No, sir. You're doing a fine job." She depresses the injector, and they both watch the cell as the vents kick into gear. Sarah and Grace cut their conversation short when they both suddenly keel over in coughing fits, scratching at their throats and heaving on their hands and knees. Mavis furrows her brow wondering if they know something she doesn't.

"Are you okay?" Bartram asks. Mavis realizes she looks concerned about their well-being.

"What? Yeah, I'm just hoping the respiratory version is compatible with their systems. They seem to be fighting it right now." They both wait a few minutes, watching them struggle through the pain and confusion of an invisible force choking them until eventually they both pass out. Mavis watches their vitals spike, chaotically going up and down until finally settling down when they go unconscious. "Still alive. Just asleep."

"Good work today, Blackwell," Bartram says curtly, then leaves just as dismissively as he entered. Mavis's stomach drops, and she watches them rest for quite a long time. She purses her lips and thinks to herself for a while. In a huff, she grabs the medical cart and takes it back to the surface. After returning it to the admin building, she needs to go for a walk.

The air outside is getting colder and windier by the night. Mavis absent-mindedly kept her lab coat on when she came above ground, which is now flapping around her high heeled shoes. As she walks along the path to the barracks, she realizes just how many new guards Bartram "hired" to patrol the grounds. There are at least three patrols roaming around the campus at any given time. Despite the crowd, she walks right past her building, crosses through the volleyball courts that Karl, Chad, and scores of other scientists that Colonel Bartram had decided to eliminate over the years used to play at, and takes a seat at the gazebo.

She looks out to the mountain behind the base, then across the desert around her. *I wonder where Kritzman wound up… If anyone would be able to get off his radar, it'd be her.* The world around her is so vast, but how much of it has she really explored? The desert is formidable, but when she contemplates the old armory shed and the general store that have weathered so much time on this base, she knows that it's survivable. A chill travels up her spine, triggering a memory she hasn't thought about in years.

CHAPTER FORTY-FOUR

December 24th, 1988

Saturday

The south wing and atrium are alive with a Christmas Eve feast. While she enjoys seeing the workforce having a wonderful time, Mavis much prefers spending her time away from large crowds. Too much noise can be distracting to her, so she prefers not to have to tune it out all the time.

Tonight, she finishes her dinner early and goes above deck to take a walk around the fort. The gazebo is a peaceful place to sit and admire the beautiful desert sunset, but just before the light is swallowed up by the horizon, Mavis is joined by an upsetting guest.

Dr. Smith hikes up his blazer and sits next to her; he hasn't shown his face around the campus much in the past couple of months, especially around her, so he's ready for her evil eye. He doesn't back down though, and the two of them spend an awkward moment in the gazebo watching the sun set. Mavis falls back on an old habit of scanning the perimeter, the mountains, and the road.

Dr. Smith picks this moment to initiate their conversation. "You know that is not your job anymore, do you not?"

"You don't get to tell me how to do my job, baby-killer. I know how to protect my people, be it with a gun or a microscope."

"Or eugenics?"

"It wasn't eugenics! Eugenics implies manipulating peoples' *reproductive rights* in order to create a more likely possibility of children having favorable traits. I don't want to take anyone's rights away. I was changing reproduction *as we know it*. Perfecting the human race. I wanted to grant our species immortality while you just wanted to make yourself look big in front of everyone."

Dr. Smith chooses not to respond. Instead, he sits back and watches the sun go down next to his colleague in a tense silence. Neither of them speaks for a while, and the cold begins to settle in. Mavis didn't bring a jacket, so she's about ready to head back to her room, but she refuses to be the first to leave. Dr. Smith takes advantage of her stubbornness.

"You know, Christmas is an interesting time of year for me. My parents were Mormon, but I was an atheist." She doesn't acknowledge his remark. "I always saw holidays as a chore. I would have to spend time and money—both precious resources back in the day—to fly out and see my family. They believed in and preached ideas that were... far from scientifically or historically accurate. I did not see the value in this until later in life."

"You don't really think I give a shit about your history, do you?"

"You probably should. I see now that those times should not have been a chore, but a chance to see the effects of history on my present. I now appreciate and remember the traditions, culture, and history from my Shoshone and Arapaho ancestors' perspectives, not just because it is customary, but because I understand their value..."

"What value does your people's history have to me?"

"History repeats itself. If you do not learn from it, it will continue to haunt your future." As he says this, Mavis takes a breath as if to retort but doesn't know how to respond. Dr. Smith continues, "I know you see me as your enemy, and... truly, I feel sorrow for the events that took place on Halloween. I wish circumstances had not led to such an outcome. However, I hope this experience teaches you who your true enemy should be."

"Don't talk to me like you understand warfare—you're not a goddamn soldier! You haven't earned that right!"

"Maybe not a soldier, but my people were warriors. Strong, noble, competent warriors who spent—and are still spending—their lives fighting to save their culture. Fighting to preserve their land and their home. Fighting to live long enough for their children to join the fight. Do you know who their enemies were?"

Mavis rolls her eyes. "Yeah, whatever."

"It is important to understand from which side of history you are viewing the present. The same people who built and looked after this fort to 'protect their people' were the ones who murdered mine."

"You tell history as if your people were completely innocent. Don't pretend the colonists were the only ones with bloodshed on their hands. Natives flayed, scalped, and raped just like the white man did."

Dr. Smith bites his lip and nods. "You are correct." Mavis side-eyes him, and he continues, "As proud as I am to be among a people whose history is such a rich and colorful tapestry, it is important for me to remember that red is one of those colors. It pains me to know that I was responsible for one of those brush strokes of red, but I rest easy knowing of my action's place in historical context."

There is quiet for a while. Mavis has a million things she wants to say but doesn't know if any of them would support her intentions.

"I know it is difficult for you to accept criticism of Colonel Bartram," Dr. Smith finally says. "But if I may—for all the tenacity, all the commitment, all the… well, the competence that Henry has displayed over the many years I have known him, do you know what trait of his presents the biggest vulnerability to this place? Makes him sloppy? Self-destructive?" Of course, she does. "His ego. It is a dangerous thing to both himself and to those who work for him."

She stands in a huff and walks away. While he watches the sun slowly dip below the horizon, Dr. Smith listens to the sound of her heels clicking against the concrete, but they stop for a moment… then she steps off again and fades into the night. Dr. Smith sighs and allows himself a triumphant smile.

THIRTY-TWO YEARS PASS within the walls of the Abaddon. Mavis is happy to serve Bartram during those years; she loves knowing that she is closing in on the ultimate form of protection—immortality. It isn't until the chill settles on her during that cool October night three decades after mourning the loss of her first batch of clones that she realizes she hadn't been protecting anyone. She kept her team, her "children," and herself in the palm of an egotistical maniac.

She tightens her lab coat and looks at the spot where Dr. Smith had sat many years ago. It feels so barren now. Focusing on the armory and general store again, she thinks to herself for a moment. *Runs With Fire was a warrior. Smarter than everyone—except for Vincent, of course. He had a better heart than anyone else, and he was stronger in every way that mattered. While Colonel Bartram was busy turning this place into a circus, Dr. Smith fought until his last breath. I can do better than them both.* She takes a decisive walk past the roaming patrols back to her office, then gets to work.

CHAPTER FORTY-FIVE

November 24th, 2020

Tuesday

The snow crunches under Vincent's foot as he steps out of the RV and finds a seat next to Tzofiya at the campfire. Dallyn offers him a cup of coffee, and they settle in for a relaxing morning. The forest around them chirps with wildlife as they watch the sun rising on the Tongass forest in northern Alaska, and the four of them take a deep breath of crisp air. Leo slides his eye patch on as they finish up a simple breakfast and prepare the equipment for today's training session.

"Vincent, you buy more ammunition yesterday?" Tzofiya asks while opening a row of pelican cases.

"No, I got busy cleaning the rifles. Let me go get some real quick," he says and grabs his wallet and ballcap from the tent, then teleports to the nearest town that sits a few miles outside the forest. After several trips to town, Vincent has managed to pinpoint the mathematics to appear in just the right spot that allows him to slyly walk into the local hunting shop and buy a few boxes of ammunition for each of their weapons.

A few minutes later, he's back at camp in the forest and places the boxes in the weapons crates where Leo is gearing up for that day's training session. Vincent silently dons his equipment and lines up next to a starting point that Dallyn drew in the snow.

"Hey, Dallyn," Vincent calls out. "Can we focus on speed for this run? Last time, I almost ended up in a tree. I need to work on that."

"Sure thing." He moves the target stands into the forest to arrange them in a confusing pattern, then returns to the camp. "You guys ready?"

In full gear, Vincent, Leo, and Tzofiya load up their rifles. "Ready."

"Three. Two. One. Go!" Dallyn fires a revolver in the air and presses a button on his stopwatch, triggering them to tactically sprint into the woods.

Tzofiya takes point, checking behind a tree as they pass. Leo stumbles at first, but he takes the rear and looks up into the canopy. Rounding the corner of a thicket, a target pops out from the opposite side of the trunk, and Vincent fires three rounds into the target. Simultaneously, a target in the canopy pops out, and Leo pulls the trigger but ends up firing wide several feet to the right for the first two rounds and hits on the third. Vincent shifts aim to finish off Leo's target, then they take cover behind the trees.

"Fuck!" Leo grunts.

"Don't worry, just do better next time." Tzofiya's words of encouragement don't really rouse him, but he gets back up anyway.

"Phasing forward to clear a path." Vincent disappears from sight. Tzofiya and Leo wait a few moments, then hear a few bullets ping against metal targets. "Clear!" Leo and Tzofiya shoulder their rifles again and push toward Vincent, who is now several yards ahead leaning against a tree. By the time Leo catches up and hears a target descend from overhead, he fires but misses all three rounds. Tzofiya picks up his slack, causing Leo to groan again.

"I still can't hit anything for shit!"

"Just get back in the game; it's okay," Vincent says calmly.

"Let's just…" He shakes his head and says, "I need more stationary target practice. I'm done. Let's just head back." Vincent and Tzofiya look at each other, unsure of what to say. "Dallyn, I'm calling it."

"Roger. Clear to exit."

Circling around the weapons crates, they debrief about the exercise, and Leo just says, "I'm still having trouble with my depth perception. I can't see shit with this fucking eye patch!"

Vincent shyly says, "I think it's in your head, buddy."

Leo slams his hands on the crate and violently points at Vincent. "It's not in my goddamn head! We've already been here for two months longer than we should have been! I just… I don't know what's happening!"

Tzofiya says, "You do great in stationary practice. Your aim still impeccable…"

Leo shakes his head and walks it off. When he returns, he still seems disappointed in himself. "How about you two just do a run without me? Might as well get through a full exercise today."

They awkwardly acquiesce and gear up for another run, Dallyn resetting their obstacle course for them while Leo pours himself a drink. At the starting line, Dallyn sets the timer and starts them off. Tzofiya takes point again as they both rush into the woods, and the first several targets fall much quicker than the three of them could have managed together. Vincent shouts, "Crossing left!" and teleports to Tzofiya's left to clear the area in front of her. He fires at a few targets while she fires into the canopy. The two of them continue this pattern of teleporting and clearing the path of targets as they reveal themselves.

Toward the end of the course, a series of targets pop up one after the other surrounding Tzofiya on all sides. Vincent's mind works hard to keep up as the math flies through his head at light speed. The first target comes from overhead, and Tzofiya takes it out easily but begins to struggle as six targets pop up in front of and behind her. She takes out the two in front as Vincent takes the three to her rear, then his magazine runs dry. His fingers struggle to handle the weapon as he tries to reload, but he drops the magazine while simultaneously the hairs stand on the back of his neck. Another target pops up from the bushes, and he instinctively tries to teleport out of the area, but then it happens.

The feeling of a sudden electrical fire bursts from his brain stem into his skull. Grabbing his head and keeling over, his vision blurs into blindness, and he curls into a ball on the ground. He shuts his eyes, but the throbbing is inescapable for about sixty seconds. He finally manages to put two feet flat on the ground to regain his balance. Tzofiya has already reloaded and taken out the target by the time his vision returns, but he pops back into his tactical stance anyway.

"You okay, Vincent?" Tzofiya asks.

"Y-Y-Yeah… I…" he stammers for a few minutes before finishing his thought. "Yeah. I'm fine. Let's finish the course."

"Already over. It happen again?"

"Yeah, I tried to jump too much, too fast. Then that last target popped up, and it—I don't know… I must have tried to move too fast or something."

"You overheat. Like car engine; you need take time and cool down."

"Yeah, well, that's alright. Let's just… let's get out of here." They return to the camp and debrief Dallyn and Leo. "It was a damn good run, all said and done, but I overdid it a bit with the teleportation."

Leo shakes his head and says, "You've become too reliant on that power of yours. We don't know how it affects you or what it could be doing to your brain."

"I know! But if we want a chance at assassinating Bartram, I need to learn how to control it."

"We never decided on assassinating him," Leo says adamantly. "That was *your* idea!"

"Yeah. And it probably should have been the plan all along. You guys had the right idea from the get-go."

"Don't remind me…"

Tzofiya interjects, "We haven't decided on what our next move is, but… leaving him alive is risky."

"Haven't we killed enough people though? Murder shouldn't still be our go-to solution!"

"It's not!" Vincent yells. "We tried doing it peacefully before. That just got Brian killed. Where is your hang up coming from? You killed plenty of people while we were down there, what happened to *that* Leo?"

Leo scowls at him but says nothing. Vincent blushes and almost cowers, but Dallyn cuts the tension. "Leo, you're not responsible for those clones." The air sits heavy for a moment, but he continues, "Bartram created them. Dr. Smith killed them—or tried to anyway. Whether or not their creation or murder were justifiable is a matter of opinion; who's responsible for them is not." Dallyn pours him another drink. "Bartram was responsible for their creation. Dr. Smith took responsibility for killing them. None of that falls on you."

Leo turns his glare to Dallyn, then a small tear sheds down his cheek. He takes the drink and says, "It doesn't matter whose fault it was. We're not killing anyone anymore."

"I want to agree with you, Leo," Vincent says. "I really do. But sometimes you have to do bad things so good things happen." Vincent pauses for a moment, "It's like lying."

"What?" Leo asks, and everybody looks at him with the same look of curiosity.

"Sometimes, you have to lie to a friend so that they'll agree to do something good."

"What are you talking about?"

"You lied to me about how you spent your time at the Abaddon, but it's okay because I get it. If I thought you were… a bad person, then I may not have agreed to work with you."

Leo glances at Tzofiya, who shrugs apologetically. He sighs. "I'm sorry I lied to you; I really shouldn't have done that—"

"Don't," Vincent says assertively. "You really don't need to apologize. I understand. You had to do something that was wrong—lying—in order to get me to do something that was right—helping you fight Bartram. Sometimes… you have to do the wrong thing so the right thing happens."

Dallyn says, "Vince, I hate to poke a hole in your argument, but… good intentions don't always validate immoral actions."

Leo agrees, "Yeah, the ends don't justify the means… especially when the means are murder."

"Look, I don't want to kill people either! But what if that's just simply not an option?"

"Then we make it an option." Leo stands steadfast against Vincent, neither of them backing down.

Tzofiya interjects, "If we want more options, we must gather intel. Let us pack up, and tomorrow, we return to Wyoming for recon, okay?"

They both nod and part ways, but Dallyn anxiously bites his tongue as he and Tzofiya exchange nervous glances.

ONCE THE TESTING FACILITY IS BACK to its former glory, the invisibility project is ready to conduct a few final experiments with their technology. Megan, Beth, and their friend Kim get the honors of donning the cephalopodic skin suits, but Mavis is personally interested in today's results. She prepares her clipboard with the various criteria that they will be testing today: elastic deformation, camouflage, and adaptiveness.

"Alright everybody!" Mavis calls out while the suits are being prepared. Colonel Bartram steps off the train and struts through the facility. "We're ready to move on to the first phase: elasticity. This should be relatively simple considering all three suits are made of polyurea elastomer-based materials designed to expand further than spandex. Our subjects will wear the same gear that our typical soldiers would wear while down range."

Tables are laid out with large Kevlar vests, bulky backpacks, and helmets. Megan, Beth, and Kim all struggle to put their equipment on. Once they finish putting it on, Megan turns to Martinez, who is standing with all of this equipment already on, and asks, "I have a whole new appreciation for your job. This has to be, like… a hundred pounds!"

Martinez, Mavis, and Bartram all laugh, but Martinez coyly says, "About seventy-five, give or take."

Once they get all settled, they begin the arduous task of putting on the incredibly light and airy elastic suit that stretches over their entire body, including the equipment loadout itself. It's a strange sensation for them, as the suit feels similar to a second set of skin; like another human had shed their own skin and now they were putting it on.

"This feels weeeeeird!" Megan exclaims.

In a deep and creepy voice, Beth says, "It rubs the lotion on its skin or else it gets the hose again!"

Megan screeches, "EW! Beth, don't say that! That movie freaked me out!"

As they fiddle with the suits, Bartram asks, "I don't see a zipper any-where. How do you get it closed around the head?"

In her normal voice, Beth answers, "Well, the polymers are self-heal-ing. So when they get cut or damaged, as long as the fabric is close to the other damaged parts, it will automatically seal you in." She demonstrates this by closing the open edges of the suit around her face, allowing the skin to rapidly heal and seal her in.

"That is truly disturbing." Bartram looks like he is on the verge of gagging, but is still impressed.

After inspecting the suits, Mavis says, "There don't appear to be any rips or tears. Let's move on to the—" but she barely gets her sentence off before the suits start getting to work. They all watch closely as splotches of color emerge, morph, and adjust upon the surface of the skin until, after about thirty seconds, the three subjects disappear completely. "The camouflage aspect of the test… wow. You guys alright?"

Megan's voice appears from the ether, "Yep, doing just fine. I can't see my own arms or anything, so it's a little disorienting, but… this is pretty freaking cool."

"Amazing. Simply amazing. Stand still, though, okay? We have a few tests to run first." Everyone in the facility begins moving around where the subjects are standing.

Bartram is dumbstruck and asks, "How is this possible?"

Beth answers, "We basically took the cephalopod's skin and improved it. They have these organs called chromatophores, which are pulled under the skin to change their color, temperature, and texture."

Kim continues, "We took that concept and created an exoskin to emulate those properties."

Mavis leads Bartram behind a thermographic camera, where they can see just the other observers in the room. "Megan, can you go ahead and rip part of your suit?" As Megan complies, the camera shows the appearance of her left shoulder, but a few seconds later, it disappears as the skin regenerates.

"Incredible…" Bartram grins.

"Final test, guys. I need you to start walking around the room. Carefully—try not to run into each other." The room falls silent as the subtle clanging of boots on metal echo around the chamber. One of the subjects' suits seems to become visible as they walk, almost as if the colors need to catch up with their movement. But once they stop moving, they disappear again.

The rest of the observers burst out in excitement, but Mavis remains steady and says to Bartram, who doesn't understand what's happening, "So, with cephalopods like the cuttlefish and octopus, their camouflage is neural, which is incredibly efficient because they can adapt to their surroundings within a few milliseconds. But it's something they actively need to think about. We designed our suits to act as both the brain *and* the skin. So the skin does the thinking for us, allowing the suit to adapt its colors, textures, and apparent temperature more seamlessly."

"What's happening with Mr. Kim's suit?"

"Well, we actually adapted some of the technology from the teleportation project—namely the computer processing algorithms that Dr. Creighton designed—into our invisibility suits. Mr. Kim is wearing the suit that we designed before adapting Vincent's contribution," Mavis says matter-of-factly while Bartram gives her a menacing look.

"Well, it's good to hear that we are able to recycle some old tech into a newer generation." Mavis ignores him and continues jotting down notes.

Once the experiment is over, the team adjourns to the atrium for a celebratory party, then Mavis cuts the rest of the team loose for the day and returns to the lab. She takes the remainder of the day to input their findings into the results section of their final report. She spends a few extra hours in the lab doing some busywork for the other projects that she's involved with, but before heading out for the day, she takes her bag of library books and lines the bottom with all three of the invisibility suits. She then takes the elevator down to the west wing and goes through her standard routine of returning a few library books and checking out a few others.

As she moves across the atrium to return to her office, she sees Colonel Bartram walking in her direction from the north wing entrance. Her heart beats in her throat when he calls out, "Blackwell!" Martinez is by his side as they walk.

"Colonel, Sergeant, what are you guys up to?"

"We were looking for you, actually. Martinez had an idea that I'd like to try out."

"An idea? This is new. What's your idea?" She nervously shifts the bag of misplaced suits from hand to hand.

Martinez takes a breath as if to start talking, but Bartram explains, "Well, those spandex suits you have must have been cut from a larger bolt of cloth, right?"

"Um, yeah, I mean we have excess polyurea elastomers, but it's basically just a super stretchy spandex until we weave the camouflage technology into the material."

"That's fine, we just want to see if we can get a sheet of the material to stretch around one of the trucks."

Mavis hesitates and stutters for a moment, "Well… I mean we don't have *that* much material. Plus, I think whatever excess we have would be better used for further experimentation rather than for one off ideas… No offense, Martinez."

"Let's just go up there and see how much extra we have. If there's enough, we'll just go take a look and return it, if not, then no harm, no foul." The two of them start walking to the west wing.

She cuts them off, "Uh, look it's already dark out there. How about we try it out in the morning? It's been a long day, and I just want to spend the rest of the night in my office. The material and truck will still be there, right?"

Bartram looks at her suspiciously. "You don't have to come with us. I've got a key for every lab. You can turn in for the night. That's okay."

She bites her lip nervously and agrees, "Alright, if you insist..." Still hesitant to leave, she slowly says, "Let me know how things turn out in the morning."

"Will do..." Bartram and Martinez share a look, then head off.

Once she is clear of their sight, she takes off for the north wing. *My timeline just got cut in half.* Sprinting through the halls and down the staircase, she runs to her office, which is littered with a backpack full of survival supplies, a set of security guard equipment, and firearms. Atop her desk, a plastic bin contains two hypodermic needles and vials of fluid. She quickly removes the library books from her bag and stashes the plastic bin inside, then she dons her security equipment, throws her backpack on, and carefully seals herself inside the suit that Megan was testing.

With no time to spare, she rushes out the door and sprints upstairs to Bartram's office, pausing whenever she thinks she hears movement of any sort. But she makes it inside his office and through to the elevator with ease, considering she's had access to Sarah and Grace's cell for occasional observation purposes. When the elevator opens, she sneaks through the hallway of prison cells where they have kept Trent and Becca, who spend most of their time asleep. *You two would make great additions to the team... but I just don't have the resources. Another time, perhaps.*

"OH MY GOD, I wish they would just get it over with!" Grace paces around their cell while Sarah unsuccessfully tries meditating on the bed due to the persistent humming in their ears. "Are you gonna kill us or not? Shit or get off the pot!"

"Don't tempt them, or they might just do it." Sarah sits up straight and rubs the bridge of her nose. "Or just keep talking, and I might do it for them."

"Sorry, I just… they've just kept us locked up with nothing to do. At least let me do some work while I'm in here!" Grace pounds on the one-way mirror, which simply reverberates back at her.

"Maybe they want to bore us into giving them answers."

"Well… it might just be working. At this point, I'll give them fake information if it means just anything *new* would happen."

"Do you think they found Vincent?"

"We've been over this, Sarah…" Grace's voice softens slightly, "I don't think he made it out."

"Then why haven't they interrogated us even once? I'm telling you, our only value to them is our association with Vincent, and if they thought for a second that he was still alive, we'd be their best shot at luring him in."

"For both of our sakes, I hope you're right about—" her thought is cut off by a sudden click and the opening of their cell door. The whiteness is disrupted, and they both back up against the opposite wall. "Hello?" Grace calls out.

"You can come out. You won't be hurt," Mavis's voice is audible from the other side. Grace eyes Sarah and slowly moves toward the open door. When she peeks around the corner into the observation room, she sees a fully geared up Mavis Blackwell looking back at her with her hands in the air.

"What's happening?" Grace's voice is much louder than she expects.

Mavis shushes her, watching the exit carefully, and whispers, "We have to be quiet. I'm breaking you guys out."

Grace looks back at Sarah, who is still kneeling anxiously on the bed, and tells her, "It's Mavis, she's… breaking us out." She looks back at Mavis and retorts, "Forgive me for not believing you."

"Would you rather stay here until Bartram has no use for you and kills you off?"

Sarah cautiously stands up and joins Grace at the door. When she sees Mavis, she starts to seeth and says calmly, "You murdered Brian."

Mavis doesn't blink. Instead, she agrees, "I did."

"How can you possibly expect us to—"

"I don't, but if you don't come with me, then you'll spend the rest of your very short lives in that cell. So which is it?" Sarah and Grace exchange an in-depth discussion through extended eye contact, but Mavis is getting impatient. "Look, we have to go now, or I'll end up being in that cell alongside you."

Eventually, Sarah nods apprehensively, then Grace turns back to Mavis and says, "Okay. What's the plan?"

"Good." She takes off her backpack and rummages through it to pull out three high-tech looking full-body condoms. "We got the invisibility suits working. I snagged them on the way down here. Put them on, and we're out of here."

As they all start donning the suits, Sarah is amazed at the craftsman-ship. "I can't believe they got them working. I thought they were still months away from the prototype."

"Well, it *has* been a few months since you were locked up, so we've had plenty of time."

"How long exactly?"

"Nearly four months."

"Oh my God… Have you heard anything from Vincent? Is he alive?" Sarah asks desperately.

"Look," Mavis says, already sealing up her suit. "We don't have time to play twenty questions. Suit up."

Sarah grimaces, but she and Grace both oblige. When they finish donning everything except the hoods, they watch the sensors calibrate, and their bodies gradually dissipate into their surroundings. "Woah… this is amazing! Wait, what's happening to yours, Mavis?"

As Mavis walks to the door, her suit struggles to keep up with the assimilation of new data. "Mine is the prototype. You two have the good ones."

"Are you still going to be able to get out?"

"Uh, we'll find out, I guess, won't we?" Sarah and Grace start talking over each other trying to figure out a way to quickly fix the suit, but Mavis knows they don't have the time for it. "Hey, guys, it's okay. I planned for this. If any of us gets caught, I'm the most likely one to break out again. Don't worry about it. Let's move."

"Wait." Grace halts them. "Before we go, I have to know… why are you doing this for us?"

Mavis pauses. "Fine… my patience with Bartram is gone. If I'm gonna cure humanity of death, I need Vincent. If there's a chance he's still alive, rescuing you is the first step in getting him to work with me again."

Sarah doesn't like that answer, but they both know she's their only chance of survival. Grace says, "Okay. Let's go."

They exit the observation room and sprint down the corridor to the elevator, but Sarah pauses as they pass the dingiest-looking barred jail cells. A man sits slumped over, chained and unconscious against the back wall of one of the cells, and the adjacent cell has an even grimmer sight—a woman with dry, bloody bandages wrapped around a stump of a left leg seems to barely cling to life in her chains. Sarah stands with her jaw wide open. "What… is this?"

"Dr. Boyce," Mavis says. "I know how you feel, but we have to keep moving."

"This is grisly! Inhumane! We have to take them with us!"

"I know"—Mavis checks her watch—"but we don't have the time or resources. Let's go!" Sarah doesn't move, but Grace takes her by the arm and drags her into the elevator. When the door closes, they rip open their hoods so they can see each other. Mavis starts barking orders, "You two, buddy system. Hold each other's hands, and don't let go. Run as fast as you can to the mountain behind the base. There's a valley just west of the gate; get there as fast as humanly possible."

"What about you?" Grace asks. "If you run in that suit, they'll see you in an instant."

"If I move slow enough, they may not be able to see me. I'll meet you out there, okay? Just run."

They nod nervously and close up their hoods. Grace takes a firm grasp of Sarah's hand. When the elevator dings, Grace launches herself forward with Sarah in tow. The surface looks much different than they remember it. There are patrols everywhere, flood lights turn the midnight sky into daylight, and the air is so much colder than they have ever experienced in the desert. But none of that matters right now; they have to get out of here. As the two of them round the corner and pass the gate guard booth, Grace gets a quick glance of the security cameras that oversee the entire campus. *Where is Mavis?* The thought passes almost as quickly as it comes though. Mavis doesn't matter right now. Nothing matters right now except reaching the mountain valley.

CHAPTER FORTY-SIX

Wednesday

Vincent can't quite figure out why it bothers him so much that Leo suddenly changed his tune about killing. "Alright, Vinny," Leo says. "While Tzofiya and I finish packing, do you mind filling up the truck? I think it's running on empty."

"Yeah, sure," Vincent says, grabbing the keys and taking the wheel. He shuts his eyes and wordlessly mutters to himself until, in the blink of an eye, the entire vehicle disappears into thin air, leaving nothing but divots in the sand where the tires were just resting.

Opening his eyes, Vincent sees a deserted, rural road stretching out ahead of him through the windshield. His fingers squeeze the steering wheel tightly, and he's frowning for some reason that he can't quite figure out. Miles of snow-patched greenery stretch out on every side of him. The key sits in the ignition, but he just stares ahead until he can hear his own thoughts.

If you're going to lie to me for a good reason, that's fine. I get it. But if you're going to lie to me about being a mass fucking murderer in your previous life, at least support me when I finally come to the realization that we need to kill a bad guy! You convert me so that I see things your way, but then you immediately change your mind? That's fucked up! Now I feel like a bad guy for saying we need to kill him! That wasn't fair...

The overcast sky threatens to snow, but nothing seems to fall yet. A recurring dream he's been having for a couple months plays in his mind. Awakening to a simpler time, he walks through his old apartment and checks his phone for a text from Sarah—there's nothing there of course, but you never know. Arriving to work before the others, he prepares the lab for the day, knowing Grace is just going to yell at Karl for not cleaning up his mess from the night before. The air conditioner never bothers him, but he brings his sweater anyway, knowing Sarah will steal it from him while she has her morning cup of coffee. Karl will try to coerce him into making a move on Sarah, but he's too afraid. He's happy being afraid though, because at least they spend every day together. There's no Trent or Leo spying on him, no Bartram threatening to kill his friends, and no Mavis tainting his mind with ideas of his great potential.

Turning the key in the ignition, he slams on the gas pedal and screams down the road until he crests the horizon to a small gas station with a single pump. A van is parked right outside the entrance to the store, but it's nowhere near the pump. In fact, the van's engine is idling with a driver in the front seat. *What the fuck?* He pulls up to the pump and sets the nozzle to fill up the tank. Then he surveys the situation: he sees two men inside yelling and screaming at the cashier, then notices the driver getting out of the van. They're all armed. Instinct kicks in, and Vincent jumps from the gas pump outside his own car to the driver side door of the van, steals the driver's revolver, and teleports again to a few feet behind him, now pointing the revolver at the guy's head. Vincent kicks out the driver's kneecaps and cold-cocks him across the base of the skull, causing him to collapse. Then he takes cover against the gas station wall.

I can't blindly teleport inside, but if I get a lay of the land it'll be easier. "What was that?!" Vincent hears someone inside shout before a series of rustling sounds. *Fuck. Go, go, go.* He teleports to the other side of the building, crouching low enough to peer through a window without being noticed. Two men wearing pantyhose as masks are carrying similar revolvers; one holding up the store owner, the other pointing his gun at the entrance. The cashier's hands are shaking as he holds them in the air.

It would take far too long to teleport him out of there. I'll have to engage the attackers. Vincent takes a deep breath and thinks to himself. *Just take your time. Nice and slow.* He then jumps back to his cover near the van. He approaches the corner and says loud enough for the hostage-takers to hear, "Your driver's out of commission. If you want to get out of here, you'll have to go through me."

"Who are you?" the one watching the entrance asks.

"Just somebody who gets uncomfortable around guns. So why don't you put yours down, and we can have a little chitchat. What do you say?"

"Not until we know who you are! You a cop?"

"Nope, no cops here. Unfortunately, I'm someone much more danger-ous. So please, drop the guns." He teleports back to the opposite window and looks inside to see them freaking out, intermittently looking at each other for reassurance. He jumps back to his negotiation spot as the watchman responds.

"We're not looking for a fight, buddy. Just trying to score some cash."

"You'll have to get a job like everyone else. You're threatening that cashier's life over what? A hundred dollars? One-fifty? Just drop your guns, and everyone will be happy." Vincent teleports back to see the watchman slowly approaching the entrance, his gun shaking in his hand. The man holding up the cashier barely has his attention on his hostage.

"Yeah, that's not really an option for us, buddy. So why don't you just scamper off, and we won't let anything happen to this poor cashier, huh?" Standing right up against the entrance, he takes a couple of deep breaths in preparation to round the corner. Vincent watches on, calculating his moves. *Three... two... one...* As the watchman rounds the corner, Vin-cent teleports over, kicks him into the wall, smashes his head against the concrete, knocks him out, then steals his gun. The hostage-taker, having just seen his friend disappear from sight, watches with bated breath.

"Oh fuck! Psycho Steve?!" he calls out to his friend. "You okay, buddy?!" He cranes his neck to get a better look, but all he sees is a body on the ground before hearing the cocking of a revolver behind him.

Vincent quietly whispers, "Drop. The. Gun."

His breath leaving him, the man doesn't budge. Instead, he responds,

"Look man, we're just trying to get by out here. It's hard for ex-cons to get jobs. You know how it goes!"

"No. I don't know how that goes, but right now you have a choice: drop the gun or die."

"I don't know who you are, man, but just get out of here, okay? No one has to get hurt!" He brandishes his gun in front of the cashier in a threatening motion.

"Three… two…" Vincent's voice is steady, and for the first time in probably his entire life, he doesn't feel nervous. Adrenaline is pumping, sure, but he feels confident that he knows what the right thing to do here is. Then the criminal makes a sudden move, jerking the gun in Vincent's direction. Vincent doesn't think twice. He pulls the trigger. "*You know the rules, pussy! When the fag gets captured, the fag gets punished.*" For a fleeting moment, Vincent feels powerful. Very powerful. But that moment is immediately replaced by… something different. Something that doesn't feel good.

A deafening yelp from the cashier brings him back to reality. Looking around the store, he realizes that he just killed a guy, and that the cashier is terrified. They stare at each other for quite some time, then the cashier says, "I didn't see anything." Vincent looks at a camera in the corner of the store, and the cashier quickly reassures him, "It's fake. Can't afford a real one."

I have to get out of here. He sprints out of the gas station, replaces the gas nozzle, and sees the cashier picking up the phone. He steps on the pedal, but he only teleports back to camp when he crosses over the horizon.

"Vincent?" Tzofiya calls out after a few minutes of Vincent just sitting in the car white-knuckling the steering wheel. When they receive no response, Leo watches curiously, and Dallyn joins Tzofiya in approaching the driver-side window. "Vincent?" she asks again and knocks on the glass.

"You okay, Vince?" Dallyn asks, but Vincent is a million miles away.

"Vincent!" He knocks on the glass again, which breaks Vincent's trance, causing him to roll down the window. "You okay, bud?"

"Uh, yeah. No, I'm fine."

Tzofiya apprehensively says, "Leo find spot for new camp. You want scout ahead? I join you, in case we have uninvited guests."

"Sure. Yeah, just… get in." Tzofiya gets inside and hands him a GPS displaying a set of coordinates sitting forty miles outside of the Abaddon's borders. Shutting his eyes, he focuses on the coordinates, feeling the quantum states of himself, Tzofiya, and the car. She waits patiently for fifteen minutes as Vincent quietly mutters until suddenly her surroundings change drastically from the snowy forest to a frost-covered stretch of desert.

After a quick walkabout to survey their surroundings and ensure they are indeed alone, Tzofiya asks, "Are you sure you're okay? Something on your mind?"

"No. I'm fine, Tzofiya. Thank you."

"You're not fine. Did something happen?"

"Nuh uh, just a routine trip."

"Okay… Listen, I know you are worried that Leo does not want to kill Bartram anymore. But don't worry. We will take him out of power, by any means necessary. Okay?"

"Right… Yeah, any means necessary…"

They do one last circle of the area, and Vincent teleports back to Alaska, leaving Tzofiya back in the desert as he wordlessly ferries equipment to Wyoming.

A few hours later, they have the camp fully set up, and Vincent prepares for a reconnaissance mission. After sunset, he holsters a silenced Glock and pockets a small knife. Leo gives him a watch, and Tzofiya briefs him on exactly what his job is. "Number one rule: stay out of sight. Learn what you can, find out security posture, what happened to Trent and Becca, and if they know our status—all of that would be nice, but most important is you remain invisible. Understood?"

"Understood."

Leo grabs his shoulder and adds, "And Vinny… be careful. I don't want to see you getting hurt."

"Thanks… I'll do my best." Vincent looks down.

Vincent soon arrives at the spot that Trent used to pick him up from every Friday night, then he gathers himself and briskly makes his way to the exterior gate of Fort Chivington. He immediately notices flood lights illuminating the grounds in a perimeter that extends about fifty yards outside the exterior fence. Several teams of watchmen patrol inside the gate. *He's increased manning since we left.* The roof of his old barracks building seems dark, so he focuses on it and a second later finds himself lying low behind the parapet.

Peeking out across the patrols of roving guards, he doesn't seem to recognize most of the faces, except for a few of the shift leaders here and there who had survived their last excursion. *I gotta get inside her room.* Lining himself up with the appropriate window, he calculates the best place to teleport without ending up inside a wall.

Popping inside Sarah's room, he realizes he was off by about a foot and stumbles to the ground. Gathering himself, he finds the place to be completely empty. All of her and Grace's belongings have been ransacked, everything clearly having been removed in a hurry. *Did they get out? They wouldn't have survived in the desert, so were they moved downstairs?*

He looks around the room for any kind of bug or camera, but it seems to be clean. *They don't care to keep an eye on the room itself. Are there any others living here?* He puts his ear to the wall but hears nothing. *Nobody's here… Still, I can't just go knocking door to door looking for anyone who's home.* He moves back up to the roof and looks around at the brightly lit grounds of the fort.

Peering over the parapet again, he checks on the various elevators that lead into the Abaddon. The armory looks to have more cameras around it than there were before, but something else catches his attention. For just a split-second, he could swear he saw a splotch of discoloration appear and disappear from inside the armory entrance. He squints to get a better look, but a sudden crashing sound prompts Vincent to lie down flat and out of sight. Martinez's voice booms from the admin building entrance, "How the fuck did this happen?!"

"We don't know, sir." Murphy tries to keep up with him as he marches. "They just disappeared! They couldn't have come this way!"

"They didn't *disappear*! You *let* them slip by you!"

"We've had patrols roving all night; there's no way they could have—"

"Well, they did! Now go get Cesar and Dolly. It's time for a hunt."

Vincent listens carefully as Martinez gathers up a couple of guards and gear. Cesar rushes out of the barracks while buckling a Kevlar vest on Dolly and marching toward the gate; Cesar has two sets of off-white bedsheets in hand and presents them to Dolly for her to sniff before getting started on their hunt. Murphy asks, "Alright, Cesar, you and Dolly ready for another ride?"

Cesar doesn't get a chance to respond before Martinez pulls Murphy by the scruff and shoves him against the admin building wall. "There's no way in hell you're coming with us, Murph. You're staying right the fuck here, and I swear to Christ, if you let another fucking rat slip through your fingers, Bartram will make sure you never see the light of day again."

"Uh, y-yes, sir," he stutters before Dolly starts barking loudly from just outside the gate.

"West!" Cesar shouts as he and Dolly load up in the truck bed.

Martinez loads up in the truck with Frank and Harry—a couple of newbies who have shown pretty good promise. Martinez shouts, "Remember! We'll stop every half mile to let Dolly regain the scent. Cesar, this is your mission! Don't let these bitches escape!" He fires up the truck and peels out, quickly rounding the corner and taking off into the desert.

Vincent peers over the parapet and sees a dust cloud billowing. *What is happening?* Immediately surveying the area, he figures the mountaintop is the best spot to follow their trail without being detected, so he teleports to the ridge.

"DOLLY'S GOT THEM. NORTHWEST," Cesar calls out.

"Alright, load up. Let's keep going," Martinez responds, prompting Vincent to follow along silently. He teleports from shadow to shadow for nearly an hour, but he gives himself enough lead to rest between jumps. Then finally, from the back of the truck, Dolly starts barking incessantly, and Cesar has to hold her back to keep her from jumping out of the truck bed. They come to a stop, then the whole crew jumps out and follows her across the sandscape, flashlights bouncing as they shine into the starlit night. *Looks like they're getting close to whatever they're following.*

He watches Dolly vigorously lead the patrol forward while someone he doesn't recognize stays behind to keep an eye out on the truck. Vincent impatiently considers his options for a while until the truck pulls up to a valley where the mountain slopes down. Cesar and Dolly jump out in front of the truck's headlights to investigate; Dolly starts pulling harder and harder against her leash until she's practically thrashing around.

"I think she's found them!" Cesar shouts as he breaks into a full sprint.

"Cesar! Stand by!" Martinez shouts, and Cesar obeys despite Dolly's impatience. "They wouldn't have made it this far without help. Blackwell is probably with them. This could be a trap." *Blackwell? They're hunting Mavis? That can't be right…*

"I see prints leading northwest into the valley. Do you want to follow them on foot, sir?" Vincent looks ahead past the cone of light emanating from the truck's headlights to see brush, Joshua trees, and small gatherings of boulders ahead of them.

"How many sets of prints do you see?" Martinez asks.

Cesar studies the sand and replies, "It's hard to tell. At least two."

Martinez takes a second to look behind and around them, then stops to think for a second. "No. Load up in the bed. We'll keep the tracks in view and see where they lead. Stay low though… and keep your eyes peeled." Martinez keeps his head on a swivel, scanning the mountain and hills on either side of the valley. For a moment, Vincent could swear Martinez lingers on the Joshua tree that he's hiding behind. "I don't trust these hills."

The truck creeps forward as it drives alongside the trail of footprints. Vincent follows along from a few hundred feet up the mountainside, keeping an eye on their progress as they go. The truck eventually comes to a halt when the trail ends at a grouping of large stones, the flat surfaces of which are illuminated by the truck's fog lights. Martinez and the rest of the guards who are inside the cab get out with their rifles drawn on the rock formation, leaving the truck running. Cesar unleashes Dolly and whispers a command before the two of them stealthily dismount the truck bed.

Martinez sidles up behind the driver's side door with his rifle resting atop the door frame. "We know you're out there!" he shouts much louder than Vincent expected, and his voice reverberates through the valley. Vincent almost feels that Martinez is addressing him directly. "You won't make it out of this desert alive! Neither will your two little scientist friends!" *Scientist friends?* He waits for a response, and Vincent listens carefully, but they hear nothing.

Martinez steps out from the protection of the truck and whispers, "Harry, let's go." He and Harry both start walking around the perimeter of the rock formation, being sure to keep their distance. Vincent watches on nervously, his heart beating faster and faster until Martinez and Harry meet on the opposite side of the formation.

Harry drops his rifle looking disappointed. "There's no one here. It was a false lead."

Martinez is unconvinced. He continues to encircle the stones and studies the tracks. "No. They're here." Martinez tentatively points the barrel of his rifle at the stones but turns his head toward the mountains and hills. Vincent's hands begin to tremble. "But if they weren't here…"

Martinez seems to be daring whoever might be watching the scene. *Is he… he doesn't know I'm here… but…* "Then it wouldn't matter if…" He slides his finger to the trigger and looks down the sights, but he keeps his peripheral vision on his surroundings. *Fuck it.*

Vincent throws his hood up and quickly jumps to a few inches beside Martinez, tackling him and grabbing the rifle. He then teleports to the driver's side of the truck to honk the horn, prompting the entire party to turn their guns on the truck in a fit of confusion. But he's already gone, returned to his perch on the mountainside.

"What the fuck just happened?!" Martinez looks around his feet for his rifle, but Vincent grins and puts the rifle on the ground, choosing instead to draw the silenced pistol from his holster. "Where'd my rifle go?!" Martinez takes a second before realizing something, "Wait… gentlemen, I think we have a guardian angel in our presence." He draws his sidearm and brings it to the ready. "Blackwell! Reveal yourself! Come with us, and you'll be welcomed back with open arms. You don't owe these scientists shit."

Vincent snarls and tightens his grip on his pistol. *What is he talking about?* Dolly starts barking, and Cesar circles back around the rock formation, stops, then announces, "There's a new set of tracks leading away from the rocks!" Vincent hears Cesar call this out and realizes there's something going on he can't see. *Someone's out there.*

Martinez runs toward him so they can follow the tracks, then calls out, "Frank, Cesar, on me! Harry, bring the truck around!" Cesar whistles a command to Dolly, and they follow the tracks. Harry jogs around to the driver's seat and jumps in, but before he can close the door, Vincent decides to join him.

Instantly appearing in the passenger seat with his gun against Harry's knee, Vincent winces and simply says, "Sorry," then pulls the trigger over each knee. If the party didn't hear the gunshots, they certainly heard the sound of Vincent thrashing Harry's head against the horn over and over until he's out cold.

"Harry?" Martinez asks, holding up a fist to halt his comrades. They wait for a response, but when the horn keeps blaring, he gestures for them to break their follow and converge on the truck. As they approach the idling truck, they see dark splatters across the windows and front windshield, then Harry's limp head slides off the wheel and against his seatbelt, his face decorated with a broken nose. "What the shit?" The three of them wince at the sight of their wounded friend.

Martinez gestures to Frank, who opens the passenger door and shines a flashlight inside the cab. He announces, "There's two shell casings on the seat. Nine mil."

A streak of anger runs across Martinez's face. He looks around the valley and shouts, "Where the fuck are you!?" But the mountains just echo his words back to him. Vincent chuckles to himself and watches them flail.

"What do we do, sir?" Frank's voice is shaking as he asks, but Martinez ignores him.

"Why the fuck isn't Dolly picking up on this attacker?"

Defending his canine companion, Cesar says, "She's got our runners' scents. But if there's a third person out here, she'll get them."

"It's Blackwell! She's trying to keep us from following the girls. Cesar, track the targets! Frank, cover his back, and don't get distracted!" The three of them take off. Martinez splits from the other two and jumps in the truck. Vincent considers his options for a minute. *Shit… if there's a scientist… if Sarah's really out here, I gotta keep these guys off their scent.*

Martinez pushes Harry's body further into the cab and shrugs off the disturbing visual, but as soon as he looks over the steering wheel, the headlights show him something that he doesn't quite understand. A hooded figure flashes into existence from thin air. This figure raises a gun to the back of Frank's knees, pulls the trigger twice, then before Frank has a chance to hit the ground, the figure vanishes into the darkness.

"What the…" he mutters to himself, but his thought is interrupted by a slight squeak as the truck bed suddenly lowers from taking on weight.

With a gasp, Martinez moves quicker than lightning to throw himself out of the truck before hearing the sound of a suppressed bullet ripping through the roof of the cab. As he falls, he reaches for his sidearm and fires at the bed, but when he looks—nothing is there. "Teleporting?" Martinez retrieves Harry's M16, then shouts at the top of his lungs, "She's teleporting!"

Randomly firing in every direction, Martinez turns about in a craze, trying to figure out how to react. Vincent, having been startled by Martinez rapidly returning fire, finds himself falling hundreds of feet above his perch at the mountainside, but he quickly teleports back to the ground. He leans against the nearest tree to gasp for breath and nurse an oncoming headache. It isn't until a few minutes pass that he realizes how cold the air is. Then he realizes why. He is no longer wearing his hoodie… nor is he holding his gun. *Aw shit…*

He looks down at the valley to see Martinez pull his hoodie and pistol from the bed. "Cesar! Get over here! Move!" Vincent scrambles for the rifle at his feet, then tries to teleport back to stop Martinez before they can act. But his headache suddenly flares up into a migraine that bursts behind his eyes, causing him to keel over. His glasses fall off, and he grasps at his head. Off in the distance, Vincent can barely hear the revving of an engine and the peeling out of tires in the sand; the searing heat pulsates in his ears for a second, then he tries to take a look at the truck, but even just opening his eyes makes him nearly choke.

It takes a few minutes for him to start recovering, but when he finally gets to his feet and puts his glasses on, he can just see the taillights disappearing off in the distance. They're gone. When his head cools down completely, Vincent does some quick math, appears at the stone formation, and looks around under the moonlit desert. "Hello? Is… Is there anybody out there?" He feels almost foolish asking the darkness, but he's starting to share Martinez's feeling of being watched. "Hello?! Sarah? Grace? …Mavis? Is anybody there?" He waits for a little while longer and sighs. "Okay… that's… that's okay." *This is not okay. They know about me, and… and I have nothing to show for it.* His chest tightens, and he rubs the bridge of his nose before letting out a scream, "FUCK!"

"Vince?"

The small voice is instant tension relief. He turns his head to see Sarah's sunken green eyes staring back at him in disbelief. She stands in ragged white clothing and unkempt, dirty, red hair with some kind of transparent suit in her hand, completely unconvinced that what she's seeing is real. Vincent takes a tentative step in her direction, then breaks into a sprint and wraps his arms around her in the first hug he has ever initiated.

"You're *alive!*" Sarah gasps. "I-I can't…" She throws her arms around his neck and buries her face into his shoulder. Breathing him in, the desert fades away, the Milky Way overhead glows brighter, and her heart flutters.

The two of them get lost in each other, and Vincent fails to notice someone else revealing herself from her shroud. It's Grace, who immediately begins to investigate the scene. She covers her mouth and takes a look at the blood in the sand.

"Is… did you kill those guys, Vince?" Grace asks. Vincent returns to the world. The emptiness of the desert falls back, and Sarah pulls away to join Grace. "How… how?"

"I didn't kill them, no. Frank and Harry should be fine, but… as for how—" Vincent doesn't know what to tell them immediately, but he knows that he has overstayed his time away from the camp. "Here, I'll show you. Take my hand."

He extends a hand to them both, and after a few moments of silent concentration, Grace asks, "Are you okay?"

"Yeah, just hold on." It takes about ten minutes of straight concentration, but in the blink of an eye, all three of them appear outside of a camp somewhere else in the desert. Vincent opens his eyes to find Sarah and Grace with their jaws agape. He steps off with a proud bounce in his step. "Welcome to our humble abode. It's not much, but—"

His sentence is cut off by the sound of shotguns cocking and people shouting, "Get on the ground!" Vincent turns to see Tzofiya and Leo pointing their guns at them. Sarah and Grace cry out, throwing their hands in the air and falling to the ground, but Vincent just throws up his hands and shouts back.

"Woah, woah, woah! It's okay! It's just me!"

They drop their rifles, but Leo immediately shouts, "Vincent! It was a *recon* mission! You weren't supposed to break anyone out yet!"

"I didn't! They were already out! I swear!"

"They were already out? How?"

"Martinez was hunting them. I followed him, but he was about to find these guys, so…"

"Oh my God," Leo mutters. "Were you seen?"

"Not exactly…"

Tzofiya interjects, "Where is your sweater? And your gun?"

"Uh, well, see, that's the thing… I got into a scuffle with them, and though they didn't *see* me, I had to teleport a bunch and… kind of accidentally left a few things behind." Behind him, Sarah and Grace are looking at each other in stark disbelief. Grace mouths the word *"teleport"* back to her to make sure she heard correctly.

"They know we're back in the desert, Vincent. They will come looking for us!" Tzofiya pulls the truck around so she and Leo can go on a roundabout to make sure they are still safe.

But before they take off, Leo says, "Hold down the fort, get these girls comfortable, and for fuck's sake, stay put!"

The truck speeds off, and after such a high-energy welcome to the camp, Sarah and Grace just stare at Vincent, who turns to them and smiles. "Like I said, welcome home."

Dallyn comes out and greets the new additions to their team by offering them some water, tea, and food while he tends to the minor scrapes and bruises they'd sustained during their escape. About twenty minutes pass while Leo and Tzofiya secure their perimeter. During that time, the four of them settle around the campfire, but when Leo and Tzofiya return, they are considerably less relaxed.

"Start from top," Tzofiya says, which prompts a lengthy conversation of everyone catching each other up on how they arrived at where they currently are. Vincent conveniently leaves out the part where he accidentally murdered an armed robber, but otherwise nothing is left off the table.

"I kneecapped Frank and Harry, but… I don't know. I just couldn't bring myself to kill either of them."

Tzofiya eyes him and says, "You had chance to keep news of incident from returning to Abaddon, but you spared two lives. I can't say I would have made same decision, but I am glad you did right thing."

"Oh my gosh!" Grace exclaims. "You guys have real food! You have no idea what it was like in the white room! They only fed us water and white rice!"

Leo laughs. "Actually I do know what it's like. I spent sixty-five years in that prison."

Grace's jaw drops while chewing a slice of salami. "You spent how long in there? And you're still sane?"

Vincent chuckles. "Well, that part's debatable."

While recounting the events of the assault on the Abaddon, Grace again exclaims, "Wait, so you fought off clone versions of yourself while Dr. Smith went to kill an army of them, then you tried to teleport away… but it exploded? Which—"

Vincent nods with a grin. "—Which did *something* that resulted in me being able to teleport on my own. Without the machine."

"You know what? Who am I to say what's crazy? The woman that Leo shot in the head broke us out of prison using goddamn invisibility suits. This is a wild world." The group shares a much-needed laugh at her observations, but away from the group, Sarah doesn't seem to be quite so distracted from her trauma.

"Can we go back to right before you guys shot down at us?" Sarah asks. "You said you saw the whole thing, right? Like, all of it?"

Vincent and Leo awkwardly nod, and Leo admits, "Yeah, uh, I saw you trying to fight off Peterson, but she was too slippery for you. So I, uh, took her out."

"That's not the part I meant." Vincent knows what she's getting at. "When Mavis held Brian at gunpoint, what were you guys doing?" Vincent blushes and sees Leo trying to keep attention off of him.

"Well, at the time, Dr. Smith was downstairs supposedly negotiating with the colonel. We were trying to avoid conflict, but when she fired the gun, we had no choice."

"Did you not see her brandishing that gun and threatening us before she actually shot Brian? There was plenty of lead up, wasn't there?"

Leo tries dancing around the answer, but Vincent takes responsibility. "I saw it. I was the one in charge of shooting her, but… I had the shot. I could have killed her before she did it. But…"

"Why didn't you? If you did, Brian would still be alive." She has an accusatory look on her face, and there's an eerie quiet amongst them. "Were you waiting for her to shoot him?"

Leo and Dallyn immediately come to his defense, "Woah! C'mon! That's not fair!"

Vincent answers for himself, "I can't say that I liked seeing you and him around, but no. I would never do anything like that, Sarah. I was friends with him, too. I couldn't pull the trigger because… I just couldn't. The thought of ending someone's life was just—it was overwhelming."

"You had a choice between Mavis and Brian, and you chose Mavis. Why?"

Vincent looks into her eyes with the reflection of the fire dancing in them. "I don't know. I know intellectually that Mavis was going to kill him… but I was hoping I could—I don't know—think my way out of it. But I froze up."

"Yeah. You did." Vincent would never have expected this kind of reaction from Sarah. Despite feeling like he deserved it in a way, her words hurt him on a level that he has never experienced before; a level that he was unaware of. Then he makes eye contact with Leo and realizes he was just on the other side of this conversation not too long ago.

Tzofiya decides to push planning their next step to tomorrow after a night of recuperation. Despite knowing that Sarah is safe and sound in a nearby sleeping bag, anxiety still manages to steal Vincent's sleep.

CHAPTER FORTY-SEVEN

November 26th, 2020

Thursday

The clanking of ice cubes against glass is the only audible sound in Bartram's living room. Martinez stands while the colonel sits in his brand new couch and sips on his whiskey. Bartram abruptly gets to his feet and walks up to Martinez, pointing an aggressive finger at him through squinting eyes. But he exhales disappointedly, then paces around the room, stopping only to admire the reconstructed atrium before taking another sip.

"Walk me through it again."

Martinez clears his throat and speaks, "We departed Fort Chivington with a hunting party to seek out the escaped prisoners—we later determined that Doctor Blackwell was amongst the escapees. Upon arrival at Dolly's final location, we discovered a rock formation in the center of the mountain valley and stopped the vehicle to investigate. Based on a set of tracks that led into the valley, it was likely we would find our targets standing on the rock formation. Unfortunately"—he hesitates—"uh… we, um, unfortunately, upon further investigation, we learned that the valley was an ambush. We were attacked by a… um…"

"Go ahead." Bartram stares daggers at him.

"We were attacked by some kind of… teleporter."

"See, that's where you lose me. What exactly do you mean by 'teleporter'?"

"I saw a human person… appear out of nowhere. They attacked Harry and Frank. We couldn't get eyes on the attacker, but there was a black hoodie and a Glock found in the bed of the truck. I'm running them for prints now."

"And what happened to your M16?"

Martinez coughs. "Well… my M16 was found in a small clearing on the mountain side, along with a few sets of footprints and evidence of life."

"Right… so… your assessment is that there was a teleporter present at the scene? Jumping back and forth between the scene of the ambush and the mountainside clearing?"

"…Yes, sir."

"Hm… and you're sure you understand the implications of this claim?"

"Yes, sir."

Bartram isn't amused by this attempt at a joke. He takes a deep breath and sighs. After a second of staring at Martinez without blinking, he downs his glass of whiskey and throws it across the room while letting out an echoing scream across the room, "FUUUUUCK!" The glass shatters on the marble wall, and ice bounces across the floor. He paces around the room trying to regain his rhythm, but then he finds himself overlooking the atrium. "He was dead, Martinez. What happened?"

"I don't know, sir."

"No, of course you don't." He lets the moment settle. "Why would he let you get away?"

"I… uh, I don't know, sir. He was pretty quick, though. Maybe he got tired?"

"Hm… maybe. Or maybe he was sending me a message."

"The whole thing was incredibly well-orchestrated; Mavis got away with the prisoners."

"If Vincent really is alive, why would he help Mavis escape? The last time he saw her, she was trying to kill him."

"Unless they've been in contact. She's been upset with the way things have been running around here since the Cultivation Center was shut down. I could see her reaching out to Vincent to help bring you down."

"But we've monitored her communications. She hasn't made a peep outside the Abaddon."

"I mean, you saw what Dr. Smith was able to do from inside that office; Blackwell is much smarter than he ever was. She's capable of pretty much anything."

"All we know for sure is this: there is a teleporter who attacked our hunting party. The only person who might be able to replicate that technology would be Dr. Creighton. If that was indeed him, he'll likely be coming back."

Martinez's radio crackles. "Martinez, this is Murphy. Sir, you might want to come see this."

"GOOD GIRL, DOLLY. You did so good today, but it was too close a call for me." Cesar gives his partner some love as they go back inside the barracks building. When they pass a certain room on the third floor, Dolly stops and begins sniffing at the air. "You okay, Dolly?" She goes to a recently abandoned room and sniffs the door. She then puts her nose to the ground and starts following a scent. Cesar looks at the door and whispers, "That's Blackwell's old room. What you got?"

He follows her through the hallways, down the stairs, and outside into the parking lot. They weave through the trucks, and Cesar calls out to Murphy, who is still standing watch as patrol supervisor. Murphy gathers the dozen or so guards standing watch, and they all silently converge on the armory building.

"What's she got, Cesar?"

"I'm not a hundred percent, but it could be Blackwell." Dolly halts and starts barking at the entrance to the armory, prompting Murphy to shine his flashlight into the wooden shack.

"There's nothing in there," he announces, but Dolly sniffs the ground and starts walking away from the armory. Cesar notices the footsteps from where their escaped prisoners ran earlier in the night, but then he notices a third set branching off behind the saloon. He makes hand movements indicating for a few patrols to converge on the rear of the decrepit building. Murphy follows the footprints until they come to a halt, at which point Dolly is going crazy, slobbering as she barks at the spot.

"We see you, Blackwell. Show yourself." After a moment's hesitation, Mavis removes the hood from her invisibility suit with a defeated grin.

"Thought you wouldn't see me if I moved slow enough. Good job, Murphy."

Murphy doesn't seem to know how to respond to that comment, but he radios in, "Martinez, this is Murphy. Sir, you might want to come see this." While arresting her, Murphy simply asks, "Why did you do it?"

She responds, "I thought Colonel Bartram was the right man to lead the Abaddon. I was wrong."

"If you didn't want to work for him, why break the prisoners out? You could have just run away. Break free."

"I needed smart people with vision to be on my side. I needed another Vincent, and they were my best bet."

"On your side to do what?"

"Dethrone Bartram, of course." Murphy looks at her thoughtfully, but continues arresting her.

WHEN THE SUN RISES, Vincent joins the group for breakfast. Everyone is quiet. Tzofiya and Leo privately discuss security matters while the others simply enjoy their plate of eggs and bacon. Vincent's attention is glued to Sarah. After a few minutes of trading glances with her, he smiles. She returns with a half-grin, then Vincent gestures to the tent. She nods, and the two of them leave.

Well aware of the eyes on them, Vincent and Sarah shyly enter the sleeping tent and take seats on either side of the interior. Vincent sits atop a pelican chest while Sarah rests in a lawn chair that's been set up next to an end table. Sarah waits a beat to speak, knowing how unconfident Vincent must feel right now, but Vincent immediately speaks his mind.

"I'm glad you made it out."

"Me, too. I really thought you hadn't made it."

"We almost didn't, but we pulled through by the skin of our teeth…" They sit in a comfortable silence for a few minutes. "I'm sorry for what happened to Brian."

"Me, too." She stammers, "I-I'm sorry for accusing you last night. That wasn't fair of me."

"Thanks… I blamed myself for it, too, even though I know Mavis was the one responsible. It's hard to make yourself let go of that guilt."

"I understand. I still feel guilty when I think about Airman Little, Stephanie, Robert, and all the others we lost during the first test."

"I'm sorry you have to go through that."

"Thanks… Have you guys figured out what you're going to do next?"

"Well, it seems we're kind of torn on that. Bartram needs to go, yes, but how? I think we all know that the best route is to just kill him, but some of us want to stop the cycle of killing."

"Are you one of them?"

"Well… I mean, we tried the peaceful way before, and look where it got us. Now we're on the precipice of another attack on the Abaddon, but we have less of a plan, less manpower, and less chance of survival than we did last time. What do you think?"

"You're right. It didn't work last time, but that doesn't mean we stoop to his level."

"So you're on Leo's side, then?"

"I'm not on anyone's side. I would just hate to see you become an assassin. You don't deserve to be a cold-hearted killer." It's a strange sentence to hear from Sarah, but it makes Vincent smile.

"You think so?"

"Of course…" She looks at her shoelaces while she talks. "As hard as it was to see Brian"—she shudders at the image flaring up in her mind again—"well… you know… I'm almost happy that it was too hard for you to pull the trigger. I know that sounds weird, but Mavis is cold. I don't want you to become cold like her."

"But me not pulling my trigger almost got you killed, too. If Leo hadn't done it for me, you'd be dead."

"Yeah… I know. But—"

At that moment, footsteps approach their tent, and Leo's head pops in, "I'm sorry to interrupt, but Vinny, I think you should come out here."

"What's going on?"

They both follow him to the breakfast table where Grace has been recounting their escape from the Abaddon, and Grace exclaims, "Sarah! Remember those disgusting cells we saw outside the white room? Those prisoners were their friends!"

"Wait," Vincent says. "You saw Trent and Becca?"

Sarah answers, "Tall guy and a short girl? Missing a leg?"

"Holy shit." Vincent nearly collapses into a nearby chair. "They made it? What about Becca? Was she breathing?"

"I mean, they were pretty rough, but I think they were both alive."

Tzofiya says, "If they were dead, why lock them up?"

"Guys," Vincent's voice has a renewed sense of vigor. "If they're still alive down there, we have to go get them. Like, tonight."

"Now, hold on there, bud," Leo tries to put the brakes on. "We can't just go charging in. From the sounds of it, they've buffed up security, put in lights, more boots on ground… I'm not sure we can get everyone inside."

Grace asks, "Vince, do you think you could teleport in? If you can slip in, grab them, and leave, that would be ideal. We could even go back for the rest of the scientists the same way."

"I don't think so. It's so deep in the ground that a single miscalculation could be disastrous. If I take the elevator down one more time though, I might be able to better judge the depth and get the math right."

"So all we need to do," Grace says with a look to Vincent, "is get you on an elevator. Shouldn't be too hard."

Vincent says, "Then I could go after the others. It'd be many, many trips, but it's a possibility."

Leo shakes his head. "Even if you could do all this without getting seen, it would take several hours to get them all above ground. Then there's the issue of retribution."

"Retribution?" Vincent cocks his head.

"The whole reason the staff works for him in the first place: their families have a target on their backs. If we help them escape, Bartram would just have their families killed. No one would *want* to leave."

"So we rile them up," Grace doesn't hesitate to say. "If we get enough people on our side, mob mentality will set in, and they'll stand up for themselves. I don't care how ruthless Bartram is; he wouldn't discard every bargaining chip he has at one time."

Tzofiya and Leo consider her idea carefully until Tzofiya finally says, "That might work."

Leo looks at Vincent skeptically. "You think you could rally everyone behind you? You would need every single scientist to stand with you. Otherwise it could all fall apart."

Vincent's eyes widen. "Absolutely not. You seriously don't think Bartram's the kind of guy to go all in on a pot that he's desperate for?"

Grace says, "Fair. He probably would. But if everyone gets away at one time, then killing everyone's family would accomplish nothing. If he did make a move, he'd have no workers *and* no leverage."

"I-I don't know… What if he catches us in the act? What if I'm too slow, and he finds us? What if I can't do it? You got a lot riding on me here. I don't know if—"

"Vince—" Grace smiles at him. "We can do this. Together."

He stops and takes a few breaths. "Okay…"

They adjourn to the main tent where Leo lays out the maps of the Abaddon, and they start planning. Tzofiya starts off, "Leo and I will accompany you on fort. We will start on barracks building where you saw Martinez leave with patrol."

Leo continues, "We'll keep an open line of communication with you on a radio headset, but we'll only be able to keep tabs on the above ground part of the fort. You'll teleport into Bartram's service elevator while wearing one of the invisibility suits. Once you reach the jail cells, you'll simply jump inside the cell, grab them, then jump back to the roof with me and Tzofiya."

Tzofiya picks up, "They know you are alive, but they shouldn't have countermeasures to your teleportation ready yet. If you are found—leave. Immediately. Do not engage." Vincent nods. "Assuming you are able to free Trent and Becca, you will then proceed to east wing and—"

"See this is where it gets fuzzy for me," Vincent says. "Am I supposed to wake them all up and rally them as a group? Or do I talk to them individually?"

Grace says, "You'll wake them up one floor at a time and rally them in the corridor. They'll be more likely to agree with you as a group than individually."

"See that's not… I don't—I'm really not that guy. That's not a job for me."

"What do you mean?" Grace asks.

"I'm not the 'rallying' guy. You want everyone to basically follow me through the gates of hell. I might be a good symbol, but I won't say the right things that I need to say in order to get them to follow me."

Leo tries to comfort him. "Hey, I know we're putting a lot on you, but if we're gonna free those guys, you're gonna need to convince your people—"

"We'll do it," Grace says abruptly, causing every eye to fall on her.

"Who's we?" Leo asks.

"Sarah and I." she looks toward Sarah with an expectant glance. "We'll do it. We'll go with him."

"No." Vincent outright denies her proposal. "There's no way I'm letting you guys risk your necks to do *my* job."

"Unfortunately, it's our decision to make." She shrugs at him.

"She's right, Vince," Sarah says apologetically. "You're right—they'll never follow you. Grace is a better leader than you, and I'm friends with most of them, so I could help connect with them on a personal level."

"No, no, no. I cannot put you in harm's way again, Sarah. I won't let that happen."

"You're not the one doing it. It's *our* decision."

Vincent tries to argue with them, but nobody is having it. Leo finally says, "Buddy, it's the right call. They're your teammates. We have to work as a team."

"Fine. But if there's even a whiff of trouble, we're pulling out. I'm getting us out of dodge immediately."

Tzofiya nods. "We expect nothing less. In fact, do you think you could get me inside security office?"

"Probably. I doubt any of your accesses still work though."

"I won't need them. There is one important part of network that is totally unsecured. Fire alarm. You need to wake up every person on a floor, one floor at a time? I activate alarm for whichever floor you are on."

"That is a good idea, Tzofiya," Leo says encouragingly. "So here's what we have so far: Vincent, you'll bring all five of us to the roof, take the service elevator down to free Trent and Becca, then bring Tzofiya to the security office before escorting Sarah and Grace—"

"One stipulation, if you two come with, you're both wearing those invisibility suits."

Grace and Sarah nod fervently. "Agreed."

Leo continues, "Down to the east wing to rally the scientists. Once you get all of them to agree to a walk out, one by one, you'll teleport them back to camp. Sound good?"

With everyone in agreement, the group breaks, but Vincent is apprehensive about the whole ordeal. *If she gets hurt… there will be hell to pay.*

CHAPTER FORTY-EIGHT

November 27th, 2020

Friday

With a swift retching motion, Sarah stumbles to her knees and reels from the teleportation, feeling Vincent's hand gently touching her back and shushing her. *I will never get used to that,* Sarah thinks to herself. From a vantage point she's never seen before, she realizes the five of them are kneeling atop her old barracks building. Tzofiya is whispering her observations of the security posture to Leo and Vincent, but Sarah doesn't quite understand what she's saying, so she just tries to settle her stomach and waits.

"You got this, Vinny?" Leo asks him, and Vincent nods steadily. Leo points to an empty spot on the roof and says, "Just bring them back right there, and we'll make sure to give you plenty of space."

"Got it."

But their discussion is immediately squashed by Tzofiya whispering, "Wait!"

"For what?"

"Look inside armory—there is light." Looking through a small pair of binoculars, she points out an almost imperceptible camera in a dark corner of the armory roof. "That is new camera. I think... I think it is thermal imager."

"Thermal imager?" Vincent says. "They've got heat vision in there now?"

Sarah cuts in, "That *is* how we broke out. Invisibility suits through the service elevator. They must have learned from their mistakes."

"Shit. What do we do now?" Vincent asks.

"Can you just jump inside the elevator itself?" Leo suggests.

"No," Tzofiya says firmly. "Thermal imager is just to see unwanted guests. If I know Bartram, he would be ready for you."

"So what? We're just S.O.L.?" Vincent asks with frustration building within him.

"We simply reverse plan. You will go to east wing first, free scientist staff, and *then* go through Bartram's office to Trent and Becca."

"That's going to take hours, while in the meantime, Trent and Becca will be lying helpless in a rotten, disgusting cell."

"It would take hours either way," Tzofiya says. "This way, you will just free scientist staff first."

Vincent apprehensively agrees, "Fine. Let's just make this quick."

"You sure you can get me into security office?" Tzofiya asks Vincent.

"Definitely, but I don't know how many jumps I'll need to do while I'm down there, so you may not have an exfil plan. You okay with that?"

"Don't worry about me—" she draws a knife from her thigh and readies herself.

"Alright. Let's do this." He takes her by the arm, and after a few minutes, they teleport directly into Tzofiya's old office. Sarah watches reluctantly as the two disappear, then the next few minutes are the longest of her life. Grace fiddles with her backpack, pulling out the two invisibility suits and handing one to Sarah. They both don their suits as quietly as they can while Leo stealthily surveys the fort, tracking patrol movements. Sarah focuses on her breathing and tries to stay cool and collected until the sudden reappearance of Vincent, who has a streak of blood across his chest.

"Oh my God, Vince, are you okay?! You're bleeding!" she whispers.

"Yeah, we ran into some company, but they were no trouble. In fact, their credentials proved to be quite useful." Vincent turns to address Leo. "Tzofiya was able to lock the guards who are still asleep in their rooms, but she couldn't get into the north wing. We think Bartram's barricading himself in his office."

"Barricading himself?" Grace asks. "Does that mean he knows we're here?"

With a grim look, Leo says, "Maybe. Or... maybe he's just being cautious. He might have even moved the prisoners. Let's just help your friends, then take it from there."

"Sounds good to me," Vincent says before addressing Sarah and Grace. "You guys ready?" They both nod "Leo, you got eyes up here. Tzofiya's got eyes downstairs. Let's keep the comms quiet unless we absolutely need something."

"Got it, Vinny. Get out of here."

Vincent takes both of them by the hands and says, "Pull your hoods up and disappear."

Sarah and Grace follow his instructions, and when Vincent finishes running the math through his head, they all instantly rematerialize directly in front of the elevator door. Though their entrance was silent, Sarah instantly hears a sniffing sound coming from the checkpoint and pushes Vincent further into the alcove so that he's hidden behind a wall. *Oh, no. Dolly can sense him.* She can hear Cesar ask, "What is it, girl? You got something?" He follows his bloodhound back through the checkpoint, and Sarah steps out to see Dolly sniffing at something invisible before baring her teeth. *Grace.* "You see something, Dolly?" Cesar asks, bringing his gun to the ready, then Dolly starts following another scent until they're standing directly in front of the wall that Vincent is hiding behind.

As Dolly approaches the corner, Sarah sees Vincent draw his silenced pistol, and adrenaline floods her veins, but he's trying to hold out as long as he can. *Maybe she'll give up... We're not here, Dolly, you don't smell anything... Just go away! Go on, get!* Then Dolly rounds the corner and sees Vincent's boots. She rears back with a violent growl, but Vincent doesn't hesitate. A single round is fired through Dolly's head, and she lets out a pathetic yelp before thudding to the ground. "What the fuck?!" Cesar draws his rifle and rounds the corner, about to fire at whatever he sees, but Vincent beats him to the punch. Cesar's brain paints the walls behind him, and he collapses next to Dolly's limp body.

Vincent stands with his pistol still held straight out in front him, his hands shaking and his throat forcing down a gasp. His breath is choppy, but he seems to be holding himself steady. Sarah whispers, "Oh my God… You killed him, Vince… They're both dead… Vince… Are you okay, Vince?"

He nods and swallows his shock. "Yeah. It needed to be done." He then radios Leo and Tzofiya, "Eagle Eye, this is Nightcrawler, uh, our entrance was a bit messier than intended. Watchdog caught our scent, and I had to, well, euthanize her. Over."

"Shit!" Leo exclaims. "It's quiet out here for now. Is Watchdog's handler out, too? Over."

"Yeah, handler's down. Over."

Tzofiya says, "Keep moving. If it gets messy, we will be cleanup crew. Over."

"Roger, Eagle Eye. Over and out." Vincent calls for the elevator, which immediately opens up. "Come on, we need to get moving." Sarah follows him into the elevator, and before she or Grace can say anything, Vincent solemnly states, "I know. That was… unfortunate. But it had to be done."

Grace says, "We know. You did good." She touches him gently, which seems to comfort him. This is strange because he doesn't usually like literal pats on the back. Sarah doesn't acknowledge the interaction.

"Hey," he says in her general direction. "This is part of it, okay? This is what they signed up for when they took this job."

"But it's not what *we* signed up for," Sarah says. "You're becoming one of them."

"I'm not, okay?" She gives no response. The elevator dings again and Vincent presses his back against the side wall, but peeks out at the atrium to see only two guards meandering about. "You two go. I'll meet you in the east wing." Sarah feels Grace take her wrist again and gently pull her along when Vincent disappears.

They move along on the balls of their feet, the guards tiredly watching the giant, empty space and admiring the newly budding flowers and other plants. Grace leads them around the corner of the elevator cove, and they quietly pass through the atrium, walking not six feet from one of the guards, who says, "Hey, Carrey. You catch the game last night?"

"Nah, man. I was on patrol duty. This shit is getting boring. How long have we been here? A few months? I didn't think I'd get burnt out so quickly."

"Yeah, it's these unrelenting mid-watches. I feel like I'm on mids every other day. My body isn't up for this shit anymore."

The east wing door randomly unlocks and opens. "What was that?" one of the guards asks and rushes to the wall panel. He scans his ID and the door closes. "Ghosts, man. These machines are full of them." Sarah and Grace are already through the threshold and waiting for Vincent to appear beside them, which takes a few minutes while the guards linger at the wall panel. They all meet back up and start down the east wing corridor.

As they walk, Grace whispers, "It's eerie seeing the atrium empty on a Friday night. This place should be bustling with music and drunken dancers."

"If all goes according to plan," Vincent says, "there should be no more parties held in that godforsaken place again. Grace, you mind scouting ahead? See if there's anyone guarding the barracks."

"Definitely." She hurries up ahead, leaving Sarah to silently watch Vincent press himself against the wall.

Unable to see where she's standing, Vincent rubs his temples, seemingly warding off a headache, and whispers to her, "Are you feeling up to this? Convincing these guys to take a stand?" Sarah contemplates his question, but refuses to answer. "Look, I know you're worried about me, but... that needed to happen. Cesar could've killed this whole thing,

390

and all our friends would be slaves to Bartram's industrial tech machine forever. He'd win."

"I know what's at stake."

"I hope so."

When Grace returns, she says, "There's two of them guarding the barracks entrance."

"On it." He draws his suppressed pistol again, but thinks for a moment, then replaces it. He sighs, then disappears. Sarah steps out to see Vincent reappear directly in front of one guard with a swift kick to the face, the back of his head cracking against the marble wall. Before the other guard can react, Vincent is already behind him, choking him out until both guards are incapacitated.

When the girls approach, he says, "They didn't need to die, so I didn't kill them." Sarah's smile is invisible to him, but he knows it's there.

They leave the bodies where they are and ascend to the tenth floor. A long hallway with dozens of rooms on either side extends in front of them. Sarah and Grace promptly take their invisibility suits off, stuffing one of them back into Grace's backpack and giving the other to Vincent.

"Alright," Vincent says. "This is it guys. Once we give Tzofiya the go ahead, she'll unlock the doors and sound the fire alarms in their rooms. Once they come out, we'll have our audience."

Grace says, "Right. This is the important one. Once we get these guys behind us, peer pressure should convince the others to back us too. Hopefully. You ready, Sarah?"

"Whenever you are."

"Eagle Eye, this is Nightcrawler. We are clear for Operation Wake-Up-Call when able." At that moment, dozens of locks all click open simultaneously, followed by several seconds of blaring, muffled alarms that stop when the doors start to open.

"What's going on?"

"Is there a fire?"

"Is everyone okay?"

Groans and grunts slowly fill the hallway, and Grace takes a step forward, stands up straight and tall, and in her most commanding voice, bellows out, "Everyone! Listen up! We don't have much time!" All eyes move front to see Grace standing with her chin held high and Vincent vigilantly watching on wearing full Kevlar armor, an assault rifle hanging at his hip next to his gas mask, and several other weapons strapped to him. Sarah is at her side with an apprehensive yet confident countenance.

"What's happening?" one of the tired eyed scientists asks groggily. "You guys are alive?"

Grace confidently shouts, "Yes. We survived! And we're here to get *you* out while you're still alive!"

"No, no, no! You saw what happened to Karl and Chad! They'll kill us! If I leave, then they'll go after my sister!"

"No, he won't. See, Bartram has a monopoly over our lives. But we fail to see the power that we still hold in our own hands. Yes, if one of us acted up or escaped, he would go after their loved ones. But if everyone rises up at the same time, then he has no power. If there is no one here to work for him, then the driving fear that he creates will have no one to affect!"

"Oh, great, easy. Let's just leave then. Why haven't we thought of that before? Oh, that's right! There's a fucking legion of armed goons standing in our way!" one of the older tenants says and starts to head back into her room while grumbling to herself.

"You're right! They are standing in our way, but that doesn't matter anymore! We have a way out. The same way that *we* came in. We can get you all out."

Megan and Beth from the invisibility project pop out of the crowd. Megan says, "Grace, it's a nice thought, but those invisibility suits were the only ones we had. When Mavis took those, we had nothing left."

Grace grins. "These were just a convenience. The real secret weapon is standing beside me." She puts her arm around Vincent's shoulder. "Vince is our man. He can get us out."

"Shooting our way out won't get us anywhere!" one of Brian's old gym buddies calls out. "One dude versus a whole army is suicide."

Vincent instantly disappears and reappears at his side, then says, "Not when you bypass them altogether." The entire crowd of scientists recoils and gasps with murmurs breaking out and spreading amongst them.

Grace shouts over them, "Vincent figured out the teleportation tech. He can innately teleport us out of here. Now it will take a considerable amount of time, but it *can* happen. If we work together, then we can—" the crowd starts talking over her, and Vincent pushes his way back to her side.

Another gym rat's voice breaks through the noise, yelling, "Even if this nerd can get us all out of here in the blink of an eye, Bartram still has our families. He can still hurt them. You say he wouldn't, but why should we gamble their lives on your word?"

Sarah answers for her, "I know it's hard… risking everything… but we are living in fear." Sarah, seeing the faces of many of her friends looking back up at her, gets a bit overwhelmed and blushes. She doesn't know what to do with her hands as she talks. "We are the last in a long line of scientists who have been held here against their will to do Bartram's bidding. If we don't stand up to him, not only will we all die serving him, but countless generations after us—and their families—will be held captive by Colonel Bartram. It's a risk, I know. But if there's any chance of us pulling this off, Vincent will be the one to free us."

Murmurs spread again, but they eventually cascade into a fiery uproar, which Grace feeds by saying, "If you want to be free, if you want your friends, family, loved ones to be free of Bartram's dirty hands, stand with us today!"

Vincent smiles as the crowd turns into an angry mob, then Grace leads everyone through the various levels of barracks rooms awakening their fellow scientists. Using the angry mob as a tool, it's easy to convince the others to follow suit. Once they've about finished, nearly half an hour later, Vincent turns to Sarah and starts to say, "I'll start ferrying people when—" but he stops speaking when he realizes Sarah isn't there. He looks all around the room and through the crowd, but there is no Sarah to be found.

"Fuck." Vincent takes off, donning the invisibility suit as he runs. Making it to the barracks entrance, he sees the incapacitated guards are missing. *They must have snuck up and taken her while we were inciting a riot.* He sprints off to the east wing entrance, but he's too late. The atrium is stark empty without a single guard in sight, but through the glass door of the north wing, he can make out a petite woman tied to a chair and being held at gunpoint in the art gallery. Adrenaline floods his system again, and though he can hear his radio crackle in his ear, his focus narrows on the gallery.

"SIR," MARTINEZ RADIOS BARTRAM from Mavis's kitchen with his portable security console in hand. "I've been locked out of everything but the north wing closed circuit systems. They're here. Over."

"Would you like to tell me my horoscope too, Sergeant? Over!"

"No, sir, but the east wing entrance opened on its own. I think they're going after the science staff. Over."

"Let them. I'm not concerned about them. Now, only update me when you have something *useful* to say! Over!"

"Roger. Over and out." He locks the console and places it on the kitchen counter, then he strolls into the living room to make sure Dr. Blackwell is still securely fastened to her chair.

Mavis looks up through a black eye and bruised cheekbones. She snarkily remarks, "Sounds like you've gone from golden boy to whipping boy."

"He's just under a lot of stress. You've really put him in a bind letting those girls go."

"Oh, is he scared of a couple of girls getting in his way? Going to the cops and telling them the whole story? They know they can't take him down. If they're not already dead in the desert, they'll probably just end up living quiet lives and staying out of his business."

"It's not the girls he's afraid of. It's the friends they're bringing back with them."

"Friends? What friends?"

"Wait, you didn't…? Don't worry about it. They'll be dead soon anyway."

Mavis curiously considers what he meant by that while Martinez turns back to his console.

Meanwhile, Bartram paces around his living room, fiddling with his single button remote. Kneeling in the center of the room and facing the atrium window, Trent wrestles with his binding, trying desperately to free himself to no avail.

"Just kill me already!" Trent shouts. "I told you, Vincent died in the accident. I'm not worth anything to you."

"Oh no, no, don't sell yourself short. Know your worth, son." Bartram says into his radio, "Murphy, you in position? Over."

"Affirmative, sir, but I think I see someone coming from the east wing. Over."

Bartram hurries over to the window, and sure enough, two guards step through the door, dragging a fiery-haired young woman behind them. "Well, what do we have here?"

"Is that Doctor Boyce? Over." Murphy asks into the radio.

"It sure is, Murphy. Vincent's main squeeze just became our crown jewel." With Bartram watching from the window, the guards drag Sarah up to Bartram's office and shove her to her knees beside a beaten and battered Trent. They both put a gun to her head.

"I didn't expect to see you so soon," Bartram says.

"What do you want with me? I don't pose any threat to you!"

"You'd be surprised, young lady." Bartram walks to a medical box atop his grand piano and prepares a needle with a mysterious purple fluid. "Now, hold still. We have plans to change."

WITHOUT EVEN THINKING, Vincent instantly flies into a rage and jumps to the art gallery, donkey kicking the guard in the nose and beating him with the butt of his own weapon, thrashing him from wall to wall across the gallery. It takes a while before he can physically hear the cries of Sergeant Murphy whimpering, "Vincent! I want to help! Please!" With Murphy's throat in one hand and a blood-covered, less-than-invisible fist raised over his face, Vincent takes a breath. "Sarah's not here!" Murphy shouts desperately.

Vincent looks over his shoulder to see a one-legged Becca slumped over in her chair, "B-Becca? Wh—" but he is quick to turn back to his prey. "Where the *fuck* is Sarah?!"

"Not far!" Murphy's voice trembles, but Vincent can hear sincerity in it. "Creighton, he knows you're coming."

"*Where* is she?!"

"He's got Trent, Mavis, and Sarah all held here in the north wing, but they've all been injected with the virus."

"What virus?"

As he asks the question, he can hear a parade of scientists storming the atrium and heading straight for the elevators. Grace sees his bloody suit through the door and looks at him with panic. He hears her radio him, "Didn't you hear? We're out of time! Let's go!" She starts ushering the staff into the elevators in the atrium and behind the kitchens in the south wing. They load up a couple dozen or so in the first volley, with Grace staying behind to make sure to get as many packed in as she can.

"Vincent, what are they doing?" Murphy starts to struggle, but Vincent holds him down. "You can't let them go upstairs! You have to stop them *now!*"

"You just held a gun to my friend. Why the hell should I trust you?"

"Because I know what Bartram's been doing. You have to stop them now! They've all been infected with the virus!"

"What fucking virus?!"

"The one Dr. Smith made! Bartram had Mavis turn it into a real, biological virus that affects humans! If they go above a certain altitude, their bodies will be transformed into organic bombs!"

Vincent can't quite tell if this is just an elaborate distraction to keep him from getting to Sarah, or if he's really trying to help. By the time he figures out that Murphy isn't running some kind of gambit on him though, it's too late. The elevator doors close, and a few cars full of scientists begin their ascent, then it takes less than a minute for the walls and ceiling above to erupt in concussive blasts and spew fire from the elevator shafts. Screams and horror fill the atrium as the staff all retreat to the gardens for refuge. Dust and debris hail down onto the survivors below, and chaos breaks out.

"Oh my God…" Vincent mutters, his hand covering his mouth.

"You have to stop him, Vincent."

"He's a monster…" Vincent stares through the glass door, seeing Grace organize the medically trained scientists to care for those who were injured by the falling debris. "They're all infected? They can't escape?"

"Listen, Mavis can disable it, but Martinez is holding her in her office. Trent is in Bartram's living room, and I would guess Bartram took Sarah back to the Cultivation Center."

"Cultivation Center?"

"Where they grow the clones—basement floor of his service elevator. He's keeping everyone separated. He thinks if they're far enough apart from each other, you won't be able to save them all." Vincent drops Murphy to the ground so that he can pace around the gallery, seething. "The worst part, Vincent—he's holding a dead man's switch. If he drops it, everyone's virus kicks off all at once."

Vincent's face contorts with a quiet sort of rage. The kind that affects his breathing. The kind that causes his vision to turn red and his mind a smoke-filled, burning building. He closes his eyes, rubs his temples, and takes a breath. When he finally opens his eyes again, his mind turns to ice.

"KEEP MOVING. If it gets messy, we will be clean-up crew. Over."

Tzofiya's voice crackles over Leo's radio. *Fuck,* Leo thinks to himself. *I don't want to be the clean-up crew anymore, goddamn it!* Leo diligently watches the patrols, keeping a mental map of every guard and every path they've been taking since he arrived. *This fucking eyepatch; I can't see straight with it or without it… I'm not cut out for this shit anymore. I need to retire.* From the duffle bag at his feet, he proceeds to gear up with their standard array. *Twenty-four guards outside. Just stay the fuck outside, and everything will be—*one of the patrols finishes their rove and begins to head inside. *Fuck. You clean up Vinny's mess, Tzofiya?*

The patrol enters the admin building, and nothing seems to happen at first, but a few moments later, the patrol comes back outside and starts asking questions to the door guard, "Hey, where's Cesar and Dolly?" *Aw fuck… Stop asking questions…* Leo posts the barrel of his rifle upon the parapet and gets ready. *Please, take care of this Tzofiya.*

"Are they not inside? They were supposed to be standing watch."

"They're not at their post." *Last chance, Tzofiya, please don't make me do this…*

"Hm… we should call this in—" but the second he reaches for his radio, Leo pulls his trigger. The door guard hits the ground, followed by the patrol who was about to turn in for the night.

It takes only a second for chaos to break out across the grounds of Fort Chivington, but Leo collects himself, tosses a rope over the side of the building and rappels to the ground, firing a few rounds at the guards standing in his landing zone. He drops the stragglers that head for the entrance gate, then turns to join Tzofiya in the security office, but he gets cut off by a small squadron of guards converging on his gunfire. *I'm so sorry, guys…* He tosses a few grenades and ducks for cover. When the grenades burst, they take a few of his enemies out of the fight and force the rest to scatter.

Once he's broken up that party, Leo advances to the admin building, which by this point has been surrounded and infiltrated by more than a dozen of the remaining guards. Once Leo is spotted, he ducks behind the gazebo for cover while the guards fire on him. They spread out, and he knows he doesn't have long before they overwhelm him. He looks around and finds his only real escape route—the entrance to the barracks building. Carefully getting to his feet, he waits for his moment, then sprints for the front door. He throws his weight into the glass door, but he feels a tickle in his hip just before the glass shatters.

When he lands, he realizes there was a shooter in his newly acquired blind spot; this shooter's bullet just lodged itself into his hip. Whether he doesn't feel the pain yet or is just ignoring it doesn't matter. The guards are closing in on him; he has to hide. *This was a bad idea.* He braces himself and drags his body out of sight, hiding underneath a staircase and drawing his pistol. *We had zero margin for error. Why did I agree to this?* A guard immediately rushes inside the building, but Leo swiftly drops him.

Normally, the recoil from a handgun barely registers with him, but at this moment, he becomes acutely aware of the effect a bullet has on someone's body. When he realizes just how much pain he's in, he loses his breath and can't catch it for several seconds. He looks down at his side to see a dark red fluid flowing from his wound. *Oh.* A footstep crunching on glass instantly causes him to fire his gun, but his vision is blurry. It takes him a couple bullets to actually drop the intruder, then the slide on his gun pulls back. It's empty. *Pressure. I need… I-I, uh, I need pressure on the wound.* He reaches for something on his person to remove, so he goes with a shred of his pants that he cuts off with his knife.

While applying pressure to his wound, he tries to simultaneously load his pistol, but he just can't seem to stay focused. Another guard breaks through his perimeter, but he barely even notices them until they have a gun trained on him. Leo takes a couple long blinks, then watches a few bullets rip through the guard's chest. The guard collapses in front of him. He then listens to a barrage of violence occurring outside until Tzofiya's voice calls out, "All clear! You can come out!"

"Yeah, I don't… don't think that's happening…"

Tzofiya pops her head in. "Shit."

"Th-there's a, a, uh, a med kit—" he barely gets the sentence out before Tzofiya sprints to the rope and is on the roof.

When she returns, she instantly analyzes the situation and starts cleaning the wound. "Bullet still inside, possibly embed in bone. We need doctor."

"Just stop the bleeding… but just… for now, let's…" Leo's blinks become longer and longer until he opens his eyes to see Tzofiya sitting against the wall opposite him. He's laid out on the ground, his head resting against one of the guards' blood-soaked Kevlar vests.

"You live"—Tzofiya's face is streaked with blood, somehow covering her chest, arms, and hands—"for now."

"Th-Thank you, Tzofiya… I-I don't know… how to—how to thank you…" he mumbles to her, but he can barely feel any strength returning to him.

"No need. Come, we need find doctor."

"Well, good thing… we have a… gaggle of… scientists downstairs, huh? One of them… is bound to be a… medical doctor, right?" He shifts his weight, sucking air through his teeth to keep from screaming, and Tzofiya takes him under the arm. Their balance is nearly thrown off when they both feel a slight vibration in the ground beneath their feet. "That wasn't a delusion, was it? You felt it too?"

"That was real. They need help. Come. We go now." She helps him hobble over to the elevator landing where one of the doors somehow got blown out and charred.

"What… the fuck… happened?"

"No time to find out. You need attention, and they need help."

VINCENT'S EXPRESSION GOES BLANK. *Bartram's dead.* Vincent cleans as much blood off his invisibility suit as he can, then sneaks down to Mavis's front door and teleports just inside in the foyer, but has to stop for a second—he feels as though an ice pick is growing in his frontal lobe. *I can't have this. I need to keep going.*

He brushes off the pain and quietly steps into the living room where he sees Mavis sitting with her hands cuffed behind her chair. Her black eye is bleeding slightly, and her lip is swollen. Vincent can't help but feel a bit vindicated, despite her desperate appearance. Martinez paces back and forth, intermittently radioing Bartram with sitreps. Vincent takes mental notes, and after sufficiently scoping out the area, he jumps his way up to Bartram's office and lightly treads past the cathedral hallway that is Bartram's gaudy foyer.

At the end of the hallway, he can see Trent knelt in front of the window overlooking the chaos-filled atrium, hands cuffed behind his back similar to Mavis. Accompanying him in the living room, the two guards who were patrolling the atrium are now lounging about. One of them—Carrey—is watching the scientific staff perform triage in the gardens while the other is lying atop the grand piano, resting his eyes.

Our country's finest. Vincent skulks through the hallway, but overhead he hears a familiar hissing sound that makes his stomach drop. *Oh, fuck...* He quickly ducks behind a column, rips his invisibility suit off as quickly as possible to access the gas mask on his hip, and tears his glasses from his face to don the mask. His breathing echoes in his ears, so he holds his breath to hear a crackle of static coming from both of the guards' radios simultaneously, "Gas. Gas. Gas."

The guards scramble to put their own gas masks on, but when they finally do, another crackle comes over the radio. It's Martinez's voice. "Orders, sir? Over."

Bartram responds, "Murphy's rogue. Execute the prisoners. Over and out."

It takes less than a second for Vincent's heart to jump into his throat. The sound of gas filling the room slows, and the smell of his rubber mask fades. Off in the distance, he can hear the pair of guards acknowledging their orders, but their voices almost seem to propagate through their air more slowly. Then they move to draw their weapons.

Five.

Numbers fly through Vincent's mind faster than the speed of light, and his brain feels like it's being dragged through rust and sandpaper, but his body instantly disappears and reappears directly in front of Mavis in her chair. Martinez's pistol is against the back of her head, and he's about to pull the trigger. Mavis barely has a chance to cough out his name, "Vi—" before he rips the pistol from Martinez's hand, throws a quick haymaker across his stupefied face, and disappears again.

Four.

In Bartram's smoke obscured office, Vincent reemerges behind Carrey, who is pulling back the action on his rifle. Vincent reacts with a panicked pull of his own trigger. Though his math is sloppy and rushed, he still sends the bullet careening through Carrey's brain stem, which causes streaks of blood to splash in all directions. Next to Vincent, the newbie gets startled and immediately tackles him, but before they hit the ground, Vincent has already jumped to Trent's side. Scrambling to his feet, Vincent fires a round to break Trent's chains. "Find a mask, or you die."

Three.

Vincent returns to Mavis's office to find Martinez charging him with a KA-BAR. He goes for an overhand strike, then a sudden flash of pain shoots across his forehead, and Vincent finds himself back in the sandy fighting ring on a beautiful night in the Red Desert. The scent of his own blood and sweat wafts across his nose, and Becca's hollering echoes in his ears. Vincent instinctively bursts forward to stop Bobby's knife hand, then manipulates his momentum to swiftly bring him to the ground. Once he returns to the present, he finds Martinez sprawled out on the ground beneath him.

Two.

Back in Bartram's office, Vincent arrives at Trent losing a wrestling match with the newbie beside a dead body that once belonged to Carrey. Vincent pulls his pistol on the newbie, but he can barely see through the smoke in the room—not to mention the growing icepick stealing his focus. It's not until Trent pulls a familiar move that Vincent finds the space he needs. Trent reaches under his opponent's mask and pulls it clean off his face. The newbie begins to choke and wheeze, allowing Trent to roll away and put the mask on himself, then Vincent takes the shot, two bullets right through the guard's heart and a third between his eyes. Without a nanosecond to spare, he vanishes yet again.

One.

Upon erupting back into Mavis's office, the room only materializes in time to fade into whiteness as his temples practically rupture, then he keels over, blacking out.

When he reawakens, his chest is heaving, and his eyes struggle to stay open due to what feels like a Carolina Reaper being scraped across his corneas—he's no longer protected by a mask. Directly over him, Martinez has mounted his prone body and is wailing on him, bloodying his eyes, bruising his cheeks, and smashing what feels like an already split skull. Vincent tries to defend himself by throwing his arms in front of his face, but Martinez manages to get through, all the while shouting at the top of his lungs, "You! No good! Pathetic! Arrogant! Loser!" Martinez grabs Vincent's jaw in a vice-like grip, and Vincent looks up at the black gas mask staring down at him through a haze. "We *had* something here! Colonel Bartram built something great, and you destroyed everything!"

Vincent's response is a simple choke and a heave.

Martinez draws his KA-BAR again and winds up to thrust it into Vincent's chest, but a sudden boom pierces the air, and Martinez gets the wind knocked out of him. Vincent takes this opportunity to thrust his hips upward, throw Martinez to the ground, pull his mask off, and put it on himself. He looks to the front door to see Murphy with his pistol still drawn on the agonizing Martinez.

"Murphy!" Vincent coughs and gags. "You saved my life!"

"Mavis! Help Mavis!"

Vincent nods and puts a mask on her, then they detain Martinez. "Looks like the paralysis has already set in on her, but we'll take her out and have Grace look after her. And Martinez's Kevlar stopped your bullet, but it's going to hurt."

"What do we do with him?" Murphy gestures toward Martinez, who gradually falls still on the ground.

"Collateral."

After reconvening with Trent, the three of them help move Becca, Mavis, and Martinez into the atrium, where Grace and a few medical doctors have stabilized the situation. Now the scientific staff waits in terror to find out what caused those explosions.

"Vincent!" Grace yells. "What the fuck is hap—oh my God! What happened to you?" she asks upon noticing his bruised and bloodied face, one of his eyes gradually swelling up.

"I'll make it. Don't worry about me. How is everything out here?"

"The elevators exploded! W-We did what we could, but we lost a lot of people—have you seen Sarah? You both disappeared before Tzofiya directed us to the elevators."

"Bartram has Sarah," Vincent says harshly. Grace covers her mouth and groans in despair, but Vincent soldiers on. "You need to stay out here with these guys, okay? Keep them calm, and for the love of God, don't let them take any more elevators."

"Stay here? Where are you going?" He just looks at her, and she knows. "No. You can't go alone. You'll need help."

"He's not alone," Trent says. His tattered clothes reek from months of being worn without a wash. In the light, Vincent can see how skinny he and Becca have become; their skin practically hanging off their bones. "I'm coming with him. This is *our* fight."

Vincent skeptically asks, "Are you sure you're up for it? Bartram's ready for us. He could have anything up his sleeve."

Trent weakly asserts, "I'm coming with you, Vinny."

"Me, too," Murphy agrees. "I've been complicit in the activities around here for far too long; I need to help you end this."

"Thank you for that, Murphy," Vincent says graciously. "But someone needs to stay here and protect these guys. If we fail, and Bartram comes after our people, you'll be our last line of defense. We also don't know how people will react to being trapped down here; an actual peacekeeper might be helpful."

Murphy reluctantly nods and stands by Grace's side. Then he asks, "Can you handle this, Creighton? Bartram's ruthless. He's a survivor."

Vincent's countenance grows cold, and he says, "Not today he isn't."

Grace mirrors his expression. "Be careful, okay?" She leans in and gives him a warm hug. "We're counting on you, Vince."

He nods coolly as if he hadn't heard her words at all, then turns to Trent and slips his mask on. "Let's do it." They hoist a paralyzed Martinez to his feet and walk back into the smokey north wing. As they navigate the labyrinth of halls within Bartram's office, they find another armed pair hobbling toward them. They both instantly drop Martinez and raise their guns. "Stop right the fuck there!"

One figure seems to be supporting the other, so they can only throw one hand in the air each. Then a female voice asks, "Trent? Is this you?"

"Tzofiya? Holy shit! You guys made it!" They meet in the middle and catch each other up on everything that's happening.

"It's wild," Vincent says. "There's this virus that turns people into bombs. I totally saved Trent's ass, and then Murphy totally saved mine."

"Oh! Murphy change team? I always knew he was good egg."

Leo tries to keep up with the conversation, but his eyes are starting to droop. Vincent catches this and notices the bandages. "Oh my God, what happened?"

"Don't worry, Vinny-boy," his words are slurred as he speaks. "I was shot, but just a little bit. Kritzman got me squared away." But Vincent can clearly tell he's bleeding through his bandages.

"That's a *lot* of blood, Leo—"

"I know. It's okay. I'm coming with you. Now where do we go?"

They head into the elevator and press the "basement" button. Vincent addresses Trent and Tzofiya. "Have you guys been to the Cultivation Center before?"

They both nod their heads with shame. Trent says, "Yeah. I used to stand watches down there…" He looks uncomfortably at Leo and adds, "And it's how Leo and I made our escape the first time." Leo closes his eyes and wretches as if he just realized something he already knew. "This is where the clones were held—in storage units. I needed a distraction. Something to buy Leo and myself some time while we made our escape. I woke up one of the clones, put it—put *him* in the subway that goes to the testing facility… and had him drive it at top speed until it crashed."

"Oh…" Vincent's jaw drops. "I'm so sorry, I didn't—"

"It's okay," he says. "The explosion killed him, but I was able to escape with the… the *real* Leo in tow."

There's a beat of silence that's broken by Tzofiya, who asks, "Do you regret it?"

Trent looks at her deeply. "No," he says. "I will carry the look of innocence and terror on his face to my grave. But… no, I don't regret it."

When the elevator comes to a stop, everyone's throat tightens up. The doors open, and Vincent feasts his eyes on the most expansive warehouse he's ever seen in his life. A massive hangar storing hundreds—thousands of metal containers interconnected by a network of computers, tubes, wires, and hoses. It's dark, lit only by a dim, green emergency light hung far above their heads.

A small opening stretches out in front of them before the grid of containers starts. Twenty feet away, Sarah stands, shivering—either from fear or the empty coldness of this place. She's unbound, once again wearing Vincent's black hoodie, which Bartram must have given her to put on since disappearing.

"Hi, Vince," she whimpers, a tear streaking down her cheek.

Vincent shoves Martinez forward and puts a pistol to his head. "It's okay, Sarah. We're gonna get you out of here." He nods to her with as reassuring a smile as he can muster, one that she is unable to return.

Instead, she mouths the word *"no"* and slowly shakes her head.

Vincent is confused at her remark, but he continues anyway, "Bartram! I'm here to negotiate!"

"*You're* here to negotiate? What are your friends here for? Emotional support, maybe?"

"Get out here! Let me see you!" From behind one of the computer terminals at a container, a single hand shoots out, holding some kind of remote. Vincent turns to his friends and explains, "Dead man's switch. He drops it; this whole place goes up."

"Good intel," Bartram says. "Sounds like my traitorous former employee has proven his worth to you." He steps out from behind the container, wearing his typical dress blues.

"That's what happens when you spend a lifetime creating a system of oppression. People stop wanting to help you."

"Are you among those people? Because I seem to recall not a few months ago, you accepted my offer of employment as my right-hand man. My own personal Angel of Death." Trent and Leo look at him, waiting for a shake of the head or some kind of indication that this didn't happen. Instead, Vincent stares steadfastly at him. "A reaper! You wanted to be a god right by my side. Has that changed?"

Vincent falls silent.

"Silly me! Of course it has! You don't need my coattails to claim power anymore, do you? You've got your own power. The pinnacle of what we ever could have hoped to achieve in teleportation technology. The ability to teleport on your own. Innately. No work necessary."

"I still do the math! I have to calculate very precisely where I want to—"

"Oh! My apologies! You need to do the *math*, perform highly complicated mathematical functions using the most unique brain of our generation." Bartram steps toward Sarah and grabs her by the waist with his left hand. "It's funny, isn't it? Your entire life, you've been betrayed by that brain of yours. Bullied, abused, manipulated—all because you couldn't understand how to appropriately socialize with others. That brain crippled you. It denied you a life with your one true love." He pulls Sarah closer to him. "And yet that same brain has now uniquely situated you to use a gift that most will only ever be able to dream of."

Vincent tightens his grip on the pistol against Martinez's head and says, "Let her go, Henry!" His voice cracks when he says Bartram's name.

"Or else… what?" Bartram asks, and Vincent threateningly pushes the barrel into Martinez's limp temple. "Oh, you think I care about that lemming?" Somehow, Vincent can feel Martinez's heart drop and his mind race. He can feel dread emanating from the paralyzed body he's holding as Bartram reaches under his uniform blouse to pull out a Glock, then swiftly fires a single round between Martinez's horrified eyes.

The warehouse explodes in a barrage of shouts and screams. Everyone behind Vincent instantly starts yelling orders and training their weapons on Bartram—who promptly tosses his gun aside. None of this noise, however, reaches Vincent's ears. All he can sense is the warmth of Martinez's blood spattered across his face before releasing his body, which thuds to the ground in a lifeless mass. Vincent recoils, and his muscles begin to shake uncontrollably. He never considered Martinez a friend, but Bartram was everything to Martinez. Bartram was infallible in his eyes. The faith Martinez had in Bartram meant nothing to him; he saw Martinez as just a tool, a thing, a means to an end.

"There. Your collateral is gone. One less thing to worry about. Now, let's get down to brass tacks."

Tzofiya unleashes a string of Russian curses at him, and Trent mutters something under his breath. Leo watches on with guilty poise. Vincent looks down at the blood he's accrued on his own hands, chest, face… everywhere.

"Oh, don't be so surprised, Vincent," Bartram says cockily. "Didn't you just kill Carrey and… the other one? They had lives that meant nothing to you, so when it came down to saving Trent or killing them, which did you choose? You didn't think twice, did you?"

Bartram is so… indifferent to human life. Nobody matters to him as long as he gets his way. Vincent becomes acutely aware of a streak of blood across his left eye—Carrey's blood. *Am I so different?*

He turns back to Sarah, whose face is streaming with tears at this point, and suddenly, he's back in the Marysworth lab, sitting in the back of the room, completely unable to stand up for himself. He's back at the Ducky Luck, where he was simply incapable of ordering his own drink. He's helpless. He's pathetic. *He's right. I didn't* think twice. *I was about to kill Murphy until he proved useful to me… I was ready to trade Martinez's life for Sarah's…*

"Here's the deal, Vinny. Hey! Hey, look at me!" Bartram snaps to get Vincent's attention, who mindlessly obliges. "Here's the deal: I'm not walking out of this room. I know that. You guys have guns and numbers against me. I get it. The only thing keeping me alive is this trigger." Vincent watches in horror, accepting every word as gospel. "But that's the thing. I don't want to stay alive. What I *want* is a successor. I want to live on *through* you." Bartram leans over to look Vincent in the eye on his level. "You have earned my spot at the table. You deserve this."

I deserve this? I… I do, don't I?

"I'm going to hand over my kingdom to you—the very lives of my employees. I will hand over this dead man's switch, and then you are free to do with me as you wish. Your friends will probably vote on killing me, but that's not their decision to make." Tzofiya and Trent choke up on the grips of their guns. "However… there's a catch, Vincent. See, you deserve the Abaddon, but you're not ready for it yet."

"What do you want me to do?" The words fall out of his mouth. Bartram's unbreakable eye contact is putting him in a trance.

"Don't listen to him, Vinny!" Trent shouts. "He's fucking with your head! You're smarter than this!"

"A god doesn't have attachments to those he rules over. He's dispassionate of the ones he controls—and you *will* control them. Your friends have guided you, misguided you, told you whatever truths or lies they needed you to hear. *They* don't threaten your rule though."

"Vincent," Tzofiya fails at getting his attention. "Shut him out. He manipulates you."

"*You* are your own biggest threat," Bartram continues. "You have this notion that human life is… valuable. It isn't. What humans can accomplish—*that's* where their true worth shines." Bartram tightens his grip around Sarah's waist, and Sarah cringes desperately. "Your attachment to human life makes you malleable. As long as you hold this notion, people will manipulate you." Vincent's throat closes up. "Your… *love* of others"—Bartram winces when he says these words—"leaves you vulnerable. You need to shed this attachment to human life, Vincent."

Sarah silently gazes at Vincent, knowing exactly what he needs to do but is unwilling to tell him. Tzofiya and Trent's pleas to Vincent are inaudible to him.

"Kill the woman you love, and my kingdom is yours." Vincent looks down at the pistol that he forgot was still in his hand, his fingers trembling. Bartram breaks his gaze with Vincent to survey his teammates, which grants him permission to look at Sarah again. He looks into her tired, green eyes, and for the first time, he sees in her what she's seen in him all along. Though her hair is greasy and uncared for after months of captivity, it shimmers. Though her skin is rough and unshowered, it glows. Though her mind is exhausted and warped, it shines brighter than any star in the night sky.

Slowly, she nods her head and whispers, "It's okay. Save the others."

Against his will, Vincent raises his gun, the barrel gradually making its way up to her. She chokes at the sight of it. The rest of his friends shout and scream and plead for him to stop, but they all know there's no alternative.

"Sa—" Vincent's voice breaks at first, but he says it again more confidently. "Sarah?"

"Vince?"

"I love you."

"I love you, Vince." His finger slides down to the trigger and gently begins to squeeze. Sarah swallows hard but doesn't look away.

"Vinny!" Leo speaks for the first time since they boarded the elevator. "Can I give you a hint, bud?" Vincent takes a choppy breath. "It's all a mind game. It's all in your head."

"Wha-What does that mean?"

"You're smarter than this, bud. You know you can't do this."

Vincent shuts his teary eyes tightly, his finger still lightly squeezing the trigger. "I've killed before! I can do this! I *need* to do this! If I don't, everyone here burns!"

"You've made mistakes, yes. Nobody's perfect. Everyone makes mistakes, but you need to learn from them. You're a scientist, isn't that what science is all about? Learning from your mistakes?"

Struggling to keep his arm up, he squeezes his eyes shut, but the moment Leo finishes his sentence, something clicks into place. The last science experiment that he actually *failed* was the very first test they performed in the Abaddon—the image of his many coworkers succumbing to an atom beam of cat-material sends a shiver up his spine. Another image flashes in his mind though: a pile of dirt. Where the cat disappeared inside the chamber, a pile of dirt reappeared. *Teleportation doesn't just move me to the target location; it brings the target to my location.* His eyes burst open, his face awash with that beautiful "eureka" moment every scientist strives for, and Leo smiles.

"Dr. Creighton," Bartram calls out, sensing the same thing that Leo does. "Focus up. Hundreds of lives are in your hands right now."

"You got it, Vinny?" Leo asks.

Vincent nods, not giving any indication of math he's calculating in his head. "I got it."

"Dr. Creighton! Listen to *me*!" Bartram's voice bellows out with fear. "Three!" Vincent tightens his trigger finger. "Two! I *will* drop this switch, and we will *all* be done for!" Bartram carefully loosens his grip on the device in his right hand. Vincent takes a deep breath and channels all the focus he can muster to stealthily activate the safety on his gun. "ONE!"

Vincent blinks. With a tug behind his navel, he opens his eyes to see that he is no longer holding his pistol. Instead, in his right hand, he's tightly squeezing the dead man's switch… and Bartram's right hand releases the pistol that Vincent himself was just holding. It takes a lifetime for the steel weapon to strike the ground—and another for everyone to realize that Vincent had just swapped places with Bartram—but when the gun clangs to the floor, Bartram is summarily beaten to a bloody pulp.

In his left hand, Vincent pulls Sarah's waist tightly against himself. His heart flutters when he realizes she's safe. The sigh of relief throughout the room is palpable. Sarah's knees give out, and she collapses into Vincent's chest. Once Bartram is in cuffs, there's a moment of shock shared amongst Vincent's team, then they promptly disable the dead man's switch. With Sarah now bawling her eyes out, Vincent wraps her in a warm, comforting embrace.

"I-I'm so sor—"

"Don't." She stops him so they can just live in the moment.

It's a long trip back to the atrium, but by the time they arrive, Mavis has awoken and begun the process of curing the virus infecting the scientific workforce. Though it takes quite some time and a great many trips, they ventilate the north wing and use the service elevator to ferry everyone to the surface. The Abaddon's inhabitants all gather in the parking lot for the first time as a whole. The night air is brisk, but most of these people haven't felt fresh air or socialized in many months. Most of them commiserate, mourning the loss of friends. Some sit together in peace and quiet. Others talk and joke about how grave and intense the night has been.

The second everyone reaches the surface, Becca and Tzofiya make a few phone calls, and by the time the sun rises, a fleet of black vans with government plates and ambulances arrives on scene. They offer medical help to those who are in need and escort the rest of the survivors out of the Red Desert—including Leo, who had become drowsy from the massive blood loss—but they're all in good hands now. A woman wearing a black suit and black sunglasses approaches Vincent and states in an official sounding tone, "Good morning, Dr. Creighton. My name is Agent Caldwell. I'm with the FBI. Would you and your friends please come with me?"

"FBI? How did you guys get here so fast?"

"We've been investigating the Abaddon long before you arrived here. Please, come with me." Vincent gathers Sarah, Grace, Tzofiya, Dallyn, and Trent, then the agent leads them to a black van that is just pulling up to the gate. The side door slides open, and an obese man sporting a comb-over, tank top, and pajama bottoms shuffles out of the van.

"Mark?!" they all exclaim in unison.

Grace rushes forward to hug him. "We thought they killed you! I thought we'd never see you again!"

"Yes, well, I'm still here."

"What happened? Where've you been?"

"Uh, long story short: after taking on the teleportation project, I was contacted by the FBI and informed of an ongoing investigation into a mysterious and deadly Colonel Bartram." They all glare across the parking lot at the colonel, who's being arrested and shoved into the back of another black van. "Apparently, he was interested in fringe projects like mine. I told them about an up-and-coming mathematician who I was sure Bartram would have been very interested in. So I hired you, Vincent. When you made your breakthrough, I rushed the press conference to get more eyes on you before he made you disappear. The world's been looking for you guys."

"You colluded with the feds to use me and the rest of your team as bait to catch a rogue—and very deadly—military officer?"

"Yeah," Mark says with a shrug. "And I'm sorry to have put you in the middle of all this, but you guys… you guys were such an amazing team. You could do anything. I knew if they failed—"

"You sacrificed our lives in hopes of stopping him?" Vincent asks more as a statement than a question.

Mark stops. "Yeah. That's accurate." Vincent looks at Sarah and Grace, who seem deflated yet somewhat understanding. "You don't have to forgive me. You can blame me for anything—everything. Karl's death is on me."

"No," Vincent stops him again. Everyone looks at him curiously. "That's on Bartram. You did what you thought was right, but Bartram pulled the trigger."

Mark holds back a relieved grin. "Thank you for saying that, Vincent."

Grace turns her wrath on the suit. "So?! What happened? You guys failed to catch him!"

Agent Caldwell clears her throat and admits, "Unfortunately, we did. We bugged your phones in hopes of tracking your whereabouts and raiding the Abaddon ourselves, but the colonel was cautious. He wasn't with you during transport, and they shook the tail we placed on them before reaching the airport. He even reverse-engineered every bit of tracking and surveillance tech we could get our hands on—which only helped him keep us at bay."

"Then how'd you find us?"

"Well, it's good to have friends." She steps aside for Becca to approach on a set of crutches. "Meet Agent Rebecca Stiles, CIA."

"Wait, what?!" Vincent and Trent are completely taken aback, but Tzofiya is unfazed. "Tzofiya, did you know?"

"Of course. See, I am not Master Sergeant Kritzman—I am Agent Kritzman. I spend decades creating persona and establishing reputation to earn Bartram's trust and get job in Abaddon. I even train Becca and Bobby. Before Trent escape Abaddon two years ago, Dr. Smith contact CIA for help. We were assigned to help you root out Bartram."

"Why wouldn't you tell us who you were?" Trent almost seems hurt, but he knows better than to mix personal feelings with business.

"We not trust you at that time. Perhaps you 'escape' as part of ploy masterminded by Bartram. Perhaps you have own agenda and use information against us in future. Keep cards close to chest. We sincerely apologize for deception."

Vincent's head is spinning. Between the firehose of information and the teleportation induced ice pick headaches, he needs to sit down. "I… I need some space." Sarah and Grace follow him, and they sit at the gazebo to reflect. "They were using me the whole time," he says to them. "All of them. They all lied to get close to me, then manipulated me, just like Bartram—"

"Hey," Sarah tries to slow him down. "It's okay. We're safe now."

"Was *any* of it real? Leo, do he and I have a real… relationship? Is Dallyn really part of Dr. Smith's tribe? Did Dr. Smith *really* trust me, or did he just trust that I would agree to assassinate Bartram? Who's really on my side?!"

"We are!" Grace says. "Vincent, we are always on your side."

"Vincent, you're not giving yourself enough credit," Sarah says. "Yes—they lied to you, and your feelings about that are valid, but… you got him. Everyone else wanted you to resort to violence—even *I* had reached that level—but you used your head. Like you always do. Hundreds of scientists are alive and free because of you. Me and Grace, we're alive because of *you*. Trent and the rest of your team, they're still alive because you chose peace over violence."

"Your mom," Vincent suddenly realizes. "We have to go to her hospital! I might be able to—"

"She's in remission." Sarah smiles. "I called her first thing. She's healthy for now. But I promised that we'd stop by and discuss an experimental surgery with her when we get home."

"Oh my God!" Vincent and Grace both exclaim and hug her tightly.

"That's amazing! I can't believe it!" As the three of them celebrate the great news, Dallyn, dressed in a long, flowy dress, comes and sits with them.

"Hey, guys, I don't mean to crash the party, but… I just wanted to give you this." From a pocket in the folds of his dress, he removes a rolled-up piece of graph paper. "I'm not a *great* cartographer, but I think I got the job done."

"What is this?" Vincent asks.

"You remember that message you relayed to me? It was a set of coordinates. Well… more like directions."

"Directions to what?"

Dallyn unrolls the paper and shows them what looks like a map of the Red Desert with landmarks that they vaguely recognize. "Dr. Smith's superpower. A unique energy converter that feeds on the warmth of our land. It acts as a generator to power the Abaddon. Apparently, it has some kind of neural interface that Dr. Smith developed with a friend of his in the sixties. It's *really* advanced stuff. This map shows you where to find the generator, and now… I'm giving this information to you. Do with it as you will." Dallyn gives Vincent a smile as he hands the map over.

"Dallyn," Vincent spits out. "I can't thank you enough. This… In the right hands, this can change the world as we know it."

"I believe *you* are those hands."

Chapter Forty-Nine

January 8th, 2021

Friday

Boom, *boom, boom!* The consistent, upbeat rhythm of a drum livens up the snow-covered, grassy field in which Vincent and scores of interestingly dressed people are standing. It's a cold, sunny day, and some people are wearing black formal wear, some look more casual, and others are dressed in varying levels of brightly colored, traditional Native American attire. The drumbeat is coming from a group of men circling around a large hide drum. They start singing a song that sounds strange to Vincent's ears. *Are those even lyrics? I can't understand them.*

At his side, Sarah is completely entranced by the music, and Vincent can tell she feels the beat pulsing through her, but he squeezes her hand and leans in to say, "This is a strange song to play at a funeral."

"It's really cool, isn't it? Dallyn said the drum is supposed to be the heartbeat of Mother Earth, and the songs are like prayers you sing to nature. Isn't that amazing?"

The painful pulsating in his head makes him want to say something negative, but when he sees the wonder in Sarah's eyes while listening to the music, he stops himself. "Yeah, it is. Pretty amazing."

He smiles silently at her, then she points at the small platform that's been set up in the field and exclaims, "Look! He's starting!"

A sporty, bright pink, frilled dress emerges from the audience and starts dancing; it takes Vincent a moment to recognize the dancer as Dallyn. It isn't the loud, acrobatic display of physicality that Vincent usually expects from dances. Instead, Dallyn takes small steps and moves with the rhythm of the drum, slowly reaching the center of the platform where a collection of hoops have been placed on the ground for him to use as props.

"What's he doing?"

"He called it a 'hoop dance,'" Sarah says, grinning proudly at Dallyn while he performs. Never one for interpretive dance, Vincent doesn't exactly get it, but he is quite impressed by Dallyn's ability to manipulate the hoops and slink in and out of them like a snake weaving through foliage. At one point, he manages to seamlessly interlock all twenty-eight hoops and dances like an eagle soaring through the air. Somehow, it makes Vincent feel… free?

Next to Sarah, Grace is also feeling the music and wants to join in, but this is more of a solo performance. Dallyn's routine starts with no hoops, then he gradually picks up more and more throughout the dance. He drops them one by one until his hands are empty again, and his performance is finished. The audience applauds, but Vincent doesn't feel it's the appropriate thing to do at a funeral.

"Thank you, Dallyn, for that moving performance," an old man says and takes to the podium atop the platform in front of the congregation. He's wearing religious regalia reminiscent of a Catholic priest or Mormon bishop robes that are designed with geometric patterns similar to that of Dr. Smith's office decor. Beside him, a large print-out of a black-and-white photograph of Dr. Smith as a child has been placed on a stand. The print-out is surrounded by several bouquets of flowers. "And thank you to everyone attending today's service. This is not the traditional proceeding for a ceremony such as this, but Runs With Fire was not a traditional man. A memorial under the open sky seemed more appropriate."

Vincent has attended his fair share of community events in his life, and whether he was at a church service, a parade, a funeral, or even just a music concert in the park, he could never get over the hurdle that was social expectations. While Dr. Smith's memorial service is no exception—in fact, being on an Indian Reservation made the feeling that he didn't belong *much* stronger—something is different here. The turnout is much higher than he was expecting. People young and old from all over the area turned up to memorialize Dr. Smith. *How could he have possibly known so many people? He hasn't been here since... at least the sixties.*

Behind him, Leo hobbles away from Mark, Tzofiya, and Becca, carefully resting his weight on a cane with each step. He rests a hand on Vincent's shoulder and whispers, "You alright? You look lost."

Vincent looks into his one good eye and shakes his head. "I'm just thinking."

The old man continues his sermon. "Runs With Fire was a mysterious figure to most of us. News of his accomplishments would spread through the community like wildfire, but from where he came was more of a myth. His family passed onto the next world long ago, but I remember hearing stories they would tell of their son—the brilliant Doctor Russell Smith."

They didn't know him. They just heard stories about him... Why are they all even here?

"He was a quiet child. Instead of playing with the other children, he would tend the fire and stare into it until the embers died out. This was frustrating to his family because he was more interested in learning about fire than he was in learning about his culture. As he grew up, he kept his nose in a book from dusk to dawn, learning how the world around him operated. His family was very proud of his academic achievements, but when he saw an opportunity to enter the rest of the world, he left. He would only return on holidays until, tragically, he disappeared completely. That is where *our* knowledge of Runs With Fire ends, but we are lucky to have a guest who knew him for much of his life. I'd like to invite Mr. Trent Carlisle to the podium."

Trent walks in from the front of the congregation and shakes the old man's hand. "Thank you, Bishop Johnson." He adjusts his suit collar and tie, stands awkwardly at the podium, and clears his throat. "Good morning, everyone." He looks out across the sea of strangers, trying to find the few friendly faces that he knows in the back. "As much as I'd like to come up here and reveal the great mystery that was Dr. Smith to you"—he smiles sadly at everybody—"the truth is… he was probably just as much of an enigma to us as he was to you. Even though I was in the Abaddon for thirty-three years—" The crowd squints at him and murmurs. He simply chuckles and keeps going, "—I didn't know very much about him. He kept to himself mostly, but on the occasions that I did talk with him, one thing was very clear to me: he was proud of his heritage."

Everyone seems slightly confused by this comment, but Trent nods in agreement. "Yes, I understand that may come as a bit of a shock to those who have heard stories about his childhood, but… you couldn't have lunch with the man without him trying to impart wisdom onto you through some story or another about his people, or his ancestors, or his tribe. He was a private guy who enjoyed his isolation, but I think as he grew older, he yearned to spend more time with his people."

As Vincent surveys the crowd around him, something strikes him as interesting: everyone is attentive. They're listening to his story as intently as Vincent would listen to his math professors in school.

"I'm not going to pretend to understand what he felt or how he thought, but he impressed something onto me that will stick with me until the day I die. The value of just a single life is… incalculable." His eyes meet with Leo's, and a thousand conversations are expressed in just a single glance.

"You've all probably heard on the news how he died." As he mentions this, many people shuffle in place and cough, but Trent continues, "And your opinions of whether or not his actions were justified are your own. However, the courage Dr. Smith displayed cannot be taken away; he died a warrior. He had a tough call to make—kill thousands of unborn clones or allow Colonel Bartram to sell those clones as weapons. It was a tough call, he made it, and the world is now a safer place for it." The bishop has a tough time accepting his premise, but he just glares at Trent.

"All of this is to say that Dr. Russell Smith was a brilliant scientist and a wise man. He valued life above all else and had immense love and respect for his people—for all of *you* specifically. He would be proud to know that so many of you came to see him off today. Thank you for allowing me the opportunity to tell my side of his story." Trent nods his head, and when he walks off the platform, Vincent sees a woman that looks about the same age as him—if not a few years older—greet him at the bottom of the stairs. She wraps her arms around his neck, but he takes a few seconds to cherish her face before they disappear into the crowd.

After the memorial, everyone meets back at the bishop's church where several tables have been set up with comfort foods and hot drinks for a feast. Sarah tells Becca to take a seat while she gathers her plate for her, which Becca resents but reluctantly takes her up on the offer. When they all sit down, Becca asks, "Is there any booze in this place? What's a good wake without alcohol?"

Sarah sucks air through her teeth and says, "Sorry, Becca. I think Mormons maintain a dry lifestyle."

Becca seems visibly offended by the idea of living without alcohol, but Tzofiya taps her on the shoulder. "Here, I got you covered." She presents a flask from her inner coat pocket, and Becca's eyes light up.

"Tzofiya! Who knew this girl could party?!"

"Have you guys seen Trent?" Vincent asks, looking around the room but not finding him.

Leo says, "Yeah, he said he wouldn't be able to come to the feast. Said something about having a lot to catch up on, so he's taking an early flight." Vincent's heart sinks. *An early flight? I can take him anywhere in the world in the blink of an eye!* Leo sees his hurt expression and comforts him, "Hey, he'll call you to hang out later, okay? He hasn't seen her in thirty-six years."

"That's true…" Vincent accepts Leo's words and smiles. "I'm glad he has this opportunity."

Dallyn joins the table, sliding his own plate of food in next to everyone else's. "Hey, guys!"

Everyone greets him with a round of applause and shouts of congratulations at his performance. Grace is especially zealous in her comments. "That was amazing, Dallyn! You're *so* going to have to teach me how to do that!"

"Absolutely! But first, what's the news? Have you heard anything yet?!"

Grace tries to stifle a smile. "We were going to wait for a more appropriate time to say something, but… yes. We have some news." Vincent and Sarah know exactly what she's talking about and suddenly feel a rush of giddy excitement. "After the clean-up and clearing out of… shall we say, 'biohazardous material', they're reopening the Abaddon!"

The table, predictably, doesn't share her enthusiasm, and Leo has a horrified look on his face. "You're kidding, right?"

"I know what you're thinking, but it's going to be a completely different place. The only secrets kept there will be government-sanctioned. The leadership will be held to ethical standards, and everything will be above board."

Leo shakes his head slowly. "How do you know that? Who the hell are they getting to run that hell-hole?"

Grace gives Vincent a smile and announces, "Us! I will be the Director, and Vincent will be my Chief Scientific Officer."

Leo's face instantly lights up. "That's amazing! You two are perfect for those jobs!" Once Leo is on board, everyone else joins in the merriment.

"First order of business will, of course, be some much-needed rebranding. Fort Chivington is dissolved, and we're looking for a new name. I suggested Runs With Fire Laboratory, but considering it will be an active military base, they wanted a name of someone who served in the military."

"That's a shame," Leo says. "Dr. Smith really deserves to be honored."

"He does… but… I wanted to check with you before I floated another name: Fort Sideris." Leo is quiet when she suggests this. "I know that's a complicated subject that deserves a longer conversation, but you endured a lot in that place. You lived there since it first opened up; I felt it right to extend the offer to name it in your honor." Grace looks at him apprehensively, almost ashamed for even asking the question.

He takes a deep breath and says, "I appreciate the gesture, I do. It's… very kind of you. But I deserved the punishment that I received there. A clean break would be best, I think."

"I understand," Grace agrees with a smile.

"Thank you though. It means a lot that you would think of me."

Becca exhales deeply and calls outs, "Your first project better be a robot leg for me! I want to be a real-life Winter Soldier! They'll call me—the Winter Agent! No, that's stupid. Six Million-Dollar Woman? The Terminatrix? We'll figure something out."

Grace laughs. "Vincent and I are already working on the blueprints for your prosthetic actually!"

Vincent excitedly shouts, "That's true! You're going to love it; it's got all the bells and whistles!"

"Yeah!" Sarah exclaims. "They wanted to have it ready by Christmas, but Vincent and I got busy moving in together." She takes his hand and leans in for a kiss.

With another round of excitement, Grace groans, "Finally! You two have been dancing around this for years!"

Vincent can't take his eyes off of Sarah. "Yeah. But you can't rush it."

"And if it's right"—her smile is radiant—"then how fast you go doesn't matter."

In her joy, Grace accidentally lets some unfiltered words slip out. "You know Karl and I had a bet going, and—" She stops and bites her lip "Damn it. I miss him."

Sarah touches her shoulder. "Me, too."

Leo leans over to Tzofiya and asks, "My friend, would you mind charging our glasses with something a little stronger? I would like to propose a toast."

"My pleasure." She pours just a slight amount of the contents of her flask into everyone's glasses, then they all raise them up.

"To our friends who aren't here to enjoy this meal with us today," Leo starts them off.

Grace leads the others by standing up. "To Karl, a brilliant quantum physicist, life of the party, and a dear teammate."

"To Bobby," Becca continues with sadness in her grin, "an exemplary agent, a loyal partner, and a real son of a bitch."

"To Brian," Sarah raises her glass a little higher, "a good man."

"To everyone who make sacrifice to protect ones they love," Tzofiya says.

"And to Dr. Smith," Dallyn adds, "without whom, you lot would still be trapped in that godforsaken hole in the ground."

"Cheers!" everyone calls out and finishes their drinks.

There is a comfortable silence for a few moments afterward until a phone starts ringing. Tzofiya reaches into her pocket and answers it. She has a hushed conversation away from the table, but when she comes back, she announces, "That was work. Mavis escape custody."

"Already?" Sarah asks. "She hasn't even stood trial yet. How did she get out? And where would she go?"

"Don't know how, but they think she want new start on cloning program. Potentially build her own Abaddon."

"Can you guys do a rush order on that leg? I want a dog in this fight," Becca asks anxiously.

Tzofiya says, "I have been assigned to hunt her down, but Vincent, I need your help."

"Me?" Vincent looks at her, flabbergasted. "You want my help?"

"You know her well. And your abilities will come in handy. Mental and physical."

"I-I'm not really the hunter type. I wouldn't even know where to start looking for her." He looks to Sarah for reassurance and asks, "What do you think?"

Sarah takes both his hands in her own. "Mavis needs to be brought to justice, the right way. I trust your judgment."

"You think I should do it?"

"Of course!" She chuckles and says, "And if you ever get in a bind, I know you'll think your way out." He smiles, and she pulls him in for a kiss.

Tzofiya interjects, "Come on, lovebug. There is meeting at headquarter. Can you take us there?"

Vincent and Tzofiya leave to find a secluded spot away from the church. She shows him their target coordinates and asks one last time, "You are sure you are up for this?"

"As long as I have my team behind me, I can do anything."

He takes her arm, and numbers fly through his head. With a tug behind his navel, they vanish.

Thank you for reading my book! If you enjoyed the story, then please help others like you discover it by leaving a review.

If would like to receive updates about my future works, then please visit my website and subscribe to my newsletter at:

www.wesleynewman.com/subscribe